The New Mother

The New Mother

JULIA CROUCH

bookouture

Published by Bookouture in 2021

An imprint of Storyfire Ltd.
Carmelite House
50 Victoria Embankment
London EC4Y 0DZ

www.bookouture.com

ISBN: 978-1-80019-659-9
eBook ISBN: 978-1-80019-658-2

This book is a work of fiction. Names, characters, businesses,
organizations, places and events other than those clearly in the
public domain, are either the product of the author's imagination
or are used fictitiously. Any resemblance to actual persons, living or
dead, events or locales is entirely coincidental.

For Di

PROLOGUE

She lifts the rock then slams it down.
    Grit, dirt, snot, howl.
    She picks up the rock and slams again.
    And again.
    And again.
    And again.

Nothing will ever be the same.

INSTAGRAM POST

rachelhoneyhill
Devon, England
paid partnership with **baby2you_**
703,356 likes

Image
- 12-week scan, cropped so it looks quite abstract. A tiny hand visible.

Text
Hello, Beansprout! Great news from Honeyhill Barn: the new chapter begins!

It's an awfully big adventure, one that is going to bring such joy to me and, I hope, the world! Join me on this, the biggest ride of all, my lovely #RRbaby.

Although I have chosen to do this on my own, with no partner, I can't do it *all* alone. I need help!

I'm looking for a special mother's helper. And who better than someone who is reading this?

YOU perhaps? I'm reaching out…

If you love babies and are up for moving in to help out here at Honeyhill, drop me a DM NOW! Qualifications preferred, but experience and loveliness are way more important.

Come and join me and Beansprout for our magical manifestation! And no, I don't know what sex my baby is going to be. That would be like peeking at my Christmas presents before opening them!

Scan at home by Sue, my lovely midwife from **@baby2you_**
private midwife and obstetrics. Helping me grow and give birth
to my baby *my* way.
#MothersHelper #BabyDays #ReachingOut

CHAPTER ONE

9 March

Abbie stops in the hallway, the key to her bedsit in one hand, her cracked Galaxy phone in the other.

She can't take her eyes off the screen, where a small white blob sits in a black circle surrounded by hazy white etched lines. It looks like a sort of abstract painting, but even without the tiny hand reaching up like it wants to wave at her, Abbie knows exactly what it is.

Her excitement overcomes even the exhaustion of the twelve-hour night shift she has just worked. RR is having a baby!

One eye on the screen, she fumbles with her key and lets herself in. Dumping her heavy rucksack on the floor, she shrugs off her fleece. Dealing with #RealLifeFirst, as RR often reminds her she should, she puts the phone down on her little dining table to say hello to Barney and open his cage. As soon as he is perched on his favourite spot – her head – she picks up the phone again and sinks carefully onto the landlord's sofa, which despite her best efforts still looks ratty and stained.

Outside on City Road, an early-morning ambulance races past. Someone screams. Abbie barely registers the sounds, which go on all the time round here.

She taps the *more…* link and expands RR's post. Her green eyes run over the lines, her breath picking up pace.

RR is reaching out!

Abbie's stomach churns, like she has just fallen in love with someone. Picking up on her shift of mood, Barney has a word:

'You look really lovely, Abbie.'

'Aw, ta, Barns.' She has taught him only to say beautiful things to her. No nasty swears here.

A Big Bang universe of possibility blooms in her brain. This could be her big opportunity!

She tells herself to calm down. She needs to breathe, get a grip. How many other people are reading this post right now? More than a million, probably.

But even so. Why not her?

She closes her eyes and whispers the RR mantra: *Think positive. You can do this!*

Excitement ripples through her belly. Perhaps she really could!

She levers off her work trainers and, phone in hand, bird on head, makes her way across the worn carpet to where her yoga mat is stashed between the rattling fridge and the cooker. Knowing this routine well, Barney flutters off and takes up his second-favourite perch, on top of the telly. He likes being there because he thinks she's watching him instead of *Pointless*.

She rolls her mat out on the clear bit of carpet between the kitchen lino and the sofa and pulls up her favourite Racheletics five-minute unwind-after-work sequence. As Rachel takes her gently through the beginning of the flow – a sun salutation so beautifully explained that it feels new every time – Abbie pictures herself on her mat on the glossy oak studio floor in Honeyhill Barn, next to Rachel, in tight proper yoga gear rather than her baggy grey work tracksuit. Instead of the skunk weed stink from the hallway she shares with eight others in this house of bedsits in St Pauls, Bristol, she breathes in that upscale scented candle burning on the ledge behind Rachel. Because of the affiliate link below the video, Abbie knows the brand. And that she can't afford even the travel size.

The sequence done, she sits cross-legged, closes her eyes and zones out the roar of traffic and inner-city fury outside her unwashed window. Instead, she fills her ears with imagined Honeyhill, Devon birdsong, a breeze riffling through trees.

'Chill, babe.' Barney returns to her head, her little guardian angel.

Despite having lived in cities since she was five years old, Abbie's still a country girl at heart. At the grand old age of twenty-six, she would love to move back, to a life free from cleaning up after office workers who don't give a moment's thought or gratitude to the silent army who move in after they go home.

She wants to be valued, to have someone be grateful for her, to not be taken for granted.

It's not much to ask, is it?

And here is the potential answer to all that. And the best part is that it's with Rachel Rodrigues!

At the very least, she has the experience and the loveliness Rachel is looking for.

This is her moment! She swipes across her phone screen to look up Posh June, who she shared a room with a few years ago and who has since helped out on the odd occasion.

'Any time you need anything,' PJ said back then. 'Remember I owe you.'

As she taps out a text asking for advice, Barney nibbles at her bleached and straightened hair.

The message sent, she tears a page out of her empty gratitude journal and writes the first item for a five-point plan:

1. Buy a nice interview suit and get your hair done.

'Who's a lovely girl then?' Barney tweets in her ear.

INSTAGRAM POST

rachelhoneyhill
London, England
paid partnership with **bluespiccadilly**
530,986 likes

Images
- Partial view through a French window, just glimpsing Piccadilly Circus
- Rachel (in BabyMama dress) and Fran, in moody luxury interior, looking at iPads
- Rachel and Fran greeting interviewees.

Text
Up in That London (help!) in my lovely **@babymama** vegan silk dress, interviewing for my special mother's helper. The blow of being in the city is softened by the luxury and glamour of private members' club and rooms **@bluespiccadilly**, with lovely #FriendFran.
So excited to meet all the lovely applicants. Wish I could say yes to everyone!!!
#FriendFran #MothersHelper #London #BluesPiccadilly #friends

CHAPTER TWO

25 April

Rachel sits back on her haunches, leans on the toilet bowl with one hand and wipes her mouth with the back of the other.

'Still,' she says to her reflection as she rinses her mouth in front of the mirror. 'At least you're not going to get fat.' Instantly she chides herself for entertaining unhealthy body-image thoughts.

Would all this be useful to share? It is, after all, a universal experience, encountered by seventy per cent of pregnant women. She laughs as she washes her hands. Throwing up is hardly on-brand, even in such a moodily lit bathroom. @rachelhoneyhill doesn't vomit. Plus, @rachelhoneyhill has been using MamaBliss Calm Tum, the anti-emetic lemon-and-peppermint herbal spray sent by the manufacturer as soon as she announced her news. As far as her followers know, this stuff really works, and she can't afford to give them any evidence to the contrary. Particularly not her new baby- and pregnancy-oriented followers.

And anyway – she eyes herself in the flattering light of the mirror – who knows how bad things would have got without MamaBliss?

Shoulders back, lovely smile, tiny breath-freshening mint and a smidge of almost invisible glow brushed on the cheeks, and she is ready to rejoin Fran to see in the next interviewee on this, the third and final day of the search for her mother's helper.

'Poor babe,' Fran says, as Rachel flops down next to her on the orange velvet sofa.

Outside the window of their suite, London rumbles. The buses are packed, overheated crowds swarm out of the Tube station across the road. It's all too much noise, too many memories of dark times, and the air here makes her want to choke. After so long in the countryside, she doesn't think she'll ever get used to being in crowds again. She itches to get back to her Honeyhill sanctuary.

But Blues offered the suite for free in exchange for a story. And it could be worse. This room, with its matt petrol-blue walls and earthy accent colours, is a perfect refuge. A little aspirational for most of her followers, but entirely on-brand. If only she didn't have to ever step outside.

'Isn't the throwing-up supposed to have stopped by now?' she says.

Fran puts a sympathetic hand on her knee. 'Some of us vom a bit longer than others. Sorry, babe.' Fran's done this pregnancy thing three times, so, as well as being Rachel's best friend, she is, in every way, her baby mentor. Rachel feels bad leaning on her too much, though, after what happened a little over a year ago with the twins. While Mila survived, poor little Noud only lived for two hours, and the catastrophe of the birth meant that they were the last babies Fran would ever have. You wouldn't know any of this to look at her today, though. She is as groomed, proud and beautiful as ever. Like nothing ever happened.

'So,' Fran goes on, 'we've got twenty minutes until the next one. Wanna recap today's lot?' She places her MacBook on the coffee table. In her hyper-organised, legal-wizard way, she has created spreadsheets for the mother's helper applicants, with headings such as *experience*, *qualifications*, *hopes and dreams* and, most importantly, *response to the Big Ask*. There is also a full-length photograph for each applicant. These snaps not only act as an aide-memoire for Fran and Rachel, but the process of taking them is secretly part of the interview, gauging, as it does, each applicant's response to that Big Ask.

Three who look awkward and uncomfortable in front of a camera are rejected without discussion. The remaining two are marked yellow, for maybe. One, Janine, beams white teeth at the camera and angles herself three quarters on.

'A bit suspiciously professional,' Fran says, pointing at the pose. 'Not sure if she's going to be natural enough.'

'And she wasn't massively experienced,' Rachel adds.

'How experienced can you be at eighteen?'

'Perhaps we need someone older? I can't be doing with having to look after a teenager.'

'Not yet!' Fran taps Rachel's belly.

'Beansprout will be the best-trained teenager in the universe.'

The other interviewee, Susie, smiles sweetly in her photograph, and holds up two fingers in a peace sign. Cute, Rachel thinks, but she got rather overexcited when she walked in, to the point of tears and slight hyperventilation.

'I can't believe it's actually you,' she had gasped, between gulps for air.

'She'd get used to you,' Fran says as she swigs from her metal water bottle.

'She's a bit small and pretty,' Rachel says.

Fran gives her *such* a side-eye at this. But while Rachel needs someone to look after Beansprout when she's born, she also needs a team member, and ideally someone who doesn't make her look and feel, at five foot ten, like a great galumphing giant. It's a sad, shallow fact that appearance counts for a lot in her world.

'I still think that Caro from yesterday is perfect,' Fran says. She brings up Caro's sheet. Her photo shows her to be relaxed in front of the camera – not too pretty, not too plain, and average height. She has au pair experience, a degree in art history and is keen on running and dance.

'But remember she didn't know that much about me,' Rachel says.

'She was so sweet about the money being so good.'

'Well, it is! Nah. I'm not that keen. She's not got any edges to work with.'

'Do you really want edges, though?'

'She looks all finished, like an *after* photo. Think about it. Where's the potential in that?'

'You'd really sacrifice the perfect girl for a before-and-after?'

'I need stories, Fran.'

Fran gives her another of her looks.

'What?' Rachel says.

They are disturbed by a waiter, who knocks and opens the door before waiting to be told to enter. The Blues uniform of unstructured linen shirt and trousers that almost blend into the walls fits him very nicely, setting off his blocky arm tats and blonde white-boy dreads.

'Can I get you drinks, guys?' he asks in broad Kiwi.

Fran looks at her watch. 'Five p.m., so a martini for me,' she says.

'Just a sparkling water for me,' Rachel says. She would murder a martini if she weren't pregnant, vomiting and officially ten years sober. But even after all this time, the tiny act of ordering soft still gives her a sense of victory, signalling that she's in control.

'Coming up. Your next one's outside,' the waiter adds, just before he closes the door. While his face betrays nothing, there's something just on the edge of snark in his voice that makes Rachel press her tongue against the back of her teeth. Is he aiming this at her? Or is it something to do with the next applicant? Or is she, as she has learned the hard way, just overcompensating for her inability to read what other people are saying?

As so often when she thinks about what the doctors call her 'neural deficit', she runs her finger through her hair and along the ridge of the six-inch scar where they had to open up her skull after The Event.

'We'll bring her in when we're ready,' Fran says to the waiter.

'Have *you* got baby-care experience?' Rachel asks him.

He frowns and leaves, perhaps a bit too quickly.

'Inappropriate, Rach,' Fran says.

'Nice arse, though.'

Rachel's assistant Wanda snippily ushers in the next interviewee, who walks straight up to them and shakes their hands. She smiles briefly, showing crooked teeth. Of average height and a little overweight, she is plainly but neatly dressed in a cheap skirt suit that has to be from Primark or Peacocks. Her shoulder-length bob is a little too stiff, and the bleach job so newly applied that her skin is still red at the hairline. Her make-up is the wrong shade for her colouring, with poorly applied contouring, and sitting above a pair of striking green eyes – her most appealing feature – her caterpillar eyebrows seriously need attention.

If yesterday's Caro was too much of an 'after', this young woman standing in front of Rachel and Fran, blushing and not quite making eye contact, is pure 'before'.

Rachel and Fran introduce themselves.

'Abbie James,' the girl says, the burr in her voice instantly recognisable. 'Pleased to meet you.'

'You're from the West Country?' Rachel says.

'I was actually born in Westbourne Parva,' Abbie says. 'Though we moved away when I was five.'

'Small world!' Rachel says. 'That's just three miles away from Honeyhill.'

'I know,' Abbie says. She swallows audibly, then says, 'I'm sorry. I'm a bit nervous.'

'You've got lovely eyes,' Rachel says.

'Thank you.' Abbie blushes. 'They're the same colour as yours.'

'Ha!' Rachel says.

'Do take a seat, Abbie.' Fran indicates the small armchair on the other side of the coffee table. Rachel knows this interruption is an attempt to stop her getting too pally, which, is, as Fran has already pointed out five times today, poor equal-ops practice.

'We'll touch first on the more unique aspects of this job,' Fran goes on. 'So if you don't like it, we won't be wasting each other's time.'

'OK.' Abbie folds her hands tidily in her lap.

Fran leans back and hooks one arm casually over the back of the sofa. 'We call it the Big Ask. We need to know that you are happy to be part of Rachel's story. This will mean that you agree to photographs and videos that contain or feature you being posted across all of Rachel's platforms – currently Instagram, YouTube and the merch website – and that you understand that you have no ownership of these images, nor any editorial control over words that may feature or mention you.'

'That's fine by me.' Abbie smiles again. 'Yeah.'

'This is reflected in the generous remuneration package,' Fran goes on. 'You won't be getting bonuses for appearances on any of the platforms. No royalties, repeat fees, et cetera, et cetera.'

'I'm good with that.'

'And you would have to hand over any existing social media presence to our control, which means that we may delete it.'

'I only use it to follow people,' Abbie says. 'I never post anything.'

'Nothing?' Rachel asks.

'Nope.'

Rachel can't quite imagine this is true. Surely everyone posts something?

Fran runs over more of the legal points, including the permanent non-disclosure agreement the successful candidate will need to sign in addition to the temporary one she has already agreed to for this interview. 'This means that you will never be able to discuss anything that you have seen or heard while you are in Rachel's employment, even after you leave the post.'

'Fine by me.' Abbie nods. She hands over her paperwork.

She is twenty-six, which seems the perfect age. Twelve years younger than Rachel, which allows for the distance of seniority without being so young that she would need looking after. And she has masses of experience as a mother's helper and nanny, all excellently documented, with glowing references. She also has a current clean DBA check. It's clear from the way she talks about her former charges that she loves babies. And going by her previous employers' testimonials, her 'ladies' appear to have greatly valued her.

In all, she looks like she would be a lot less challenging than certain of Rachel's previous employees.

Abbie settles back in the armchair, her capable hands folded again in her lap, her sturdy ankles crossed. She appears to be perfect in every way.

But still. But still. Rachel can't get over the social media thing. And she certainly doesn't ever want to be referred to as one of Abbie's 'ladies'.

She tells herself to stop being such a snob.

To make amends, she leans forward and gives Abbie one of her best glowing smiles. 'What are you up to at the moment?' she asks her. 'The last childcare job on your CV finished six months ago.'

'Agency work. I like to wait for a job that suits me. Not just go for the next offer.'

'And you realise that this post may last longer than the usual mother's helper job?' Fran says. 'If all went well, you could become part of Rachel's story for a long time.'

Abbie nods vigorously. 'More than happy with that.'

'And you're fine to uproot yourself and move to the country-side?' Fran asks.

'I dream of getting back there,' Abbie says. 'I've had enough of Bristol.'

'A lovely city,' Fran says.

'Some parts, yes.'

Indeed, when they move on to the next section of the interview, Abbie defines her hopes and dreams as a desire to live back in the countryside, to be of service and to be in close contact with animals and children.

'How did you hear about the job?' Fran asks.

'On Rachel's channel. I check in every day,' Abbie says. 'I do the yoga and workouts, and all the food stuff. And the meditations are great. I'm pretty calm, but they keep me proper grounded.'

'Ah! A fan!' Rachel says.

Abbie nods and smiles. 'A big fan! Working for you is my dream job.'

'It's more than just childcare, you know,' Fran says. 'You'll be expected to help out generally around the house and cook some meals for Rachel, and for baby when they turn up.'

'Beansprout,' Rachel adds.

'I'd love to do that,' Abbie says. It turns out that she has the vegan chef diploma from Ethical Eats Org, which, fittingly, she discovered when Rachel ran some partnership posts with them. As real knowledge of vegan food preparation is such a rarity, this is a massive bonus, although Rachel doesn't want to talk about it in too much detail because of her delicate pregnancy vom situation.

Finally they take a photo of Abbie for Fran's spreadsheet. The confidence she shows by standing straight, her shoulders pulled back, is undercut by those hard-working hands – Rachel noticed the clipped nails and roughened palms when they shook hands – which she holds awkwardly clasped in front of her, against her cheap skirt, like she isn't quite as sure about herself as she makes out.

It's exactly what Rachel is looking for. She has just one issue.

'Is it me, or is her face a bit blank?' she asks Fran.

'It's just you, my love,' Fran says, putting a kind hand on her knee.

They see one more candidate –a definite no-no. Then Juno arrives for the photo shoot for the @bluespiccadilly story for Rachel's Instagram.

And then it's decision time.

INSTAGRAM POST

rachelhoneyhill
on a train, England
630,520 likes

Images
- Shot from train window, the English countryside blurring past
- Rachel selfie, with cup of herbal tea.

Text
Me and Beansprout really glad to be heading home, after three days up in the smoke.
Interviews done, met thirty beautiful people.
I wanted to say yes to everyone!!
Spirits high. BIG NEWS soon!!!
#MothersHelper

CHAPTER THREE

Fran's eyes blur over the less interesting parts of Belgium as they pass the window of the 18.10 Eurostar St Pancras to Rotterdam.

Rachel, Rachel, Rachel. Because of what happened to them when they were teenagers – The Event – they are so bound up together, it's sometimes hard to know where the space is between them.

It wasn't so much falling in love with Wim that made Fran move to the Netherlands. A typical down-to-earth, laid-back cloggie, he would be happy to live anywhere, and their respective jobs mean that location really isn't an issue. More important was the physical space the shift put between her and her old school friend.

It's not that she doesn't love Rachel. It's just that, on top of work and the children, the subtle but constant support she has to provide drains Fran right out. At least giving it mostly over Zoom and text means that it now occupies a purely Rachel area, which she can fence off when it's not being used.

It's been a long haul, getting Rachel pregnant, and she's delighted that they've been successful at last. This baby will give her friend a chance to focus on someone other than herself. Which is important, because however lucrative it is, however much Rachel professes it is simply her job, Fran fears that all that selfie-taking is leading Rachel to an excessively inward focus, and that this will further isolate her. This idea – Fran's, of course – of a live-in helper/placeholder for her own presence, a halfway house between friend and employee, was a stroke of genius.

She hopes this one doesn't go the way of the other staff who have passed through Rachel's hands. Fran has had it with policing post-resignation gagging orders. She has had to keep her eye on all three of Wanda's predecessors, a photographer, a gardener and, of all things, a window cleaner.

It's hard work being employed by Rachel. She hopes this Abbie survives. She'll need a thick skin, possibly literally as well as metaphorically. She wonders also if Rachel's insistence on having her start so early is such a good idea, whether 'getting to know each other' might not be more of a negative than a positive. She doesn't want to lose Abbie before there's even a baby to look after.

Fran rummages in her backpack and pulls out her lipstick. Using her phone as a mirror, she slides it on, then leans in and examines the crinkles around her eyes. What's that down to? Three children in five years? Four, she silently corrects herself, discounting the possibility of adding grief to the list. The human rights lawyer work? Or Rachel?

It's all such a responsibility, her shoulders hurt.

Shut up, she tells herself. You treat a thirty-eight-year-old woman like she's one of your children.

'Well, she is, kinda sorta,' she says out loud to her image in her phone, forgetting about the middle-aged businessman across the aisle from her, who shifts in his seat and – at last – removes his gaze from her.

It's the sense of duty she feels towards Rachel that's the worst part. If she were supporting her purely out of choice, then it wouldn't be so hard. But she's also doing it because she owes her. Big time. Twenty-two years is quite long enough, though. She loves Rachel, but surely there must be a limit to feeling beholden to someone. Even if that person not only saved your life, but also shoulders the heavier part of your shared secret.

She scrolls on to Instagram, noting with mild alarm that Rachel has put up a new post. She pulls it up, but is pleased to see that

her wayward friend hasn't got overexcited and broken their mutu-
ally agreed embargo. It's a relief, because Wanda needs the time
to follow up references and let the other applicants down gently.

Fran winces at Rachel's breathless 'I'm on the train' post. She
hates the name Beansprout. And all those exclamation marks.
But then Rachel's whole shtick is so anti-cool it *is* cool. It's why
young women like her so much, and God knows, if there's one
thing Rachel gets, it's what her audience likes.

Fran really needs to stop feeling so proprietorial about that
baby. Let it go.

The thought alone stings the scar where her belly was ripped
open.

Have they made the right decision about who will look after
this precious new life?

'Abbie's the one, then,' Rachel had said as they took their seats in
the restaurant across the road from Blues.

They had both decided that a change of scene would be a good
idea for the end-of-day decision-making. Plus, after the waiter
brought Fran a second martini, and a first for Juno, who was
clearing up after the photo shoot, Fran knew she wouldn't be able
to put up with his flirting one moment longer. Rachel had given
him an inch and he clearly thought the mile was his for the taking.

'Really?' Fran said. 'She's sweet. But don't you think she's a bit
dull, a bit puddingy?'

'No.'

Rachel looked a little green round the gills as she read the menu.

'Let's just get you some plain pasta with a bit of cream sauce,'
Fran told her. 'That used to be my morning-sickness go-to.'

'But carbs,' Rachel said.

'You need them right now. You should be putting on weight,
not losing it.'

'If you say so, Mama. What do you mean about dull, then?'

'What do the two of you have in common, for example?'

'Is that important?'

'Are you compatible? You're going to be spending a lot of time together.'

'It's a big house.'

'What about that Caro? Have we completely discounted her?'

'Once the baby comes, she'd be running rings round me,' Rachel said. 'I'm too competitive for that. It'd be exhausting.'

'Perhaps we should reach out again?' Fran said.

'Wanda and I went through over a thousand applications. We shortlisted down to fifty for the first-round questionnaire, and this thirty we've just spent three days seeing in person are the final lot. We're not going to find someone better than Abbie.' Rachel sipped her fizzy water. 'And anyway, I don't have to make her my best friend.'

'Absolutely not! That post is already filled.'

'And just think of the content I can make about improving her fitness and appearance. My followers will love her – she is literally one of them.'

'But is that a good enough reason—'

'And she comes from just round the corner. It's a good omen! I mean, she's not some city girl who's going to be all scared or bored stuck out in the countryside.'

'True.'

'That would be a nightmare. No. She's perfect.'

And that was it. There was no telling Rachel once she'd decided on something. After the meal, they returned to the Blues suite and phoned the numbers of the two past employers Abbie had given as references.

'Wanda should be doing this,' Rachel said. 'Where is she?'

'You sent her home, remember? Said you wanted to travel back on your own?'

'Oh yeah.' She nodded. But she had clearly forgotten. This worries Fran. Is this blackout thing getting worse?

As the train pulls out of Antwerp, Fran looks back over the notes she took when they spoke to Abbie's former 'ladies'. The first, a hair salon owner, sounded as one would expect. But the second sounded more like some sort of gangland matriarch than the businesswoman she claimed to be.

Remember, Fran tells herself, it takes all sorts. And Abbie's references, whoever they come from, are madly, wildly glowing.

But something inside her, some over-honed lawyer's bullshit detector, makes her spend the next twenty minutes searching online. The only relevant hits among the hundreds of results returned for 'Abbie James' are those two empty social media accounts. Despite this, her nose still twitches; the lack of trail rings yet more of her alarm bells.

She tells herself to chill. The dark parts of humanity her job shows her – on top of the history she shares with Rachel – have turned her into a fidgety old cynic. Perhaps this Abbie is just not an online person. Which is something Fran would find easier to believe if she were older than twenty-six.

No. She needs to roll with it. Peel off a couple more layers of responsibility and hand them over to Abbie, who is going to be, whatever Fran may feel, think or say, the new mother's helper. Dull and sweet is good. It means that if things go tits up – which Fran reckons is seventy–thirty in favour – there will be a lot less fuss than usual.

'I mean,' she says, again out loud, 'what's the worst that can happen?'

This time, the middle-aged businessman takes up his briefcase and jacket and moves to another carriage.

INSTAGRAM POST

rachelhoneyhill
Devon, England
paid partnership with **willowitch1**
875,246 likes

Images
- Soft-focus Rachel with Wanda in the Honeyhill garden, picking lavender and placing it in a basket she has in the crook of her arm
- Rachel and Wanda indoors at Honeyhill enjoying home-made cupcakes from a vintage tea set.

Text
Spent the afternoon with lovely **@wandawoo** in my gorgeous Honeyhill Barn garden, picking lavender for my gingham sleep pillow craft project. If you're having difficulty sleeping, a lavender pillow can be as effective as prescribed sleeping pills. Why not give it a try?
I love my rustic basket from **@willowitch1**. It makes little tasks like this so much more romantic.
And afterwards, what could be nicer than tea and cupcakes from my own special gluten-free recipe.
Head on over to the YouTube channel to see how to make your very own pillow and cupcakes.
Link in bio.
#Lavender #crafts #crafting #cupcakes #cookery #baskets #rustic #Willowitch #friends

CHAPTER FOUR

6 July

Abbie pays the young taxi driver and stands by the roadside until he has driven away. She enjoyed, in the face of his nosiness, operating the discretion that is now her contractual obligation. Of course, it was easy to be mysterious when met with 'What's she really like?', because she doesn't actually know the answer to that one yet.

But she is pretty certain that RR is really like how she appears to be on her channel. If a person were a hashtag, Rachel would be #authentic.

The other thing Abbie had to be careful with when the chatty driver picked her up from the little railway station on the other side of the village where she was born was his insistence that he must have met her somewhere. He was sure he recognised her.

She most certainly did not recognise him, but she does know that a strong likeness runs in her family, on her father's side. The green eyes, of course. And there are a fair few iterations of her slightly upturned nose knocking around the area, too. She knows it sits better on some of her half-siblings than on her – for example, her beauty-queen half-sister Gina, in Plymouth. Something of a loser in the genetic lottery, Abbie's own face is more a mismatched selection of her father's cast-off features, muddled with the worst of her mother's.

It's partly this acceptance of her own ordinariness that made her initially disbelieve Fran when she called to say she had got the job. She had tried so hard to keep her cool in the interview and to look natural and pleasant when they took her photo. But she has very little experience of being in front of a camera, and was certain her nerves had shown. She thought she had blown it.

Surprised as she was, she doesn't like to think what she would have done had she not been successful. To say she had her heart set on it is something of an understatement. This is her dream come true.

Bending to extend the handle of her brand-new wheelie suitcase, she peeks under the cover of Barney's cage, which she has set on the ground beside it. He's still calm, thankfully.

She read on the internet that cannabis oil was good for sedating birds. While that was too expensive for her – she hasn't yet received her first wages and had a lot of other expenses to get herself here – she bought a quid's worth of skunk off one of the stoners upstairs and crumbled it into Barney's seed bowl. He seemed happy enough with it, and it stopped him talking on the journey, which she would have found mortifying. What goes on between her and Barney is private.

Sweat trickles down her back. The air is thick with humidity and she can feel the crackle of electricity that suggests the afternoon is melting towards a storm – although that could just be her excitement.

Then she notices the smell. If you ignore its tall security fence, Honeyhill Barn looks as picturesque as it does in Rachel's posts – all old brickwork and timbers and modern steel and glass, with creepers up the front. Even the fence is softened by honeysuckle and jasmine. But the sweet scents promised by those flowers are killed stone dead by the fruity, malty stink that Abbie instantly identifies as pig farm.

Before she buzzes the entry phone to open the gates onto the driveway– as part of her contracted discretion, she thought it best for the taxi driver to drop her off outside the property – she looks to her left, where muddy tractor trails lead along the deep country lane towards a sizeable but ugly modern bungalow surrounded by working farm buildings.

It's not quite as picturesque as Rachel's Instagram would have you believe. As Posh June used to say, relishing the irony, 'There's always a serpent in paradise.'

It's not that Abbie thinks the countryside is like a picture off a biscuit tin. Quite the opposite, in fact. She knows it's stinky and muddy, and that it's not all rich folk. She knows, too, that it can sometimes be dangerous. But even so, this scruffy workaday-ness takes her by surprise.

She pats down her hair, which she had specially – and expensively – cut and styled for starting the job, and presses the button on the gate.

It's Wanda who buzzes her in through the gates and meets her at the door. This is a bit of a let-down. Abbie had always pictured Rachel giving her the big welcome.

In the past nine weeks, after finally believing Fran and accepting the job offer in the un-coolest way ever, with a big whoop followed by grovelling thanks like some sort of hyperventilating fangirl – which, to be honest, wouldn't be too far from the truth – she has had a lot of contact with Wanda.

It was Wanda who took her through the legal side of things, which was a proper job of work, involving signing fourteen different documents.

'Never sign anything you've not thoroughly read through,' Posh June once told her, so it took her ages to go over them all. And then there were questionnaires about Abbie's 'story', her preferences and requests for food, drink and toiletries, as well as vital statistics, weight, shoe and head size. Abbie is surprised they didn't ask her for a DNA sample.

That would have been interesting.

Anyway, the process was a bit of a mess, because Wanda kept on losing track of what she'd sent and what Abbie had signed. Abbie, who has a natural aptitude for administration and might well have excelled at it were it not for her lack of formal education, wasn't impressed.

Before the interviews, she had seen Wanda on Rachel's feed, where she sometimes appears laughing like she's one of her friends rather than her PA. Now she stands in the Honeyhill Barn doorway, dressed head-to-toe in what Abbie considers to be RR gear – a cropped soft cotton orange hoodie over bum-sculpting leggings that neither shine nor wrinkle. She's thin as a whip. Her hipbones jut under the edge of her top, which must make some of the yoga/Pilates positions where you have to lie on your front quite painful. From the look she's giving her, Abbie suspects she might have work to do to get Wanda to like her. She's no doubt feeling threatened by this invasion of her little kingdom.

Well, that, as Posh June also used to say, is *her* problem, not Abbie's. Abbie hasn't had many chances to shine in this world, so she's taking this one with both hands and giving it her all.

'Ah,' Wanda says, the look on her face entirely illustrating Abbie's theory. 'You're not expected yet.'

'I got an earlier train,' Abbie says. 'But my phone's out of battery, so I couldn't call.'

Wanda eyes the birdcage in Abbie's hand. 'What's that?'

'Barney. My budgie.'

'Did we know about that?'

'I thought it would be OK.'

Wanda's shapely eyebrows come together in the middle of her forehead. 'Rachel's allergic to feathers.'

'Oh. Sorry.'

The two women stand on either side of the Honeyhill threshold, looking at the cage. Abbie won't give up Barney, whatever the stakes. He's her best friend.

In the end, Wanda rolls her eyes.

'I'll have to tell her. Just keep it in your room and don't let it out of its cage.'

'OK. Thanks.'

'You'd better come in, then.' Wanda's accent matches Abbie's, so she must also come from somewhere round here. But her brown eyes and straight Roman nose make it pretty clear they don't share a father. That would have been awkward. 'We do outdoor shoes off in the house,' she tells her.

Abbie lifts her little suitcase and brushes gravel from the wheels with her toe, then kicks off her trainers and puts them in the space Wanda points out in a shoe rack. After checking it's OK to keep her socks on, she follows Wanda across a flagstoned hallway to a staircase.

'Rachel's just having a nap,' Wanda tells her, pausing at the bottom of the stairs. 'So if it's OK with you, I'll show you to your rooms. She said not to disturb her until five.'

Rooms. Abbie likes the sound of that plural. 'Do you stop here too?' she asks.

'No!' Wanda says it like Abbie has asked her if she eats dog turds.

As Wanda turns to climb the stairs, a black-and-white sheepdog skitters across the stone floor, head down, tail wagging, to greet the newcomer.

'Hey, Sam!' Holding Barney up high, Abbie bends to scratch the dog behind the ears. She knows him so well, she feels a small sense of ownership. A regular presence on Rachel's channels, he video-bombs her stories, getting underneath her Downward Dogs to lick her face, skipping around her HIIT burpees and gratefully licking any proffered bowls during the baking vlogs.

Wanda ignores Sam and continues on up the stairs, confirming Abbie's suspicion that she is a heartless soul. You can always judge a person by how they are around animals.

'You and I are going to be great buddies,' she says to the dog. Buddies in a way that she already knows she and Wanda won't be.

'Is that all you've got?' Wanda says, turning and eyeing the suitcase as Abbie lugs it up the stairs behind her.

'Yes.'

'Just as well, probably. Rach got in a whole load of stuff for you from Flow & Glow so you can dress like us. In your size, of course.'

Abbie can't work out if this is bitchy or just factual, but she doesn't really care. All she knows is that since Rachel started wearing F&G she has spent far too much time on their website looking at all the luxe sportswear and workout gear in recycled fleece and cashmere. But there's no way she could have afforded to actually buy it. She thought about getting a headband, just to have *something*, but forty quid for a bit of stretchy sweatshirt to wear on her head? No thank you.

Wanda hurries her on to the end of the corridor and up a smaller, more winding staircase.

'Don't wander around downstairs at night, or you'll set the alarms off,' she says as she leads her along the landing.

'Alarms?'

'We've had issues.' Wanda stops in front of a door with a Yale key in it. Dangling from the key is a gold – or golden, at least – RR-branded key ring.

'This is your place.' She turns the key and opens the door. If you discount Rachel's suite in Blues, this is the nicest room Abbie has ever seen. It's a broad and long attic room, with a slouchy sofa, a nice big telly and a small kitchen area. The sloping ceilings are more window than anything. Steamy grey storm clouds fug the view at the moment, but Abbie imagines what it will be like on a blue sunny day. Or at night! Lying on that sofa, looking up at the stars and the full moon!

She puts Barney's cage down on a nice old scrubbed-pine dining table, which, with its wonky old candelabra and handmade bowl of rustic apples, looks what Abbie thinks of as *very Rachel*. She can't help noticing, though, that there's a layer of dust on it all. Her fingers itch with the urge to deal with it.

'Bedroom's through here.' Wanda leads her into a second, equally large room with the same sort of skylight thing going on. At the far end is a bed so massive that it sends a proper thrill down Abbie's spine.

She's twenty-six, and by no means a virgin. But she's never, ever slept in a double bed. She wants to run and launch herself at it, dive onto the sheepskin cushions scattered near the headboard, wrap herself up in the chunky knitted blanket that covers the end. Roll about in the crinkled linen sheets and duvet.

But she won't give Wanda the satisfaction. Won't let her see how excited all this makes her. She wants to appear more sophisticated than that. So she just nods and smiles. Keep it cool, she says to herself. And that goes for when she meets Rachel again, too. She doesn't want her to think she's just some little overexcited fan.

'Bathroom's through there.' Wanda points at a door at the far end of the room. As casually as she can, Abbie strolls over and peers in. There's a rainfall shower like the one Rachel sometimes features in her posts – although this one has blue tiles, whereas the one she uses is set in limestone. And – Abbie can hardly contain her excitement – there's a whirlpool bath!

If more signs were needed that she has arrived, she doesn't know what it would be.

Apothecary's bottles of bubble bath and shampoo stand ready for action. They're Malachi, a brand Rachel has been using of late. It's all Abbie can do to stop herself stripping off, running a bath, and pouring it all in.

Behind her, Wanda coughs.

'Nice,' says Abbie, cool as a carrot.

'We've put the clothes and stuff in the drawers and wardrobes,' Wanda says, leading her back into the living area. 'There's enough coffee, tea, et cetera to keep you going, a sourdough in the bread bin and Rachel's jam and some vegan butter in the fridge. If you need anything else, just WhatsApp me – I'm making a housekeeping group for you and me. You'll be eating your meals with Rach, at least until Beansprout arrives.'

'Which is in eleven weeks,' Abbie says, proud that she has done her homework and is on top of Rachel's estimated due date.

'Ten,' Wanda corrects her. 'While some of our more spontaneous posts are instant, most are lined up a week in advance, just in case of unforeseens. We've decided to keep the whole pregnancy story one week behind, too.'

Abbie is surprised at how shocked she is at this reframing of such a central part of her world. She doesn't quite know what to say. She's still casting around for words when Wanda drops the key ring into her hand.

'This is yours, Abs,' she says.

'I prefer Abbie, if that's OK,' Abbie says.

Wanda looks her up and down, a half-smile on her face. 'OK, Abbie. I've got to get the month's accounts finished before I go home, so get settled in. Rach will be expecting you down for supper at seven sharp.'

She turns and pads towards the door. Abbie notices that she is wearing Magic Stones, the alpaca-felt slippers that Rachel has featured on her Instagram that contain nano particles of jade to wick heat and moisture from the feet.

Abbie wants those slippers.

'Oh,' Wanda says, her hand on the door. 'There's a new iPhone and iPad for you on the kitchen worktop. I've set up accounts for you, so you won't be needing your old phone.' She holds out her hand.

'Eh?' Abbie says.

'You can give me your old phone if you like. So we can recycle it.'

'I'd rather hold onto it,' she says.

Wanda's lips disappear into a thin line. 'I'll have to tell Rachel.'

Abbie's not sure what sort of power trip Wanda is on, wanting to take her phone, but she's not going to rise to it. 'OK. Thanks, Wand,' she says.

'It's Wanda.' She turns and goes, leaving a waft of orange-blossom perfume that just about overrides the slurry stink from next door.

Alone, Abbie looks around at the unaccustomed luxury of her rooms, and for one second feels absolutely tiny. Rachel is placing a lot of trust in her. She hopes she can meet her expectations.

'Can I do this, Barney?' she asks her bird on the table.

'Course you can, darling.' He knows what to say. It's an old routine of theirs.

She throws her arms wide, and, full of joy, twirls around in the vast space of her new living room, imagining she is Julie Andrews in one of her favourite films, *The Sound of Music*.

Abbie has landed.

INSTAGRAM POST

rachelhoneyhill
Devon, England
paid partnership with **shrink_rap_** counselling
832,634 likes

Images
- Rachel looking a tiny bit stressed and tired
- Close-up of Rachel's wrist as she taps it.

Text
Tapping the body can create a balance in your energy system and treat pain. It can also help whenever you feel like you've just had enough, when you're anxious, addicted or lonely.
For more information, check out **@shrink_rap_**, who have pages of resources. They also run group and individual tapping and therapy workshops.
What do you do to combat stress?
#stress #tapping #anxiety

CHAPTER FIVE

Rachel wakes and finds herself lying naked and soaking wet on the floor of her en suite. Rolling onto her side, she surveys the damage. The wall cabinet mirror is smashed, ripped toilet paper litters the tiled floor and an extravagant smear of blue toothpaste adorns one wall.

She looks at her hands and sees the horror of red, and thinks, *Oh no*, and, *Not again*.

What has she done this time?

Even though it's rarer these days, there's no knowing when it's going to happen.

She feels no pain, so that's a good sign.

She checks her Beansprout bump and says a little prayer of thanks.

She puts her fingers to her nose. Instead of rust and copper, she smells lanolin and perfume.

Slowly she drags herself to standing and checks each limb. Just two bruises this time, one on each arm.

She turns to face the shower. A lipstick scrawl covers the limestone surround. In among a string of obscenities, a sort of graffiti Tourette's, she deciphers *RR LOVES WIM*.

Jesus.

In the shower tray, several stubs of her rarely used Chanel lipsticks lie like spent bullets.

'Really?' she croaks, looking at her wrecked face in the cracked mirror and seeing that she has a clown smile painted over her lips. 'Really?'

Unable to immediately deal with the carnage, she staggers like a woman with a bad hangover into her bedroom. Reaching the bed, she climbs onto the duvet and collapses, making sure to keep her hands and face off the white linen.

'None of that stuff you wrote in there is true.' She says it out loud, in her firmest voice.

She checks the rest of the room. At least there is less damage than sometimes, and it's only to inanimate objects. Nowadays she locks herself in her room when she sleeps, to make sure she can't get out. She doesn't know what she would do if, say, she were to stumble into Wanda or Sam with this rage, this vile urge to destroy, coursing round her damaged nervous system.

Fran is right. She really should seek professional help. She didn't look after herself during her lost years in London – didn't see a doctor or a dentist – so her medical record sort of fizzled out, and her current GP has no idea of her condition. In any case, she mostly has it under control with techniques like tapping, counting and chanting, and it happens infrequently. She's frightened that if anyone official finds out about her episodes, they'll stop her driving, even take her baby away from her.

She can't allow that.

She lies still and lets the last fizz of electricity leave her brain and limbs.

Then she remembers that Abbie is arriving today.

She has a lot of clearing-up to do.

INSTAGRAM POST

rachelhoneyhill
Devon, England
paid partnership with **veggiedog66**
637,970 likes

Images
- Sunny day. Rachel riding Cal with Sam running along the cliff path beside them
- Sam sitting beside a cross-legged Rachel, looking like he's joining her meditation
- Rachel feeding Sam a bowl of kibble.

Text
Sam and Cal say hi!
A healthy dog is a happy dog!
Sam loves running alongside his best bud Cal and me as we trot along our glorious Devon coast path. He also loves helping me out with my yoga and meditation.
But what he loves most of all is his **@veggiedog66** kibble.
He loves it because it tastes so good, and I love it because it contains all the vitamins, minerals and amino acids an active dog needs, without harming any animals or the planet! Win-win!
After all, there's no point in having an animal if you don't give it your best self, is there?
Sam and Cal truly are my spirit animals. Who's yours? Post your pet pics and tag me so Sam and I can meet them!
#instadogs #vegandog #vegan #dog #Samdog #VeggieDog #HappyBoy

CHAPTER SIX

'You look gorgeous!' Rachel levers herself up from the living room sofa and sticks out a hand to welcome Abbie. 'Give us a twirl.'

Abbie has made ample use of the lovely things in her new rooms. She poured a generous slug of the Malachi Incense & Woodfire bubble bath into the tub, slipped in and set the whirlpool going. It frothed up like nothing she had ever seen before, made her feel like she was at one of those foam parties in Ibiza that you see on social media, except that she was all alone in her bathroom in the countryside near Westbourne bloody Parva. Not *in* Westbourne bloody Parva, though, she reminded herself as she soaked.

When she got out of the bath, she wrote it all up in her gratitude journal. Rachel has always recommended keeping one, and Abbie has tried, but until recently never had anything to put in it. Now, though, she couldn't have more to be grateful for.

After her bath, she riffled through the new clothes in her wardrobe, enjoying the box-fresh smell, and selected a grey F&G Winona cashmere lounge set, which she knows, from seeing it on the models on the website, is meant to be looser than this one is on her.

She steps back from Rachel and, holding the pink glittery gift bag she has brought down with her out to her side, awkwardly twirls to show her the outfit.

'We'll get Wanda to make them send another Winona in a size up,' Rachel says. 'If they do it. You can never have enough Flow & Glow, can you! Have you settled in?'

Abbie nods. 'It's very nice, thank you.' Which is the understatement of the year.

'Hope you don't mind being in the attic,' Rachel says. 'I thought it would be nicer for you to be self-contained.'

'I love it.' Abbie looks around the vast open-plan living space. It's surprisingly untidy, with used mugs, discarded clothes, tubes of cream, magazines and books everywhere. The sofa cushions, which she is used to seeing immaculately placed and plumped, are scattered around the room, some on the floor, others piled up on the sofa as head or back rests. And the wall behind where Rachel was sitting has a dent, like someone has slammed their fist into it. Despite the drifts of dog hair on almost every surface, the actual dog doesn't seem to be around. 'Where's Sam?' she asks.

'You've met him already?' Rachel says.

'We said hello when I arrived.'

'He's with Alice. He'll be back in an hour or so.'

'Alice?'

'The dog walker.'

Abbie tries to keep her face still as she takes this in. Rachel *pays someone else* to walk Sam? If she had a dog, she'd have to be paid to *stop* walking him.

'Take a seat, please.' Rachel gestures to the sofa. As she lowers herself back to where she was sitting, she winces. Abbie tells herself she needs to be more understanding. Of course taking a dog all over the hilly Devon countryside is just not practical at this stage of pregnancy.

'You like animals, don't you?' Rachel asks.

Abbie nods. 'I'm looking forward to meeting Cal, too.'

'And you shall. Wanda told me about the bird. It would have been good to have known before you arrived.'

'Sorry about that.'

'It's fine. Just I have this allergy, so it'd be great if you kept her in your rooms.'

'Him. He's called Barney.'

'Sweet. What sort of bird is he?'

'Budgie. I got you this.' Abbie thrusts the gift bag towards Rachel. It's a bit graceless, but she's not all that practised at giving gifts. Or receiving them, for that matter. 'For Beansprout.'

'How lovely!' Rachel unties the pink ribbon on the top of the bag, then pulls out the contents, which Abbie has wrapped in pastel-blue tissue.

'I've used both pink and blue because you told us you don't want to know Beansprout's sex. You said it's like unwrapping your presents before Christmas. I really liked that.'

'Thank you. And that's very sweet.' Rachel puts the still-wrapped gift down and places her hands on her bump. 'Keep it under your hat, but I'm certain Beansprout's a girl.'

'Really? How?'

She smiles. 'We mothers just know, Abbie.' She unwraps the tissue to reveal the dinky peach-coloured crocheted matinee jacket. It's not new, but Abbie has hand-washed it with tender care, and it smells beautifully of Fairy non-bio. She can't let Rachel know the significance of it right now, but it is a massively big deal that she is giving it to her.

'That's lovely!' Rachel says, fingering the delicate crochet work and the ribbons that Abbie loves so much. 'Completely gorgeous! Did you make it yourself?'

Abbie nods. She put a lot of love and work into it.

Rachel folds the jacket and puts it back in the gift bag. 'You're so clever! Hey, would you like a drink before dinner?' Leaving the bag on the sofa, she gets up and leads Abbie across the messy living part of the room – half glass box of modern bifold doors, half ancient stone-walled barn – towards the tidier poured-concrete surfaces and dark-painted cupboards of the kitchen area. Abbie knows this part of the house well from Rachel's cooking videos, although this evening it doesn't look like it's been used at all, which is odd, because she thought they were going to be having dinner together, and her stomach is growling. Rachel opens a big wall cupboard to reveal a cluster of bottles. 'I've got wine, beer, gin…'

Abbie blinks. 'I don't drink,' she says. 'Like you.'

'Oh, that's a pity. I love to watch other people pack it away. Now that I can't.' Rachel indicates her belly.

'You stopped ten years ago,' Abbie says, keen to show her knowledge.

'Indeed! Soba sista 4 eva!' Rachel holds up her fingers like a Girl Guide salute. 'What do you want, then? Can I recommend booch with a splash of Montmorency cherry? Tastes like ropy red.'

Abbie only understands about half of that, but she nods yes anyway, and Rachel herds her onto a bar stool.

'So how long have you been alcohol-free?' she asks, while she fills two glasses with ice from the fridge-door dispenser.

'Only two years,' Abbie says. She has always wanted one of those ice things.

'That's fantastic! Why'd you stop?'

Abbie blushes. 'Because you showed me how good being sober can be.'

'That's nice.' Rachel pours some blood-red syrup on top of the ice. 'Me, it was because of my mum's drinking. I don't remember much about her, but I do know I didn't want to end up like she did, drunk and dead in a car crash of her own making.'

Abbie knows this story well; it's part of why she loves Rachel so much. 'My dad was a heavy drinker as well, so I suppose that had something to do with it for me too,' she says.

'That surprises me.' Rachel is now sieving some liquid that looks like piss from a jar with a thick, flat disc of something mushroomy in it. 'I didn't get that impression from what you told us about your background.'

'He was great, though, when I was growing up.' Abbie could kick herself. In her rush to be a kindred spirit, she has veered from the rose-tinted biography she penned for Wanda – that her dad is a successful builder who set up his own double-glazing company – and dangerously towards the less idyllic truth. 'I never knew when I was a kid, of course. We were very happy as a family.'

'You're so lucky.' Rachel looks wistful as she pours the liquid into the glasses. 'Happiness is all you need, isn't it?'

'I'm sorry. I didn't mean to rub it in…'

'It's fine. I know you know my story. It was tough losing my mum so young, being dumped on grandparents who really didn't know how to love.' Rachel hands Abbie her drink, her eyes shining. 'But I'm a big girl now.'

'Yeah.' Abbie gestures at the smart kitchen, like it's a symbol of survival. She holds her glass up to the light and watches little bits of something moving around in the liquid. She hopes it's because the drink is fizzy, rather than what it actually looks like, which is tiny worms.

'Go on, try it!' Rachel says.

Abbie takes a sip. It's weird. But she will get used to it, she supposes.

She perches on the bar stool and watches as Rachel pulls four cartons of packaged ready meals from the oven. Before she can change the frown on her face, Rachel turns and catches it.

'What is it?'

Abbie blushes. 'It's just you always cook from fresh.'

'But these *are* cooked from fresh. Just not by me! They're brilliantly balanced fresh meals. I'm giving them a go for a month for a prospective partner. If we like them, we'll be featuring them.'

She pulls a couple of plates from a low cupboard and piles cutlery on top. 'Can you give me a hand getting these to the table?'

*

The food – by a company called Pimp Those Plants – doesn't really taste of anything. Abbie has been eating vegan like Rachel for over a year, but she still occasionally falls off the wagon for bacon and cheese, neither of which she can resist. And the occasional Burger King Whopper.

After arranging some candles around their plates and taking a couple of snaps, Rachel picks up a block of what Abbie takes to be fake Parmesan and grates fine, wispy clouds over her plate.

'Could you pass that, please?' Abbie holds out her hand.

Rachel gives her an apologetic smile. 'It's cow, I'm afraid.'

Abbie gasps.

'Sorry, sorry, sorry! Now I'm over the morning sickness, I've just got these cravings at the moment. Uncontrollable!'

'Self-denial is self-betrayal,' Abbie says, quoting one of Rachel's mantras.

'Very good! Would you like some?' Rachel holds the cheese up for Abbie like the serpent tempting Eve with the apple.

'Oh, go on, then.' Abbie is surprised by the relief she feels as she grates cheese onto her own food.

Rachel forks the beany, creamy mush underneath the cheese. 'This really is tasteless, isn't it? I'm going to tell Pimp Those Plants I can't work with them unless they up the seasoning.'

'It's nice with the cheese,' Abbie says.

Rachel laughs. 'We can't tell them that!' She scoops the cheese off the top of the food and pops it into her mouth. 'You're disappointed, aren't you? You're probably thinking "Why ready meals? Surely that goes against everything she stands for?"'

Abbie blushes and stammers. 'No. I'm sorry, I—'

Rachel holds up her hands. 'No! No! Say it how it is. It's part of the brand shift we're working on – the "busy new mother" angle:

"You may be too busy to cook, but that doesn't mean you have to give up good food."'

'I can cook for you.'

'I'm really looking forward to it! I love that you have the vegan chef diploma.'

'I learned so much.'

'Get a shopping list to Wanda if there's anything you need for your creations.'

Abbie nods. It's going to be a steep learning curve. But then how difficult can vegan cooking be anyway, with Google as your friend?

'We're going to have such fun!' Rachel lifts her glass of whatever the drink is called. 'To our beautiful partnership.'

She sits back and watches Abbie eat, which makes her feel a little uncomfortable. 'Wanda said you've still got your old phone,' she says.

'It's got all my contacts on it. I'd like to hold on to it, if that's OK.'

'I understand,' Rachel says, scraping fluffs of cheese from the grater and licking her finger. 'Of course I do, but it is wasteful to have two phones on the go. As soon as you've transferred the contacts, do hand it over to Wanda. We're part of this great recycling scheme where phones are refurbished and donated to children in need.'

'Nice,' Abbie says.

'Hope you haven't unpacked everything.' Rachel's perching on a bar stool while Abbie clears the kitchen. Alice the dog walker quietly returned Sam to the boot room while they were eating, and he's licking the plates as Abbie stacks the dishwasher. It's not behaviour she'd personally encourage, but it's Rachel's house and Rachel's rules.

'Not yet,' she lies.

'Good! Because we're going away tomorrow. A little surprise trip. For you to experience the perks of being part of the @rachelhoneyhill family.' Rachel holds up her hands and closes her eyes. 'Don't ask me any more, because I won't be drawn. Wanda should be WhatsApping you a packing list tonight.'

'For me to do for you?' Abbie asks. There's nothing she would like more than to help Rachel with her personal belongings, ironing and folding them, placing them neatly in a smart suitcase.

'No! I can look after myself. No, for you. Because how will you know what to wear if you don't know where we're going?'

This is not a problem that Abbie has ever encountered before, but it's one she's happy to entertain. Except for one point:

'Will I need my passport?' she asks, as casually as she can, because she has no idea how she could admit to Rachel that she hasn't got one.

'I'm not flying now Beansprout's so big. Strictly UK only.'

Abbie lets her breath out slowly, trying not to show her relief.

'Though,' Rachel says, scrolling through something on her phone, 'why don't you give your passport to Wanda to keep in the safe? Just in case.'

INSTAGRAM POST

1 year ago

rachelhoneyhill
Devon, England
paid partnership with **ejeep**
1,850,993 likes

Images
- Rachel in her turquoise eJeep, the top down, the wind in her hair, driving down a country dirt road
- Rachel in her eJeep, the top up, driving through a city street
- Rachel sitting on her eJeep bonnet, parked up by a sandy Devon beach, surfers on the waves behind her
- Rachel plugging her eJeep into the Honeyhill charger
- Video of Rachel inside the eJeep, driving and talking through all the features, music on the stereo.

Text
Look at my lovely new wheels! I love the colour, the fold-down roof, the way it handles the rough Honeyhill roads as breezily as the motorways and looks at home in the city, the countryside and at the beach.
But most of all, I love that it is 100% electric, clean and green! It gets me wherever I need to go on the planet, without harming the planet!!
Sound on for **@kudublue**, the coolest electro funk in the world.
#eJeep #electric #greencar #cleancar #KuduBlue

CHAPTER SEVEN

7 July

Rachel turns the eJeep through two tall brick gateposts and up a long gravel drive. A peacock in the middle of a jewel-bright green lawn lets rip with a camp nasal hoot and unfurls his stunning feathers.

'Ta-dah!' she says to Abbie, who sits still and silent beside her.

Abbie's not exactly chatty, and that unnerves Rachel. On the way up, the eJeep top down, a Mazda full of girls recognised her as they passed on the motorway. They swayed so dangerously close, waving and trying to take photos, that Rachel had to slow right down and eventually was forced into pulling a sudden exit into a service area to shake them off. As she sat there in the stopped car, trying to gather her composure, she wondered, not for the first time, whether a less distinctive vehicle might lead to more sane journeys. But what can she do, when they give it to her expressly to make it famous?

For a couple of seconds the buzzing in her ears started and her hands began to go numb. She tapped the side of her arm and silently recited the alphabet backwards. If she kicked off here, she'd have a lot of explaining to do to Abbie. Thankfully, the moment passed. Yes, she does have it under control. To frighten this new employee off after just one day would be even more shameful than the one week it took her to scare that poor bruised and battered young Charley away.

She turned to Abbie, who had been sitting beside her through all this, seemingly oblivious. Had Rachel read it wrong about those girls in the Mazda, then? Had she overreacted? That would be typical.

'Let's get a Starbucks,' she said.

As she was leaning on the counter, ordering oat milk cappuccinos, Abbie tapped her on the shoulder. 'Shouldn't you be having decaf, though?'

'It's my one remaining vice, and I'm sticking with it,' Rachel said, turning her back on Abbie and ordering a double shot for her cup, just to show her. Over the last couple of months, her nausea has been replaced by cravings for strong flavours: coffee, Parmesan, chilli, which is perhaps why she's finding what she perceives as Abbie's blandness so challenging.

Sweet and dull. It pains her to admit it, but Fran may have been right.

Throughout the whole journey, Abbie showed not the tiniest bit of curiosity or excitement about where they were going. Admittedly Rachel had told her that it was a surprise and she wasn't going to tell her however much she begged, but to show no interest at all? Just weird.

Instead, she just sat there answering Rachel's questions about her family and where she grew up after leaving Westbourne Parva. They moved around a lot, apparently, because of her dad's job – although why double glazing would lead to multiple relocations is beyond Rachel. And she had a 'normal' upbringing with both parents, two brothers and one sister in 'nice, detached' houses.

Rachel yearns to have had that level of normal in her background. But perhaps she should be grateful that what she did have at least turned her out with a bit of spark – even if it gets a bit much at times.

With Abbie's unmoving shape in her peripheral vision as she drives the car past two more peacocks, she thinks about how long they are going to be living in each other's pockets – until Beansprout is six months old at the very least. A numbness smothers her heart at the prospect.

Perhaps that Caro would have been a better choice.

No. She's thinking too far ahead. Jumping the gun.

Perhaps this solid presence is what she needs. Perhaps Abbie is just shy and will bloom, given time. Rachel needs to follow her own advice and #bepositive. At least, she tells herself pointedly, Abbie is going to be easier to control than certain other people she has employed.

She pulls up in a small car park to the side of a low-level minimalist modern building that appears to stretch for a glass mile beyond them. She notes that the van is there: a satisfying sign that The Team has already arrived.

'Where are we, then?' Abbie says.

At last! Some curiosity!

'BabyMoon at Pinehurst,' Rachel says. 'I'm trialling it in exchange for stories, and they've allowed you in as an extra. My treat. A sort of welcome, and we can get to know each other on neutral ground. It's going to be such fun!' She's going a bit full on with the positivity, but she needs a reaction.

'Thank you,' Abbie says, and Rachel fights a sudden urge to smack her. *Show a bit of fire*, she wants to scream at her.

'BabyMoon, like a honeymoon,' she says instead. 'Clever, huh?'

'Yeah.'

They step out into the hot midday sunshine. The familiar spa scent of ylang-ylang and chlorine hits Rachel's nostrils. The sweetest smell in the world, and a welcome antidote to the pig stink from Honeyhill Farm at home. She makes a mental note to tell Wanda to get the solicitor to follow up on how the odour control enforcement is going.

'Is Wanda going to be here?' Abbie asks.

Rachel suppresses an irrational flash of outrage that she might have been reading her mind. 'Wanda's strictly admin. Only you get to come along with me on the fun gigs.'

Abbie moves her face in a way that suggests an actual smile.

They climb the stone steps to the front door and ring the doorbell. 'Hope they come soon,' Rachel says. 'I'm dying for a piss.'

At that exact moment, a glowing young woman opens the door and catches her words.

'Rachel!' she says, her beaming smile overriding any awkwardness. She touches a hand to her heart. 'Sunita. I feel I know you in here.'

To make up for her idiocy, Rachel gives her most ethereal namaste back.

They take off their shoes and follow Sunita along a long glass corridor to a jasmine-perfumed sunken area, all low-level squashy sofas, big pot plants and views out on the tropical-style garden at the back, with tantalising glimpses of water, steam and Japanese-influenced wooden buildings. The post-drive buzz that hangs around Rachel's shoulders and jaw is already melting away, and they haven't even checked in yet!

If this is what being a mommy influencer is like, bring it on.

Sunita hands her an iPad showing Pinehurst's new BabyMoon media pack, then sweeps Abbie away to check her in. The process is particularly thorough, involving weighing, measuring and drawing blood, as well as an extensive medical questionnaire. Sunita will be handing over Abbie's stats so that Rachel has a thorough 'before' picture of her for her planned transformation programme.

For herself, Rachel signed the Pinehurst disclaimer for VIPs who prefer to keep their personal data private. She agreed, though, to being photographed going through the motions of check-in to show how exacting it is. This will instil trust in any pregnant followers tempted by the ten per cent discount she will offer on her affiliate link.

Apart from The Team – who, Rachel notes with a little tic of annoyance, are conspicuous by their absence right now – there is no one else staying here at the moment. After a *lot* of work pitching and positioning herself, Rachel has been chosen as brand ambassador, a gig that, on top of the perk of this exclusive visit, is worth good hard cash. She can also return whenever she feels like it, although she will in future have to share the place with paying guests. This is fine by her. She imagines lots of reciprocal photo opportunities with wealthy patrons, even some potential partnerships. With minimal work on her part, she could make this *the* place for pregnancy networking.

She swipes on through the literature. BabyMoon is a new venture for Pinehurst, which formerly ran spa retreats/rehabs for wealthy patrons who demanded discretion. Now they are rebranding into a wellness resort for women who are pregnant, who want to be pregnant or who have been pregnant. To cover all bases, they're also offering menopause retreats – FullBloomMoon. The thought brings Rachel to an involuntary shudder. She is so thankful she has managed to get Beansprout in before it is too late.

Even so, a tiny part of her wonders if she has the staying power to continue on her influencer trajectory until her own FullBloom-Moon rears its head. It's not like there are any precedents for longevity in this game. How long, after all, can you go on flogging your life by living it? Sometimes she feels weary just at the thought of what she has to do. And she's beginning to wonder whether the flogging has taken over the living. Does she record her life, or does she live her recording? It's hard to remember a time when she did something because she really *wanted* to. Her actions seem to be based on whether they'll make a good story or not. She can't recall when she last took a photo just because she wanted to capture a moment for herself rather than tell the world about it.

Beansprout kicks inside her, and she pauses this depressing train of thought to say hello.

'I got you because I really wanted you,' she tells her. And that's true. She had to go to all sorts of extreme measures. And yes, so what if she intends to monetise the process of pregnancy, childbirth and rearing? She has to make a living, after all.

She sits back on the comfortable sofa and lets her eyes defocus on the calming Buddha water feature in the sun-drenched atrium in front of her. The Sanskrit mantra that her meditation teacher whispered to her plays in her mind. Because of the oath she took to keep it to herself, it's one of the very few things in her life she hasn't shared with the world.

'All done!'

Rachel jerks awake. She blinks, marvelling how pregnancy has turned her into a power-napper, before taking a tiny check around to make sure nothing has been destroyed. Thankfully, it's all good. Abbie's standing in front of her in a special Pinehurst BabyMoon-branded towelling wrap, and the shining Sunita is saying something about a guided tour of the facilities.

Blearily, Rachel drags herself up to standing. She pulls herself together enough to take a couple of snaps of Abbie looking awkward in her robe before Sunita leads them down the staircase to the basement, where, once more, the spa smell fills her with the sense of possibility.

Even though she is only really thinking about taking a proper nap in her sure-to-be-luxurious bedroom, she still finds her breath being taken away by this other-worldly network of rooms. Abbie trails around with her, eyes like saucers. The twelve interconnecting treatment areas cover every imaginable way water could be used as a therapy. There's heat, ice, colour, waves, bubbles, steam, jets and all sorts of plunging, soaking, swimming and immersing possibilities. Some rooms are heavily scented – all, Sunita, says, using organic, baby-safe essential oils – others full of pure ozone. There's a shining cave room encrusted with salt crystals – thanks to a yoga teacher in Brighton, Rachel has already run a story about the beneficial effects of salty breathing – and another where you bathe in green tea, which Sunita says is very good at replenishing antioxidant levels. Discreet, soothing ambient sounds thread through the low-lit tiled and stone interiors. Rachel snaps away with her phone camera for the more informal 'wow, wow, wow' story already forming in her mind.

When they finally climb the stairs back to the sunlit ground level, it feels as if they have been down there for a year. She's surprised it's still daytime.

'That's incredible,' she tells Sunita. 'I've never been anywhere like it.'

'We are rated one of the best spas in the world,' Sunita says, and Rachel believes her.

'What's outside?' Abbie asks.

Rachel turns to smile at her, pleased that she's found her tongue. Her face is flushed with the heat from the spa rooms, and she is slightly out of breath.

Getting her into better shape is going to make such a great story. Her slightly retroussé nose could actually be quite pretty if everything around it were rearranged. Indeed, it reminds Rachel a little of her own. Abbie just needs to grow out that terrible bleached hair into something looser and more organic, get rid of the stark colour job, match her foundation to her skin tone, sort out her skincare routine, stop painting on those marker-pen eyebrows and tighten everything up body-wise.

That's how Rachel's mind works. Honed on bettering herself, she's always looking at how to improve others. It's not being bitchy. It's just searching for the best in the people around her. The deep irony of the 'be happy with what you are' mantra she shares with her followers is that to reach that state takes so much damn work.

She can honestly say, though, that she can find nothing to refine in Sunita, who, with her swishy black hair, glowing skin and shining eyes, looks like she takes every advantage of the facilities around her.

'Two jet spas,' Sunita is saying to Abbie. 'A long pool for laps, a bubbler basin, two oak-barrel saunas, two plunge pools, four hot tubs and a circle of rapids, although we've slowed that one right down for BabyMoon.'

'Pity,' Rachel says. 'I love a good swirl.'

Sunita touches Rachel's arm and stage-whispers to her, smiling, 'Just for you, we can speed it up a bit.'

Looking at her standing next to Abbie, Rachel wonders what it would be like having Sunita for her mother's helper instead.

'My team has checked in?' she asks as they make their way towards the accommodation zone.

'Hey,' Abbie says. The sudden animation in her tone makes Rachel and Sunita pause and turn. 'What team?'

INSTAGRAM POST

rachelhoneyhill
Devon, England
paid partnership with **flow.and.glow1**
256,346 likes

Image
- Abbie in a Flow & Glow tracksuit by a swimming pool, smiling happily at the camera. No make-up, hair blonde, straightened, unwashed.

Text
Hey everybody! I'm so pleased to introduce my wonderful angel Abbie James, who will be helping me in every way imaginable before and after Beansprout is born.

Doesn't she look lovely in her **@flow.and.glow1** trackie? Well, let me tell you, not only is she beautiful on the outside, but she is also one of the sweetest people you are ever likely to meet! Abbie has asked me to help her out with a new Racheletics fitness schedule so that she can be in peak condition to keep up with the Honeyhill lifestyle. Watch this space to keep up with her progress!!

#AbbiesJourney #fitness #MothersHelper #Racheletics

CHAPTER EIGHT

Abbie lies flat on her back on her bed looking at an arty mobile turning in the breeze from the half-open bifold doors. This room is even posher than the one at Honeyhill. She can't quite believe she's here. Clean, bare wooden floors with old Persian rugs, a vast bed, fabrics that feel expensively organic to her touch, a lovely smell everywhere and a bathroom bigger than her entire flat back in City Road, with a big copper tub, colour-changing misting shower and towels as fluffy as clouds.

So why, she thinks, as she turns her head and gazes out at the afternoon sun playing on a Japanese lily pond that falls away like an infinity pool to a backdrop of rolling green hills, is she not feeling two thousand per cent happy? She's living her dream.

It's *The Team* thing.

She thought it was just going to be her and Rachel. She was so excited about that. She played it cool as they drove up the motorway past Gloucester and then out into the wilds of the Cotswolds, hiding the unsophisticated part of her that was bursting to ask 'Wherearewegoing? Wherearewegoing?', the excited little girl who despite everything still manages to live on inside her.

Instead, she just quietly followed their journey on Google Maps on her phone, looking at the satellite images of all the big houses and gardens and swimming pools and trying to contain herself.

She enjoyed telling Rachel the Abbie-growing-up story, though. It calmed her to think of all those five-bedroom executive houses with their big gardens, the loving housewife mother and the busy, successful – if slightly alcoholic, she reminds herself with a groan – father. And there she is, Abbie, in the middle of that happy family, with her two protective brothers and role-model big sister.

And when they arrived, she couldn't believe her eyes. She was here, with Rachel Rodrigues, just the two of them, the whole place to themselves! She can see why Rachel has decided to work with the spa. As that snooty Sunita showed them round and Rachel took photos with her iPhone, Abbie started looking forward to perhaps even taking some snaps herself for the RR Instagram.

She always thought Rachel did it all herself, that the life she presents to her followers is how it is, that only she is involved, that she makes all the choices on what to show and how to show it.

But she doesn't. Abbie lifts her foot and taps the mobile, setting it dancing.

The Team means it's not just the two of them here. The whole nature of what she was imagining has been upended. It's not just a getting-to-know-you sort of trip. There are hair and make-up people here, a stylist, a photographer. And while that sounds glamorous and exciting, it's *so* not what she had in mind.

'It's always work, I'm afraid,' Rachel said once they were in her suite, which is even lusher than this one. Sunita had finally left and Abbie was unpacking Rachel's luggage, taking great care with every item, folding, smoothing and putting away. 'We'll have plenty of time to ourselves, though, in between shoots. It's what pays the bills. What pays your wages.'

What could Abbie say, confronted with that? 'Where do you want these?' She held up a cotton bag containing supplements and special teas. Rachel told her to put them by the kettle, which was already surrounded by bottles and jars of all sorts of weird healthy stuff.

'We must get you on some of those goodies,' Rachel said, pointing at them from the bed, where she was lying with her swollen legs up on a pillow. This is a trick she, Abbie, has shown her, Rachel Rodrigues. Who'd have thought it?

She looked like a mermaid lying there with her dark hair fanned around her. Abbie wishes she could look so good with so little apparent effort. She knows it's down to keeping to routines and using the right products, but she's rubbish at the former, and she's never been able to afford the latter.

'Cool,' she said.

'The check-in will give us the data we need, and we'll have you in top nutritional order in no time.'

'Sounds expensive,' Abbie said.

'My treat. Or rather, BabyMoon's treat. They're providing us both with six months' supply of their own branded supplements.' Rachel waved at the stuff arranged around the kettle: little cardboard packages with names like *Dragon's Breath*, *Pull Your Weight*, *This Is What You Need* stamped on them with something like a kid's John Bull printing set. Abbie knows that if a beauty product looks like someone made the packaging on their kitchen table, she's not going to be able to afford it.

'So why have you brought your own?' she said.

'I know what works for me. It's what works for *you* we have to find out.'

Abbie can't wait to have her own cotton bag full of products.

'That's for you,' Rachel said as Abbie took a parcel from the suitcase. 'A welcome present.'

Speechless with delight, Abbie unwrapped it to reveal two beautiful silk dresses in exactly her size.

'For the smart-casual dining code,' Rachel said.

'Oh, thank you,' Abbie managed to say. 'Thank you so much, Rachel.'

She has hung the dresses on the outside of her wardrobe, like flags from this new country she's found herself in.

Her phone buzzes. It's Wanda, checking everything is OK. Abbie emojis back a thumbs-up. Then Rachel WhatsApps her. *Come and meet the guys!*

Abbie quickly slips out of the BabyMoon towelling robe and into the Flow & Glow tracksuit she wore on the way up. She takes her time over her make-up, though, making sure she gets the contouring right, and straightens her hair so that it hangs around her head like fused straw.

The living room of Rachel's suite – which Abbie left so neat and tidy after unpacking – has been taken over by three wheeled racks of activewear, kaftans and bikinis. The surfaces are covered with more make-up than most women would use in a lifetime.

Rachel perches on a small hairdresser's chair that has somehow magically appeared, an apron clipped around her, while a thin person in tight jeans and a skinny cropped Breton-striped top trims her ends.

'Hi,' Abbie says from the doorway. There's so much going on in the room that she doesn't know where to look.

'Abbie, come and meet Cyn,' Rachel says.

Cyn pauses working on Rachel's hair and looks her up and down. 'Hello, Abbie dear.'

'I've seen you on Rachel's posts,' Abbie says. She had thought Cyn – @cynthem – was a friend, but it appears they are also Rachel's hairdresser.

'See what you mean,' Cyn says to Rachel.

'Rude!' Rachel taps them on the arm and turns quickly to Abbie. 'I was just saying what wonders Cyn could work with your hair and make-up, Abs.'

Abbie smiles.

'Hey, Zander, come out and say hello,' Rachel says.

A tall man in a short kimono jacket pops his head out from between two of the clothes racks, making Abbie jump. The tape measure round his neck wriggles like a snake as he holds out his hand and says, 'Hey!'

Here's another friend from Rachel's posts who also seems to be working for her.

'Zander's got a great idea,' Rachel says, while Cyn carries on snipping tiny millimetres from the tips of her hair.

He holds up a linen jumpsuit. It's in orange, Rachel's signature colour, with her RR branding embroidered in dark grey on the left lapel. 'It's a sort of uniform,' he says, in a lovely French/West African accent that Abbie thinks – because it's very like that of one of the women she worked with cleaning offices in Bristol – might be Ghanaian. 'But more chic.'

'Thank you,' Abbie says.

'Try it on!' Rachel says.

Abbie looks around her. 'Is there somewhere I can get changed?'

Everyone laughs.

'Our whole job is about seeing birds in their undies, darling,' Cyn says. 'Don't mind us.'

Blushing, Abbie turns her back to the room and peels off her tracksuit bottoms. She steps into the jumpsuit, then edges off her top and slips the sleeves onto her arms. Behind her, she can almost hear the looks on their faces as they watch her trying to hide herself. She's never been comfortable stripping off in front of strangers. There are things she likes to keep private, and her body is one of them, especially the scars.

The jumpsuit fits her loosely. She fastens the fabric tie around her waist, then turns to face three critically appraising pairs of eyes.

'Perhaps this.' Zander steps forward, undoes the tie and pulls it away.

'Turn so we can see you sideways, Abbie,' Rachel says.

Abbie does as she is told. The silent criticism she picked up on intensifies. She wants to run away and hide.

Cyn sighs. '*Prisoner: Cell Block H*.'

'You're right.' Rachel laughs. 'As you were, Abbie.'

'Sorry, my love.' Zander hands her back her tracksuit.

Mortified beyond belief, Abbie slips out of the jumpsuit.

'Can I touch her hair now?' Cyn asks Rachel, as she turns back to face them.

'Not yet!' a woman's voice cries out behind Abbie.

'And this is Juno, my photographer,' Rachel says, as a small, possibly Japanese, woman strides into the room holding a digital SLR camera as big as her own head.

'I need my befores,' Juno says.

'Befores?' Abbie says.

'It's just for a thing,' Rachel tells her. 'Juno will take care of you.'

'Come with me, my dear.' Juno takes Abbie's hand and leads her out of the glass doors to the little private swimming pool on Rachel's terrace.

'You have a very characterful face,' Juno says, as she makes Abbie hold a big circle of mirror fabric on her lap and look slightly to the left of the camera. She's got her perching on a neat wall made of the local stone, which looks a lot smoother than it feels to sit on.

'Is that a good thing?' Abbie says.

'Depends.'

'OK.'

'Can you smile now?'

Abbie has a go.

'Looking good in a picture is a skill you have to learn, Abbie,' Juno tells her. 'Don't worry, you'll catch on. Just don't fret about getting it perfect. Think of something nice instead. Your favourite place, a time when you were happiest.'

This is easy for Abbie, who closes her eyes and casts back to when she was taken to Spain when she was eight years old. It was a time of endless sunshine, sand between her toes, hours spent watching lizards running along the terrace outside the hotel room she shared with Carly, another half-sister, back when she and Carly used to speak to each other. It was a time of special Spanish chocolate milk, Chupa Chups and temporary tattoos, of getting pruney and shivery in the swimming pool, of being well fed and just being allowed to play all day under the watchful eyes of caring grown-ups.

'Now open your eyes!' Juno is laughing in front of her, and Abbie smiles back. The camera clicks. 'You really found your happy place. Look!'

She shows Abbie the picture she has just taken. Abbie doesn't recognise herself. She looks like a little girl in Spain.

'That's the perfect snap,' Juno says. 'I'll just check it with Rach, then we can let Cyn loose on you.'

Abbie's still wondering what a 'before' is.

Two hours later, after an extensive amount of pulling bits of Abbie's hair through a plastic cap, painting on and washing off colours and mumbling about who on earth put these highlights on her, Cyn finally turns the chair to face the mirror so that she can see what's been done. The cut and colour she spent forty pounds on two weeks ago has been replaced by what Cyn describes as a 'loose bob, back in your own brunette, with some reddy hints in the lowlights'.

Cyn stands behind her, working product into her curls to make them stand out more. 'See.' They point first at her eyes, and then at her chin. 'It softens here, and sharpens here. And the colour is so good on you. Takes years off.'

Abbie has to admit, despite the lifetime battle she has fought against her natural curls and colour, her hair looks quite good like this. Almost, if she half closes her eyes and imagines six more inches on the ends, like Rachel's.

'Thank you,' she says to Cyn. She is genuinely grateful.

'This is the beginning of your "after",' Rachel says as she admires Cyn's work in the mirror.

And finally Abbie gets it. 'What else are you going to do with me?' she says.

As Rachel talks on through make-up and what Zander can do with 'those eyebrows', and then on to diet and exercise, Abbie's excitement grows. She is going to have a makeover, like they do on the telly, but for free. And the best part of it is that in the end, she imagines that she and Rachel will look like peas in a pod.

Even with The Team, everything is turning out better than she could have dreamed.

INSTAGRAM POST

barbara_celeste
Manchester, UK
2,324,862 likes

Image
- Split-screen photograph:
- On the left: Rachel Rodrigues by a pool, pouting at the camera, her pregnant belly neat in a silver bikini, an alcohol-free cocktail in her hand, Abbie James a little behind her on a sunbed, smiling
- On the right: Barbara by a paddling pool, pursing lips at the camera, her not-pregnant belly unruly in a silver foil bikini, can of Special Brew in her hand, a French bulldog a little behind her on a dog bed.

Text
Got my bitch, yo, ready to go.
#BarbaraCelestechallengeaccepted #funny @rachelhoneyhill

CHAPTER NINE

10 July

It has taken three days of BabyMoon bliss to relax Rachel.

Big shades over her eyes, silver bikini straining across her blooming body, she reclines on one of the spa garden loungers, sipping a celebratory sparkling elderflower. The peacocks screech from the front garden, and a tree nearby vibrates with a cluster of small birds. The Team has left, and tomorrow she'll be driving herself and Abbie home.

It may look like she's lazing in luxury, but the iPad balancing on her bump means she is, in fact, working. She smiles to herself. It can be *so* tough being an influencer.

The BabyMoon break has been a great success workwise. Representing this brand is a smart move. Using her Apple Pencil, she notes down, in her GridSmasher post-planning software, phrases she might use – the odd word here and there, hashtags that need to be researched for their impact.

She lifts her sunglasses and, for inspiration, taps her way to the photos Juno has parked on the @honeyhill Dropbox.

Partly thanks to all the throwing up, Rachel still looks good in a bikini shot, despite the big bump on her front. Her arms and legs appear unchanged – toned and buff – and she has *finally* got a pair of tits. Even so, Juno's going to run the images through

PerfectMe to filter out the red Nile Delta of stretch marks on the underside of her belly. She will also be getting rid of the dark linea nigra that looks like she has a seam running down her middle, and those tiny hints of visible veins at the top of her thighs.

Other than these blemishes awaiting their digital excision, the pictures are so perfect that she hopes they might be picked on by one of the big Instagram parody accounts, perhaps even Barbara Celeste. In the past, these 'funny' women were the bane of her life, digging holes in her online self, making her look controlling, idiotic, a farce of white privilege – all of which, a part of her knows, is fair comment.

It got so bad once that she felt obliged to trigger a pile-on of her followers. It turned out so brutal that the offender had to freeze her account and has since disappeared into social media oblivion. Rachel sometimes feels a twinge of guilt about that. After all, the woman was just like her, just trying to get by. But did she really have to be so cruel? Anyway, Rachel's hardly responsible for what her followers do. If she told them to jump off a cliff, etc.…

Her eyesight flickers and a sharp white pain jabs her skull. *Z, Y, X, W, V*, she recites to herself. Just in case. The moment passes.

She relaxes her lips, which she realises have bunched up into a tight cat's-arse. Bad not only for wrinkles, but also for the soul – an embodiment of negativity.

On the bright side, now that she's pregnant, these jokers have taken a gentler approach. After all, kicking a woman with child is not a good look. And if they treat her kindly, she will be able to respond graciously, with good humour, and then everyone will do well out of it.

She's a big enough girl to know that even if it hurts at the time, a little bit of light pwning is good for exposure – there's always an uptick in her own follower numbers after a post like that. She manages to retain many of them long after it all blows over, because people coming to her expecting shallow narcissism are surprised.

Her offer goes a lot deeper than other influencers with all their gloss and conspicuous consumption. She's far more tasteful than a lot of the trash out there.

She glances over at Abbie, who is lying on the next lounger, gormlessly scrolling on her phone, and tries to start up a conversation.

'It's been great, hasn't it?'

'It's been fantastic, thank you.' Abbie looks up from her screen. She's snacking noisily on the smoked almonds that came with the elderflower.

'What was your favourite part?'

She smiles. 'I liked it all, thank you.'

Rachel sighs and goes back to her iPad. That's sweet enough, but she wishes Abbie had accepted the champagne the waiter offered her earlier. It might have made her more interesting.

She sips her own drink and tries to imagine that instead she is swallowing a mouthful of her old friend and foe, Proper Alcohol. She blurs her eyes on the light playing on the jet pool in front of her and casts her mind back to bars and pubs and laughing and tipping out into Soho streets and waking up not quite remembering where she had been or what trouble she'd caused…

Oh, sigh.

How did that girl she once was end up here?

By the skin of her teeth, she tells herself sternly. Or else she would have been in a different place altogether. A far, far worse place. Dead, even, like her mother.

And it's not as if she doesn't still have blackouts and comes round wondering what she's done. Her fingernails sinking into someone else's cheek flashes before her as an image of an act that, despite handsomely paying off her victim – a sure indicator of guilt – she has no memory whatsoever of carrying out. It's only there – so vividly – in her mind because people have told her about it. Endlessly.

It's just that she has lost the alcohol-induced variety of blackout.

She shakes herself and turns back to the iPad and the photos of Abbie. Has Juno managed to discover some hidden depths?

They aren't actually too bad. Generally Abbie's gaucheness tends to set off Rachel's put-together casual vibe quite nicely. At its best, the juxtaposition of the two of them – Rachel in her skimpy silver bikini, Abbie in the hidden-control black one-piece Zander put her in for all the swimwear stories – makes Rachel look generous, like an encouraging big sister showing her younger sibling the ropes.

There's a lovely candlelit snap of them smiling together over a salad. The real story is that the object of their amusement is a poor waitress who, out of shot, had just accidentally tipped beetroot soup down the front of Cyn's white kaftan. The moments after the photo involved a rather nasty dressing-down delivered to the poor girl by an outraged, sodden Cyn.

Knowing how vicious things can get when Cyn goes off on one, and wary of a potential PR disaster, Rachel intervened, which was just as well, because it turned out that this was the kid's first job, and that she, a big RR fan, was beside herself with nerves in the presence of her idol.

To make the most of the situation, Rachel allowed the girl to take a selfie with her. She scrolls on to the photo Juno took of the moment – the excited, grateful, uniformed waitress holding up her own phone to capture herself, her face pressed like a lover's next to Rachel's. It's a sweet picture and Rachel might use it.

In some of the Rachel/Abbie photos, though, Rachel appears to be acting like some smug, let-them-eat-cake queen, consciously outshining her servant. In others, Abbie gazes at her like a mother-less puppy, full of adoration and wonder. Like Rachel is telling her the full meaning of life, rather than, for example, which vegetable to juice for maximum vitamin C.

These photos are irredeemable, even with the PerfectMe pixel magic.

Rachel turns to the pictures where Abbie is on her own. These are even less promising. In almost every single image, she looks directly at the camera, which is all wrong for Rachel's informal brand. There is one nice one, though, of her smiling by Rachel's private little pool. She looks plain and dumpy, and neat and sweet and happy. A perfect 'before' picture.

Rachel puts a black flag on the unpromising images – most particularly those where she looks like a stuck-up Marie Antoinette – so that Juno doesn't waste time touching them up.

Lifting her sunglasses, she glances again over at Abbie, who is scrolling on her phone, her bottom jaw a little slack, her tacky home-made arm tattoos on full display: 'Zayn', 'Harry' and 'Taylor'. When Rachel asked her about them when they were in the whirlpool, Abbie looked a bit shamefaced and explained that she had been a massive One Direction fan in her teens and a friend did them for her.

'What about Taylor?' Rachel asked.

'Swift. She went out with Harry.'

Rachel knocks back the last of her elderflower.

Is it really going to be possible to share her life with this woman?

Suddenly and solidly, Beansprout kicks her, a little foot, or elbow, or whatever body part it is, rippling under her skin. Rachel places her hand on her drum-tight belly and feels her baby: part of her but not part of her. An independent life, brought into the world entirely of her own making, out of her own desire.

Sometimes she thinks this is the first real thing she has done – far realer than she thought at the time of conception. Back then, she saw it more as a game, a way of diversifying, of shaping herself into a new Rachel, to give her greater potential, leverage, some longevity. She saw becoming pregnant as more of an idea than anything else, an abstract concept, a shape, a new arrangement of light and shade on her body. A – dare she even think it to herself – career move, hit upon after a session with a brand consultant.

But now Beansprout is here, all but talking to her. And she realises the massive responsibility she has taken on. One that goes far, far beyond herself. Imagine!

The only babies she has ever held are Fran and Wim's, and she didn't manage to get to see any of them until at least a few weeks after their birth – which meant she missed meeting poor little Noud altogether. And, of course, she's never had sole care and control of anything. Even Sam came to her ready-trained.

With her experience of looking after babies and their mothers, Abbie will surely come into her own when Beansprout arrives. Despite all Rachel's misgivings, the thought that this stolid presence will be beside her when the birth happens has shrunk the terror that used to grip her every time she thought of the sheer bloody bodily mess of it.

The problem is, Abbie's role goes a little beyond that of staff, but she's not quite a friend. With Rachel's challenges over relating to other people, this is the difficult bit. She knows she's overfamiliar with The Team, and that she's possibly too distant and formal with Wanda – who she finds as difficult to understand as Abbie. She is also aware that she is over-intimate with and leans too heavily on Fran, her best friend in all the world.

She sighs heavily. Why is everything so complicated?

Abbie pops her head up above her phone. 'You OK?'

Rachel smiles brightly, puts on her public persona. 'I'm feeling like a new woman, aren't you?' She holds up her iPad. 'Juno's got so many great photos.'

'Nice.'

'How did you get on with The Team?'

'Very well, thank you.' Abbie pauses for a second, then goes on, 'I never knew it worked like that.'

'That what worked like what?'

'Your posts and that. All those people doing all that stuff. I thought it was just you.'

Rachel smiles at her innocence. 'It *was* just me at the beginning, but I have higher production values now.'

'So that lot dress you up and do all your photos now?'

'They come in once a week to shoot my new stories. I've also got Drew, who does the sound and filming for the video segments, but he's expensive, so we tend to work in batches for those. One day a month or so.'

'So you don't take any photos yourself?'

There's something quite intense about Abbie's frown when she says this, something that reminds Rachel of her look in some of those solo photos. Is Abbie cross with her for some reason? She wishes she was equipped to tell.

'Of course I do! I mix it up – there are the more product- and client-oriented shots that I do with The Team, and then I pepper that with selfies, and my own landscapes and pictures of the animals, my meals and so on. Though I have to use PerfectMe all the time on my own snaps.'

'PerfectMe?'

'A filter app that makes you look just like you are, but more so.'

'What?'

'Everyone uses it, all the time.'

'Do they?'

Rachel lifts her sunglasses. She has killed some of the magic for this poor fan, she knows. 'Everyone at my level has stylists and photographers and filters. After all, I have clients relying on me making a good impression.'

Abbie chews on another nut.

That blank face. Unreadable. Rachel is suddenly exhausted.

As she hauls herself to standing, she feels sorry for Abbie. It must be like when the lights come up in the cinema and you see all the popcorn and soda spills on the floor.

'You look a bit tired, Rachel,' Abbie says.

'I'm going for a nap. Wake me at five, will you? I've got a Zoomer with *The Styler*.'

'Zander?' Abbie asks.

'No. The *magazine*.' Rachel tries hard to keep her voice sweet.

But really. Is she going to have to explain everything?

THE STYLER ONLINE

Baby, Save Me

by Jane Roberts, editor

14 July

Image
- Cartoon of Rachel pushing stroller full of money down an idyllic country lane.

Text

British social media lifestyle influencer Rachel Rodrigues – or RR, as we are encouraged to call her – sits in an extremely nice bedroom in **Pinehurst Spa,** just outside Cheltenham, where she is trialling their new **BabyMoon** concept. When I booked the interview, her spiky assistant Wanda told me that it would be granted on condition that I mention and link to both the spa and the concept. There you go, Wanda. Job done.

I don't get to experience the luxury, though, because we meet over Zoom, rather than IRL, because, as RR says, 'It is what it is.' Make of that what you will.

She will probably need no introduction, but if you have been living with your head in a non-recyclable plastic bag for the last five years, let me enlighten you. RR is an Instagram star with over a million followers. She also has an online shop, HoneyhillMerch.me, and a YouTube channel dedicated to her cookery videos and the hybrid Pilates/yoga/HIIT mix-up she has called Racheletics. Imagine, if you will, a downmarket English Goop, mixed in with a shabby-chic version of that

UK daytime TV classic, *Escape to the Country*, and a middle-aged Simply Ella. According to the most recent Instagram Rich List, RR's net worth is two million dollars, and if you want her to push your product, it will set you back two thousand dollars per post. She hates, however, to talk about money.

'It's not what motivates me at all,' she says, shaking out her trademark long dark curls. She tells me she's wearing a Flow & Glow sweatshirt and Natty Dread earrings, although she won't disclose the terms of her sponsorship deals with those companies. 'I've just thrown them on to talk to you. In any case,' she says, 'I only feature products I truly love and would wear or use for pleasure whatever the circumstances.'

Whoa, RR. Why so defensive?

When Rodrigues first came to social media attention ten years ago, her offer was somewhat different to the health, beauty and simple-living shtick she peddles today. If your thumbs are up to it, you can scroll back that far through her early posts to see what we mean. Or look up @soberachel, her first profile, mothballed six years ago.

'Yeah, I was all about sobriety at first,' she tells me. 'I'd seen some dark times, being a party girl in London. I was hooked on booze, took far too many recreational drugs and my mental health really suffered. It was straighten out or die, so I chose the former, moved out of the city and started to heal myself. Initially my feed was just for me, documenting my mood and coping strategies, but it just sort of took off.'

'And the yoga and so on?' I ask. 'The "Racheletics"?'

There are nasty rumours in some of the darker corners of the internet that RR isn't qualified to lead yoga or Pilates sessions, but, I have to say, I like her workouts, and as a devoted yogini of two decades' standing, I find she's certainly not the worst teacher I have ever had.

'I moved out of the city, and as it happened, the woman who owned the cottage where I rented a room was a yoga teacher, and she taught me. I even went on and qualified, doing an online course with Manu Chakraborty, a teacher in Agonda, Goa. I also undertook Pilates teacher training with Anna Morales in Kensal Rise.'

The details are so specific, who am I to question them? Indeed, I follow them up after our chat, and they do check out. There are some nasty rumour-mongers out there, aren't there?

'I've always had a bit of a knack for photography,' Rachel goes on, sipping a smoothie offered to her by a younger woman – also in F&G leisurewear – with loose, flowing brown curls just like her own. 'And I guess, with @rachelhoneyhill, I was just offering the right thing at the right time – a way for people to reconnect with themselves and with nature, at the moment when that sort of thing was becoming the zeitgeist. It just sort of grew from there.'

'But why the countryside thing?'

'That's the truly unique part of my offer. I grew up in the countryside, and always felt that it was my spiritual home. I wanted to share it with people who haven't necessarily had that experience.'

Time here to fill in the bit of background integral to the Rachel Rodrigues story. Her mother was the actress Janine Rodrigues, more famous for the life she led away from the fictional world of *Up the Junction*, the now-defunct TV soap in which she starred.

Mostly snapped tipping out of clubs at 3 a.m., flashing her gusset, with her make-up on the wrong parts of her face, Rodrigues senior met an untimely end in a horrific car crash. This was possibly partly caused by the paparazzi hot on her tail, but it was more likely down to the fact, revealed by the post-mortem, that she was four times over the drink-driving limit.

Rachel was just three years old. Thus orphaned – the identity of her father remains unknown – she was brought up in rural poverty and obscurity, somewhere in the West Country, by her strict religious grandparents, who considered her more a burden foisted on them by their estranged daughter than their own flesh and blood.

'It's not something I really discuss any more,' Rachel says when I press her on these circumstances. 'It's all there on the internet if you want to find out about it. I have nothing more to add.'

That aside, her amazing rags-to-riches rise is well documented. From renting a room in a rural cottage, she has gone on to buy and extend Honeyhill Barn, now the gorgeous backdrop to many of her Instagram posts. Her love of nature, the changing seasons, her horse, Cal, and her dog, Sam, are all part of the RR brand, and, some may say bizarrely, young urban women have been signing up to lust after the lifestyle in droves. All you need for happiness, she tells them, is good simple food, a bit of green space, time to meditate and move, and a few choice ethically produced items to wear and possess.

'Beauty is important,' Rachel says. 'Who wants to surround themselves with ugly objects? But if I sell things, I do so incidentally. My real mission is to give hope, encouragement, positivity to my followers. The recurrent theme I pick up from followers who DM me is that over the recent difficult years we've had in this world, I have provided those who need it with a sense of purpose, a reason to get up in the mornings.'

It has to be said, Rachel's offer has proved surprisingly popular. And in many ways, it provides a welcome antidote to the plastic Californian princesses holding up more blatantly unattainable standards of beauty and consumption. RR touches on the yearning for authenticity and connection that to some degree every one of us has felt these past few years.

We move on to the new development in the RR world: the reason why the lovely Wanda – who incidentally regularly appears on Rachel's Insta, posing as 'friend' @wandawoo – contacted me about this interview in the first place. Rachel looks down at her belly and strokes it.

'Yes, Beansprout,' she says.

I refrain from asking about the cutesy moniker and ask her instead why she has decided that now is the right time to get pregnant.

'I've always wanted a baby, but my twenties were too focused on partying. It's taken me this far into my thirties to feel that I can provide a secure enough future for my child. I take financial security very seriously, given what happened to me when my mother died.'

'You're keeping the identity of the father very quiet,' I say, before asking the question that has been on everyone's lips since the announcement. 'Is there a secret partner in your life?'

Rachel laughs. 'No! I have no time for a man.'

This, too, of course is part of the healthy Rachel Rodrigues brand – that women can do it on their own, that we don't need boyfriends and husbands in our lives unless we positively choose that path. That there is no stigma in being, like RR, independent and unattached. If the current Youth and Social Attitudes Survey is anything to go by, she is reflecting – possibly even playing a part in creating – a marked social trend. Over the past three years, there has been a twenty per cent drop in the number of young women who say they hope one day to find a partner.

'So you used a sperm bank?' I say.

'Please.' The smile has gone from her face. 'I don't wish to discuss Beansprout's conception.' Once again, she touches her belly. 'This is going to be a real person, and that information is private.'

'Did you feel at all conflicted then about posting your scan?' I ask her.

Rachel appears to be confused by this. She asks me for clarification.

'Isn't there an issue of consent about posting your baby *in utero*?'

She starts to laugh. But she refuses to answer my question.

'So how do you see "Beansprout" impacting on @rachel-honeyhill, then?'

'I hope my followers will come with me on this incredible journey,' she says. 'In a way this baby belongs to them as much as to me. I'm planning loads of great events over the next few months leading up to the birth.'

'How long is that?' I ask her.

'I'm twenty-nine weeks,' she says. 'So not long now.'

'Do you think it's advisable for an influencer with such a young following – the average age is eighteen – to advocate getting pregnant alone?'

'This is my life,' she says, looking straight down the camera at me. 'I'm not advocating anything.'

'You have lost quite a few followers since you made the announcement. Do you know why?'

Rachel says she doesn't, and that in any case, she's all about living her authentic life, rather than numbers. Before I can draw her out on that, she turns away from me and beckons to someone off screen.

'I want to introduce a new person in my life,' she says, holding out a hand. The woman with the matchy-matchy hair comes to join her in shot, obediently sitting beside her. 'This is my friend Abbie James,' Rachel says. 'She's come to live with me to help me out with the baby when he or she arrives.'

'She answered your ad,' I say. 'The one you put on your feed.'

'She did. She's a follower, aren't you, Abs?'

'I am, Rachel.' Abbie leans forward and nods. 'I'm her biggest fan.'

'And my followers are going to see a lot more of her over the coming months, as she settles in and gets down with the RR way of life,' Rachel says, chipping in over the top of her.

I ask Abbie how she feels about that. She says she feels very excited.

I begin to ask Rachel if Abbie, being younger, is part of a strategy to retain followers of that demographic, but she cuts me short. It is, she says, time for her evening meditation. She suggests I go to her channel to find one for myself. It will, she says, teach me kindness.

Follow Rachel and see what she does with – or to – Abbie on Instagram: @rachelhoneyhill. You can also find her on YouTube here and buy her wares here.

CHAPTER TEN

14 July

Rachel's roar makes Abbie bang her head on the clothes rail.

They've been back at Honeyhill a couple of days, and as part of her campaign to get everything in the house sorted for life after Beansprout is born, Abbie is tidying Rachel's walk-in wardrobe. It's a right old mess, nothing in the right place, lovely clothes just screwed up and stuffed onto the shelves or fallen off coat hangers into a tangled heap all over the floor.

As encouraged by Abbie, Rachel is having an hour's rest in the bedroom next door with a cooling gel eye mask over her eyes and her feet up on pillows.

At least Abbie thought she was.

She pokes her head out of the walk-in wardrobe. 'What's the matter?'

Rachel has flung her iPad across the room. Luckily it's landed on a floor cushion. The patchouli from the essential oil atomiser on the dressing table just about manages to smother the pig-farm stink, but it does little to cover the odour of outrage coming off her.

'That fucking two-faced Jane Roberts so-called journalist is the fucking matter,' she says. She lies back and tugs the eye mask over her face.

Abbie stands in the middle of the room, blinking, trying to work out how to fit this rage onto her Rachel.

'She's made out I'm some inauthentic money-grubbing cow,' Rachel says from behind her mask. 'Read it.'

Abbie picks up the iPad and sits on the side of the bed. Before she starts reading, she takes a breath and reminds herself that even though all this anger is unsettling, she is here, in RR's actual bedroom, being called on for by support by RR herself!

After the treatments and all the water therapy at the Baby-Moon, Abbie feels as if she has shed three layers of skin. Whenever she thinks it was all a dream, she just looks at her feet. A woman knelt in front of her for over an hour, cutting, filing, plucking, buffing and massaging. And now these soft things at the end of her legs, with their perfect shocking-pink toenails and smooth round heels, look like they belong to someone else.

Someone better than her.

Someone, through this great gift of being with Rachel, she will become.

She has to remember, though, never to take any of it for granted. If she does everything well, her life – and Rachel's, and Beansprout's, of course – will shine bright, forever.

She mustn't get lazy and fall back into all this comfort.

She's barely read the first paragraph of the article before Rachel sits up and pulls off her eye mask again.

'You lose all power with interviews. They just print what they like. I said afterwards that I didn't want any mention of numbers, and look what she's done. I swear it's the last one I'm doing. She makes me out to be a cynical bitch.'

Abbie scans on through the piece. She likes the mention of her hair. It's the first time she's ever been interviewed in a magazine.

'It's not so bad,' she says. 'She likes Racheletics.'

'"As a devoted yogini of two decades' standing, I find she's certainly not the worst teacher I have ever had"? Talk about damning with faint praise. What a class wanker.' Rachel grabs her phone, rolls off the bed and marches over to the other side of the room. 'Look as if you're reading it for the first time,' she tells Abbie.

That won't be hard, because Abbie really *is* reading it for the first time.

'And look cross, or a bit pissed off.'

Abbie tries her hardest, turns her mouth down, frowns.

'Lift your chin a bit,' Rachel says, and snaps her.

Abbie carries on with the article. She doesn't read all that much apart from social media, and anyway she's used to taking things at face value. But perhaps Rachel is right. Perhaps this really is a nasty article.

'Are your numbers really going down?' she asks, looking up.

Rachel sighs, steps over to the window and looks out. The view is lovely, out west over misty hills where the sun is setting, blazing a pink as bright as Abbie's toenails. Shepherd's delight.

'I've had a bit of a blip,' she says. 'Some of my younger followers thought I was going to leave them behind. And then some of the older women and the Christians disapprove of me going it alone. I'll gain new pregnant followers. It's just a matter of time.'

'You'd never leave your true followers behind, though, would you?' Abbie says.

'I'm not going to turn into one of those sappy influencers whose post-baby feeds are all adoring movies of their cutesy offspring, if that's what you mean. I know why people value me, and I'm not turning against everything I've worked so hard to build up over so many years.'

'Thank you,' Abbie says. If she were still a mere follower in her bedsit on City Road and Rachel's feed changed in a way that excluded her, she would have felt as empty and low as if someone had died.

She looks over at Rachel's bump, outlined by the blazing sunset outside the window. The future, she knows, is golden. She takes a deep breath and asks the other big question thrown up by this magazine article.

'*Do* you know who your dad is?'

Rachel does a double take. 'What?'

'She says here that your father remains unknown.'

'As you know, I'm all about truth and authenticity. I have no idea who my father was, and I could kill that Jane Roberts for digging that up yet again.'

Abbie wishes she could comfort her. 'That must be hard for you.'

'It would be hard for *you*, coming from your nice secure family background, but my whole childhood was defined by uncertainty. Everything seemed temporary to me. I didn't dare even imagine that anything I saw, touched or loved would last. That's why this baby is so important to me.'

She looks so beautiful saying this, standing there bathed in that light, in her full pregnant bloom. Like a goddess.

Then Abbie realises that Rachel is not now looking at her, but at her own reflection in the large mirror behind her.

'Quick.' She holds out her phone. 'Take a photo.'

Abbie does, and shows her the result.

'That's going on the feed, Abs,' Rachel says, hugging her.

Abbie's face goes beetroot with joy.

'We'll show that Jane Roberts how authentic I am,' Rachel says. 'The snotty cow.'

'You mustn't let her upset you. It's not good for Beansprout.'

'I really want to hurt her.' Rachel looks at Abbie. 'Badly.'

Oh, there's a mad bit of steel in her eye when she says it. A mad bit of steel Abbie recognises all too well. She wants to take a tissue and ease it out, like a stray eyelash.

'Why don't you put your feet back up?' she says. 'And I'll go and make you a nice cup of chamomile.'

INSTAGRAM POST

rachelhoneyhill
Devon, England
paid partnership with **fitsofitso**
215,603 likes

Images
- Abbie smiling, holding up her wrist to show off her FitSo tracker on a bubblegum-pink strap
- Rachel and Abbie smiling, holding their FitSo tracker wrists together. Rachel's has a stainless-steel strap
- Abbie on the SmartStep scales, smiling as Rachel weighs her
- Rachel tracking the FitSo data on her iPad as Abbie works out in the background.

Text
Abbie and I are **@fitsofitso** sisters! We're both kitted out with the latest awesome state-of-the-art tracker that lets us see all our stats at a glance.
Abbie's FitSo even has a special trainer tracker function, so that I can see exactly how she's doing.
No cheating, Abbie!
Using the SmartStep scales we can also keep track of Abbie's progress in reducing her body fat and building lean muscle!!
Truly taking personal training to the next level!
Don't you love her new hair, too? I'm weaning her off the straighteners!
#AbbiesJourney #fitness #MothersHelper #Racheletics #friends #naturalhair

CHAPTER ELEVEN

15 July

Rachel's in the kitchen, blasting up two post-workout peanut-butter vegan-protein raspberry wheatgrass oatmeal smoothies. She casts her eye over at Abbie, who is in the living area, slumped on the sofa gulping water, her eyes closed.

Perhaps she should have gone a bit easier on her.

But kudos. Little Miss Please and Thank You is determined. To sprint on the treadmill until you literally throw up, that's really something. The past couple of days in the gym have proved that this girl does appear to have some grit in her. Perhaps Rachel can turn it into a pearl.

As she passes Abbie the smoothie, Wanda strides through the door, clearly trying her best to look efficient. Sometimes Rachel has to work very hard not to slap Wanda.

'You look nice and sweaty, Abs,' Wanda says as she passes her.

Rachel wishes she could tell what Abbie thinks about that.

Wanda places the basket of opened packages and letters on the kitchen worktop. 'No turds or condoms today, Rach.'

'Phew,' Rachel says.

'What's that?' Abbie asks.

'Haters,' Wanda says.

Abbie looks at Rachel. 'What?'

'People out there whose only purpose seems to be to try to upset me. It's not too hard to work out the address here, so…' Rachel sifts through the mail.

'That's disgusting,' Abbie says, with surprising force.

'She used to open it all herself,' Wanda says. 'But now I do, so she only sees the nice stuff. And hence all the security systems. In case anyone gets any bigger ideas…'

'Enough, Wanda, I think. Ah. Finally.' Rachel pulls a small cardboard box from the pile of packages and letters and hands it to Abbie. 'Present for you.'

'For me?' Abbie says, her face turning red. 'Thank you!'

'Ooh.' Wanda slides her bony arse onto one of the breakfast stools.

'Thanks, Wanda,' Rachel says. 'You can go now.'

Wanda leaves, huffily. Rachel would like to get rid of her, truth be told, although Fran says that three fired assistants in as many years – and one of them quite badly scarred – is not a good look. And of course, despite all the NDAs in the world, even an unscathed ex-employee knows where the bodies are buried, and therefore poses a security risk.

Abbie takes the box – the suppliers have gift-wrapped it, which is sweet but not surprising considering the exposure they are going to get out of Rachel using it on Abbie.

'It's a top-of-the-range FitSo,' Rachel says.

'Blimey. Thank you. Like yours,' Abbie says, holding the unwrapped box as if Rachel has just handed her an engagement ring.

'"Taking personal training to the next level". And they've sent a choice of straps, too.'

She shows her the three on offer: a matt-black neoprene, a silver metal and a hideous bubblegum-pink rubber.

Abbie chooses the pink.

'Hold it up!' Rachel says, once they've fastened it on her wrist.

It takes ten shots to arrive at the right snap: Abbie smiling, looking happy, not daunted.

'Right then, let's get it all set up,' Rachel says, grabbing her iPad. 'You should aim for ten thousand steps every day.'

'How far is that?'

'Depends on your stride, but about seven kilometres.'

'I can't do that!'

'You'll surprise yourself. Hey. No time like the present.'

'Should you be going for such a long walk in your condition?' Abbie says, as they head out along the lane from Honeyhill. Sam bounds on ahead, off the lead.

'I don't know what your other women have been like, but pregnancy isn't a disease.' Rachel adjusts her silk bandanna to catch the stray wisps of hair blowing into her mouth. 'Women who exercise at least thirty minutes a day throughout their pregnancy have easier, faster labours, they feel better post-partum and their recovery is much quicker.' In fact Rachel is walking below her normal exercise pace, but Abbie is already slightly out of breath. 'It also reduces the odds of developing depression by sixty-seven per cent.'

'How do you know all this?' Abbie stumbles along behind her as she turns into the footpath between the farm and the barn.

'I like to do my research,' Rachel says.

'But you don't do all that sweaty stuff you made me do earlier?' Abbie picks up a stick and throws it for Sam.

'A bit of strength work, but it's mostly yoga and stretching at the moment.' To demonstrate how physically able she is, Rachel takes a stile extra-smoothly. 'I still run, but I've cut it back to just three times a week.'

'Just three times!' Abbie hauls herself over the stile with a lot less grace.

Rachel reaches out a hand to help her down. 'Do you run?'

'They tried to make me do a cross-country thing when I was at school, but I fainted.'

'You managed on the treadmill.'

'That's different.'

'You just need to build up to it slowly. Then you'll wonder why it took you so long.'

They carry on, walking across a large field full of oilseed rape in full bloom. Yellow pollen dances in the air. Abbie sneezes and Rachel hands her a tissue.

'Thank you. I get a bit of hay fever,' Abbie says through streaming eyes.

'We'll get some local honey down you. Strictly speaking, we shouldn't, as vegans, eat it, but it's from a small supplier, and it really does work wonders.'

'Thank you.'

'I thought we'd call in on Cal on the way,' Rachel says, as they follow a narrow track through a small copse. 'I normally drive to his stables, but this route takes us right past.'

'I was wondering when I'd see him. Why's he not at Honeyhill?'

'I don't have the time to be looking after a horse. It's a massive commitment.'

'But all those pictures of you grooming him, feeding him, mucking him out…'

'Oh, I like to do all that,' she says, as breezily as she can. 'Just not every day. Sometimes. Here we are.'

She sails over a five-bar gate and waits on the other side for Abbie and Sam to join her.

With Sam now on the lead – which Abbie rather sweetly begged to hold – they stride past paddocks fenced off by electric wire. Rachel loves it here at the stables: the wide-open green pastures, dotted with horses and set off by the hills in the background. The sweet smell of horse, leather and earth at once excites and relaxes her. If ever she feels hemmed in by all the responsibilities of her life, or when the ghosts of her past become too insistent, this is where she comes.

Horses understand, and they don't pass judgement.

That's not to say she's here often, though. She's too ashamed to own up to Abbie that this is her first visit in over a month. But so what, she tells herself. The stables are excellent, and she has a good thing going on with them. Just one story last year featuring a group hack filled up their riding lessons for twelve months. She is confident that Cal is in the best possible hands. Better than hers, to be sure – she is not proud of how slack things got before she stabled him here.

'Why have they got those horrible masks on?' Abbie says as they pass a group of particularly lovely mares.

'To keep the flies away from their faces.'

'Hmm.' She doesn't look convinced.

As they arrive at the yard, Julie, the manager, comes out of her office to greet them, striding, as usual, as if she still has a horse between her legs. 'Hello, stranger,' she says.

Rachel winces. 'How's he doing?' she asks. She realises, too late, that she should have said hello and introduced Abbie.

It's all OK, though, because, attuned exclusively to equine needs, Julie barely registers Abbie's presence. 'He's such a lovely boy,' she says, pointing them to where Cal is stabled.

Rachel hopes Abbie likes Cal. She's going to add coming down here to visit him as another item on her job description, thereby assuaging some of her guilt about not doing so herself. A picture forms in her mind of Abbie pushing Beansprout down here to say hello to Cal, and then she sees Beansprout, a little older, being held up on his back as she learns to ride.

She is already framing these fantasies about her unborn child as Instagram posts: #Horseyfun, #GeeGeeBaby. She's not going to feel bad about it, though. This is partly what the baby's for, after all. Crudely put, it's like a glamour model having a boob job to enhance her employment prospects.

Rachel opens Cal's stable door and steps in. Abbie hangs back with Sam on the other side of the threshold.

'Hello, boy.' Rachel strokes his velvet muzzle and holds out some horse nuts for him to nibble on. 'Come and say hi, Abbie. He won't bite.'

Cautiously Abbie steps forward. She actually looks terrified. 'He's so big,' she whispers.

'Here.' Rachel palms some horse nuts into her hand. 'Hold it out, fingers flat, so he doesn't mistake them for something tasty.'

There is something of the child about Abbie as she does as she is told. Her tongue pokes out ever so slightly at the corner of her mouth. The world seems to go silent as she and Cal stand there, joined by horse nuts.

When he's finished, she sighs. It's a big, fluttering-out breath. 'That was lovely,' she says. 'Thank you.'

'Stroke his forelock,' Rachel says, showing her how.

'I love you, boy,' Abbie says.

Rachel finds this encounter deeply heartening. With a toddler Beansprout there, it would have made an excellent post.

Soon, soon, though.

She's finding that she's getting quite fond of Abbie, with all her pluck and gratitude.

It's rather cute, really.

INSTAGRAM POST

rachelhoneyhill
Honey Hill, England
paid partnership with **getyourglowoneu**
102,516 likes

Image
- Selfie taken by Rachel of herself and Abbie on Honey Hill, with Westbourne Parva in the distance. Abbie's hair is windblown, her skin pink, her eyes bright. In her hand she has a Get Your Glow On bar, a bite already taken.

Text
We're out in the glorious Devon countryside, 8,000 steps into a walk (say our **@fitsofitso** trackers) and we're in need of fuel! What could be better than an all-vegan organic **@getyourglowoneu** apple salted-caramel protein bar? Just what your body and soul needs.
Abbie says 'Yum!'
#AbbiesJourney #fitness #MothersHelper #walking #vegan #snack #GYGO #friends

CHAPTER TWELVE

They've walked for forty minutes since leaving the stables, and as they labour up a steep, grassy hill, Abbie is beginning to wonder if they'll ever turn back towards the barn. Her FitSo says she's done eight thousand steps already.

She's stripped right down to the sports vest and shorts she had on for that killing workout, but if it weren't for the sweat holding her skin together, she would be exploding with the heat. Worst of all, it's gone lunchtime and Rachel shows no sign of stopping for the snacks in the rucksack squelching around on Abbie's perspiring back.

She feels like crying and saying she can't go on, but she's not going to show weakness. So she pushes herself upwards, past prickling clumps of pina-colada-scented gorse, her eyes on the scabby cluster of hawthorns at the top, where hopefully they can stop for a rest. Sam doodles around her ankles, like he is egging her on. Sweet Sam. He and she are turning out to be big buddies.

How can Rachel leave a beautiful creature like Cal for someone else to look after? What's the point of owning an animal if you don't give it your best self? That's what Rachel said on her Instagram. Abbie remembers that 'best self' post really well. It even had Cal in it, with Rachel riding him, the sunshine behind her making her hair all shiny and lovely. It was because of that post that Abbie got Barney.

'Phew,' Rachel says as they reach the top. 'Pass us the water.'

Gratefully, Abbie stops, swings the rucksack off her back and pulls out Rachel's water bottle. 'Is it OK if I have one of the snack bars, please?' she asks. All she's had all day is that smoothie, which was OK, but she'd hardly call it food.

'I'm not your keeper!' Rachel smiles and puts her hands on her haunches to stretch her back out.

Before she can get the food in her mouth, Abbie has an attack of dizziness. She bends over.

'Are you OK?' Rachel says.

'Yes, thanks. Just a bit… Ooh.'

Rachel takes her hand and talks her through some stabilising breathing exercises to get oxygen back into her body. 'In, two, three, four. Hold, two, three, four. Out two, three, four. You're doing great!' She is so incredibly fit and agile, even at nearly thirty-two weeks pregnant, and here she is being lovely, concerned for Abbie's well-being.

Abbie can feel the energy coming from her touch. Finally her breath stabilises.

'Yes!' Rachel high-fives her. 'Now eat something. You need to replenish your stocks.'

Abbie unwraps a Get Your Glow On bar. Because they are one of the more affordable products RR endorses, she has tried most of the range. They're actually not too bad. Indeed, the apple salted-caramel one she's tucking into right now is one of her favourite healthy foods.

'Look up, Abbie!' Rachel says. She's standing behind her, her phone up in front of them.

Abbie obeys, and Rachel snaps a selfie of the two of them.

'See,' she says, showing her the screen. 'You look like a different person already!'

Abbie squints at the image. Rachel, of course, looks gorgeous. But she doesn't look quite so bad herself. Apart from her chin – she has a thing about her chin, which is at best weak in photographs – she hardly recognises herself. She looks so healthy and – yes – happy. She could almost be one of Rachel's friends.

She stops herself. She *is* Rachel's friend. She. Is. Rachel's. Friend.

'And you're holding the GYGO bar so that the wrapper is entirely visible,' Rachel says, putting her arm around her so that Abbie gets a whiff of fresh sweat and salty deodorant. 'You're a bloody natural, Abs. One for the 'Gram, no doubt about that.'

The praise makes Abbie glow so much that she's sure she can be seen from the little village in the valley beyond them.

'Where is that?' she asks.

'Westbourne Parva,' Rachel says. 'Place of your birth. Today's destination.'

Oh no, Abbie thinks to herself.

They come to a halt by the little playground tucked away at the edge of the village green, against some tall poplars. The lawn has been freshly mowed; the peppery, grassy smell scratches Abbie's nostrils, and again she sneezes.

'Bless you.' Rachel hands her another tissue. 'I know you left when you were tiny, but I bet you haven't forgotten this.'

Abbie remembers the playground only too well. And the village: she's come back here on several occasions, none of them particularly happy. The swings and slide look so much smaller now. The ancient oak beside them, having been around longer than anyone on the planet, nods in the breeze like it has seen it all. It's all so beautiful, but it was hers for such a short, awful while. She feels like crying.

'Where did your family live?' Rachel asks her.

'The Meadows,' Abbie says, mentioning a famously upmarket cul-de-sac of executive homes built in the late 1980s on the other side of the village.

'Oh, la-di-dah,' Rachel says, and Abbie smiles. She opens the gate and leads Abbie through to the playground. 'Grandmother used to leave me here when she went to the village shop. Though back then it wasn't fenced off, and there was a dangerous hard surface. I broke my arm once, falling off that slide.'

'Your grandparents lived close by, then?' Beyond it being somewhere in the West Country, Rachel has never let on publicly exactly where she grew up. But because of her own family stories, Abbie does know that Janine Rodrigues hung around the area when she was young, so it stands to reason that it wasn't far from Westbourne.

Rachel looks at her. She's smiling, a little shamefaced. 'OK, so I'd better tell you this, because it sort of links us.'

Abbie starts. 'What?' Her voice comes out almost as a squeak.

'I need you to remember your NDA.' Rachel laughs. 'Keep this firmly under your hat, or else I'll have to kill you.'

Abbie nods. A prickle of anticipation runs up her sweating back.

'Let's take the weight off our feet first, though.' Rachel points at a bench, placed for parents to keep watch over their children. A bench, Abbie thinks with a thrill, where she will soon be sitting herself, watching children. Rachel loosens her trainers and pulls them off, followed by her socks, then she wriggles her perfect toes. 'Jesus, that's better.'

Abbie doesn't follow suit. Beautiful as they are after the pedicure, her own sore feet will be stinking after all the sweating. Instead, to cover her impatience to hear what Rachel has to tell her, she gets her water bottle out of the backpack and takes a swig.

Eventually Rachel takes a deep breath and holds out her little finger. 'You have to promise not to tell *anyone*. Pinky swear.'

Abbie curls her own little finger around Rachel's. She is so excited she thinks she might pee.

'OK, then. My grandparents owned Honeyhill Farm, and that's where I grew up.'

Abbie blinks and gasps. This isn't the revelation she was expecting. She tries and fails to fit this into what she knows about Rachel. That beautiful house, all that land. 'But you said they were poor!'

'They were. Cash poor. They had the farm – they lived in that horrible bungalow at the end of the lane. You've seen it, yeah?'

Abbie nods. 'The pig farm.'

'It was arable in their day. But by the time I lived with them, they had stopped working the land – they were too old to do much, so they had nothing coming in. I was only a kid. All I knew was that the house was always freezing, the food was cheap and rubbish, and they said they had no spare cash for anything beyond the basics. No toys or books for me.'

'So they left it to you when they died?'

Rachel nods. 'Not officially. They didn't have wills. It passed to me as I was the only living descendant. I sold the farm and land and used the proceeds to do up the barn.'

'Really?'

'Yes. Why?'

'I thought you bought it with your own money, that you'd earned yourself.'

'Have I ever said that explicitly?' Rachel's tone slightly reminds Abbie of how she was when she was angry about that magazine article.

'No. I suppose not.' Abbie hates to think that she might have upset her. 'Sorry.'

Rachel looks away, over to the poplars swaying in the hot breeze, their leaves rattling. 'Believe me, Abbie. If anyone earned that place, it was me. Jesus Christ.' She closes her eyes.

'Sorry.'

But Rachel doesn't respond. Instead her lips move like she is counting, and her fingers beat a sort of rhythm on her arm. Eventually she breathes out slowly and rubs her face. 'Can I have the backpack, please?' she asks, her voice tight and small.

Abbie hands over the bag. Rachel pulls out a tin box containing a bunch of grapes. She sits and stares at the daisy-carpeted grass, snapping off the grapes one by one and throwing them into her mouth.

'So you must have gone to the village school, then?' Abbie tries to steer onto safer ground. 'I was there just for reception, although it would have been a few years after you were there.'

'I went to school nearby.' Rachel snaps the lid back onto the tin box.

'Oh?' Abbie takes a swig from her bottle.

'Mothcombe.'

Abbie nearly chokes on her water. 'The posh school?'

'Look. It may sound posh, but it wasn't, OK?'

'But how could they afford to send you there if they were so poor?'

'Probably the only sensible thing my mother did in her entire life was to put some money by for my education. It was all she left me, apart from this.' Rachel holds out her hand to show Abbie the signet ring with her mother's initials, JR, engraved into it. Abbie knows it well: Rachel wears it all the time, and her hands appear so often in her cookery and crafting videos that she recognises them as readily as her own.

'Even though the school is so close to the farm,' Rachel goes on, 'my grandparents decided to send me as a boarder. They had as little to do with me as possible, while still fulfilling their duties as "good Christians".' Her perfect upturned little nose wrinkles when she says this.

It wouldn't be an exaggeration to say that these revelations have rocked Abbie's foundations. But she goes on, as lightly as she can manage, 'Aren't you afraid of people finding out? I mean, they know your surname, your mum was famous…'

Rachel turns to face her. 'Is that a threat?'

Abbie holds up her hands. 'I would never grass you up, Rachel. I want you to know that right now. Anything you say goes no further than here.'

'Of course you wouldn't.' Rachel puts a hand over her heart. 'I know I can trust you. I feel it in here. You're a good person.'

Abbie finds herself blushing again. Rachel's words have instantly smoothed down the disappointment building inside her. A good person. No one has ever said that about her before.

Rachel pulls two bananas out of the bag and offers one to Abbie.

Abbie takes it. She could eat a cow right now.

'You see.' Rachel bites the very tip off her banana and nibbles the tiny mouthful as if she is counting the times she chews. 'My mother used a stage name and I've taken it on. Hard, therefore, to trace.'

Abbie is amazed. 'I never knew.'

'Course you didn't!' Rachel laughs. 'I keep my secrets close. Don't get me wrong. Despite how it sounds, it was a far from luxurious childhood. From when I was eleven, I didn't even go back to my grandparents' house in the holidays.'

'You stayed at the school?'

She nods. 'My mother's money allowed it. There were a few of us whose parents were either too busy or too dead to have us with them. It's hard for you to understand, Abbie, coming from such a stable family background, but it's tough not having anyone to love you.'

Abbie nods. She does understand this only too well, of course. But if Rachel can have secrets, then so can she.

'At least I had Fran there,' Rachel says.

'You were at school together?'

'Yeah. And her folks were busy, important people back in Senegal, so she hardly ever went home either. We got up to all sorts.'

'It must be nice, having a best friend like that,' Abbie says.

'I couldn't live without her, nor she me.'

Abbie takes this in.

'All that is too difficult to explain for it to be @rachelhoneyhill's story. She's more about the present than the past, anyway.' Rachel stands and holds out her hand for Abbie's banana skin. 'Done?'

Abbie hands it to her and pulls the rucksack on. At the moment, she's just the mother's helper. She has no illusions about that. But she is going to do everything in her power to join Fran as someone Rachel can't live without.

All she needs to prove herself is a bit of time, a bit of luck and a fair wind behind her.

'We weren't really supposed to come to the village at all during term time,' Rachel says, as they pass the council estate. 'Out of bounds, they told us. Fran and me, though, we were the naughty ones. We'd disguise ourselves so no teachers would spot us and we'd come down and meet a couple of lads, that sort of thing. Always up to no good. But even we avoided the appropriately named Dicklands estate. You probably wouldn't know about it, coming from the posh side of the village, but there were a few of "those sorts" of families living here, if you know what I mean.'

Abbie nods.

'Still looks pretty rough,' Rachel goes on. She leans in to whisper to Abbie. 'I mean, look at that.'

A furious-looking woman in her mid-forties has burst out of the front door of the end of the first terrace of houses. She stamps grubby slippers across the messy shared front garden. It's gone midday and she is still in a faded pink dressing gown that looks like it hasn't seen a washing machine its entire life. In one hand she has a fag, and in the other a clear plastic bag with a dog turd in it.

She's heading towards her next-but-one neighbour, who's leaning in his doorway in a stained grey tracksuit, smirking at her and smoking. An Alsatian and a pit bull bark wildly in his front window.

'What the fuck do you call this? What the fuck do you call this?' she yells at him.

'Stupid bint,' the man says, the casual threat of violence in his voice making Abbie's spine prickle.

The woman throws the bag at the man's feet, then turns to go back to her own house. As she does so, she catches sight of Abbie and Rachel and stops short, her fag dangling from her open lips, staring at them.

'She looks like she's seen a ghost,' Rachel says, laughing.

'Perhaps she recognises you,' Abbie says.

But Abbie knows that the reason she's staring at them has nothing to do with Rachel, or a ghost. Not that sort of ghost, anyway.

'State of it. Come on,' Rachel says. 'Let's get out of here before she starts flinging dog crap at us, too.'

Abbie is only too keen to leave. Her FitSo is now at fifteen thousand and they've got to walk all the way back.

INSTAGRAM POST

rachelhoneyhill
Devon, England
paid partnership with the **gbnurserypaintco**
534,902 likes

Image
- Rachel and Zander paint the nursery wall a sage green, behind the handmade wooden cot, which is fully made up with mobile and teddies positioned on the bedding.

Text
Only another three months to go, and **@zanderbabe** came over to help me get ready here at Honeyhill!
I'm so hands-on!
Don't you adore the colour we're using on Beansprout's nursery walls? It's called Baby's Breath and it's by the Great British Nursery Paint Company, who make the most fabulous toxin-free paints to give our children the healthiest starts. I'll post later so you can see the nursery in all its finished glory. I'm choosing green because it is the colour of nature, and it is gender neutral, something very close to my heart.
I can't wait to lie little Beansprout down in this fabulous cot! It's handmade in Cirencester by **@cotsandco**, who also make these adorable matching mobiles and this totally organic bedding.
Admittedly, it's not cheap, but you want to give your baby the very best start in life, don't you?
#baby #cot #nursery #paint #green #organic #GreatBritishNurseryPaintCo #friends

CHAPTER THIRTEEN

16 July

Rachel knows she shouldn't be doing this.

She's telling herself that it is just about getting to know her employee better. Talk about a closed book. Abbie has been here for ten days, and Rachel has shared almost all her secrets with her, but has had virtually nothing back in return. There's still something about Abbie that she can't put her finger on. It's not that she mistrusts her or anything – indeed, she admires the way she has so far pushed herself physically with the eating and exercise plan – but she knows that still waters run deep.

What, she thinks, as she watches Abbie on the house cameras, is going on behind that pale, blank face?

Knowing Fran will be able to read her better, she presses the record button on the console with the idea of running some of the footage past her, see what she thinks. She'll no doubt get a long spiel about how she's invading Abbie's privacy, legal implications, blah, blah, blah, but when it comes down to it, what are she and Fran if not partners in crime?

The cameras are there because security is important to Rachel. She has had numerous dealings with the unbalanced: Vial of blood, anyone? Requests for used tampons? And she doesn't want to get started on the grievance-fuelled vitriol of certain ex-employees. She is vulnerable.

She has endured two unwelcome incursions into her home. The first, one Friday three years ago, was when one of those ex-employees, Charley, forgot to activate the system when she went home. That evening, Rachel turned round from her NutriBullet to find a stocky freckled man standing in her living room in muddied clothes, his mouth open, his lower jaw hanging a little sideways, eyeing her.

'All right, my lover,' he said.

Having peak physical fitness on her side, she sprinted to her bedroom and activated the panic-room doors. By the time the security firm arrived, the intruder had disappeared, but the damage was done, horrific trauma had resurfaced for Rachel, and Charley went on to pay a possibly inflated price for her stupid, idiotic, moronic mistake. Rachel didn't call the police that time. She tries, wherever possible, to avoid contact with the law.

The second time was a year ago, when an intruder managed to get into the house posing as a representative from a vitamin brand interested in partnering.

Wanda let her in, and while she was waiting in the living room for Rachel to appear, she took off all her clothes and arranged herself naked on the sofa, a remote-controlled camera on a tripod in front of her. When Rachel entered the room, the camera flashed, making her cry out in shock. It perfectly captured the outrage on her face, showing her utterly unmasked, all her defences down, out of control.

She shudders even now when she thinks of it. She was at a very low point at the time, getting over a miscarriage that nobody knew about. She can't remember much about what happened in the seconds following the flash, but she knows it wasn't pretty.

Luckily, it was a video day, and Drew, who is not what you would call a small man, heard the girl screaming, came charging through to see what was going on and managed to pull her away from Rachel, who apparently went on to grab the camera and rip out the memory card.

Before Rachel could stop her, Wanda called the police. It turned out that this person claimed to be a big fan of multiple influencers. But she was also an art student and was making staged interventions in the lives of her heroes. Her naked pose was supposed to be something to do with high and low culture, artifice and reality.

After the girl had been taken away, Rachel found a tiny chunk of what looked like skin under the nails of her right hand. Fearful that she might be accused of assault, she quickly said she didn't want to press charges, an act that had the added benefits of both making her appear gracious and cutting off any more contact with the police. Instead, she got Fran to take out an anti-harassment injunction, and to further mitigate any potential damage to her reputation, she sent the girl a replacement memory card, a signed photograph and a hundred-pound voucher to spend on the F&G website.

One intruder was bad luck. Two was a fault in the system. She needed something further to reassure her. Hence the hidden cameras and microphones, which wirelessly transmit the goings-on from every room to an app on Rachel's iPad. She now regularly checks each room, and monitors every visitor before she goes to meet them. Indeed, she often has the grid of feeds up on her monitor as she hangs out in her bedroom, just to keep an eye on things.

For honourable, ethical reasons – and because Wanda knows about the system – she doesn't watch Wanda in her office. Also, since Abbie's arrival, Rachel has turned off the feed from the cameras and microphones in the nanny flat. She is aware that greater integrity could be shown by also physically removing them, but she didn't get round to that before Abbie arrived, and it would seem odd now to alert her to their existence.

She has eyed the black spaces where the images should be on her viewing grid and has been sorely tempted. It's a bit like standing on the edge of a cliff and finding yourself fighting the irrational urge to throw yourself off. To flick the switch on those cameras would be equally destructive, though, both to Abbie's privacy and to Rachel's standing as a human being who deserves to walk the earth.

But it's all right to watch Abbie as she sorts out the baby's room. She would be there herself overseeing if it weren't for this overwhelming fatigue that has poleaxed her since their walk yesterday.

She overdid it going all the way to Westbourne Parva and back, she knows, but she really wanted to see Abbie's reaction to return-ing to the village where she was born. She hoped that it would bring her guard down, but in fact, of course, it just led to Rachel running her own mouth off, exposing her own secrets and lies.

Not that she suspects Abbie of having secrets and lies.

She doesn't think she's that interesting.

Perhaps it's the frisson of the transgression, but she can't keep her eyes off Abbie as she stands in the middle of the large room destined to be Beansprout's nursery. Something, surely, has to be going on in there?

'Blooming mess,' Abbie mutters to herself.

Rachel can't argue with that. Apart from one corner, dressed for a recent photo shoot to look like she and Zander were painting the walls, the nursery is currently a dumping ground for all the stuff Rachel gets sent that she doesn't want to use. It started off as a reject pile, and now it's a reject room. Well, rooms, really, because there are equally large stashes in two other bedrooms, the garage and the loft.

Her plan is that one day she will give it all away to charity, but what might seem a simple, generous act is fraught with difficulties that have completely stalled her.

Is she planning to do it out of the kindness of her heart, or is she doing it because it might make a good story? She honestly can't tell. Even if her motivation is goodness, is she just doing that to make herself feel saintly, or to atone for her sins, or is her urge genuinely to help other people? Is it possible for both to exist in the same person, the same act?

Again she is stumped. If she takes the good-story angle – and she hates to say it, but this tempts her sorely – then how can she show it without revealing what freebies she doesn't want to hold onto and pissing off the brands and the PRs that sent them to her?

It's a stagnant minefield, and Abbie is standing right in the middle of it. As a sort of initiative test, and a perfect way to have the decision taken out of her hands, Rachel has told her that it is up to her to determine what to do with all the stuff. She can keep what she wants and give away or recycle the rest. So if anything backfires, it's not Rachel's fault.

But Abbie's still just standing there, in the middle of the room, looking at it all – cardboard boxes piled up against every wall with *FOR CHARITY?* scrawled on each one, like a statement of intent. There are also stacks of clothes dumped on the floor and a crammed line of makeshift metal garage shelves that Wanda's predecessor put up in a short-lived attempt to organise toiletries, foodstuffs and supplements.

All this is beyond Abbie's job description, admittedly, but she didn't object when Rachel mentioned it. So.

Finally she rolls up her sleeves, takes hold of the big cardboard box nearest the door and upends it onto the floor. She kneels to start sorting through the contents – mostly sports and yoga gear, all unworn and still in its packaging.

But when Rachel sees what else is in the box, she lets out an audible squeak.

If she could reach through the camera and whisk it away, she would. She toys with the idea of hauling herself up and sprinting the entire length of the barn and up the stairs to distract Abbie long enough to grab it.

But just as she's rolling herself up from the bed, she sees Abbie freeze. For a tiny, hopeful moment, she thinks the feed has packed in. But no. Abbie's hand reaches out and picks up the matinee jacket she gave Rachel when she arrived.

Everything about that little coat filled Rachel with horror. It was badly hand-knitted, for one. The wool was highly synthetic, and it was a depressing pastel peach colour with nasty ribbons that surely shouldn't be allowed on baby clothes. If she had believed that Abbie had knitted it specially for Beansprout, she would have taken greater care of it. But it was clearly second-hand. It stank of nasty chemical washing powder, and worst of all, there was a tiny baked-in shit-coloured stain on the inside back.

Rachel knows that Abbie would want Beansprout to wear it. So to avoid actually throwing it away, she discreetly handed the thing to Wanda, asking her to deal with it. Her hope was that, when the time came and it was nowhere to be found, she could blame it on her assistant.

She did not expect Wanda to put it in one of the *FOR CHARITY?* boxes.

Damn bloody Wanda.

She peeps from between her fingers to see what Abbie is going to do with this discovery. Is she going to come charging to her room, waving it and calling her names? In a way, she deserves that.

But no. Ever so slowly, Abbie stands. Holding the thing to her face, she breathes in the artificial scent of it. As she turns to the window, her face is entirely visible to the camera, and Rachel sees that her eyes are watering. Perhaps it's the chemicals coming off the jacket.

She can't watch any more. She feels as dirty as the mean little voice inside her – a constant companion after The Event – tells her she actually is.

But just as she is about to turn the camera off, the feed from the microphone crackles as Abbie sniffs and wipes her nose with the back of her hand. She's muttering something, her lips moving. Rachel puts her ear to the iPad speaker, but it's too quiet to make out what it is.

INSTAGRAM POST

rachelhoneyhill
Devon, England
paid partnership with **babymama**
104,236 likes

Image
- Rachel twirls with arms out in a new BabyMama silk dress in the middle of the expansive Honeyhill lawn, the tree ferns behind her and the blue sky above. Sam plays around her feet.

Text
People often ask me why I choose to live in the countryside. I consider it a privilege to be out here in nature, with the wide-open spaces as well as freedom and security. I love twirling like this in my fabulous **@babymama** organic silk dress.
Even if you live in the city, do yourself a favour and seek out green places. Your soul will thank you for it!
We are what we are, not what we do.
#countryside #green #nature #soul #feedyoursoul #inspiration

CHAPTER FOURTEEN

When she's pulled herself back together, Abbie folds the little matinee jacket in what she thinks of as 'the shop way'. She swipes a load of toiletries off one of the metal shelves. After using her sleeve to wipe the shelf clean of dust, she puts the tiny piece of clothing in the middle, all alone.

It must have been a mistake. There's probably a box in the room that's for Beansprout's things, and someone put it in one of the charity boxes by mistake. It's the only explanation Abbie's going to allow to enter her head.

She's got to stay positive.

'It was probably Wanda,' she says to the little jacket.

As if to confirm her suspicions, her iPhone buzzes. It's Wanda on the housekeeping WhatsApp. She's been nagging on and on at Abbie with this since she arrived:

Abbie, what do you want me to order from Goodfoods for next week's dinners?

Abbie, will you make sure you have the baby room clear for the decorator at the end of the week?

Abbie, can you make sure Rachel gets back to Cots & Co? They're not happy about the 'not cheap' comment, and thought they were getting a standalone post, not being tagged on to the paint company.

Abbie, can you help Rachel decide on the newborn layette offer from Littles? They're a potential partner and time is running out.

Abbie, I *really* need to know what you want me to order from Goodfoods for next week's dinners.

Abbie hasn't replied to any of these beyond a thumbs-up. It feels very much to her that Wanda is trying to queen it over her, and she's not going to play along. While she is happy to do all of these tasks – indeed, she is beyond excited at the thought of going through baby products with Rachel – she will only take instruction from Rachel, not her Skinny Minnie minion.

This new message is yet another one about Goodfoods. Apparently Wanda has to get the order in by six today.

Or what? Abbie thinks. The whole world will fall in?

The baby's room is more of a mess than when she started, but as Posh June says, you can't make an omelette without cracking eggs. And anyway, finding the jacket has killed her enthusiasm for the project. She'll come back at it full blast later, once she's had it out with Wanda.

She heads along the corridor and past her own rooms towards the stairs, thrilling again at the thought that Rachel wants the baby's room to be up here so that she can do the nights.

She is itching to smell a baby's head again. She really misses it.

Wanda is in her office off the entrance hall, where she's working at her computer, sitting at her desk and facing the door. From the screen reflected in the window behind her, Abbie can see that she is doing something on an online bank account.

She's a messy mare, Wanda. Every surface is covered with used coffee cups, hair bands, little golden twists of empty Werther's Originals wrappers, hand cream, make-up, socks and all sorts of other crap. There's even, Abbie notes with disgust, an earwax-coated cotton bud just by her mouse mat.

What if there were an unexpected visitor and they got a glimpse of this stinking pit? How would that be for RR?

'I could tidy up in here if you like,' she says.

'Oh, hi, Abbie.' Wanda looks up from her screen, goes bright red and quickly clicks shut the window she's working on.

Like she's got something to hide.

'Have you done the Goodfoods order?' she asks.

'I don't like being nagged,' Abbie says.

Wanda looks shocked. 'Sorry?'

'It'd probably be easier if I did it myself direct, on the website.'

Wanda's mouth makes a prissy little moue. 'I'm afraid I'm the only one authorised to use the account.'

'I'm sure Rachel would trust me.'

'I'm sure she would, Abbie. But there has to be accountability, and if it's spread too thinly…'

Abbie rolls her eyes. Wanda's clearly desperate to cling on to every little bit of power she possesses.

'I looked in the freezer,' Wanda goes on, as if to prove Abbie's point. 'There are only two more Pimp Those Plants meals.'

'Yeah. We've been working our way through them. Well, I have. Rachel's not all that hungry at the moment.'

'You have to make sure she keeps her intake up,' Wanda says.

Fine one to talk, Abbie thinks. Those sweets are probably the only thing that bag of skin and bones eats.

'The Pimp Those Plants meals aren't all that tasty,' Wanda goes on. 'I took a few home for myself, just to try—'

Thief, Abbie thinks.

'—so we'll not be partnering with them.'

'Rachel prefers smoothies,' Abbie says.

Wanda rolls her eyes. 'I've told her so many times that she can't live on smoothies. You really need to start using those *marvellous* cookery skills of yours.'

So that's what this is about. Wanda doesn't believe she can cook. She's setting her up for a challenge.

'And for that,' she goes on, 'you need *ingredients*.'

Abbie leans in the doorway – she doesn't want to move even a foot into this filthy tip of an office. Wanda is talking to her like she's a naughty teenager, or a suspect in the interview room at a police station. 'Whatever,' she says under her breath, looking up at the ceiling.

'Sorry, what?' Wanda waggles her short blonde curls and smiles in that irritating passive-aggressive way that's typical of women like her.

Abbie looks over her shoulder just to make sure that no one else is around. Then she turns back to Wanda. 'Did you put the matinee jacket I gave Rachel in one of the charity boxes?'

Wanda goes a satisfying Merlot shade. 'Sorry?'

'Did you put the matinee jacket I gave Rachel in one of the charity boxes?'

'Did I?' is all she manages. It comes out as a squeak.

'I think you did. I gave that to Rachel as a special present, and I think you tried to hide it from her because for some reason, me being here threatens you.'

Wanda smiles and waggles her head so much Abbie imagines – hopes – it might be in danger of flying off.

'In future,' she goes on, 'I would like it very much if you kept your nose out of what goes on between me and Rachel. If you don't like me being here and being so close to her, well, Wanda, you're just going to have to lump it.'

Wanda makes a strange little noise, a bit like a dog's whimper, picks up a random pile of papers littering her workstation and bangs them on her desk to square them up.

'I'll get your Goodfoods list to you in the next hour,' Abbie says. 'Is that soon enough for you?'

Wanda gulps and nods, and Abbie swaggers her way back up to her rooms, wondering what the stick insect is up to with online bank accounts.

*

When she's back in her room, she doesn't work on the shopping list. Let Wanda sweat. No, this business with the little coat has unnerved her so much that she begins to see how delicate her plans are. There's some very important admin she needs to be taking care of, some early steps that she's been avoiding up until now.

'Hello, beautiful.' Barney greets her very nicely as she lets him out of his cage.

She feeds and waters him, then, bird on head, she fishes out her private Galaxy phone from the back of her knickers drawer, connects it to the house Wi-Fi, and looks in her contacts for Ms Ayo Dafé, the woman who holds the key to her happiness.

It's time to start asking, yet again, for contact.

INSTAGRAM POST

rachelhoneyhill
Devon, England
326,701 likes

Images
- Looking over Rachel's shoulder as she and Fran Zoom each other.

Text
It's so good to talk to friends. Even though she lives in another country, #FriendFran and I Zoom each other at least four times a week, just because it's good to see each other and hear each other's voices.

Connection is what makes us human.

So stay in touch, even if you don't have anything pressing to talk about.

#friends #connection #love

CHAPTER FIFTEEN

22 July

For the first time in Fran's memory, Rachel's magnificent living room looks tidy and clean in the background, its surfaces clear, its floor uncluttered.

'Abbie magic,' Rachel says when Fran comments on it. 'Unlike her food. We've had one attempt so far, a stir-fry. Inedible!'

Rachel is laughing, but Fran is worried.

'What about that vegan cookery diploma?'

'If she really has one, then she's forgotten everything.'

'Do you think she was lying?'

'She doesn't have the imagination to lie, Fran.'

'Hush now.'

'Not like you and me, Frambles.'

Fran ignores this overture. Since she got pregnant, Rachel has gone over and over her transgressions as if she is sorting through a button box of guilty secrets. In particular, of course, she keeps returning to The Event, re-examining every awful detail. But Fran never wants to talk about it again. Certainly not on a Zoom – who knows how insecure their connection might be? – and most definitely not while she's at home, where Wim or the children might overhear her.

'What are you eating, though?' she says. 'You need to make sure our baby is getting enough nutrition.'

'Sorry?' Rachel leans towards her iPad. There's an annoying time lag, and as ever, she's growing impatient with the failings of the technology. 'Is there something wrong with your internet?'

'No.' Fran rolls her eyes. She has super-fast efficient Dutch internet in her warehouse conversion in the old port area of Rotterdam, one of the best-connected cities in the EU. Rachel has creaky English Wi-Fi in a remote Devon barn that doesn't even get phone or data reception. Whose fault is the poor internet connection? Not Fran's, that's for sure. But as always, Rachel blames it on her. It is one of her less endearing qualities, this inability to see that problems can sometimes stem from her own hallowed self.

'Don't worry about Beansprout. In the absence of edible real food, I had Abbie get Wanda to order me some WeAll.'

'WeAll?'

'A pregnancy version of MeAll, the meal-in-a-glass. You know, the people I partnered with last year? "For when you're busy but need the noms"? This one's offer is "Three glasses a day meet Mumma *and* Bubba's nom needs".'

Fran shudders. 'So you're partnering with them again?'

'Nah. They didn't bite, for some reason. I'm actually paying money for it and pointedly not mentioning it on my feeds.'

'Ha.'

'But honestly, Fran, who screws up a stir-fry? I mean, you just throw everything in and bam, yeah? She burned everything but somehow managed to have it all raw as well. Thickly cut raw onions, euch. She put the noodles in dry, and apart from an overwhelmingly large amount of chilli – three bird's eyes, she told me afterwards! – there was nothing to add any extra flavour, not even salt.'

'Sounds rank.'

'Understatement. And look at this!' Rachel flips from selfie view, takes the iPad over to the kitchen and picks up a charred wok from the range cooker. 'I'll have to throw it away! It concerns me, Fran. She's supposed to be cooking for me so I can go straight back to work after the birth. And for Beansprout, when weaning comes round. Plus I'm not sure if I like having someone else around all the time. And Abbie's so different to me. I've tried everything I can to pull her out of her shell…'

As she speaks, she makes her way back across the living space to the mid-century sofa Fran picked out for her in a flea market in The Hague. She's got it nicely positioned, with its back to the room, looking out through the bifold doors, which Fran sees are wide open today. She's clearly rattled, though, because, when she switches back to selfie view, Fran sees that she has brought the wok with her.

'Put that down, Rach,' she says.

'What?'

'The wok.'

'Oh yeah!' Rachel puts it on the coffee table in front of her.

'It's good practice for you in advance of the baby,' Fran says. 'The disruption of having someone else around.'

Rachel cuts her off with a dismissive wave of her hand. 'Oh, you always make it sound so difficult. How hard can it actually be, one tiny baby?'

'Just you wait.'

Rachel can be such a child sometimes. If she's having difficulties sharing that massive house with just one other adult, then she's got a nasty shock coming when a baby's thrown into the mix.

Five years ago, when Luuk, her first, was born, Fran was outraged at how her freedom had been taken away from her. How it was no longer possible for her even to take a pee on her own, let alone go out at night with her husband. She wouldn't swap it now for the world, of course, and misses the added chaos her poor fourth child would have created so badly that it physically hurts her. But she worries how Rachel, after thirty-eight years of doing exactly what she wants, is going to take being the subject of a tiny demanding child.

'The worst thing is…' Rachel says.

She goes quiet. For one moment Fran thinks it's her dodgy internet again.

'What is it?'

'Abbie makes me feel bad about myself.'

Not this again, Fran thinks. Enough of the self-flagellation already. If Rachel could actually admit to herself that she has a disability that sometimes affects her behaviour, it would be such a relief to everyone. 'What do you mean?'

'She's just too quiet and too nice and too polite.'

'Sounds good to me.'

'But all the time? She hardly says anything of substance.'

'Probably just shy.'

'I feel I could do anything – I don't know, cut her pay entirely, tell her to lick the toilets clean, pull out her fingernails – and she'd just say, "thank you".'

'Please don't.'

'Look at this.' Rachel leans in and shares the video of Abbie discovering the little jacket in the nursery. She tells Fran the story and how evil she felt about trying to get rid of it. 'Is it just me, or is there no way of knowing what she's thinking? Even on her own like that? Wouldn't her face show some sort of emotion? Wouldn't she be angry about me throwing away her gift?'

'She looks really upset to me, Rach.'

'Does she?'

'She's crying!'

'Is she?'

'Yes!' It's so obvious to Fran that she worries that Rachel is somehow deteriorating, that the neural pathways damaged in The Event have given up a few more of their connecting fibres. She would love to get her to a doctor about it, but she knows better than to bring that particular issue up again. Not after last time. However, there is something about this video that needs to be addressed.

'Should you really have been watching her?'

Rachel looks at her. 'Don't you start making me feel bad, too.'

Again, turning it round to being anyone's fault but her own. Fran gives up on that one, too. 'What's that she's saying at the end?' she says instead, watching Abbie's tearful muttering.

'No idea. Creepy, though, isn't it?'

'Looks more sad to me. Send me the vid and I'll let Marieke look at it.'

'Marieke?'

'A deaf colleague. Ace lip-reader. Perhaps whatever she's saying there is the emotional hook you're looking for.'

Rachel taps her screen a couple of times and Fran hears the zip of a video arriving in her inbox.

Another thing for her to do for Rachel. Why does she agree to all this? Oh yes. She owes her life to her, that's why.

'The other people here seem to have difficulty with Abbie too,' Rachel says. 'John the cleaner has resigned. Although I can't really imagine her doing it, he says she told him he wasn't doing a good enough job. When I asked her about it, she said it was a good thing he'd gone, and that she'd do it instead.'

'Wow.'

'She's doing it brilliantly, I have to say.'

'I can see.'

'And she's rubbing Wanda completely up the wrong way.'

'That's hardly a challenge…'

'The worst thing is, though, Frambles, we have absolutely nothing in common.'

Fran so feels like saying 'I told you so', but what would be the point in that? And really, with the big case she's working on at the moment, and the deadline of the baby arriving, the last thing in the world she wants is to have to go through the whole search for another mother's helper. In any case, she's almost entirely certain that at least ninety per cent of the problem is actually coming from Rachel rather than Abbie.

'Nothing in common except that she's supposedly my biggest ever fan. She's just… she's just…' As she often does when she's trying to speak the truth, Rachel screws her eyes up tight, like she's attempting to find the words in the darkness. 'She's just so lumpy and awkward, and never… I feel like everything I say is just absorbed and swallowed up. I never get anything back, Fran. You know what I mean?'

But Fran doesn't respond. Instead, she is watching in horror as Abbie comes into the room behind Rachel. She steps just out of view of the camera, but she is definitely there, hearing every word that is being said about her.

'Rachel!' Fran tries to interject, but once again, the reception is lagging.

'The sad fact is that Abbie's dull,' Rachel is saying.

'Rachel, Rachel, stop!'

'Dull, dull, dull. Sometimes I just wish I'd listened to you and gone for that Caro instead. Someone with a bit of spark.'

'Rachel!' Fran hisses it so forcefully, it scours her throat.

'What?' Rachel says.

'Hi, Abbie!' Fran gives Abbie one of those manic online waves, as if Rachel has not been bad-mouthing her, as if, rather than mortified, she is completely delighted to see her.

'Oh, hi, Fran,' Abbie says. 'How are you?'

If Fran were Wim, her straight-talking Dutch husband, she would just bring out into the open the fact that everyone has been party to this awful moment of indiscretion. But despite her Senegalese heritage, she was brought up in the English manner, so the possibility of anyone addressing the elephant in this particular room does not exist.

'How are you getting on, then, Abbie?' Fran says, as Rachel turns back to the camera and pulls a face of shame – which, Fran wants to tell her, Abbie can see, because although she's out of shot she's still looking at the screen.

Rachel gathers herself to turn and pat the sofa next to her, for Abbie to come and sit down.

Abbie squeezes in and waves at Fran.

'I like your hair,' Fran says.

'Thank you. I'm slowly becoming an after.'

'What?'

But Abbie has picked up the burnt-out wok from the coffee table and is smiling at Fran. 'I don't know if Rachel told you, but I had a cooking disaster.'

Fran wonders exactly how long Abbie had been standing behind the living room door before she came in.

Unable to give the situation any more of her mental space, she draws the call to a close, pretending that Mila, her baby, is crying in the background. Almost as soon as the screen goes blank, she texts Abbie.

Hi Abbie! I'm so sorry about what just happened. Rachel didn't mean what she said. She just really doesn't know how to behave around people. Could we have a call in the next couple of days? Just to check in? And I could explain then.

A lot of the problem is that because Rachel is poor at reading people, she doesn't quite get Abbie, who, given the circumstances, has just behaved quite gracefully. After all, John the cleaner *was* pretty rubbish, and Wanda frankly does need a firmer hand. And not everyone wears their heart on their sleeve like Rachel, so that could explain Abbie's lack of reaction, her silences. Those referees were all so positive about her, after all.

Mila really does start crying, and Fran puts her worry back into her Rachel box, saving it for the call with Abbie.

Which she will forget about for several weeks.

INSTAGRAM POST

3 years ago

rachelhoneyhill
Devon, England
paid partnership with **crockagold**
2,756,993 likes

Images
- Charley and Rachel peering into a bubbling pot of vegetable tagine
- Charley and Rachel at the candlelit Honeyhill dining table, their plates empty.

Text
Eat real food, people! It's easy when you know how.
No time to cook? Get your mitts on a **@crockagold** slow cooker and your weekly **@fullalove** veg box.
A light bit of chopping, then throw everything in before you skip off to do your thing for the day.
When you get home, *voilà*! Hot, super-tasty, super-healthy supper, all waiting for you, as if you had your own personal chef. It's a brilliant way of staying on track with your healthy eating. Prep like a queen and you'll be in it to win it!
@charleywarley and I did that just today when she came round, and look what we made! Not a scrap left over for poor Sam, either.

Head on over to the RR YouTube channel for a how-to on one of the tastiest veggie Crockagold slow cooker tagines in the WORLD!!! Link in bio.

#Crockagold #slowcooker #vegan #recipe #vegbox #Fullalove #vegandog #preplikeaqueen #friends

CHAPTER SIXTEEN

'Fancy a hot tub?' Rachel says to Abbie, the minute Fran hangs up on the call.

'Now?' Abbie says. 'I thought I'd carry on with the baby's room.'

The mention of Beansprout's bedroom doubles Rachel's already intense cringing, making her feel quite dizzy with shame. But instead of showing it, she smiles so brightly it hurts, and steers Abbie towards the back door. 'Oh, let's knock off for the day. Hot tub's a great thing, Abs. You must use it whenever you like. It's fantastic for DOMS.'

'DOMS?'

'Delayed onset muscle soreness, which, with your workout this morning being quite so full on, you'll be feeling pretty strongly right now.' She reaches past Abbie for her iPad. 'See, your FitSo stats. You burned nearly a thousand calories in forty minutes. That is truly some workout.'

'Thank you. I nearly threw up again,' Abbie says, a touch of pride in her voice.

'Well done!' Rachel doesn't tell her that she already knows this, because as well as watching the FitSo stats, she was also following Abbie's workout on the gym cameras. 'You animal.'

Abbie flexes her bicep, which does look a bit firmer. 'Touch it,' she says.

Rachel gives Abbie's arm a press, which is a bit weird, but not as weird as the fact that Abbie hasn't said anything about what she overheard just now.

'Shall we get supper on while we're waiting for the hot tub to warm up?'

'Supper? But it's just gone breakfast.'

'Ah, but there's this.' Rachel digs out her Crockagold and a sheaf of really easy vegan slow-cooker recipes that she got Wanda to print out and laminate. They are so simple that even Abbie won't be able to balls them up. Surely.

'We'll make my vegetable tagine,' Rachel says.

'I like that one,' Abbie says.

'You've made it?'

'I've watched the video.'

As the cooking-supper-together session turns into more of a cookery lesson, Rachel wonders if Abbie has ever handled *any* of the ingredients before. She doesn't even know what to do with couscous, or how to properly chop an onion. When Rachel introduces her to that vegan stalwart, nutritional yeast – or, as she calls it, nootz – Abbie takes one sniff and gags. Admittedly, it can smell rank if you're not expecting it, but no worse than Parmesan.

By the time they've got everything in the pot, the hot tub is ready, and they go off to their respective rooms to change.

'You didn't get the lid off by yourself, did you?' Abbie says as she gingerly climbs the wooden steps to join Rachel in the steaming tub. She's taken an inordinately long time to get changed into her F&G swimsuit, whereas it was a matter of seconds for Rachel to slip into her bikini.

Not that it's a competition, of course…

'I got Wanda to do it for me,' Rachel lies. But why shouldn't she do it herself? She's pregnant, not a cripple. In fact, she feels as strong as she has felt in her entire life, if not stronger.

Leaning her head back against the hot tub cushion, she tries to relax. She half closes her eyes and squints up at the sky, a brilliant blue filtered through the leaves of the tree ferns that her garden designer put in a cluster of pots at the back of the tub. But despite the colour-changing lights, designed to soothe away all cares, her lingering shame washes over her far more insistently than the bubbling water.

'This is what it must be like in a birthing pool,' she says, to try to think about other things.

'Probably.'

'Giving birth is going to be such a cosmic experience.'

Abbie says nothing.

'I'm going for all-natural. No interventions, no drugs, just Sue the midwife on hand. And you, of course.'

'It's painful,' Abbie says, 'giving birth.'

Rachel doesn't want to think about that. And what would Abbie know anyway? She lies back and tries to let go, but the silence feels too difficult. 'Seems like years since we sat in that tub at the BabyMoon,' she says.

'It does, doesn't it.'

Through the edges of her sunglasses, Rachel can see that Abbie is sitting upright rather than relaxing into the bubbles, and staring at her like a fangirl in a restaurant. She has another shot at conversation. 'The Team are coming tomorrow for an activewear shoot.'

'Great.'

They both watch the water move, swirling from Rachel to Abbie and back again. The awkwardness of the situation, of the two of them sitting in their swimwear in a pool, with nothing to say to each other, propels Rachel to come out with it.

'I'm sorry if you heard me being awful about you while I was talking to Fran.'

Abbie stays so quiet that Rachel has to go on, which she does, moving her hands through the water, trying to catch the bubbles as she speaks.

'It's just that I spend so much of my time being good, happy, positive Rachel, Rachel in the exercise videos, Rachel in the cooking videos, Rachel in the photographs, that I store up all the real-life Rachel stuff. The only person I can be myself with is Fran, so I sort of download when I speak to her, and nasty Rachel sometimes takes over.'

No response from Abbie.

'Do you understand that?' Rachel asks.

Abbie nods and says nothing. So Rachel just keeps on speaking.

'I'm just a normal person, just like you, just like Wanda. And this thing I've done with myself, and what people expect of me, sometimes it's just all too much. I'm actually really vulnerable. All this' – she waves at the massive barn, with its glass box extension – 'is built through me not showing that part of myself to the world.'

Beansprout suddenly does a massive turn in her belly. It feels like her insides have been caught by a huge wave. It takes her breath away and makes her stop talking, as if it's a message from her baby to shut up.

And Beansprout is right. This apology to her silent new employee has turned into a pathetic poor-me monologue. Are there no depths to which she will sink? Apparently not. She is grabbed by an almost visceral longing for Fran to appear at the glass wall at the back of the barn, to slide open the doors, stride capably over to the tub, help her out of the water, tuck her into bed and take care of everything for her. Make Abbie go away.

Make Abbie go away? Is that what she wants?

Her head throbs. She realises she is gasping for air, on the edge of an attack. She pleads: *Please don't let it happen here*, imagining drowning, gasping for air, her nails this time deep in the flesh of Abbie's cheeks.

'Are you all right?' Abbie shifts her position, readying herself like a backstop ready to catch a ball. Rachel realises she is that ball.

Beansprout's big shift is followed by a good deal of elbow and knee action, like Sam, she thinks, when he decides he wants to make a nest for himself in the sofa cushions. And suddenly, that thought combines with the shame and the self-pity and the shame *at* the self-pity, and she finds herself sobbing big fat wet tears into the hot tub.

'Oh no, oh, Rachel.' Abbie shifts into the seat next to her and puts her hand on her knee. 'What is it?'

This unexpected tender touch breaks Rachel. She is handled daily by the people who work for her, preparing her for photographs, placing her for optimum effect. But it's been so long since someone put their hand on her with no other motive other than to give her support, back her up. Even Fran is not a tactile person.

She is, she realises, so alone.

She puts her hand on Beansprout. Poor Beansprout. Has she made the worst choice ever, bringing her into her life?

'Of course not,' Abbie says, making Rachel realise that she has spoken aloud. 'Having a baby is a lovely thing to do. The best thing.'

'If I left it any later, my time would have started running out. I might have missed the boat.'

'You're not that old.'

'But you never know how hard it's going to be, particularly when you're not ever going to get pregnant by accident.'

'You got lucky, then.'

'It took a while. Two years. Not constantly, of course!' Rachel laughs through her tears.

'Well, you've got Beansprout now, and we're all lucky.'

'Eh?'

'You're lucky because you're going to have a lovely baby, and I'm lucky because I get to be here and help you out. And Beansprout is lucky because she gets you as her mum and me to look after her.'

The water stops bubbling, as it does every now and then for the motor to rest. After the noise of the jets, the silence so focuses sound and light that Rachel feels like she has gone into a cave. The sun moves behind the big horse chestnuts at the back of the garden, and a rook caws and launches itself like ink flung into the deep blue sky.

'I can't believe you're being so nice to me when I was so vile.'

Abbie takes her hand. 'We all make mistakes.'

This kindness sets Rachel off again. She hasn't cried like this for years.

'You're so lucky,' Abbie says. 'You have this lovely home; you're going to have a lovely baby. You have the best job in the world, where you get to earn good money and are given lovely things just for being yourself. And best of all, your followers love you!'

'I've dropped nearly one hundred thousand since I told everyone I was expecting,' Rachel says, not liking her almost whiny tone of voice.

And perhaps this is it. Perhaps this – rather than being overheard by Abbie, rather than the weight of being Rachel Rodrigues, rather than the hormones and the responsibility of Beansprout – is what is really getting to her.

'You'll pick them up again, remember? It's just a temporary blip, all the oldies and the Christians and the young girls…'

Rachel reaches to get her phone, which has been waiting beside the tree ferns for a glamorous selfie of the two of them in the hot tub. After the ugly crying, there's no way *that's* going to happen.

She pulls up her Instagram analytics tracker and scrolls back to when she started to lose followers, which was at midday on 10 March, just over nineteen weeks ago, the day after her scan photo.

She opens the post that kicked it all off and shows it to Abbie. Although Juno actually took the photo, it's supposedly a mirror selfie. In it, Rachel is wearing knickers and an unbuttoned long white man's shirt. Her little belly and sunken eyes are what first strike the viewer, followed by the thigh gap that she thought made her look sweet and vulnerable.

'I remember that,' Abbie says. 'You do look a bit tired.'

'We did that when I was at the peak of my morning sickness. I wanted to show my vulnerability. "Like a tiny lift of a bride's veil", as Zander put it. Hence the white shirt.'

'I think you look lovely.'

'Thank you. I wanted to share the struggles I was going through with my pregnancy. But it was a massive mistake. People don't like to see negativity on my feed. That's not what they come for.'

'I seem to remember it did get some nasty comments,' Abbie says.

'We leave some of the milder things up so that it doesn't look too censored, but we take down the really awful stuff. If we didn't, people would start wondering if there might be some truth in it – where there's smoke there's fire sort of thing.'

'How bad did it get?'

Rachel calls up the comments archive and starts a search. 'We store all the comments, nasty and nice. The police told us to do it after my first stalker about six years ago, in case things ever got to the stage where evidence was needed.' She's tried always to tuck that thought into the back of her mind, but sometimes she remembers, and it chills her.

'I don't get stalkers,' Abbie says.

'Crushes gone horribly wrong. It's sad, really.   Here.' Rachel shows her the comments she and Wanda pulled down. Abbie reads them through, shaking her head and tutting.

'As you can see,' Rachel says. 'They start by wondering if I'm OK, but then people start saying that I must have an eating disorder. Then see how someone starts using #SickRachel. That brings in the professional trolls, who talked about me looking like a Belsen victim.'

'Sickos.'

'Tell me about it. See: this one says I need a good fuck to sort me out. And this one says I brought it all on myself, slutting about and getting myself pregnant.'

'Disgusting.' Abbie continues to shake her head as she scrolls down through the comments.

'They're like slugs, living in their mothers' basements, sliming out to spew poison over good people,' Rachel says.

'They don't deserve to live,' Abbie says.

'I hear you. So that's when I started losing followers.' Rachel looks up from the screen. 'Am I doing the right thing, Abbie? Will I be able to take you young women with me as I move into motherhood?'

'I'll never stop following you,' Abbie says.

Rachel laughs, but when she looks at Abbie, she can't see a smile on her face. 'Each follower leaving me is like a death. I guess, with my mum passing away at such an early age, I've always had a thing about loss. I want to scoop all my followers up and hold them to me forever. It's why I can't get rid of stuff,' she adds. 'It's why there's piles and piles of things in every spare room. I lose track of it all, everything gets in a mess.'

Once more she finds herself crying.

'There, there,' Abbie says. 'I'm here now. I'm going to help you sort it all out, put everything in the right place.' She shifts herself slightly over towards Rachel and gives her the extended stiff hug of someone unused to displaying physical affection.

Rachel clings on, and the tears just keep coming.

Abbie clasps her even tighter. Rachel sniffs, closes her eyes and sinks against Abbie's chest. Some memory deep inside her is stirred, for the first time. In the warmth of the tub, the swirl of the trees and the sky above them, she hears her mother's voice, singing to her.

Then, in a whisper, barely audible above the sound of the bubbles, Abbie speaks. 'If anyone wants to hurt you or Beansprout, they're going to have to deal with me first.'

True fire. Rachel didn't see that coming.

Will she never learn how wrong she can be about people?

INSTAGRAM POST

rachelhoneyhill
Devon, England
paid partnership with **seen.**
303,993 likes

Image
- Rachel runs along the edge of a cliff at night, Sam at her side. The moon is full over the sea behind them. Sam wears a glowing collar. Rachel wears a body torch over a silvery running jacket that reflects every scrap of light back at the camera.

Text
Have you ever gone for a run or walk at night? If not, give it a go. Without the distractions of the daylight world, you can really focus on what's going on inside.
The world is different in the dark. It's just you, what your feet touch, and your very immediate surroundings. You are free to commune with your sprit, relax and concentrate your attention on what's important, blanking out the chatter of your normal daytime mind. It's important, though, to be safe while you're out, and the main way to address this is to be visible. **@seen**. night gear is the perfect way to be seen! It's your one-stop shop for night running. Look how I glow in this picture! And the body torch makes sure I can see where I am going to place my foot. And doesn't Sam look handsome in his Seen collar?
Post your photos of your night-walking adventures and tag me so I can see them!
#nightrunning #nightwalking #bodytorch #nightdog #full-moon

CHAPTER SEVENTEEN

24 July

Abbie sits on a stool in the boot room and pulls on her trainers, getting ready to head out into the darkness for what Rachel calls *the spiritual communion of night-walking*.

Abbie is glowing. After the hot-tub meltdown two days ago, she feels she has finally won Rachel's trust; they now have nothing but good things to look forward to. As she ties her laces, she softly sings a hymn she remembers from when, as a teenager, she was forced to go to church.

'*Amazing Grace, how sweet the sound,*
That saved a wretch like me.'

She is happy that, instead of Jesus, the one saving her from wretchdom is Rachel. And just as Jesus was a human, and fallible, so, she is learning, is Rachel. Reality isn't as perfect as dreams, it never can be. But she can work with that. Another thing she took from those enforced church visits were the words handed down by the snooty vicar from his pulpit:

'*The gate is narrow and the road is hard that leads to life, and there are few who find it.*'

That reading hit the young Abbie – a difficult, angry girl at the time, slouching in her pew seat – like a calling. She repeated the words in her head until she got home, and wrote them on a piece of paper that she carried in her wallet until, four years later, some junkie lifted it.

She would crawl across broken glass to achieve her end goal of a permanently blissful existence with Rachel.

'*I once was lost, but now I'm found,*
Was blind but now I see.'

'Nice song, Abbie,' Rachel says as she joins her in the boot room.

'Thank you.' Abbie blushes and fiddles with her laces.

'Put this on.' Rachel hands her a lightweight waterproof jacket with a hood. It's made from a sort of holographic silver-grey fabric, like fish scales.

'It's not raining,' Abbie says.

'But it's pretty blowy up on the top, and you don't want cold air blasting through to your skin. Particularly if we've worked up a sweat. Plus, the hood will be useful. The wind up there can give you an awful earache.'

'What do you mean, the top?' Abbie says.

'My surprise. Come on!' Rachel helps her on with the new waterproof, which is smooth and close-fitting. In its silvery sheath, Abbie feels like some sort of alien in an old sci-fi movie, but she's pleased to see that Rachel is now putting on an identical jacket.

'Look,' Rachel says, turning her so that they are both reflected in the full-length check-yourself-before-you-go-out mirror on the boot room wall. 'We could be sisters!'

She hands Abbie a body torch, which, partly because she is in a bit of a daze of bliss, takes her a while to figure out how to put on.

She straps her bum bag around her hips and she's good to go.

Rachel beckons an eager Sam out of the house. There is no missing him either, with his LED collar. Outside the gates, Rachel opens a flap on a grey box secured to the fence. Underneath is a screen that glows blue light onto her face. 'As we're leaving the place empty, let me talk you through how to lock up. Along with an app on my phone, this box here – plus a couple more inside – controls all the external doors and windows. It overrides all the keypads and manual locks, so you can't open anything without using your fingerprint either here or on my phone.'

'Can I do it?'

'Not yet. Wanda's got the master unit. I'll get her to put you on the system.'

Is it strange, Abbie thinks, that she's been here over two and a half weeks and she's not even able to leave and re-enter the building on her own? *The gate is narrow, and the road is hard.* It's probably just an administrative oversight. No doubt Wanda's fault.

Rachel presses her finger onto the box. 'I'm also setting the perimeter fence. If anyone tries to break in, it sets off a hideous alarm and calls out a response team from Plymouth.'

'That's a bit of a way.'

She shrugs. 'Best we can do out here. It would take them thirty minutes at night, but the system also alerts me on my phone, so I can use the safe-room lock on my bedroom door.'

'Have you ever had to do that?'

'Only once, when an ex-assistant forgot to activate the perimeter when she went home.'

'What happened?'

'I'd really rather not talk about it.'

'What happens if the Wi-Fi stops?' Abbie asks. 'Or if there's a power cut?'

'The whole security system, the cameras, everything is on its own circuit, with a generator backup. Whatever happens, we're secure.'

Rachel sets off, faster than Abbie could comfortably call walking, along a track down the side of Honeyhill, heading in the opposite direction to the village. There's a full moon, so with that and the stars, the darkness isn't as pitch as she had imagined it would be. Still, she's glad for the little beam of her body torch, which lights the way for her, making sure she doesn't trip into a rabbit hole, or stumble over a tree root.

As far as she can remember, this is the first time she has been out in the dark, away from street lights. The smell – a sort of grassy dampness, all honeysuckle and nettle – makes her want to stay here forever.

An owl hoots. Abbie hasn't heard one in real life before. A dark shape takes off, making her jump as it rattles the trees at her side.

'He's found something,' Rachel says. 'Wait…'

They both pause, their ears tuned, until a tiny sound, like a scream from the world's smallest woman, pierces the air around them.

'He got it then, I suppose,' Abbie says.

'Nature red in tooth and claw,' Rachel says, turning to her with glittering eyes. 'I'd be happy to die out here, wouldn't you? So far away from everyone and everything else. I love it. Sometimes I feel like I've had it up to my neck with other people.'

'I get like that too,' Abbie says. More proof, if proof were needed, that she and Rachel are bound together. Out here it feels like they are the last women on earth, and anything is possible.

They head off again. After about forty minutes, the wind builds and a new sound starts stroking the silence. 'We're heading to the sea,' Abbie says. 'That's what you meant by the top. The clifftop!'

Rachel, a silver spook in front of her, turns and temporarily blinds Abbie with her body torch. 'You got it.'

Ten minutes later, she stops. 'We're at the edge,' she says, beckoning Abbie towards her. 'Step carefully.'

Abbie draws up next to her and angles her torch down. Thirty metres or so beneath a sheer drop of dark cliffs, the sea foams and curls, white froth on inky blue, slapping onto shining wet rocks. It looks, she can't help thinking, like hell. Sam jumps at the back of her legs, nearly pushing her forwards and over. Heart racing, she grabs his flashing collar. 'Have you got his lead?' she asks Rachel.

'Oh, he's fine. He knows this path too well to make a mistake.'

Abbie still holds onto him. 'Do you come here often at night?'

Rachel laughs. 'No! I'm far too scared of the dark.'

'But I thought you were an expert at night-walking.'

'Oh, I'm very good at sounding like I know what I'm saying, because I do my research. I'm doing a story for these jackets.' She points to a boulder perilously close to the edge. 'Stand on this, will you?'

'Really?' If Abbie wobbles when she's up there, she could fall backwards. The thought of skull meeting rock makes her scalp prickle. 'Why?'

'Photo. Only for a minute. You'll be fine.'

Rachel helps her up and gets her to take a burst of pictures as she and Sam walk past her. 'I scouted this out the other day. It's a perfect angle from where you're standing, with the moonlight on the sea down there.'

Her legs shaking, Abbie steps gingerly down from her perch and shows Rachel the results.

'Let's try again,' Rachel says.

It takes three more nerve-shredding attempts before she declares one of the snaps usable.

'Let's go down to the sea,' she says. 'There's a path over there.'

Abbie looks at the steep fall away of the cliff. 'Is it safe?'

'Course it is. Come on!'

For someone so afraid of the dark, Rachel seems pretty bold. Perhaps, Abbie thinks with a thrill, it's her being there that's giving her courage. They take a precarious crumbling and sliding route down the edge of the headland, until they land on the sand in a small cove. The tide is on its way out, and it has left a smear of jellyfish on the shore that reflects opal light back at Abbie's torch.

Down here, a sea fog slightly hazes the air, bringing a welcome chill to her face.

'We used to come down here to smoke dope and drink cider. Me and Fran.' Rachel's voice echoes in the heavy wet air. She points up the dark valley that leads inland. A couple of palm trees silhouetted against the sky make Abbie think of Caribbean islands and pirates. 'Our school was just up there.'

With that information, Abbie knows exactly where she is. 'This is Red Anchor Bay, isn't it?' she says.

'Yes, it is!'

She turns and looks at the sea, which right now looks like it would only give you a gentle buffeting if you were to go in, rather than drown you and beat your body to a pulp.

'My uncle was found here.'

'What do you mean?'

'He was found here dead. On this beach.'

Rachel gasps. 'No.'

'His head was all mashed up. By the waves, they thought. They said he'd fallen in. He was only twenty-two.'

'Poor man. What was his name?

'Daz.'

'He lived in the village?'

'Yeah. My mum took it badly. He was her big brother. She never believed it was the sea. He was a strong swimmer – a fisherman. He knew not to take risks.'

'So she thought someone killed him?'

'He messed with the wrong crowd.'

'Your poor mum.'

'Yeah.'

Rachel's face, framed by her silver hood, looks like it has shrunk. She has her hand on her belly.

'Are you all right?' Abbie asks her. 'Do you want to get back?'

'I'm fine. It's just a bit… When did this happen?'

'Don't know exactly. When I was little.'

They stand still again, listening to the water. Abbie doesn't like this place and would never knowingly have come down here. She kicks at a piece of bladderwrack with her toe. The salty freshness of the air is spiked by the stink of rotting seaweed, and something else, something animal, also decaying.

Uncle Daz's death did her mum in and smashed up her own life – her entire childhood, in fact. Not wanting to think about it, she crosses the cove to investigate a lump lying just where the waves slide across the sand. It's a dead porpoise, its face eaten – or beaten – off, right down to the skull. That's where the stink's coming from. She squats to take a closer look.

Behind her, Rachel, who has followed her over, shudders.

'Let's go, Abbie,' she says. 'You talking about your uncle, well, it's raised the ghosts, I think.'

Abbie looks up. Rachel is casting around her, like she's expecting to see something come out of the fog at them. Sam has obviously picked up on her spooked mood; he is whimpering, and everything in his body language says he wants to leave, too.

'Can I hold on to you?' Rachel says. 'To get over the rocks? I always think about slipping and smashing my head here. And now I know about your uncle…'

Abbie holds her arm out. Rachel puts her hand in the crook of her elbow, then presses her close. 'See,' she says. 'The darkness holds all sorts of horrors, doesn't it? I'm so glad you're here, Abbie. So glad.'

INSTAGRAM POST

rachelhoneyhill
Devon, England
paid partnership with **fitsofitso**
72,934 likes

Image
• Rachel and Abbie running through a field with Sam.

Text
Look how my girl Abbie is coming on! The **@fitsofitso** recorded a 3K run/walk today. I'm going to have to pace myself. What with Beansprout growing and slowing me down, Abbie's going to start outrunning me!

Honestly, if you think you can't run, you're wrong. Just follow one of the FitSo training plans. Individually tailored to your very own fitness levels, they start you slowly, build you up gradually, and you're running 5K in no time.

If you don't believe me, take it from Abbie: 'I've never even run for a bus before,' she told me. 'And now I feel like I can just keep going.'

#AbbiesJourney #run #running #5K #FitSo #friends

CHAPTER EIGHTEEN

Still holding Abbie's arm, Rachel leads the way up the valley towards her old school.

The urge to flee bears down on her like a giant hand at her back: *Just go back the way you came. Run away!*

But she can't. That would be too easy.

This valley is sheltered on all sides from the wind. The thicket of trees at its mouth eats the sound of the waves, so, but for their footsteps, all is silent.

Rachel knows the land here intimately. It is full of ghosts. Apart from her London years – her lost years, she calls them – she has been coming here at least once a week, almost her entire life. It is one of those almost tropical enclosed spots only found in Devon and Cornwall.

The original owner of the grand house at the top of this valley – later Mothcombe, the school that was more of a home to Rachel than anywhere else in the entire world – probably recognised this, hence the palm trees and giant gunnera that tower over them as they move onwards. The smoky fog and the native ferns – which grow to almost obscene proportions in this warm, damp little enclosure – just add to the effect.

'It's like we've stepped back in time,' Rachel says to Abbie. 'To a prehistoric age.'

'Like *Jurassic Park*,' Abbie says. 'Dinosaurs and that.'

Beasts from the past.

After what Abbie told her on the beach, Rachel needs to look a few things up – dates and times, names and places. She has a strong feeling, though, that this is a piece of research that, unusually, she is going to put off.

She will conveniently allow it to be forgotten, buried by the hundred tiny tasks and worries of her daily life. As if to remind her of this, Beansprout does another giant flip inside her, walloping her cervix and making her gasp.

'Are you OK?' Abbie puts her hand on her arm, and Rachel realises that she has stopped with one foot over a low dry-stone wall. If it weren't for Beansprout's continued activity, she would be worrying right now about having slipped into a lost moment.

'Um…' she says.

'We need to get you back,' Abbie says. 'You really shouldn't be overdoing it.'

'I'm not an invalid,' Rachel snaps, pulling her arm away.

'OK.' Abbie steps back. 'Sorry.'

'And anyway,' Rachel works to soften her tone, half her brain doing the backward alphabet thing as she speaks, 'it's just as far to go back as it is to go on.'

'Here.' Abbie reaches in her bum bag and pulls out a small paper bag. 'I packed these for an emergency. I think this is the time.' She points to the wall and empties some cashews into Rachel's hand. 'Sit for a few minutes.'

Rachel perches on the wall, but she doesn't feel comfortable here, so she's still counting letters backwards. The fog swirls up the valley like so many ghosts, still chasing her after all these years. In the silence, she can almost hear herself and Fran sneaking down here with a spliff and a couple of bottles of whatever they'd managed to swipe from the village shop. On nights like this. On a night like this.

'You look great there,' Abbie says, pulling her phone from her bum bag. 'Shall I do a pic?'

'Can I just see if I'm presentable?' Rachel holds out her hand for the phone to check herself in selfie mode. Abbie hands her an old Galaxy, which makes her frown. 'Where's your iPhone?' she says. 'Is it broken?'

'No. I… er… I must have picked up the wrong one when I came out.'

'You didn't hand this one in to Wanda, then?'

'No, I—'

Rachel frowns at the screen. 'You've got a message.' She holds up the phone so they can both see it.

Just swung it for that visit. U can come next Friday. Da x

'Is that your dad?' Rachel hands the phone back to Abbie. 'What's this about a visit?'

'It'd only be for a day. Can you spare me?'

'Course I can!'

'Thank you, Rachel.'

'Where is he?'

'Other side of Reading. You sure?'

'I *can* live without you, Abbie. Hey. You can take the eJeep if you like,' Rachel says.

'Really?'

'Of course. I'll put you on the insurance. I've been meaning to ever since you joined me.'

'That would be great. Thanks.'

'I'm going to need you to be able to drive when Beansprout arrives. If not before.'

'I can run errands for you. Go to the shops, pick people up from the station, take you places when you don't feel like driving.'

'All of that.'

'Cool!' Even Rachel can see that Abbie's smile is now one of pure joy.

'Take that picture, then,' she says, glowing at the pleasure afforded by her generosity.

Abbie snaps her. It's a good one.

'Come on.' Rachel says, slapping her thighs and standing up so quickly her vision goes blurry with the blood returning to her head.

They carry on up the valley until the school looms above them, a dark shape against the night sky. As they get closer, they can see the barbed wire, the empty dark windows. The security fences are plastered with signs saying *Keep Out*, *Dangerous Building*, *Beware of the Dog*, *Hazard! Electric Fence* and *Patrolled by Watchers Guarding Agency*, followed by a local number. Rachel knows that every single warning is complete crap.

'It's closed,' Abbie says, rather unnecessarily.

Rachel nods. 'Yeah, it was shut down about five years ago, after a scandal. Turns out one of the older teachers was a kiddy fiddler. He'd been there when we were, and we always thought he was a wrong 'un, but we never had any idea what he was really doing. I couldn't believe it when I found out. Those poor girls.'

'It's amazing what people get up to behind your back,' Abbie says. 'The things they don't tell you.'

Rachel's scar burns. 'Come on,' she says quickly, aiming her torch at the gap in the fence that she knows is there because she made it herself.

'Should we, though?' Abbie is hovering behind her.

'Honestly, there's no security whatsoever,' Rachel says. 'Come on!'

Like a good employee, Abbie obeys.

INSTAGRAM POST

rachelhoneyhill
Devon, England
paid partnership with **baby2you_**
92,715 likes

Image
- Rachel in the moonlight, surrounded by giant ferns and palm trees, her hair loose and curling around her face.

Text
What did you do for your baby's birth? Did you have a plan? Did it all work out? I'd love to hear your experiences. Comment here, or post and tag me.

I'm planning on a home birth at Honeyhill. Of course, I'm lucky to be in the excellent care of Sue from **@baby2you_**, who guarantee the same midwife from pregnancy test to postnatal care.

I'm researching birthing pools at the moment, and putting together a **@spotify** playlist of soothing birthing sounds, which I'll share with you when it's done.

I'll post my findings here, but in the meantime, here's a snap Abbie captured of me when we were out night-walking, looking a bit like a Madonna!

#birthplan #homebirth #birthingpool #spotify #midwife

CHAPTER NINETEEN

Abbie looks up at the school building. It's like a Greek temple, all pillars and ivy and high-up arched windows. Very different to the places she grew up in. But she's not going to let that get her down. Not now that she's got the visit to Da to look forward to. She can't wait to let him know what she's up to.

Like standing here, for example, with Rachel, in front of the posh school.

'Do you want to go inside?' Rachel says.

'Isn't it all locked up?'

'I've got this.' She shows Abbie a key she's wearing on a ribbon round her neck. 'Me and Fran stole one each so that we could sneak in and out at night. It's for the door round the back. Come on.'

Once in, they creep along a narrow corridor, past a big kitchen and cloakrooms with their pegs and shoe cages still in place – even a couple of ancient drawstring gym bags dangling from the pegs.

'Spooky or what,' Abbie says.

'It's the first time I've dared come down here at night,' Rachel tells her. 'I don't think I could be here on my own. So many ghosts.'

The corridor opens onto a grand hallway with a sweeping staircase up one side.

'This was strictly for teachers only,' Rachel says as they climb the stairs. 'We girls had to use the shabby one at the back, but that's all rotten and fallen-in now.'

She leads Abbie along a dark, damp corridor that seems to go on forever, until they reach a door at the very end. 'Stay there,' she tells her, as she opens it.

Using her torch, she makes her way across the room and switches on a lamp sitting on a table against the far wall. 'There are no overhead lights, but for some reason the sockets still work.'

Abbie whistles. It's a big room – about the size of a tennis court. The parquet floor, worn uneven by decades of feet, is covered with thick white dust from the partially collapsed ceiling. Twenty beds line the walls, weirdly still made up with greying pillows and brown blankets that look like they would scratch you to death if you slept under them. The room smells of old laundry, damp, and rotting wood.

Rachel points to one of the beds. 'That was mine. I slept there for seven years.'

The set-up is entirely familiar to Abbie. But they kept the posh girls like this too? 'You were crammed in here all them years?'

'You moved in the fifth form, so you only shared with one other in a study bedroom.'

'You shared with Fran, I suppose?'

'Of course. It looks pretty grim in this light, and the windows are all boarded up with those squatter-proof shutters, so even in the daytime it's hard to get an idea of what it was like. But they opened out to the sea, and it could be quite beautiful in here. I didn't like sharing with so many, though. And some of them weren't so nice to me either. Can you imagine trying to go to sleep next to someone who is a total cow to you all day long? Someone you just don't trust?'

Abbie says nothing. She knows exactly how that feels, no imagination needed.

Because of the elevated position of the building, she can hear the sea in the distance, like someone whispering outside. Something scratches inside the internal wall – a mouse, perhaps, she thinks with a shiver. She loves animals, but even pet mice and rats have always turned her guts. She's had enough of this place. Rachel's scared of the dark, goes on about ghosts, and yet she brings her into this spook hole?

'It's gone midnight,' she tells her. 'We really should get you back home.'

Rachel nods silently, but she doesn't move.

'If I were to call anywhere in the world home, this would be it. Despite that bad apple, there were some kind teachers, more like parents to me than anyone else I knew. Here.'

She takes Abbie's hand – bringing a lump to her throat – and leads her to a good-sized side room, with a bed and an en suite shower and toilet. She goes into the bathroom, runs the tap and takes a drink.

'Water's still on, too. This was Miss Chamberlain's room. Our house mother,' she says, wiping her mouth.

'Your what?'

'She sort of stood in for our parents. Looked after us. She was the kindest person I have ever known. "You can do this" was her motto. She died in this room, years after we left. They say she's still around.'

'Don't!'

'Oh, if she's a ghost, she's a good ghost. That's why, I think, I decided to move into the barn when my grandparents died. To be close to this place. To her, perhaps.'

'You could do a post about it.'

Rachel laughs. 'As you know, boarding school isn't exactly part of the RR brand. Over eighty per cent of my followers are young women aged sixteen to twenty-two, almost all of them state-educated, almost none of them gone through higher education.'

Abbie nods. That makes sense. It's basically what she is, give or take a year or two.

'They have a bit of cash,' Rachel goes on, 'not masses, and feel that following accounts like RR elevates them. Knowing I went here would alienate them massively. Part of the Beansprout plan is to retain that lot, but also lure in a few more ABs into my CDE following.'

'Eh?'

'Marketing speak, sorry. I'm after middle-class, slightly older yummy mummies, stuck at home after childbirth. More grown-ups.'

'Why? What's wrong with the younger ones?'

'I'm not getting any younger. I can't compete with someone up and coming in their mid-twenties. And to be honest, the new audience I'm going for has greater spending power.'

'More money?'

'It's a compelling business case, I'm afraid.' She taps her belly. 'Gotta feed the kid.'

Abbie sighs. She hates it when Rachel speaks like this. It spoils the magic. Rips it apart. Makes her weary.

It feels like a betrayal.

Rachel suggests that they head back home.

With it having been her idea in the first place, Abbie is all up for that.

THE STYLER ONLINE

20 July

- Portrait of Jane Roberts.

Text

The Styler is offline today in memory of our editor Jane Roberts, who died last night in what appears to be a hit-and-run accident on Curtain Road, Shoreditch, while she was cycling home from a night out with friends. The police are appealing for witnesses.

A great journalist and a great friend.

We will always remember you, Jane.

Full obituary to follow.

RIP.

CHAPTER TWENTY

27 July

'I just get these great waves of hostility from her.' Wanda spreads her hands and wrinkles up her face. She has interrupted Rachel's personal yoga time to complain about Abbie. Apparently it's the only opportunity to speak to her alone, while Abbie is doing her workout in the gym.

'You just need to get used to her,' Rachel says from her mat. 'She's actually really sweet.'

'All I've had from her is cheek. She doesn't like me. I can tell.'

Rachel decides to give up on her yoga. Why Wanda couldn't have waited the half hour for her to finish, she doesn't know. Another example of her own useless boundary-setting and inability to assert her personal needs, and why she should probably never employ people. Surely in her position she should be able to tell Wanda to go away and come back when she's finished?

But no. She's too lily-livered, too English, to speak her mind like that. Instead, she employs that other less than admirable British trait of passive aggression, and pointedly stands and rolls up her mat.

'Why wouldn't she like you?' she says, silently adding, *Let me count the ways*. Indeed, as they head from the studio to the kitchen, they are met by a prime example. After making her mid-morning smoothie, Wanda has left the work surface covered in banana skins, chia seeds, squashed blueberries, a green drift of spirulina and gobbets of the smoothie itself. The dirty NutriBullet, *three* chopping boards, five knives, a clutch of spoons and the un-rinsed dishcloth have been dumped in the sink.

Wanda is anorexically controlling about food – odd hours, odder ingredients – and a total mess in the kitchen, her office, her car, whichever space she happens to be in. While Rachel is no paragon of good housekeeping – indeed, Fran calls her a messy mare – Wanda takes disorder to another, deeply disturbing level. Rachel has tried to have a word with her, but it's in one ear and out the other.

'I don't think I can go on with her in our space,' Wanda says, providing two other perfect examples of why not to like her. First, an incredible lack of self-awareness about how irritatingly high-handed she can sound. And second, it is *Rachel's* space. She does not share it with Wanda.

Wanda acts like she has colonised Rachel, who right now wants to turn round and tell her to get lost. Or possibly punch her in the face.

She finds herself almost maternal in her urge to defend Abbie from this onslaught. Sweet, funny Abbie, who is just beginning to come out of her shell, who is trying so hard with the health and fitness programme. Who, Rachel knows instinctively, has her corner in a way that Wanda, who finds it impossible to put her own ego aside, will never manage.

'Abbie is perfect to help me with Beansprout,' Rachel says, surprising herself at her directness. 'I really like her.'

Wanda winces. Rachel knows she finds her foetus's nickname irritating, but it's also clear, even to Rachel, that she has just realised how excessively she has misjudged her employer's allegiances.

'Can we clear up the kitchen?' Rachel adds. She's really kicking arse today.

'Can we just go through this morning's business first?' Wanda says. Touché.

So, ignoring the kitchen carnage, they sit at the dining table, and Wanda readies her laptop. 'There's a partnering request from an anti-sag neck cream.'

'Really?'

'I've done my research. It's been tested on animals. I recommend we turn it down.'

'Of course.' Rachel rolls her eyes. On all counts this is not a suitable product for her endorsement, and even mentioning it to her is a classic Wanda tactic, stemming back to a time when, without checking, she agreed to Rachel featuring dog chews that turned out to be made from animal tendons – not a good look for a vegan, even if they were organic.

After that, Rachel asked her to run everything past her, which Wanda now does to excess.

'Twenty-two requests for signed photos,' Wanda says, wrinkling her nose and handing Rachel a Sharpie and some prints. Rachel reties her hair in its scruffy updo and bends over the photos, while Wanda spells out the names for personalisations.

Wanda refuses to see how it's these little touches that really keep the followers onside. If she had her way, there would be no sending stuff out. She has complained more than once about the cost, itemising how much it is to mail to, for example, Massachusetts: postage, photo print, the envelope, her own time schlepping to the post office.

'How's the BabyMoon contract going?' Rachel asks as she works on the photos. 'Is there anything for me to sign yet?'

'Soon-soon.'

'And how's the income going?'

'All good.' Wanda looks up at her. 'Do you want me to print out the current cash-flow spreadsheet?' She words it more like a threat than a request.

'It's fine. I trust you.'

'That's not what I meant. Everything's fine, Rachel. No need to worry about anything.'

Rachel hands back the stack of pictures. 'And MamaGlisser?'

'Still waiting for them to get back with the contract to sign.'

'So slow.'

'Tell me about it. Right. On to DMs,' Wanda says, opening a new window on her MacBook.

Every day Wanda picks out DMs that require more than the standard generic replies from her phrase database, and Rachel dictates her personalised messages.

'It's OK to feel sad, Carla,' she says, in response to a girl who has written to her about the death of her beloved dog. 'Little by little, you will start to feel better.'

'Ah, another dead dog. Can I put that in the database?' Wanda says. 'For other bereavements?'

Rachel shakes her head. 'I still want to see them. It connects me to my followers.'

Wanda raises her eyebrows, then bends over the laptop to type the response. As she does so, Rachel pulls a screwy little face and secretly sticks out her tongue at her.

A snort from the other side of the room makes both of them look up. Abbie is there, Sam at her feet – which is fast becoming his favourite place – leaning in the doorway.

'What?' Wanda says, hostility seeping from every pore.

'Phew,' Abbie says, heading across the kitchen. 'That was a sweaty one.' Her vest and shorts are testament to that, with dark patches under her arms and at her groin.

'Did you enjoy it?' Rachel asks. She has upped the reps and weights on Abbie's gym session. Even after these few weeks, her body is looking more defined.

'Rachel, can we get on with this, please?' Wanda taps her laptop.

'It was great!' Abbie says at the same time. Just for good show, she flexes her bicep.

'Impressive!' Rachel says.

'Rachel!' Wanda touches her arm. 'We need to do this.'

'I'll clear up here,' Abbie says, standing by the sink, knocking back a pint of water. 'You just get on. Don't mind me.'

Wanda rolls her eyes at Rachel.

Rachel just smiles back at her.

'Did you see the news about that poor *Styler* journalist woman, Jane Roberts?' Abbie says as she clatters about at the sink.

'No, what?' Rachel grabs her phone and googles.

Wanda sits, waiting excessively patiently to get on with business.

'Oh my God,' Rachel says, clamping her hand over her mouth.

'Horrible, isn't it?' Abbie says, rinsing the chopping boards.

Wanda, who has moved closer so that she can read the article on Rachel's phone, puts her hand on her knee. 'It's like it's payback for that bitchy piece she wrote, isn't it?'

'Don't say that,' Rachel says. There are tears in her eyes.

Abbie picks up a sharp knife and scrapes dried-on chia seeds from the work surface.

INSTAGRAM POST

rachelhoneyhill
Devon, England
216,072 likes

Images
- Rachel serving up a Greek spinach and vegan-feta pie to Zander, Cyn, Wanda and Abbie at the outdoor dining table
- Everyone laughing as they eat it for lunch, in the sunlight.

Text
Today was a beautiful day. The Gang turned up unexpectedly, so I threw together this impressive but oh-so-simple pie, a vegan take on the Greek spanakopita – spinach and feta pie – with a gorgeous heritage tomato salad with herbs from the Honeyhill garden.
We whiled away the afternoon nibbling, chatting and laughing, until dear Sam took us all for a walk!
Head on over to the RR YouTube channel for the how-to for the pie!
Link in bio.
#pie #veganpie #Greekfood #fresh #vegan #recipe #friends

CHAPTER TWENTY-ONE

2 August

Abbie knocks back the last of her coffee and taps 'Buy Now' on the three Georgette Heyers she's sending to Posh June, who loves a historical romance. June has done so much for her, helping her get this job and other stuff, that she deserves a little thank-you gift.

It's the day before she is due to visit her father. She's just finished clearing up after feeding The Team, who left a few minutes ago after spending the whole morning on a 'Rachel and Wanda have fun in their new Natty Dread earrings' shoot. Rachel is upstairs, having the afternoon nap Abbie has mandated now she is thirty-four weeks.

As she's going to spend some time in the turquoise eJeep tomorrow, she has decided that her next job is going to be giving it a proper clean and clear-out.

She also needs to keep busy to calm the irritation she is still feeling about the pie she served up for what Rachel called 'an al fresco family lunch' with The Team and Wanda.

There were loads of gratifying oohs and aahs when she brought it to the table. It had, after all, taken her ages to research, plan and make.

'That looks so beautiful, so glossy and flaky and spinachy,' Zander said.

Rachel turned to Juno. 'Shall we feature it?'

'Sure!' Juno ran indoors to get her camera. 'The light's perfect, too.'

Abbie's flush of pride soon cooled when Rachel took the oven gloves from her and held the pie up for the camera as if she had made it herself. Juno danced around photographing her putting it on the table, with Zander, Wanda and Cyn all replaying the appreciation they had shown Abbie first time round. When they'd finished, Rachel even asked Abbie for the recipe to accompany the post!

Abbie opens the driver's door of the eJeep and marvels at the sea of mud, discarded disposable coffee cups, food wrappers and receipts around the central console and the door pockets. It's almost as bad as Wanda's office.

The bad feelings still scratching inside her are saying, 'What a slut!' But her loyalty to Rachel is telling them to shut up. Rachel may be flawed – and every day brings more evidence of that – but Abbie can, and will, save her. And one of the ways is by fighting her general untidiness and Wanda's manic chaos by instilling order in the house, building a clean platform for the new future that's coming Abbie and Rachel's way.

For example, the kitchen is now nicely arranged, with all the outdated tins and jars and packets thrown out. Rachel's attempts at plastic-free bulk-buying had resulted in haphazard mystery storage in whatever empty receptacles came to hand. Abbie has standardised all the dry goods into a line of identical Kilner jars, ranged on alphabetised labelled shelves in the pantry. She has cleaned out the fridge and freezers, sorted the cupboards – which formerly had no logic – into tins, packets, sweet, savoury, nuts and seeds, spices and flavourings, cereals and drinks. In addition, she has commandeered the old dairy, one of the many clean and dry outbuildings on the property, for catalogued storage of excess merchandise, and Beansprout's room is now clear for the decorators, who are due to come in next week.

She has, in short, spun the Abbie magic method she used during her childhood to win over an adult's heart. It always worked brilliantly, until, as was her habit back then, she blew it up in everyone's faces.

'It's like you've lifted a weight off my soul,' Rachel said, when Abbie showed her the system for finding things on the shelving she had installed in the dairy.

Abbie had been shocked to find, after the immaculate facade of the photographs, so much disorder in Rachel's home. The Team come by twice a week or so, and before she took control, every single shot had involved a load of shoving stuff aside in the background.

From watching Juno work, and researching on YouTube, she has begun to get a strong idea about how to compose and shoot a good photo. It's paying off. The more informal snaps she takes of Rachel while they are out walking or exercising are increasingly appearing on the RR feed.

Perhaps, one day soon, it'll not only be tidying that becomes redundant for photo shoots, but also Juno. How hard is it, after all, to point a camera and press a button?

The back seat of the eJeep is heaped high with clothing, books and bags thrown over from the front. There's even a bunch of dead gerberas buried under a couple of coats. Attached is an adoring message from a fan.

'Bit disrespectful, after she went to all that trouble,' Abbie says. Indeed, the whole car could be seen as the vehicle of someone who doesn't have much regard for anything. Someone whose outlook is that someone else should clear up after them.

Trying not to allow this train of thought to develop, she opens the boot. But the state of it crystallises all the little things that have begun to disappoint her about Rachel.

She looks at the filthy dog cage, which is clumped with dried-on mud and leaves. 'Poor boy,' she says to Sam, who is, as ever, sitting loyally beside her, watching her every move. 'She doesn't look after you properly, does she?'

This, to Abbie, is the most inexcusable part of Rachel's behaviour. She thought that Sam was bound up with her, that they were best buddies and barely ever apart. But she now realises that he is lured into Rachel's Instagram world with treats and bribes. When he's not working, he shows Rachel as little interest as she does him.

'Fancy living here with all these lovely fields and footpaths, yet paying for someone to take you out for walks,' Abbie tells him.

Well, that's not happening any longer, because she took it upon herself to tell Alice the dog walker that her services were no longer required.

'What about socialising with other animals, though?' Alice asked.

Abbie had to breathe slowly in and out. Exploiting poor lovely Sam with rubbish about him needing to spend time with other dogs? Why does he need to do that with Abbie here to look after him?

She sent Alice packing. She won't be back.

Rachel hasn't asked about her yet, but she never dealt directly with her anyway. That was the other shocking thing. Alice had fingerprint access to Honeyhill. She just walked in and found Sam, no knocking, no saying hello, nothing. It was like Rachel didn't even know or care if he was being taken out.

Abbie visited Wanda's office the night after she sacked Alice, and, using the master unit, removed her access privileges. You can't be too careful.

And as for Cal. Poor horse. Virtually ignored and left to that bandy-legged Julie at the stables. Abbie has since visited him every other day. She has told him that one day, when she plucks up the courage, she will ride him.

She hauls out the dog cage and hoses it down, leaving it out in the sun to dry. She then sets to clearing the car of all the rubbish, starting at the front.

It's not seemly to examine someone else's litter, but because of the familiar smell, Abbie can't help smoothing out some of the plastic wrappers she finds stuffed in the driver's-door pocket. They are from a particular brand of pasty that she used to love before she went vegan to be like Rachel. It seems that Rachel is partial to the very same snack herself.

This similarity in taste is yet more proof that Abbie will be able to hold up to Rachel when the time comes. So in that way, it's a good – a great – thing.

On the other hand, Abbie has been denying herself these pasties because of all the meat, the animal fats, the processed white carbs and the earth-unfriendly packaging. And yet here is Rachel, stuffing her face with them.

She checks the sell-by dates, and some of the wrappers are over eight months old, which means there's no chance of them being an uncontrollable pregnancy urge. The dates also show that it's been a long time since anyone showed this beautiful car the love it deserves. In fact, since it has last year's registration, it has probably never been cleaned at all.

If Abbie ever has a car of her own – which she's certain she will, one like this but in a shade of green to match both her and Rachel's eyes – she will keep it lovely.

She stuffs the wrappers in the bin bag she has ready on the drive for unrecyclables. 'She wouldn't even let *you* eat that sort of rubbish,' she says to Sam, who sniffs at the wrappers with great interest. He has vegan dog food, courtesy of one of Rachel's partners, poor thing. However expensive and fancy it is, Abbie thinks it is just plain wrong to feed a dog soy and banana blossoms.

Especially when you don't follow a strict vegan diet yourself.

Hypocrite, hypocrite, hypocrite.

'Breathe, Abbie,' she tells herself.

The other surprise on the driver's side is a stash of Mars bar wrappers wedged into the sunglasses holder. This feels like a double desecration to Abbie. Not only does Rachel stuff herself with non-vegan, high-GI, empty-calorie sweets, she also crams the wrappers into a fancy sunglasses holder.

'What are we going to do with her, eh, Sam?' she says, as she moves round to the other side of the car. She's still trying to joke about it, still trying to be like a little sister tutting at her older sibling's misdemeanours. Trying not to let the disappointment fester.

It's less of a mess here. Perhaps throwing rubbish into the passenger footwell is just too much effort. It also explains why Abbie wasn't particularly aware of the dire state of things when they drove to the BabyMoon; either that, or she was still on her RachelMoon at that point, still star-struck and awed by her employer – a state from which she realises she is emerging.

'She is, after all, only a human being,' she says to Sam, who looks back at her with the unconditional love that only dogs offer. 'She can't be perfect.'

But even as she voices this argument, a little flame of anger is kindling inside her. Rachel *should* be perfect. Or she should show what she's really like on her feeds. Her WHOLE THING is about being authentic.

Her temper not improving, Abbie opens the glove compartment and rolls her eyes to find it rammed with yet more junk: hand cream, a *Vogue* magazine – mainstream fashion? Really? But then she finds a cardboard box that makes her mouth turn down at the edges, her heartbeat quicken and her hands shake.

She straightens up and holds it in the sunlight just to be sure she's not jumping to conclusions. She's not. It's prescription meds, made out for Rachel. Not just any prescription, though. It is the exact same antidepressant Abbie once used herself. The exact same antidepressant that, because of Rachel's stories about how it is possible to cure your negative thoughts through meditation, yoga and good nutrition, Abbie stopped cold turkey.

That stopping led to a bad run that culminated in one of the worst days of her entire life, one so bad that she doesn't even want to think about it.

The doctors said that in order to avoid another such event, and for her to stand any chance of reversing the awful consequences of that day – something she wants beyond anything else in her life and something she is actively working towards right now – she needed not only to stay medicated, but also to take a new, stronger drug. So, of course, she did.

But because of Rachel saying she balances herself naturally, every morning that Abbie wakes up and swallows her daily capsule, she feels like a failure.

She squints at the date on the packet. It is six months old. Although she didn't read the leaflet that came with the packet when she was taking it – and no doctor ever flagged it up – she now knows what it says by heart: 'May cause birth defects, miscarriage or neonatal death.'

Rachel messing with her followers is one thing, ignoring her dog another – and both are bad enough.

'But endangering our baby?' Abbie says to Sam.

She has to stop this. Leaving the car doors open, she storms into the house to find Rachel.

'This,' she says to Sam, who trots at her side, as if she and he are a delegation of Beansprout's representatives, 'is too, too much.'

INSTAGRAM POST

18 months ago

rachelhoneyhill
Devon, England
1,356,215 likes

Image
- Rachel selfie on the cliff at Red Anchor Bay, the sky above her, the sea beneath her. Intense gaze at the camera.

Text
It's OK to be on your own. You have so much to connect to, even inside yourself. You are what you are, not what you do. You are never alone.
You have it within you to heal yourself. You just need to find it.
#motivation #motivationalquotes #positiveminds

CHAPTER TWENTY-TWO

Rachel knows what Abbie has found. She has been lying on her bed watching her on the driveway security feed. Because there are no mics on the external cameras, she can't hear what she is muttering to herself, but she knows it's not good.

Her unmistakably heavy footsteps come thundering up the stairs and along the walkway towards Rachel's bedroom, making the floor bounce like a drum skin.

Rachel quickly flips to her own website and, absurdly, sticks a pencil between her teeth, to look like she's working.

The door appears to shake with the force of the three short raps Abbie gives it.

'Yep,' Rachel says, as casually as possible.

Abbie steps in. She holds out the empty white cardboard box. Her hands are shaking.

'You say you don't take drugs,' she says. Her voice is about an octave lower than usual.

'What?' Rachel tries hard to look as if she hasn't noticed what Abbie is holding in her hand.

'These. The happy pills.' Abbie waves the packet right in her face.

'Where did you find them?'

'Cleaning out your car.'

'OK.' Rachel closes her eyes and takes a deep breath. 'I had a bad spot, Abbie. I won't lie. In the months leading up to getting pregnant, I realised I was sliding. I'd been trying for so long, and I had an early miscarriage, and—'

'Pills are unnecessary, though. You tell us we can do anything we like with the right nutrition, exercise and meditation.'

The tears in Rachel's eyes as she looks up at Abbie are genuine. 'You have no idea what it was like for me,' she says.

'But these are really dangerous for Beansprout.'

'I'm not on them any more! Look at the date. It's for well before Beansprout joined me.' She takes the box from Abbie's hands and shows her. 'The next time we tried to get pregnant, I made sure I was well clear – I started tapering two months before and was completely clean when the time came.'

Abbie turns to look at her. For Rachel, her eyes are like a clean sheet of paper, saying nothing and hiding everything underneath. 'You have to be really, really careful to look after your baby.'

Rachel nods. 'I know. I am. Believe me, nothing is more important to me.'

'Good.' Abbie takes the box back from her and puts it in the waste-paper basket. 'And you're totally clean now?'

'Antidepressants aren't dirty,' Rachel says. 'For people like me they can be life-savers.'

Abbie sits on the bed. She's looking at the floor, frowning. 'So why don't you tell us that?'

'What?'

'On your posts. Why do you tell us that we can do it naturally?'

'Because most people can!'

Abbie looks back at her with those damn eyes that feel like they're scraping the surface off her. 'What if we can't? What if we're like you?'

'If you're like me, you should be getting professional help, not taking advice from a social media influencer.'

The air in the bedroom – normally crisp and light – feels so thick that Rachel has to work harder than normal to get air into her lungs.

'Why don't you tell us the truth?' Abbie says at last, so quietly that Rachel has to bend closer to hear her.

'I don't lie,' she says.

'But you don't tell us everything.'

'People don't want the whole truth, Abbie. They want something to aim for, proof that it is possible to be perfect in an imperfect world. If I show them weakness, they stop believing in me.'

'We loved it when you did that post about loneliness.'

'Which one was that?'

'January the twelfth last year. "It's OK to be on your own. You have so much to connect to, even inside yourself." There was a lovely photo of you on the cliff, with the sky above you and the sea spreading out in front of you.'

Rachel looks at Abbie open-mouthed. 'You can quote it?'

'I printed it out and put it on my wall. It meant a lot to me.'

Rachel can't remember the post. It was, as she has just explained to Abbie, a bad time. A very bad time indeed. And she was so, so alone. 'That was a positive message, though. It was me trying to make myself feel better, and in doing so, hoping that I could help other people. That's what I'm here for, to help, to make people feel good about themselves. Like you, printing my post out and putting it on your wall.'

'What if the person is on antidepressants themselves and you tell them that you managed to make yourself better all by yourself, that they shouldn't take their pills? Does that make them feel good?'

'Abbie, I have never, ever said that it's wrong to take pills. If that's how you've interpreted it, then I'm sorry. But it's really not my intention. If I didn't say things for fear of someone getting hold of the wrong end of the stick, then I'd have to be completely silent.'

'It's like how you leave out the junk from the photos in the house. How you have your team to help you with how everything looks. Like how that photograph of you on the cliff wasn't you on your own. Juno was there, wasn't she?'

'And Cyn and Zander, too.'

'I didn't even think about that when I saw it.'

'Show me the post,' Rachel says.

It takes Abbie two seconds to find it on her phone, which means she must have it bookmarked. It's a good photograph. And Rachel looks brave in it, a survivor, which is, of course, a large part of her story, both public and private. She remembers when it was taken, and how she'd just had the miscarriage, and how desperate she felt, how doomed to a life alone, and how she wished that she could be like everyone else and have real friends who were part of her everyday life, instead of just Fran and Wim in Rotterdam, her paid employees and her faceless legion of followers. She remembers thinking she would have liked to have thrown herself off that fucking cliff.

'That photograph was taken just before I started those meds,' she says to Abbie, who has taken her phone back and is sitting on the edge of the bed, looking at the picture as if it were someone she had just found out had died.

She feels awful for causing such devastation.

'So you're really not taking them any more?' Abbie says.

'I'm not.'

'Do you swear on Beansprout's life?'

Rachel nods, silently.

She's really not taking those pills any more.

She can't bring herself to tell Abbie the full truth, though. That her doctor has put her on a different brand that is acceptable in pregnancy, 'when,' as the doc said as she wrote out the prescription, 'you thoroughly weigh up the risks and benefits'.

'Good. I just want what's best for us all,' Abbie says.

'Yes,' Rachel says. 'I know.'

'Who's we?'

'What?'

'You said "The next time we tried to get pregnant". Who's the "we"?'

Rachel looks away, her face stupidly flushing like a teenager caught out. Having sworn on her baby's life, she has to continue with the truth. 'Beansprout's father,' she says. 'Please don't ask me any more. It's too complicated to explain.'

Abbie looks at her, and for a long, painful moment, Rachel thinks she's going to insist on more. Beansprout's father would be way more difficult to explain away than the pills.

But instead she slaps her thighs and stands. Then, as if her business is completed, she changes gear completely and smiles. 'I'm making your car look lovely for you. Giving it a proper clean-out.'

'Great!' Rachel says. 'I hope you don't find anything else incriminating.'

'Even if I did, I'm not the police.' Abbie smiles and leaves.

Rachel knows that she has seen the food wrappers.

She should feel awful after all that. But although she feels like she has been partially filleted, she also feels somehow cleaner, as if Abbie has shone a light right inside her, revealing who she truly is. Something no one else other than Fran has ever dared to do.

She flicks away from the security camera feed over to Instagram and scrolls through all the younger influencers she is following – the younger women whose numbers are going up while hers are, at best, static.

She's been noticing a growing trend for them to show their lives warts and all – quite literally in the case of one person called @marysmoles. She looks at selfies of dark rings under crusty eyes, dirty fingernails, stomach rolls. One even asks her followers: *Is there anything better than a really good poo?* The question generates over three thousand responses, nearly all of them positive.

In the mommy influencer camp, there's a strong stretch mark/ saggy tits theme, and she doesn't have to look far to find quite prominent influencers going on about urinary incontinence after a vaginal birth. Even piles feature, although thankfully not in the imagery.

Is this what people want now?

Is her own softly brushed content old hat?

She hauls herself to her feet, lifts her kimono and looks at herself naked in the bedroom mirror. Yes, there are stretch marks underneath that belly. Yes, her face is a little swollen, and yes, her Zeppelin breasts are three times the size they used to be. Would it do her a favour to not worry too much about losing her baby weight, tightening up and getting back to her old body? Could this be part of the new RR?

The possibility, while terrifying, also carries a whiff of relief about it.

She lies down again, flicks back to the camera feed and watches Abbie power-wash her car. That young woman there is her model follower. Rachel needs to listen to her and learn.

Abbie will save her from her greatest fear: oblivion.

Inside her, Beansprout lets off a volley of kicks, right against her bladder, as if to ram home Abbie's lesson about who and what is important in life. She only just makes it to the en suite on time.

As she sits on the toilet, watching herself in the mirror opposite, she wonders how she can swing her brand round enough to talk about the feeling of blessed relief that comes with a really good piss.

INSTAGRAM POST

rachelhoneyhill
Devon, England
80,209 likes

Images
- Janine Rodrigues' last headshot
- Janine in character for *Up the Junction*
- Janine with Rachel when she was a toddler.

Text
Happy birthday, Mama! You would have been 60 today.
I'm so sad you aren't here to see how your little grandchild is growing. I miss you every day.
I never knew who my father was. Perhaps things would have turned out differently if I had. And if that had happened, perhaps I wouldn't be here today, living the life I love! Accept and build. It's what I tell myself, and what I will tell my Beansprout when they are growing up.
#mother #beautiful #JanineRodrigues #RIP

CHAPTER TWENTY-THREE

5 August

Abbie swings the now-pristine turquoise eJeep out of the Honeyhill Barn drive and sets off down the lane on the long drive to visit her da. Apart from her stable trips and dog walks, it's the first time she has been out of the house without Rachel, and it's like she has had an arm cut off. Like a mother going out for the first time without her baby.

An electric car is a new thing for her. She's not driven anything for years, in fact, and even then it was a basic elderly Fiat Panda with a manual gearbox. The crash that wrote it off was one of the outcomes of her own adventures with alcohol, mental health challenges and bad times. It also gave her one of the scars on her belly, when they took away her spleen.

She is a proper survivor, in every sense of the word. And now, she thinks, as she gets the hang of the car in the little lane, her Lady Gaga playlist kicking in, blue skies ahead, she's on the edge of glory.

The car is surprisingly easy to operate. You just press a button, and it goes. With its newly sparkling interior, it is the symbol of the soon-to-be-born Rachel-and-Abbie combo, who are going to take on and conquer the world!

As she hits the main road, she turns up the volume so that the car vibrates as though she's inside a drum. It's like she's in the movie of her life, watched by millions.

She stops at Leigh Delamere services and spends a while working out how to charge the eJeep. The charging point reckons it will take thirty minutes, so while she's waiting, she makes full use of the credit card Rachel has given her – the company card, as she calls it – in the M&S and Smith's.

Taking her discovery of Rachel's pasty wrappers as permission to relax her own dietary rules while on the road, she picks up two of Da's favourite BLTs – one for her, one for him. She also chooses a lovely chocolate cake, a big bag of crisps, a pork pie – another passion of Da's – and, as requested in a text from him a couple of days ago, a plastic bottle of tomato ketchup, a large bottle of Coke, six packets of Gold Bensons and a small bottle of gin that she's to put at the bottom of her handbag.

As she's buying meat, she thinks she might as well get some proper dog food for Sam, so into her basket go four cans of meaty beef chunks. It's such a joy not to have to worry about how much her grocery shop is costing.

Her last job for Da involves the cashpoint. Using the credit card, she draws out three hundred quid. Petty cash, she'll tell Rachel if she ever asks her. So unused is she to having money, it doesn't even cross her mind that she could easily take that sort of sum out of her own account, which is currently in the healthiest state of its entire existence.

Hoarse-throated with accompanying La Gaga, she finally turns the car into the new visitors' car park. It's the first time she's felt able to visit Da for four years. Now she has so much to be proud about, she needs to let him know.

This recently opened building is so different to the Victorian pile she was brought to during her childhood. It looks very architectural – there's even a little something of the BabyMoon spa about it. Indeed, when it first opened, there was a lot of talk on social media about it being too good for people like Da. But Abbie's line – sometimes, in her past, so stridently voiced that it got her into fights – is that Da can't help who he is. Circumstances, genetics and brain chemistry dealt him a tough hand, and it would have been more surprising had he not ended up in trouble of some sort or another.

As Rachel says: 'We are what we are, not what we do.' If Abbie were to have her own personal mantra, that would be it. She finds it reassuring.

The security checks for visitors are not what she remembers either. It's more like an airport, with X-ray scanning machines and gloved female guards to pat you down. On the other side, her shopping is taken away.

'We're now a tobacco-free environment. And you can't bring food in,' the guard says. 'For your own and their safety. Could you just open this for me, please, madam?'

Abbie unzips her handbag, which has just come out of the scanner.

'I'm afraid two hundred's the limit,' he says, having counted the cash. 'We'll put the extra aside and you can claim it back with everything else when you leave. Ah.' He holds up the little bottle of gin with a raised eyebrow, like she's deliberately been naughty, which of course she has.

'Oops. I forgot about that,' she says, pretending it's emergency personal alcohol, like she used to carry about with her.

Finally, after fingerprinting, iris-scanning and having her FitSo, phone, make-up mirror, happy pills and paracetamol taken off her, she is given a visitor's badge and taken to the visit room.

Her uniformed escort opens the door and passes her over to another one inside, who wordlessly ushers her in.

'All right, my lover?' Da says from behind the table where he is sitting. There's no hint of recrimination about the time lapse since her last visit. After all, he's probably not short of visits from his many other acknowledged children. It's not as if she's special.

She sits facing him, and with a look at the guard sitting in the corner to check it's allowed – the rules change over the years – she takes his hands, which are soft and dry. Everything about him seems to have faded since she last saw him. His hair still has its curl but while it used to be tighter, like hers and Rachel's, it's now fuzzy and grey. His green eyes are now muddied, his lips less red.

'Hello, Da. How you doing?'

'Can't let the fuckers get you down.'

He smiles at her, wrinkling his little snub nose, which, with his freckles, sits so incongruously in his otherwise manly face. His teeth are strong and white, better than Abbie's. He has, after all, benefited from twenty years' worth of the good dentistry afforded to patients here, whereas she was rarely taken to a dentist her entire childhood.

Indeed, it was on a trip to a surgical orthodontist three years ago that he managed to escape. He'd got as far as Westbourne Parva by the time he was picked up. The papers speculated that he had taken the opportunity to do a bit of digging and revisiting.

Abbie thinks all that is nonsense.

'You look good,' he says. 'Lost a bit of that weight, yeah? And I like what you've done with that hair.'

Abbie blushes. Pleasure fills her from her toes up to the very tips of her now officially fabulous, gorgeous hair.

'I got a new job,' she tells him. 'With Rachel Rodrigues.'

Her dad's mouth opens, his lower jaw hanging a little sideways in the way it does when he's thinking about sex. Unlike probably every other man of his age, he knows exactly who Rachel

Rodrigues is, because one of his contributions to family legend is, as he puts it, 'I 'ad her mother.' Before he was arrested, this connection with the TV actress Janine Rodrigues was his only claim to fame, so he milked it at every opportunity. He has followed Rachel's rise to stardom as much as anyone can with highly restricted access to the internet.

Abbie tells him about Beansprout and her role as mother's helper.

'Mother's helper? Sounds more like bloody lady-in-waiting.'

'I'm just helping her out.'

'Don't let yourself be a doormat,' he says. 'You're too much of a pushover. If she's anything like her mother...' He leaves the ending of the sentence hanging, along with his jaw.

He ''ad' Janine Rodrigues when he was, as he put it, 'a handsome and randy young buck'. His story goes that they had a scorching affair when, at the height of her fame and beauty, she came down to Devon for a bit of a holiday – 'read rehab' is what he also says.

Not seeming to mind that his audience might be his own children, some of them very young, he has, over the years, recalled in graphic detail what happened with his famous conquest. She walked into the Shepherd and His Pack in Westbourne Parva, he bought her seven Bloody Marys, and then they 'shagged like beasts' in some field on the edge of the village.

'Older woman,' he would say. 'Knew all the bloody moves.' He'd stick his tongue in his cheek. 'Proper good blow-jobs.'

She was up there, the undisputed queen of his thousands of conquests. As he got older, and went with other women, he got more violent and insistent. A few years down the line, when living in Bristol, he 'dallied' with the women he describes as 'the whores' who contributed to his incarceration here, their versions of events involving a lot less consent than his own. 'They say no, but they always mean yes' is his general line of defence.

The stories of these women – or victims, as they were described in court – helped the police build a case against Da while pursuing him for what he did to at least three other, even less fortunate women who 'couldn't take the rough stuff'. These three victims, being buried up on Lee Moor above the village of his birth, were in no position to tell any stories at all. Even more silenced are the ten or so women police believe are still up there. Abbie dutifully sides with Da when he says he has nothing to do with those disappearances.

'I love my job,' she tells him like a little girl twirling in a tutu, desperate for his approval. 'It's so glamorous. We do such exciting things. And Rachel is lovely. Just like she is in her posts. We get on so well, like sisters.'

She lets that hang in the air, half a smile, eyebrow cocked.

'Well done, old Abs. Who'd have thought it of you?' He cracks out one of his massive throaty laughs. When it's not aimed at her, Abbie loves it when he does this.

'Da,' she tells him, so conspiratorially that she can feel the guard in the corner prick up his ears, 'the dates work out. I've done the maths. She was born nine months after you had that Janine Rodrigues.'

'I know,' he says. 'I've always had an idea. But she was a right slapper, that Rodrigues. Could have been any number of fellas, probably.'

'But we look so alike, me and Rachel.'

'Nah.' He shakes his head. 'She's much hotter. More like Gina.'

'Well then,' Abbie says, a little stung. 'More proof.'

Beauty queen Gina's mother had once been a beauty queen herself. According to the extended family gossip machine, Gina senior now earns a fortune doing live internet porn. Abbie takes more after her own ma, whose extreme youth, rather than any beauty or glamour, had attracted Da's attention.

'But we've got the same eyes and hair,' she says. 'Our noses are a bit the same, too. And we like the same things,' she adds, thinking of the pasties. 'There's no way we're not sisters.'

'Fuck me,' he says, smiling.

'She trusts me, Da. She really trusts me. When the baby's born, I'll be living in a proper family for the first time, and anything will be possible. There's this beautiful converted barn she lives in near the village—'

'I know it,' Da says.

'—loads of countryside and space, and horses and a dog. Money to do whatever we want. And then I'll be able to...'

But he has stopped listening. He grabs her hand again. 'She's proper loaded, yeah?'

Abbie nods.

'Then let's say she's mine.' He nods, like it's finished business. 'Play your cards right, girl, and we could be onto a winner. She'd surely like to look after her poor old da, wouldn't she?' He cracks another perfect smile.

Abbie hesitates. As she knows when it comes to her own feelings about Da, blood is thicker than water. But she wonders how Rachel will take being told that Wayne Speakman is her father. She's also confused about how she's going to tell Rachel the truth after spinning her the tale about her fictional family with a double-glazing professional at the helm. But the truth is the truth, and her plan is that one day, it will all out. No more secrets. No more lies.

'Of course, Da,' she says. 'We'll remember you. Always.'

Da leans forward and winks at her. 'You know what I say, Abbo: Do whatever it takes, girl. Whatever it bloody takes.'

Abbie nods.

'Good girl. Good girl.' He rests his back on his chair and yawns. 'Tell me about those kiddywinks, then.'

'Oh, you know.' Abbie doesn't want to talk about that. It's another reason why she hasn't been to see him for so long.

'Be nice to see them some day.'

'You will, one day soon. After the baby's born.'

'Good girl. Where's my stuff, then?' he says.

She explains that it was taken off her at security.

'Bunch of fucking arseholes,' he says pointedly at the guard.

The journey back is a victory drive for Abbie. Now she's said the words out loud to Da and got his blessing, her plan feels more formed than ever.

She bombs down the M4, yelling along with Lady Gaga. So loud is her music, so busy is she imagining the vast crowd in front of her at the O2, that she doesn't hear or see the siren and blue lights of the police car bearing down on her until it is alongside, the two officers waving her over onto the hard shoulder.

She toys with the idea of outrunning them, but even though the eJeep has just amply proved itself capable of a hundred miles an hour, she doesn't think she stands much of a chance.

So she pulls over and waits, her heart thrumming, as one of the officers gets out of the car and strolls along the hard shoulder towards her.

'In a hurry?' he asks her.

'I'm so sorry,' she says. 'I've just heard my sister is in labour.'

'That's great news,' he says. 'But I'm sure she'd prefer you to arrive alive, and not having caused an accident.'

Abbie nods, summoning every bit of meekness she possesses.

'I'm going to have to book you,' he says, pulling out a notebook. 'Name?'

'Rachel Rodrigues,' Abbie says.

He looks at her for a long beat. Does he know who Rachel is? Does Abbie look sufficiently like her, even on a bad day, to get away with it? It seems that if he does, she does, because he goes on: 'Are you the registered owner of this vehicle, Ms Rodrigues?'

'Yes,' Abbie says.

'May I see your licence?'

'Sure.' She reaches into her bag and pulls out Rachel's driving licence. Not having one of her own, she secretly borrowed it for her trip, just in case something like this were to happen.

The policeman looks at the photograph of Rachel on the plastic card, squints at Abbie and, to her enormous pleasure and relief, nods and hands it back to her.

The ticket will be sent to her home address, which means that Abbie will have to intercept the post before Wanda gets to it, which will be a real pain, involving getting up early and hanging around the front-garden mailbox to catch it before she arrives.

In fact, Abbie thinks, as she drives westwards at a steady seventy, it would be better for her – and therefore better for Rachel, in the long run – if that Wanda were out of the picture entirely.

INSTAGRAM POST

rachelhoneyhill
Devon, England
paid partnership with **fitsofitso**
15,765 likes

Images
- Abbie in crop top and shorts in the Honeyhill gym, working out like a demon at the free weights. Her tattoos – Zayn, Harry, Taylor – are visible
- Abbie swinging a kettlebell. Her growing six-pack is exposed, as well as several nasty-looking scars
- Rachel and Abbie in identical cropped workout gear, standing smiling, their arms around each other's shoulders.

Text
Isn't she doing well! Just look at those abs and guns!
The stats are FANTASTIC! 5 kilos gone, and a 10% reduction in body fat. In just FIVE weeks!
@cynthem even said when they popped by the other day that we almost look like sisters!
What do you think?
Me and Beansprout are so proud of her!
#AbbiesJourney #sisters #friends

CHAPTER TWENTY-FOUR

12 August

'Abbie! Abbie!'

Rachel runs away from Wanda's tip of an office, crying. Wanda is on her heels, bangles rattling as she waves her hands around, trying to calm her down.

'It's not so bad,' she's saying, the ghosts of stale butterscotch sweets riding on her breath, making Rachel feel like throwing up. 'We knew this was going to happen.'

Rachel stops and turns so suddenly that Wanda runs right into her. 'Death threats?' she says. 'We knew *death threats* were going to happen?'

'Not quite that, granted—'

'Twenty thousand followers gone in a day?' Her voice is so high that Sam comes running, wondering what all the dog-frequency fuss is about.

'—but we knew there were going to be negative reactions and that they were going to build to a certain critical mass until we swung things around.'

'Oh, shut up, Wanda. Did I send you on that marketing course just so you could spout bullshit at me? I want Abbie.' Rachel's hands are tingling, and her vision is swimming.

Wanda breathes in so deeply that her tiny pointy tits rise almost level with her chin. 'You need to calm down, Rach. For the baby. You're getting it all out perspective.'

'Out of perspective? This is my *life*! Abbie!'

Rachel is by now far from calm. On her scalp, her scar throbs. Inside, she's the little girl who heard that her mother had just died.

'I'll take it from here, Wanda,' Abbie says from the doorway to the gym, where she has been doing her workout.

Quite by accident, Rachel and Abbie are both wearing the same Gossip Yum yoga pant/hoodie combo, in exactly the same pattern, Día de Muertos, which is tattoo-like white skulls on a red background.

Rachel blinks. Have the negative commentators on her most recent post got it right? *Is* she colonising Abbie? Making her into her own mini-me? *Has* she run out of ideas, so that the only thing she can show the world is self-replication?

Why do other people have to complicate everything so much?

Abbie sweeps across the room and puts an arm around Rachel. 'Honestly, Wanda,' she says over her shoulder. 'You're really not needed. You can get back to work.'

As she lets herself be led towards the sofa, Rachel can smell Wanda's face go sour behind her back. Abbie sits her down, holds her hands and talks her through her breathing.

'What is it, Rachel?' she asks, once Rachel is calmer.

Rachel turns and looks at Abbie, who has a massive spot on her chin that it's hard not to stare at. At least, though, for a brief moment, it takes her mind away from her troubles.

'I'm getting some horrible haters, Abbie. And we've taken a heavy dip this week in followers. It's like a snowball. Once it starts rolling, it just gets bigger and bigger. And today the stats have gone over a cliff edge. I don't see how I'm ever going to crawl back from this.'

Abbie gets up and grabs the kitchen iPad. 'Show me,' she says.

Rachel logs on to her Instagram stats tracker using facial recognition. She points to a graph that indeed shows a steep downward slope for the past week with an almost ninety-degree drop for today.

'Why didn't you tell me?' Abbie says.

'It's not your area.'

Abbie gives her a look like she has been a naughty girl, like she has in some way disappointed her. 'It's *all* my area, Rachel. I'm here to make sure that both baby and mother are fine. If there's anything wrong with you, I need to know about it so I can help make it better.'

The tide of panic that has swept Rachel since she was in Wanda's room now begins to turn. Abbie does this, she realises. She gives her perspective.

'Here.' She pulls up the comments below today's Abbie's Journey post. 'The trolling kicks off here.'

Scotty2002 *You dressing your new dolly up, Rachel? Got nothing better to do? #emptybitch*

'It's not still up?' Abbie says.

'This is the archive. Wanda pulled it, but not quickly enough. It caused an almost instant pile-on. All the haters, drawn out on my supposedly narcissistic arse.'

Abbie squints at the first troll's handle. 'Do we know anything more about this Scotty2002?'

Rachel pulls up the profile and they look through Scotty's history. He's fairly newly arrived to Instagram, and his one aim seems to be to spread poison about Rachel. The actual account only contains five innocuous and badly taken photographs: two of a car parked in a driveway, its number plate blurred out; two of a soccer match taken from within a crowd, and one of a dirty-looking burger and fries.

Acid scratches up Rachel's throat as she expands his profile picture. All you can tell is that he's white and spotty. The rest of him is covered by a black beanie, fake Ray-Bans and a black face mask. 'If that's even him,' she says. 'Unlike those of us who put ourselves out there on the line, these bastards are usually too cowardly to show themselves in full.'

They scroll through the one-hundred-plus Scotty2002 comments removed from Rachel's posts. They start with the usual slaggings-off: words like *slut*, *whore*, *bitch* – so common on social media that, shockingly, they have almost lost their potency. Then, as he realises he's getting attention, he degenerates into frankly libellous stuff:

RR's on smack.

RR's so skank I wouldn't poke her even if she paid me and begged me.

RR should end it all now. I'll lend her my piece.

'Nasty little creep,' Abbie says.

'He really hates me.' Rachel remembers what the police said about storing troll comments in case evidence is ever needed, and shudders.

'So what are you going to do about this?'

She could swear that Abbie's eyes become darker as she says this.

Rachel shifts on the sofa, puts her hands on her belly and strokes what she imagines is Beansprout's head. 'There's nothing I *can* do. We've blocked him and reported him to Instagram, so he won't be able to post any more – at least as Scotty2002. But there's nothing to stop him opening another account and getting at me again. In fact, they almost always do that, to retaliate after you block them.'

She screws up her face, puts her hands in her hair and yells.

'Rachel, Rachel, you have to relax.' Abbie puts her hand on her knee. 'You can't let the fuckers get you down.'

Hearing Abbie swear shocks Rachel into silence.

'We're going to sort this.' Abbie takes her hands. 'First off, I'm going to do a film and you're going to post it.'

'What?' Rachel has never, ever taken creative lead from anyone on her content. She's quite shocked that Abbie's even suggesting it.

'Come on!' Abbie takes her hands and pulls her up. 'Bring the iPad.'

'Hi, I'm Abbie,' Abbie says to the iPad camera.

After tidying her hair and make-up, she had positioned one of the garden chairs under the tree ferns and angled a reflector board on the grass to uplight her face. It's like, Rachel thinks, she has been studying how to set up a photograph.

'I'm here to help Rachel with Beansprout when he or she is born. But I am also one of Rachel's biggest fans, if not *the* biggest.' Abbie laughs, something Rachel has never seen her do before. Watching her on the iPad screen as she films, Rachel marvels at how she is so stilted that she looks natural, like an improvising actor. She has none of that slickness that can make a video look staged or unnatural.

This is pure authenticity.

'My official job title is mother's helper, but I do just about everything here to keep the ship ticking over.' She gestures awkwardly with her hands. 'When I first arrived, I was pretty out of shape. Years of poor eating and lack of exercise had made me put on weight, and I got out of breath just going up the stairs. I asked Rachel to help me out, and she very generously put together a bespoke exercise and nutrition programme, tailored specifically for me. Aren't I lucky?

'She's also been giving me hair and make-up tips. I honestly had no idea about any of that when I first came here. Now I know how to make the most of myself, and here at Honeyhill, we're all ready and waiting for Beansprout to arrive!'

Abbie's face settles into a smile. After almost exactly ten seconds, she calls, 'Cut!' and Rachel turns off the camera.

'That was brilliant,' Rachel says. 'You're a natural.'

'When shall we put it up?'

'Soon,' Rachel says.

But she can't use this film. Despite Abbie's authentic look and feel, the whole thing is over-earnest and corny. It's so off-brand, her remaining followers would think she'd been taken over.

Trouble is, Abbie's going to be waiting now, expecting the post to go up. Rachel hates the idea of disappointing her. But she dislikes even more the thought of telling her that her idea is naff. As she returns to the house, she's too busy worrying about this to remember the small step up to the terrace, and she trips and stumbles, taking the fall on her right knee. The shock stings her entire body, and Beansprout startles like a little earthquake inside her.

'Rachel! Are you OK?' Abbie, who tried to catch her and failed, is on her knees beside her.

The tears come – partly because of the shock, mostly because of everything else. Pregnancy has stretched her skin so thin.

'Oh dear.' Abbie puts an arm around her shoulders and helps her up. 'Let's go in and see to that knee.'

'You do look a bit peaky, you know,' Abbie tells her as she cleans the graze on Rachel's knee and puts on a plaster.

'Do I?' Rachel glances at her reflection in the living room window, which Abbie has closed because now the sun has gone off the back of the house, there is a chill in the air.

'You've allowed yourself to get too upset about this troll business. You really need to start taking things a bit easier now that Beansprout's nearly cooked.' She touches Rachel's belly.

Rachel hates people touching her bump and has to fight the urge to whack Abbie's hand away. Instead, she closes her eyes and nods. She does feel indescribably weary all of a sudden.

Abbie takes her hand. 'Where's your signet ring, Rachel?'

'Over on the kitchen surface with my chain and my earrings. I took them off for my yoga.'

'You shouldn't leave your valuables lying around.' Abbie fetches the jewellery and puts it on her. 'They might get lost. Hey, why don't you go and have a lovely bath? I'll tell Wanda to take the rest of the afternoon off, and in a bit I'll make you a tasty supper and bring it up on a tray and you can have a nice early night. What do you say?'

While Rachel is steaming in the deep, hot bubble bath, her phone, which she is scrolling through, pings. It's a message from Fran.

Marieke says she thinks Abbie's saying 'bad sister' in the nursery video. Does that mean anything?

Rachel shrugs and taps out her reply.

Weird. Perhaps Marieke's not so hot at reading English lips. LOL.

INSTAGRAM POST

rachelhoneyhill
Devon, England
paid partnership with **tetradiajournals**
1, 930,253 likes

Image
- Rachel writing in her Tetradia Journal, by candlelight, in her nightdress in clean white bedlinen.

Text
If you're ever feeling down, just writing what you have to be grateful for can be helpful.
Reading it back can also be a tool for lifting you out of a low period.
Value your writing by keeping a beautiful journal. Here's my vegan leather book, painstakingly handmade in Dorset by **@tetradiajournals**.
I like to use a dip pen, too, for the added romance, and only ever write my gratitude journal in bed, with the curtains open so that I can look at the sky for inspiration.
#gratitude #gratitudejournal #veganleather #handbound-book #inspiration

CHAPTER TWENTY-FIVE

Abbie leaves Rachel tucked up in bed and drains the bath in the en suite, watching as the expensive bubbles slip away down the plughole. How can one woman having one bath make such a mess? Is this how she would have been herself had she not had tidiness drummed into her as a means of survival? Or is it a genetic legacy from Rachel's mother?

She gathers up the towels to take down to the wash, wipes the toothpaste from the basin and screws the lids back on Rachel's face creams and serums, which are scattered around the vanity unit. There is no space inside the mirrored cabinet to put them away, though. It's jammed with hundreds of pounds' worth of creams, all sent to Rachel. There's enough there to cover a face night and day for two lifetimes. Abbie takes out a particularly large pink jar and a couple of other smaller pots and hides them in the towels to take to her own room. Then she puts the stuff Rachel has been using in the newly emptied space.

'Much better,' she says. Rachel will never notice the missing pots.

And after all, this is what little sisters do – borrow their big sister's cosmetics.

'Who's gorgeous? You are.'

When Abbie gets back to her bedroom after clearing up the kitchen and walking Sam, Barney greets her in his usual flattering manner. She lets him out of his cage and gives him a handful of dried worms as a reward.

She showers and smooths one of her newly acquired creams into her skin. Then she wraps her bathrobe around herself, grabs her gratitude journal, her iPad and Galaxy and sits on the sofa with the telly on in the background. Barney settles on her head.

'We've got work to do,' she tells him.

'You are lovely,' he says.

She opens her journal and starts to write her reasons to be grateful. She's grateful that Rachel is her sister. She's grateful that she is becoming indispensable to her. Most of all, she is grateful that she has finally had an email back from Ms Ayo Dafé, saying that although they still do not think it is in the best interests of Harry and Taylor to see her at present, she is hopeful that she will get permission from the review board to visit Zayn.

It's not perfect, but Zayn is the one she misses most, as he was seven when he was taken from her. She had hardly got to know Harry, who was only one, and of course Taylor she only had for a couple of days after she was born.

But she'll show them what a good person she has become. She'll get them all back in the end, now she's with Rachel.

She notes all this down. Underneath the writing, she draws a picture of herself, Rachel and the children, all smiling together on the sofa with Sam and Barney. It's not great art or anything, but it says it all really.

She puts her journal aside and strokes the iPad open. The rest of the evening is going to be all about a hunt. Thanks to Posh June, who spent many hours passing on some of the knowledge she acquired over a lifetime of committing major fraud, Abbie has surprisingly advanced research skills.

Because of this, she knows how easy it is to leave an online or paper trail that could trip you up, and has adjusted her own identity accordingly. She has, for example, changed her name from her father's – Speakman – to her mother's – James. This means that no one will discover how she met Posh June, which was some six years ago, after an unfortunate incident when a man called Kieran got on the wrong side of Abbie and came off very badly for it. Abbie spent two years in Eastwood Park, a women's prison just outside Gloucester, and she and June were cellmates.

What with what happened with the children and everything when she got out, Abbie hasn't ever put the skills June taught her to use. She did become part of PJ's 'outside' network, though, looking after certain items when necessary. Hence the reason June helps her out on occasions.

But it is these skills she plans to use to locate Scotty2002.

First, she looks at the car photos on his account. They're of a modified Citroën Saxo with custom paint job. She looks it up and discovers the make and model. Sadly, it's a common car, but she can narrow it down to two years, as this particular version was only in production between 2002 and 2004, it's a right-hand drive, and there's a British pelican crossing behind it. So UK, definitely.

She zooms in on a picture taken from the house side of a driveway. The car number plate is blurred out, which suggests Scotty-boy reckons he knows a thing or two about covering his tracks. But it turns out he's not as clever as he thinks, because, in the background, on the other side of the road, there's a takeaway called the Codfather.

A bit of googling tells Abbie that there are twenty-five fish and chip shops with that name in the UK, so she just has to go through each one on Google Street View. By the thirteenth, she has found the right Codfather and therefore the address of the house opposite. It even has the stupid Saxo sitting on its driveway. It's easy then to find the postcode, search the electoral roll – which costs a few quid but is, in Abbie's view, worth it – and find out who lives in the house. The result comes as a bit of a surprise: three women.

A short time on Facebook narrows it down. Two of the occupants – an elderly woman and her middle-aged daughter – can be discounted. After checking on football team allegiances – the soccer photos were taken from the home side of Plymouth Argyle FC, who feature prominently on the remaining account's home page – Abbie is pretty sure she has bagged her troll.

Scotty2002 is a twenty-three-year-old, slightly built, car-mad girl with acne and facial scars called Charlotte Williams.

And conveniently, she lives in Exeter, not an hour's drive from Honeyhill. Abbie thinks of once again calling in a favour from Posh June, who has ways of connecting with associates on the outside. But when she did that with that Jane Roberts, things went a bit pear-shaped – teaching a lesson got taken a step too far. With Charlotte's direct social media connection to Rachel, that kind of action isn't such a great idea. All Abbie wants to do is make her pay, and stop her posting ever again.

'No. I can do this myself,' she says. After all, as that Kieran can attest, she is pretty good at teaching a person a lesson.

'You're so clever,' Barney tweets from the top of her head, where he has sat all this while.

She zooms in on Charlotte Williams' scarred face and thinks she's seen her somewhere before. But before she can work out where or when, her iPad buzzes with a message. It's Fran, asking if she's free for that long-promised call at ten tomorrow morning.

INSTAGRAM POST

rachelhoneyhill
Devon, England
paid partnership with **wombsplash**
12,215 likes

Images
- Abbie and Rachel laughing over something on an iPad
- Rachel giving Abbie a cup of tea
- Abbie and Rachel cooking together in the kitchen
- Abbie and Rachel running together on the cliffs, with Sam
- Rachel leading Cal with Abbie on his back
- Abbie and Rachel reading the instructions while erecting the birthing pool.

Text
I can't tell you how happy I am to have Abbie in my life. She came as my employee, but now she is so much more to me. In return for me guiding her on her journey to fitness, she helps me in every corner of my life. It's so good to see her unfolding here, in the green Honeyhill peace.

We had a lovely time this afternoon putting together my fantastic new **@wombsplash** birthing pool.

Beansprout and I can't wait to show you pictures of it in action! And yes, Abbie will be with me, being my doula, along with Sue, my lovely midwife from **@baby2you_**

#MothersHelper #birth #baby

CHAPTER TWENTY-SIX

13 August

'Hey.' Fran does her friendliest smile at Abbie. She's heard from Rachel how reticent she can be, and she wants to get the best out of her today, while Rachel is in her private yoga practice.

'Hello, Fran.' Abbie smiles back.

'I'm so sorry it's taken me so long to check in. I've been rushed off my feet here.'

'That's fine.'

'You're OK after that call you overheard?'

'Yes.'

'So I just wanted to see how you were settling in after your first month.'

'It's all going well, thank you.'

Fran leans in and squints at the screen. 'What's that on your head?'

'Barney. My budgie.'

'He looks very sweet. Hey, you know Rachel has a feather allergy, don't you?'

'She's perfectly happy to have him here, so long as he stays in my rooms.'

'And do you like your rooms?'

'They're very nice.' Abbie pans the iPad around what used to be the attic. Rachel's done a good job on it, and Abbie is keeping it nicely, not a thing out of place.

'You're looking well.'

'I've lost five kilos, body fat's down to thirty-four per cent, and I can do ten press-ups in a row without stopping.'

'That's amazing after such a short while.'

'And I can hold a plank for three minutes.'

'Your hair's looking good, too.'

'Cyn's going for a more natural look. More like Rachel's.'

'The eyebrows, too.'

Abbie runs her fingers across her brows. She's clearly looking at herself on the screen, just like Rachel does, and the gesture itself is very Rachel indeed. In fact, the transformation that has taken place in the past five weeks has been little short of miraculous, and not a little spooky, in the way that Abbie is looking more and more like Rachel. A bit *Single White Female*. Except, unlike in the film, it seems this shape-shifting is entirely Rachel's creation, rather than Abbie doing it secretly behind her back.

'We're documenting my progress for Instagram. Hashtag Abbie's Journey.'

'I've seen it.'

'"If she can do it, anyone can" kind of thing.'

Fran had doubted the whole transformation project – whether the person they picked for the job would be up for it, and whether they would stick to it – but she's been proved wrong. This is a remarkable achievement on Rachel's part. But then Abbie's determination is there on full show too: the set of her jaw, the intensity of her gaze, the confidence with which she speaks. Even the fact that she has a bird sitting on her head can't undermine all that.

This young woman is far from puddingy, as Fran once thought. She has edges like hard crackers.

'I was wondering if you would be up for doing me a favour?' she asks Abbie.

'What's that?' Abbie says.

'Would you be my eyes and ears on Rachel?'

'What do you mean? *Spy* on her?' Abbie sounds shocked, even a little disgusted.

'No, not spy. Care. I know Rachel really well, and—'

'Yes, you've been friends since school.'

'That's right. I speak to her most days. And she just doesn't seem herself at the moment.'

'She's fine.'

'She just seems quite vulnerable.'

'She's eight months pregnant. It can be a vulnerable stage.'

'Tell me about it. Been there three times.'

'Well then, you would know.'

Fran wonders if she might be paranoid, but she's sure she can detect a touch of hostility. Yes, she would bloody well know. Unlike Abbie.

'She's not happy with how things are going on Instagram,' Abbie goes on.

'We've talked it through, and we've developed a strategy.'

'A strategy?'

'If you're worried about her meds, don't be. She's fine without them.'

'Meds?'

'The antidepressants? When she had the miscarriage and felt everything was sliding?'

Miscarriage? Fran needs to take a couple of moments to digest all this, away from Abbie's face and its low-key, pleasant smile, which – and she hopes this is more paranoia, but fears it's not – makes her look like she's scoring points. Like she is revelling in knowing more about Rachel than Fran does.

'Could you hold on for just one moment, please, Abbie?'

'Of course.'

Fran mutes her microphone and switches off her camera. Her hand to her belly, she gets up and walks across the scarred and pitted wooden floor of her office on the first floor of her warehouse conversion. Downstairs, Wim is messing around with Luuk in the open-plan living space. It sounds like there's a rowdy game of pool going on. And three-year-old Lotte is, as ever, rattling her little toy car up and down the entire length of the apartment. No sound from baby Mila, who must be back to sleep after a *hideous* night. Fran slides open one of the gargantuan windows that look out over the steely water of the Nieuwe Maas, steps out onto the balcony and takes a breath. The usual crowds loiter in the sunlight outside the Fenix Food Factory, snacking on frikandellen and fancy microbrewery beers.

So busy here in the middle of a city at the gateway to Europe. So quiet and disconnected in Devon. Fran, who has found her place in the world by powering forwards and away, has never felt happy about Rachel moving back down there, despite her argument that to her it was home. Never having had any notion before now of what 'home' actually meant, Fran couldn't understand. But then since The Event, there's been quite a lot she doesn't understand about Rachel.

Poor Rachel.

But things seemed to settle, and Fran came round to believing that Rachel had finally found her place, that everything was going fine and she was going to be able to stop worrying. Clearly, if Rachel has been going to the doctor's and asking for pills to help her to bear living, Fran has been deceived.

She has certainly never been told about a miscarriage. Was this before or after she lost Noud? Was Rachel shielding her from bad news? *Rachel* looking after *Fran*?

Since The Event, it has always been the other way round. When Rachel was struggling with life after the lost years that followed, it was Fran who suggested keeping herself on course through diet, exercise and meditation. It worked for her, after all. But then, she thinks, as she hears the laughter from downstairs, she has all this. A family, a home, a real sense of purpose with her job.

As she has just discovered, it seems a DIY strategy for good mental health wasn't enough for Rachel.

Millions of women are on antidepressants. It shouldn't be a big thing. And after all, Rachel's business is Rachel's business. But why does she feel she needs to hide things from her best friend?

Plus, given Rachel's condition and her past with alcohol and recreational drugs, she has to be very careful indeed about what she puts in her body and her mind. Fran knows for a fact that she won't have mentioned anything about her history or her episodes to the doctor who prescribed those pills.

In the background, she hears Abbie speaking.

'What's she up to, Barney? Has she forgotten about us?'

'You're a stunner.'

Fran does a double take. Was that the *bird* speaking? Telling herself to get a grip, she heads back to her laptop, switches on the camera and the mic.

'Sorry – just had a bit of a domestic emergency.'

'If you're worried about the baby,' Abbie says, 'she tapered before she got pregnant.'

That thought hadn't even occurred to Fran. And there she is, with her special investment in this child. She needs to be able to trust Rachel to look after it, both before and after the birth, but she's not entirely sure right now whether she can. It feels like the reins are slipping through her fingers. What else is Rachel not telling her?

'I'm so glad I've got you next to her,' she says to Abbie. 'Can you make sure she's happy? That's the most important thing.'

'Of course. That's my job, and my job is my life.' Abbie smiles, and the bird takes off from her head, a flash of green and yellow.

'Can we just keep this conversation between ourselves, eh?'

'No worries. Oh. You were going to explain to me why you think Rachel "really doesn't know how to behave around people".' Abbie is reading the message Fran sent her after she overheard Rachel bitching about her.

Again there appears to be a level of insolence in Abbie's tone. Fran doesn't want to get high-handed, but she really doesn't feel like talking about The Event, Rachel's brain injury and her violent dissociative fugues right now. It would feel too demeaning, like she was engaging in a tit-for-tat, *I know more about Rachel than you do* competition. If anything, a not very admirable part of her is hoping that Rachel goes off on one in front of Abbie. With any luck, if Abbie is unprepared, it might set her packing like it did that dim little admin girl Charley, who, with her attempts to break her NDA, is still a thorn in Fran's legal side.

Fran's saved from having to wriggle out of it by an alert popping up on her screen. Speak of the devil. Rachel must have finished her yoga and wants to connect. 'Abbie, I'm really sorry. I've got a work call coming through.'

'On a Saturday?'

'No rest for the wicked.'

'I've got to go and walk Sam anyway.'

'Is that really your job? What about the dog walker?'

'We decided to let her go. I love Sam and I'm happy to take him out.'

'OK.' Fran supposes that's fine. She just worries what will happen when Abbie leaves, as she intends her to do at some point after Beansprout's birth. But she can file that away until later. 'Gotta catch that call.' She does the Zoom farewell dance, disconnects, and watches as Abbie freezes and disappears.

She decides not to confront Rachel about the pills. What good would it do? And anyway, she can't have her knowing she's been speaking to Abbie behind her back.

'Hi, Rachel,' she sings. She unplugs the laptop to take it downstairs so that the children can say hello.

INSTAGRAM POST

2 years ago

rachelhoneyhill
Devon, England
paid partnership with **spiral_d.n.a**
1,367,432 likes

Images
- Rachel balancing a pot of Spiral DNA face cream on her outstretched hand
- Rachel smoothing the cream onto her skin
- The back of the jar, with Rachel's unique DNA result, rendered as a mandala.

Text
Did you know that your DNA affects your skin?
The famous DNA double helix has thousands of variations called single nucleotide polymorphisms: SNPs.
16 of these SNPs, handed down through the paternal line, are responsible for the composition of your skin. They provide the key to formulating the perfect skincare routine, just for you.
@spiral_d.n.a has captured this technology and created a method of formulating a unique, luxurious face cream for your very own particular SNP composition.
You send off one hair and in just two weeks you get a beautiful hand-blown blue glass jar, with your DNA result expressed as a spiritually uplifting mandala on the label, and a heavenly scented bespoke cream inside that is scientifically guaranteed to have amazing results!

It's not the cheapest product I have featured, but it's worth every penny! Follow the link in my bio and use the code RRSNP for a 10% discount!

#facecream #skincare #DNA #spiraldna

CHAPTER TWENTY-SEVEN

15 August

Sam sits like a good patient boy on his lead at Abbie's side while she waits, in running gear and trainers, by the mailbox just outside the Honeyhill Barn gates. It's over a week now since she was stopped on the way back from visiting her dad, and she's expecting the fixed penalty speeding notice to come through any day now. She hopes it's today, because she is not a morning person, and she can't really be doing with these early starts.

It's all Wanda's fault, of course, for being such a pain-in-the-butt jobsworth. There's no way Abbie could explain why the official letter addressed to Rachel is actually for her to deal with, without Wanda going off bleating about it.

The sound of a vehicle bumping down the lane pricks both Abbie and Sam's ears.

'Is it Postie?' Abbie asks Sam.

It bimbles into view and instead reveals itself to be Wanda's stupid little yellow Fiat. Abbie lifts one side of her top lip in a look that would be more fitting on the canine face at her side.

'What's she doing here this early?' she says.

She could just play this by pretending she was taking Sam for a run, but instead she holds her ground and gears herself for a confrontation.

Wanda acknowledges her without a smile and, using the blipper in her car, opens the gates and turns into the driveway. But she comes to a halt just inside the gates and winds down the window.

'Hi,' she says. Her body language fails to convey an actual greeting, however. It comes out more as an accusation.

'Morning,' Abbie says.

'You don't need to get the post,' Wanda says. 'That's my job.'

'I'm happy to do it.' Abbie ruffles the top of Sam's head.

'Right.' Wanda switches off the engine and gets out of her car. She hasn't yet got any make-up on and is in a pink linen dress that looks more like a nightie on her skinny frame. From the look of her, she's not a morning person either. She strides over to Abbie and faces her, standing far too close, right in her space.

'What's your problem, Wand?' Abbie says.

'My name is Wanda.'

'Oh yeah.'

'Abbie, I think we're having some boundary issues. You are here to help Rachel with the baby, and anything she may need in that area. You are not her friend, nor are you anything to do with her work life.'

'She thinks I'm her friend.'

'You are her employee. She pays you – well over the odds, I may add – to do a job here. Which does not involve picking up the post or bringing it into my room and moving everything around.'

'I'm just tidying it up for you.'

'I like it how it is. I know where everything is.'

'Rachel hates the way you have it.'

Wanda's mouth becomes so small that Abbie can barely see her lips. 'It's my room,' she says, her voice a strange strangle.

'It's Rachel's room,' Abbie says. 'If you think about it. And she's embarrassed that it's the first thing a visitor might see.'

'So you're her mouthpiece, are you?'

'She trusts me, Wand.'

The hatred with which Wanda looks at Abbie is gratifying. She has to be removed.

'Nice bag,' Abbie says, reaching out and fingering Wanda's Mulberry, which she knows for a fact is worth over a grand. It's leather, so not something Wanda would have picked off one of Rachel's vegan freebie piles. 'Is Rachel paying you "over the odds" too, then?'

Wanda looks like she might just explode any minute.

Abbie knows she's up to something. She knows the type, and Wanda is it.

At that moment, the postman's van appears. When both she and Wanda hold out their hands for the mail, Abbie is delighted that, after sizing them up, the postie gives the stack of letters and packages to her.

It's a sign.

She grabs the evil-looking brown envelope.

That night, after Rachel has gone to bed, Abbie finds her little pile of jewellery, which she left on the kitchen counter as usual before filming a late-pregnancy yoga session with Drew.

Abbie rather likes Drew, who is six foot four and has the sexiest forearms. It's the first time she's felt any interest in a man since Dean, Taylor's dad. Not that he knows he's Taylor's dad. After him, she decided she'd had it with men. Perhaps these feelings she has for Drew are a sign that now her plan is falling into place, things are picking up for her in other areas, too. It's all academic, though. He only has eyes for Rachel, and Rachel, of course, is completely oblivious to that fact.

Among the silver bangles, chains and rings on the kitchen counter, she finds what she's looking for: Janine Rodrigues' signet ring. Her eye is also drawn to a chunky amber number that, although Abbie has seen it a couple of times on Rachel's hands when she posts, doesn't often get an outing. It's a dome of golden stone so shiny that it makes Abbie think of boiled sweets, and it has a perfect spider embedded in it. As she holds it up to the light above the worktop, she knows she has to have it.

She pockets both rings and tiptoes along the corridor to Wanda's dump of a room, where she slides the signet ring into the desk drawer, slipping it under a muddle of make-up and skincare items, no doubt snaffled from Rachel's stocks of freebies.

Where there's smoke, there's fire.

That dirty little thief, Wand.

The other ring stays in her pocket and gets taken up to her room to join a growing stash of personal treasures she has found around the house. It's not stealing when Abbie does it. It's more meaningful than that. It's *collecting*.

The next morning, she has to comfort Rachel, who is devastated about not being able to find her signet ring. Abbie is pleased to note that she isn't even aware that the amber spider was in her jewellery pile.

'It's got to be somewhere,' Abbie tells her. 'It's bound to turn up.'

'But I feel so bare without it,' Rachel says, looking all lost in her dressing gown, which barely covers her bump now. 'Losing it is a bad sign. A really, really bad sign.'

'You mustn't let yourself get worked up.' Abbie hands her her morning cup of chamomile tea. She's been weaning her off caffeine, and they're down to just one Americano now, but that's not allowed until mid-morning. 'For Beansprout's sake.'

But Rachel *is* worked up. So Abbie puts her back to bed. 'Try to just sleep,' she says.

'What about The Team?' Rachel says from underneath her duvet. 'They're due in at eleven.'

'I'll take care of everything. You need a day off. Dr Abbie's orders.'

'What about my posts, though?'

'You've got plenty lined up on the GridSmasher, haven't you?'

'Yes.'

'Well then. You can just let them go live when scheduled and take some time off. And by that, I mean proper time off. No screens except TV.'

Abbie gathers up Rachel's phones and iPad and takes them downstairs.

True to her word, Abbie does take care of everything. She calls and cancels everyone, even Wanda.

'What?' Wanda says on the phone, scandalised and suspicious.

'Rachel's not feeling all that well. She's asked for an empty house today, just so that she can rest without any pressure.'

'Can I speak to her?'

'Did you not hear what I said, Wanda? And don't try calling her – she's not got a phone within reach.'

Wanda still doesn't sound convinced, so Abbie dangles a dual-purpose carrot in front of her.

'She also says have the day off and use your company card to take yourself and a friend to Bannon's for a lovely spa day and lunch.'

That does the trick, and, finally, greedy Wanda agrees not to come in. It's grudging, though. And there's Rachel offering her a spa day in the most expensive hotel in the area. The ungrateful little bitch.

Now, that's a phrase Abbie has heard many times in her life. It's refreshing to be able to use it against someone else.

*

'I feel so much better,' Rachel says as she appears for the iron-rich spinach crêpes with creamy mushrooms Abbie has cooked for their supper. It took her three lots of mixture to get pancakes that weren't like lumps of Play-Doh. The final versions were a little on the thick side, but Rachel wolfs them down.

'A digital detox is such a good way to go,' she says as she wipes her finger around her plate and licks it. This fills Abbie's heart, showing as it does both her enjoyment of the food and that she doesn't worry about table manners with her.

Just like sisters.

'Does a day really count as a detox?' Abbie says, doing the same finger-licking thing.

'Does for me! I might even do a story on it, although it's kind of biting the hand that feeds me.' Rachel smiles, but as she reaches for her plate again, she sees the space where her favourite ring should be. 'Where can it be?' she says, holding up the empty finger.

'We could search for it now,' Abbie says. 'It's always good if you've got a problem to feel like you're doing something about it.'

'You're so full of wisdom.'

Abbie shimmers at this and entertains a brief fantasy of being Rachel's mantra-writer one day, before getting back to business. 'You're completely sure you left it on the counter?'

'A thousand per cent.'

'I've been through the bins and it hasn't been accidentally thrown away. And it definitely hasn't been knocked on the floor, because I've done an eye-level search for it. And I'm certain that Sam hasn't swallowed it, because he would have passed it by now and I know for a fact that he hasn't.'

Rachel makes a face. 'You'd do that for me?'

'So we're down to someone moving it.'

Rachel nods. 'I think we are.'

'You took it off yesterday morning, and you definitely left it there and you definitely didn't put it back on.'

Rachel nods and looks miserably at the white line on her finger. 'That's my system. All my jewellery off or all my jewellery on. I don't do it by halves.'

'Who was in the house yesterday?'

'You, of course.'

Abbie smiles. 'Apart from me.'

'Drew – but he was with me all the time. Alice the dog walker.'

Abbie nods. Rachel still doesn't know that she has dispensed with Alice, and now isn't the right time to tell her. 'But she doesn't come in here, does she? Sam hears her and boom, he's at the door.'

'And Wanda. She was the only other one.'

Abbie stays still and quiet for a moment, just to let that thought sink in with Rachel.

'You trust Wanda, though, don't you?'

'I mean, yes, I…' Rachel spreads her hands out in front of her. 'She's been coming here for two years, does a good enough job.'

'Apart from keeping her office nice.'

Rachel laughs. 'I mean she handles all the money, all the correspondence with partners, travel details, everything. If she's not trustworthy, then I'm doomed.'

'We could just take a look, couldn't we?'

'What?'

'In her office. Just take a look, in case…'

'But that's her private room.'

'It's in your house.'

Rachel thinks about this, then nods. 'But if – and I mean *if* – she has taken the ring, she'd take it home, surely?'

'As you say, she controls all your money. If she really wanted to steal from you, she could just do that, couldn't she? When did you last check your bank account?'

Rachel goes pink. 'I can't remember.'

'You just rely on Wanda's word?'

She nods.

'It might be worth taking a look, when you have time. If Wanda really wanted to steal, she'd be creaming cash off that way, not nicking rings. I'm not saying she is at all – just that if she *has* moved the ring, it wouldn't be because she wants it for herself.'

'I don't see why not. It's a lovely ring.'

'And I'm not saying that either. I'm just saying that she might've hidden it to upset you. She may even be planning to have it show up again, make you think you're going mad.'

'But why would she want to do that?'

Abbie takes a deep breath. 'I hate doing this.'

'What?'

She takes Rachel's hand. 'Do you know how she talks about you behind your back?'

Rachel shakes her head, horrified.

Abbie holds her body tightly, her shoulders up around her ears. It's not a bad impersonation of Wanda. '"She wants me to be her photograph friend again",' she says in an approximation of Wanda's wheedling voice. '"Saddo."' She rolls her eyes like Wanda might if she actually said things like this.

'What?' Rachel's mouth is wide open.

'She hates me just as much. She ignores me most of the time. I don't mind it. I mean, it's not really my job to be in close contact with her. But I don't like there being an atmosphere in the house. It's not good for you, or for Beansprout.'

Rachel is now looking suitably appalled. 'I had no idea.'

'Well you wouldn't. I hate to say it, but she's pretty devious.'

Rachel stands. 'Let's search her office.'

It takes half an hour of hunting, Rachel saying that she can't believe she's doing this, for her to find the ring.

She opens the drawer and starts lifting out the essential oils and hand creams that Wanda has helped herself to.

'I was wondering where these had got to,' she says. 'They're by MamaGlisser, a prospective partner we've been waiting forever to get back with a contract. "Calming products for new mothers".'

'They were sent for you to use?'

Rachel sighs and nods. 'I thought they hadn't arrived. I was going to chase them up. But even so…' She piles yet more MamaGlisser products on the desk. 'We're a little loose about who gets to keep the goodies. I should have been clearer about it to Wanda. I know she likes nice smells.'

'Even so,' Abbie says, echoing Rachel, 'she shouldn't be—'

She is cut off by Rachel's yelp as she finds the ring. It's part joy, but mostly outrage.

'The fucking ungrateful little cow!' she says.

'Wow,' Abbie says, all scandalised. 'What are you going to do?'

Rachel shakes her head and slides the ring back on her finger where it belongs. 'I don't know, Abbie.'

'You're not going to let her stay?'

'I can't, can I?' She bites her lip.

'I'll deal with her in the morning,' Abbie says. 'If it's too painful for you.'

'Would you? It's just I'm so bad at confrontation.'

'I can also stand in until you've got space and time to get someone else in,' she adds. 'I was a secretary for my dad before I did my childcare training, so I'm pretty good at admin. And I know exactly what you want. It'll be far easier for me to step in until Beansprout comes, and then you can think about what to do. You may even find that we can manage without anyone else. You never know.'

Rachel is looking at her with wide-open eyes.

'Is there no end to your brilliance, Abbie?'

Abbie lets her have one of her rarest gifts. A smile.

INSTAGRAM POST

rachelhoneyhill
Devon, England
paid partnership with **gossipyum** organic yoga gear
82,915 likes

Images
- Rachel in Warrior 2 pose, wearing Gossip Yum Día de Muertos yoga pant/hoodie combo
- Rachel in Tree pose, with Sam sitting at her feet
- Rachel in Cobbler pose.

Text
Nearly ready to pop!
Beansprout and I are well into the third trimester, but that doesn't mean we can't do our body work.
There are many yoga poses that are so good for us at this stage of our pregnancy: Cat Cow, Warrior 1 and 2, Bridge, Cobbler, Child, Tree, to name but a few, and I've incorporated these into five great new Racheletics sequences for third trimester.
Hop (or waddle!) on over to the RR YouTube channel to see my full Racheletics for pregnancy playlist.
#yoga #pregnancyyoga #thirdtrimester #Racheletics #yogagear #GossipYum

CHAPTER TWENTY-EIGHT

17 August

Rachel traces the initials on her signet ring. This bit of jewellery is the one thing she has left of her mother. While it was missing, she was unanchored.

She is so grateful to Abbie for helping her find it.

After a terrible night's sleep, she still can't get comfortable. Beansprout is now so big that lying on her back or sitting propped up on pillows puts pressure on her spine and makes the backs of her legs tingle. Her hands, too, are all pins and needles. She asked Sue the midwife at her thirty-four-week appointment, and she said that sciatica and carpal tunnel syndrome are very common in the third trimester. No one tells you about that. While she's truly appreciative of Abbie's care, she wishes Fran were with her, or at least someone who has actually been through pregnancy and childbirth. Just for the reassurance it would offer. But she worries that Fran might find it too upsetting to be with her, what with what happened with Noud. And then of course there's the issue of Beansprout's father…

The whole thing about letting Wanda go exhausted her last night. She can't believe that her assistant, her right-hand woman, betrayed her like that. But then because she finds it so hard to read people, she always defaults to a position of trust.

At least she can be absolutely sure that Abbie has her back. For example, because of all the stress, her thoughtful mother's helper has ordered another offline day of rest.

'The key thing,' she said as she tucked her in last night, 'is that we need to make sure you have enough energy to build Beansprout as strong as she can be. When we work from home, we need to make an extra effort to switch off. So you need one more digital-free day, where the only thing you think about is what I'm going to cook you for supper.'

Rachel, who, for years has spent every single day thinking about work, found herself nodding like the obedient child she never, ever was.

Trouble is, she can't face it.

She reaches under her bed, pulls out the iPad she smuggled upstairs and switches on the camera feed from the room she needs to stop thinking of as Wanda's. To make herself feel less guilty about doing this, she mutes the sound on the feed. There's Abbie, sitting at the desk, all businesslike, her hair pulled back in a scrunchie, her face the usual blank canvas it is to Rachel. She must have been up early, because she has already worked wonders in there. All the junk has been cleared out, the shelves reorganised, and the desktop is clear of everything except the computer, a mobile phone and a pad and pen.

Abbie sits concentrating on the screen in front of her, a slight frown on her face. Occasionally she bends over the pad and writes some notes. She must be playing music, because every now and then she gets up and dances like no one's watching, mouthing words, waving her hands in the air. Rachel finds all the activity comforting to watch, to see her whole life being put back in order…

*

'Hey.'

Confused for a second, Rachel thinks perhaps she is in that Japanese horror film about a well, and a ghost has just walked out of the screen to get her, her hair hanging creepily over her face. She tries to punch her assailant off, but quickly comes to and realises that it is Abbie, in the flesh. She is standing above her holding her fists and stopping her punches, her hair flying loose from the scrunchie, which is now on her wrist. As Rachel looks wildly around her, she sees, on her bedside table, a cup of the horrible chamomile tea Abbie insists on making her drink, sitting on top of a folder thick with papers.

'You're online, Rachel,' Abbie says.

Rachel pulls her hands free and grabs for the iPad, but Abbie, who has not just woken up, is quicker than her and gets hold of it first.

'I was just watching a movie. It was more comfortable on the iPad because I can lie on my side with a cushion between my knees…'

But Abbie holds the iPad up to Rachel's face to open it, and there in front of them both is the security camera footage of the empty office.

'What's this?' Abbie says.

Rachel tells her, her eyes shut, her mouth downturned, an ice rod down her spine. If Abbie had walked in on her masturbating to torture porn, she would have felt less ashamed.

Abbie flicks through the cameras, seeing the feed from each room, the gardens, front and back. The bathrooms.

'It's for security. I never watch them,' Rachel says. As if that makes a difference.

Abbie fiddles with the app. 'These?' she says, holding the screen up to Rachel. It's her own rooms. The bird sitting in its cage, the neatly folded nightdress on the pillow. 'Do you watch me when I'm in there?'

Rachel shakes her head wildly. 'No! I had those feeds switched off. You've just turned them back on.

'Easy, though, isn't it?'

'Honestly, it's for security. If a feed is live, it sends an alert when movement is detected in a room. I only look when that happens, just to keep us safe. I was just taking a quick peek to see if you were in Wanda's room—'

'*My* room.'

• 'Your room… I was just taking a quick look—'

'A look so quick that you fell asleep while you were taking it?'

Defeated, Rachel turns her back and, as far as she can, curls into a ball.

Abbie says nothing. Rachel hears the small accent chair by the window being dragged across the floor, then the springs squeaking as Abbie sits down.

'OK,' she says at last. 'You've made a mistake. But we're going to have to stop this spying.'

Rachel nods. 'I know.'

'You have no need to watch me.'

'No.'

'I only have your best interests at heart. That's what I'm here for.'

'I know.'

'And that's why I came to see you.'

The gravity of Abbie's tone makes Rachel haul herself to sitting and turn to face her. 'What is it?'

'I'm afraid…' Abbie takes a deep breath, as if she is just about to tell her that someone dear to her has died. 'I'm afraid Wanda hasn't been keeping you properly informed about how things are going money-wise.'

'What?'

Abbie puts the folder on the bed, pulls out a handful of pages and hands them to Rachel, who sees that they are her last three months' bank statements and a profit-and-loss statement.

'I pulled this off your accounting software,' Abbie says. 'I've got to check all the details, but it seems that in the last quarter, your income has dropped by eighty per cent.'

Rachel gasps. 'That much?'

Abbie passes her a dozen or so printed-out emails. 'Quite a few brands have been getting back saying they don't want to partner with you any more, as your numbers are going down and your demographic has diluted.'

Rachel scans the emails, her frown deepening. 'But we've been working so hard at growing new brands to work with…'

Abbie shakes her head gently. 'You've had a lot less success than I think Wanda has led you to believe. MamaGlisser turned you down, although she hasn't told you that, I suppose?'

Rachel shakes her head.

'And I'm afraid to say BabyMoon have cancelled.'

'What? But we'd sealed the deal.'

Abbie shows her another sheaf of paper. 'The contract. Still in Wanda's in-tray, I'm afraid.'

'No!' These partners were the backbone of Rachel's transition to her new identity. She throws back the duvet and starts levering herself out of the bed, but Abbie gently puts a hand on her shoulder and holds her back.

'Don't get upset,' she says. 'I'm going to see what I can do to save all this.'

Rachel wants to resist, wants to stand up and take charge, but Beansprout gives her a series of elbow punches and knee kicks, and she finds herself gasping and lying on her side, allowing Abbie to wedge a cushion behind her to prop her up.

'May I?' Abbie gestures to the spare side of the bed.

Rachel nods, and Abbie sits next to her, her own iPad in her hands. She pulls up a spreadsheet.

Rachel lifts her head to look at the grid of numbers. 'Wow.'

She has no idea about spreadsheets, financial management, administration. She is more of a creative soul. 'More free-spirited' is her frequently aired expression.

'Yeah. I like all this stuff,' Abbie says.

'So why are you working in childcare and not this? I mean, you could earn loads more with those skills.'

'You pay me well enough,' Abbie says. 'And anyway, looking after babies and children is the most important job in the world. But the great thing is, now Wanda's gone, I can use my knowledge of both areas to support you.'

'Will you have time, when Beansprout's here?'

'Believe me, Rachel' – Abbie puts the iPad down, clasps her hands together in front of her like an angel in prayer, and looks Rachel directly in the eye – 'the work Wanda spent all day fiddling around at will only take me two hours tops. When I set my mind to do something, I give it my all. I'll not be down there painting my nails and sucking sweeties.'

'I can't believe how she pulled the wool over my eyes.'

'People like that, they just take the mick. Always.' Abbie scrolls through the figures and Rachel's eyes blur over. 'There are these sums here, and here, big chunks that she's been paying into a mystery account.'

'I can't believe it!'

'I afraid to say it's true. I need to check out where it's actually gone, but don't worry, I'm sure I can get it back for you without too much bother. And you know she's been misusing the company card, too?'

'No!'

'I've checked the statement. Just yesterday she spent over three hundred pounds at the spa and restaurant at Bannon's.'

'She *what*?'

'I'll obviously go back further, make a list and make sure she pays everything back. But just in case she thinks she can carry on, I've removed her privileges and changed the pin.'

Rachel feels horribly hot. 'Thank you.'

'You're well shot of her. Anyway…' Abbie pulls her attention back to the figures. 'I've got a few suggestions to deal with your cash-flow difficulties, but they actually fall quite nicely into a strategic plan. You said you wanted to be more authentic with what you posted…'

'Did I?'

She puts the iPad down again. 'That's what you've been all about, ever since I first saw you on Instagram. Perhaps not in so many words, but I read between the lines, see? I know what you want.'

Rachel feels once again like she is a tiny child, this time being told how things are by an adult. She's not sure how much she likes it, but she doesn't really have a choice. She shouldn't have let Wanda mismanage things so badly.

Abbie once more brings her back to the iPad. 'The major part of your outgoings are in this column, see: fees and wages. We can sort it all out by cutting everything out of here – except me, of course!'

'But—'

'That means letting The Team go, but really, Rachel, are they actually helping you deliver the real you?'

Rachel frowns and rubs the scar in her hair. Perhaps Abbie's right. Perhaps—

'So the best way forward, in every way, is to be true to yourself. You tell us that so often, but how true are you really? Look. I've been watching Juno and Cyn and I can honestly do everything they do, just as well. It won't look so slick, but slick isn't what you want to put across, is it? It will look real and natural.'

'But real and natural are quite difficult to achieve…'

Abbie lets out one of her rare, strange laughs. 'Will you listen to yourself! Look at you. You're in bed, no make-up, your sweet bump… The light's coming through the window, all lovely. Stay there.'

She pulls the scrunchie off her wrist, takes the iPad and jumps off the bed. As she moves around Rachel, sizing up a shot, the look of concentration on her face is so like Juno's she could almost be her. 'Move those,' she says to Rachel, pointing to the balled-up tissues on her bedside table. 'We don't want to be quite *that* real. Not yet anyway.' She holds up the iPad and takes a photo.

'There,' she says, swinging onto the bed and showing Rachel the result. It's not bad. The side light works well on her cheekbones, and there's a story in her gaze. It lacks the refinement of light and form of Juno's work, but already Rachel is forming captions – *Every moment is an adventure*, perhaps.

'It's almost usable,' she says to Abbie. 'We'd need to use PerfectMe to smooth a few things out here.' She points to a little line at the side of her face. 'And we could burn out the bit where the light comes from the window, make it stronger, more contrasty.'

Abbie shakes her head. 'Or we could really go for it. Hashtag nofilter. No retouching, guaranteed. You could be starting a revolution. Showing your life how it actually is!'

Rachel rubs her fingers across her forehead. 'I don't know, I—'

'Think about it. We'll post this today and see how it goes. I've got to go and let the others know that we won't need them any more. The sooner we break off with them, the sooner we can start turning things around. And I'll let Alice go, too. I'm more than happy to walk Sam. Oh, and I'll take that.' She holds out her hand for Rachel's iPad.

'Why?'

'I'm going to take down all those nasty cameras, Rachel. It's not good for your mental health to be so paranoid. You've got security enough around the building. Honestly. You're safe.'

Rachel's brain feels like jelly. What's happening here? Her mind leaps from the art student who conned her way in and took off all her clothes, to the muddied freckled man standing in her living room, to her current online abusers and what sort of real-life threat they may pose. She can't join up the lines. 'But what about the trolls?'

'I'm dealing with that. Don't worry. You just rest, and after lunch you can get up and we'll do a bit of yoga. Then I've got to run a couple of errands, and you can get on with your posts for the day.'

Abbie breezes off, leaving, Rachel notices, a scent that reminds her of her Spiral DNA moisturiser, which she has been using since she featured it a couple of years back. This in turn reminds her that she seems, typically, to have lost the improved pink-jar edition they sent her for a further set of posts, and because of that she will lose the income. No packshot of that lovely big new jar, no dosh. It's her own fault.

Again her jelly brain, now geared to see her own failings – that she loses expensive cosmetics – leads her to think what a strange coincidence it is that Abbie's perfume smells so like that cream.

But then a brilliant solution to the missing special moisturiser issue comes to her. She inspects Abbie's discarded scrunchie and finds one of her hairs. She'll send it off and get a jar for Abbie as a present. Say sorry for watching her on the cameras. And expensive as it is, the cost of one jar is nothing compared to what she can earn by using it to replace the lost one in a story.

Secretly, it will also be a thank-you gift. From Rachel to Abbie for helping her see that she needs to be more authentic. Wasn't she just thinking that herself the other day, when she was in the bathroom?

Yes, Abbie is right.

This is the change she needs.

Greater authenticity will halt the emptiness that, despite the very real fact of Beansprout growing inside her, still gnaws away at her.

She wraps Abbie's hair safely in a tissue and turns and lies on her side. She wants to sleep again, so badly.

INSTAGRAM POST

3 years ago

rachelhoneyhill
Devon, England
paid partnership with **flow.and.glow1**
1, 817,543 likes

Image
- Hazy dawn. Rachel standing upright in a field in Flow & Glow workout gear. Beside her, Cal, looking noble, and Sam at her feet, looking loyal. They all gaze at the distant sea.

Text
Have you ever stood in nature and watched the sun rise? Set your alarm and get out here. We're waiting for you, me in my **@flow.and.glow1** layers, just perfect for peeling off as that glorious sun heats the beautiful earth!
Don't downgrade your dream to match your reality. Upgrade your vision to master your destiny.
#dawn #Samdog #nature #horse #inspiration #inspirational

CHAPTER TWENTY-NINE

Abbie trundles the eJeep down the lane. She stops at the postbox at the end to mail her signed fixed penalty notice. She's opted to just pay the fine and accept the points on Rachel's licence rather than attend a speed awareness course. She can't commit to being away from home for too long. Rachel needs her.

She's going to be out now for a good three hours, but it is, broadly speaking, a work trip. And Rachel has plenty to get on with, having missed three days of post-writing. Thanks to the one-week insurance lag, she has enough content lined up on the GridSmasher scheduler for now. But she needs to get next week's stories ready, or she'll fall behind, which would just add to her stress, particularly with the birth coming up. As Abbie knows only too well, babies can come early – although it's better if, like Rachel, you look after yourself properly during pregnancy and don't, for example, take antidepressants that are bad for your baby. It's also better if the dad isn't a no-good, do-nothing, violent drug-taking twat.

She is excited about seeing the film of herself talking about Abbie's Journey go live. Perhaps Rachel will even swap out one of this week's posts to get it up sooner. It'll go a long way to shutting up all the nasty troll chatter.

But that alone won't do it. Other factors need to be taken in hand.

She glances over at the basket she has put on the passenger seat. It's one that Rachel has featured many times – classic hand-woven willow, with a handle just the right size for hooking over your arm. With it beside her, Abbie feels like she is featuring in a soft-focus version of Rachel's online life.

Except that when it's photographed with Rachel, it's full of nice things, like lavender 'from the garden' – although Abbie knows that it was actually bought from Amazon for that particular shot.

Today, though, its contents are quite different.

Today, under a pullover she has brought along just in case she ends up staying out later than intended and the evening turns a bit chilly, Abbie has hidden a roll of duct tape, a pair of scissors, a 5kg kettlebell, the hair straighteners she no longer uses, an unused boning knife sent to Rachel as a gift from a prospective partner who hadn't done their homework, and a bottle of spirits of salts – or hydrochloric acid, which, because it is a more scientific name, is how Abbie likes to think of it. On top of the pullover she has laid a pair of silvery @seen. running gloves she found when sorting out Rachel's winter wardrobe storage.

While she was gathering the evidence of Wanda's mismanagement of Rachel's affairs, one thing she didn't tell Rachel, because she didn't want to further upset her, was that after the blocking of Scotty2002, that nasty Charlotte Williams has resurrected herself as Steve2002. The lack of imagination disgusts Abbie almost as much as the evil rubbish 'Steve' spouts about Rachel. 'He' has also taken to bad-mouthing Abbie in a horribly personal way, commenting on her tattoos and scars and insinuating all sorts of sexual stuff between her and Rachel. That last part particularly gets her goat. Even thinking about it right now spikes her FitSo heart rate number.

She eyes herself in the rear-view mirror. 'Why can't everyone just be lovely to each other in this world?' she belts through the open windows, outdoing Lady Gaga on the in-car entertainment system. As she overtakes a cyclist, he wobbles, nearly falling off his bike.

Abbie blocked Steve2002, logged the posts on the comments archive and has been firefighting the outbursts the posts ignited ever since. 'He' is clearly a catalyst for all sorts of nastiness, and there'll be no stopping him unless something is done.

Which is why she's driving to Exeter.

Otherwise, things are going brilliantly. She is particularly proud that she is helping Rachel get rid of all the fake stuff around her online persona. No one will ever again be disappointed in her, because she will show the world what she actually is.

'What *we* actually are!' she sings, glowing with everything that 'we' embodies.

As she crawls up the A38 – it's clogged with summer traffic, so she has to slow right down – she reflects on how amazing it is that she is in this position. Her, little Abbie James, née Speakman, living with Rachel Rodrigues!

She first discovered Rachel nearly ten years ago, just when she was kicking off her SobeRachel healthy living and exercise journey. Sixteen at the time, skinny and undeveloped, with cropped bleached hair, Abbie had just been handed back into care by her last-ever lot of foster parents. Like all the rest before them, they couldn't cope with her. Thinking back to everything she did, she can hardly blame them.

The children's home she was living in at the time had ferried a vanload of teenagers to Calstock for a weekend festival for looked-after children arranged by some do-gooder charity. It was totally lame – a couple of local posh-kid bands doing their whiny indie shit, and a really, really brain-numbing play by what looked like a bunch of drama students about teenage refugees or some such dross. There were also hippy crap workshops – drumming, crafts, cookery and fitness.

Abbie thought about bunking off with some of the others. But as they were walking past the main marquee, a lady on a little stage inside smiled and waved at them.

'Hi, guys.' The lady beckoned them in to join the ten or so kids she already had in front of her. 'We're just about to start. Come and join us.'

Abbie's companions sniggered and swore and sloped off.

But Abbie stayed, transfixed. That lady was the most beautiful person she had ever seen, and she was smiling at *her*. It was a golden moment in a life otherwise made up of base metal.

'Grab a mat from the pile!' the lady said.

Abbie was, in fact, glad of an excuse not to go with the others. Newly arrived at the children's home, she had been doing her usual marking of her territory by being hostile and borderline scary to everyone else. It was important, she believed, to let other people know that you wouldn't take any shit.

But being like that is exhausting, and doing the lady's class – whatever it was – would give her a break from her scary alter ego.

Not so much of a break, however, as to stop her giving a bit of attitude to the other kids in the tent as she picked up a mat and strode across the grass to the spot the lady was pointing out to her, down at the front.

That workout was life-changing for Abbie. The teacher lady was, of course, Rachel, in her SobeRachel incarnation. She gave out such a feeling of calm, and moved so beautifully, like a ballet dancer.

Even though Abbie had no idea who Rachel was back then, she could feel the connection, the fact that they had something that linked them. Right up at the front like that, she saw how their eyes were that same rare green. It was hands down the most important moment of her life.

At the end of the workout, Rachel had them all lying on their backs in what Abbie now knows is Corpse pose, then they all sat up and did namaste. This made a couple of the other kids giggle until Abbie shot dagger stares at them. At this point, the stage crew, who had been waiting at the edge of the marquee, moved in and started setting up for the next band, an unwashed load of heavy-metal village gits.

'Thanks, guys. Can you all roll your mats, please, and leave them in a pile over there?' the teacher said.

Abbie pulled out her phone. 'Miss!' she shouted. A few of the girls behind her sniggered.

'Me?' The teacher pointed at herself, smiling.

'Can I have a photo, please, Miss?'

'Of course.' She stuck her rolled mat under her arm and smiled.

'What's your name, Miss?' Abbie asked.

'Rachel. Rachel Rodrigues.'

'Anything to do with Janine Rodrigues?' Abbie asked, remembering the family story about the TV star and her blow-jobs.

Rachel smiled. 'She was my mum, in fact.'

Abbie's mouth fell open. She wanted to tell her about her da, and how he'd 'ad Janine Rodrigues, but before she could find a way of introducing it, a lady in a posh frock swept Rachel off to a building with a sign on the door saying FESTIVAL STAFF ONLY.

Abbie still has that photo on her phone. It's a memory that will never, ever leave her.

The episode could have changed her there and then, could have stopped her going through the next five years of shit. But unfortunately, life isn't like that. Those five years happened: homelessness, drink and drugs, the prison spell...

It wasn't until eight years later – two years ago – when she was in hospital on bed rest, that she finally came across Rachel again.

Vicki, the dim girl in the bed next to her, also with pre-eclampsia, was an Instagram addict. Abbie had never been all that bothered with it before then – all those glossy pictures never really seemed to have much to do with her own life.

'She's so peng,' Vicki said, holding up her tablet to show Abbie a photograph of a woman standing in a field in workout gear with a dog and a horse. 'So real.'

Abbie instantly recognised the woman. 'What's her name?'

Vicki ran her acrylic nails over the screen. 'Rachel Rodrigues, but we call her RR.'

'We?'

'Her followers.'

When Vicki was next asleep, curled up around her bump, Abbie dragged her drip stand across to her bay. Slipping the tablet away, she returned to her own bed and disappeared down a wormhole of RR research. Looking at her date of birth, she did the calculations and realised that, given Da's story, there was a strong possibility they could be sisters. Of *course,* then*,* they had a connection that time in Calstock! Abbie signed up to Instagram, started following Rachel, and over time became more and more convinced.

But again, life got in the way. Following Rachel's lead and giving up her meds was the final straw, really. Everything fell apart after that. One day she got so angry that she nearly threw the new baby across the room. Instead, she took what, in her confused state, she saw as the better path and ran out of her tiny flat, leaving all three children home alone while she got off her face. She returned two days later to find that a neighbour had rung the police, who were at her flat, in the process of taking Zayn, Harry and baby Taylor away.

It wasn't the first time something like this had happened, but it was the last, and it was the end of life as she knew it.

Only RR kept her going after that. Plus the thought that one day she would be able to meet her and tell her the truth about their connection.

All she needed was the opportunity.

And now here she is, in Rachel's car, turning off the M5 northbound to head towards the St Loyes area of Exeter to help

Rachel put her own life back together so that the happy ending Abbie deserves – her sister, her three children, her new niece, all in one big house in Devon – can happen.

Briefly – because she is driving – she closes her eyes to picture that perfect family that one day will be hers. All of them bound up together in so many ways.

'Whatever it takes, Abbie. Whatever it takes,' she says, remembering one of Da's fine sayings, her eyes once more on the road.

She checks the sat nav. Twenty minutes and she'll be outside Charlotte Williams' crappy little house, ready to get her to see sense and desist.

'When life gives you shit, fling it back.' That's another one of Da's.

INSTAGRAM POST

rachelhoneyhill
Devon, England
8,230 likes

Image
- Rachel, sidelit by the morning sun filtering through her window, curled on her bed with her hands on her bump, looking into the distance like she's looking at her future with the baby.

Text
Love yourself, take time and truly live every moment.
#dreamy #baby #pregnant #pregnancy

CHAPTER THIRTY

'We're nearly, nearly there!' Fran sings along with Luuk, Lotte and Mila, all neatly strapped into the hire-car company's child seats. They're not actually nearly, nearly there at all. They've just hit the end of the M5 and have another hour at least to go, more even with the summer tourist traffic.

But in terms of their long journey, started at dawn that morning when Wim dropped them off at Schiphol, they are pretty close, and singing the 'nearly there' song at this point in the drive down from Bristol airport is a family ritual, started when Luuk was Mila's age.

After the call with Rachel four days ago, Fran knew she had to come. Rachel had still been in bed in the middle of the morning, and she looked so depleted, like she had shrunk. She has always maintained that lie-ins are for losers, and was less than sympathetic when Fran, in her various pregnancies, wouldn't surface till late.

Perhaps this is all just a sign that Rachel is a pregnant human being, and it's all normal. But Fran knows she's been having a few number and troll woes, so perhaps she's getting down again. Mostly, though, she is worried that Rachel hid a miscarriage and meds from her and Wim. If there's one thing Fran has always demanded from Rachel, it's that she is straight with her. The viability of their lives is built on mutual trust. Take that away and what do they have, really?

And then there is Abbie. The call with her set Fran's alarm bells off. Nothing obvious; just her proprietorial air, the feeling that she was subjecting Fran to a game of one-upmanship. And that damn bird sitting on her head. In retrospect, it just felt a little arrogant. A little weird.

Anyway, Fran knew she wouldn't rest until she found out for herself what was going on. Wim is up to his ears in work – he's in the last few days of post-production on a TV series – so she had to bring the children with her, although that presents more of an opportunity than a hindrance. For one, they always cheer Rachel up. But they also might be handy for a little test she has in mind for Abbie.

As she pulls out to overtake a frustratingly slow caravan hogging the middle lane, her eyes are drawn to a distinctive turquoise eJeep bombing down the other side of the motorway. She stops singing – much to the annoyance of the children – and tells Siri to call Rachel. Surprise visits are all very well, but it would be a total bore if they were to arrive at an empty house.

Sue the midwife answers Rachel's phone, and for a second, Fran is terrified that something's gone horribly wrong.

'Oh no, Fran love.' Sue laughs. 'Rachel's just doing me a pee sample for her thirty-six-week check. Everything's lovely here, baby and mum doing well. She's a little tired, but that's to be expected at this stage.'

'Tell me about it,' Fran says.

'And she completely forgot I was coming! But again, that's not unusual either.'

'Is Abbie there?'

Fran wonders if she's right in thinking that Sue's voice loses a little of its usual warmth. 'No, dear. She's gone out, apparently.'

'Where's she taking the car, then?'

Fran settles down on the sofa with Rachel, who she found all alone, sitting at the dining table working on her posts. She's keeping an eye through the wide-open bifold doors on Luuk and Lotte, who are running round the garden with a football. Little Mila is, at last, sleeping on the other sofa, her arms flung wide. Oh, to have the trust in the world of that little girl. Fran's feeling something quite the reverse at the moment. She can smell something wrong in this house.

Rachel shrugs. 'She said she had a few errands.'

'She was nearly at Exeter!'

'I know.' Rachel shows Fran the FitSo tracker app on her phone. Abbie's dot shows her to be somewhere on the outskirts, on the far side of the city.

'What's she doing there?'

'No idea. But it'll be something useful. She's been very busy since she took on Wanda's work.'

'Wait – what? Where's Wanda?'

Fran listens with growing horror as Rachel tells her about the stolen ring, the appalling state of her finances, the lost clients.

'But she seemed so competent!'

'Perhaps anyone would after that dim Charley.'

'Oh my God, yes. She was a nightmare.'

'Yeah, well, perhaps I did go a bit far with her.'

Fran takes her hands. 'It's not your fault. You had an episode, that's all. And now Wanda's let you down, too.'

'I should have guessed. Did you see the state of her room?' Rachel says.

Fran glances over at the dining table, strewn with mugs, paper, banana skins and enough Apple products and associated cables and accessories to stock a small shop. 'Untidy desk doesn't always mean untidy mind.'

Rachel follows her gaze and smiles. 'Abbie's very efficient, though. She's got it all in hand.' She looks down at her bump and heaves a deep sigh.

Fran takes her hands. 'What is it?'

Rachel takes her time to reply. But in the end, she comes out with it. 'I just don't feel myself any more.'

Fran looks her in the eyes. 'This is how we get when we are pregnant. You will still be Rachel, but soon you will be someone else, too. You'll be your baby's mother. It's like being possessed. It takes time to adjust, like a branch grafted onto a tree. But you will come out of this a happier, more fulfilled and complete person. Look at all this lot. Believe me, Rach, I wouldn't go back to how I was before, not for anything or anyone.'

'But I don't think I'm up to it,' Rachel says.

'Course you are. You're RR, remember. You're a survivor.'

'But that's all bullshit.' Rachel waves a hand over at the desk with all her work laid out on it. 'I'm trying to put together next week's posts, and I'm looking at it all and it's all just fake and nothingness. It's not me, Fran.' She thumps her chest. 'Not really me.'

'Where's this come from?'

'I don't know who me is. I've no right to—' Her words are swallowed by a great choking sob.

Fran holds her friend, who by now is crying uncontrollably, to her chest. She thinks about broaching the whole antidepressant and miscarriage thing, but she still doesn't want Rachel to know she's been speaking to Abbie.

'Why are you thinking like this? Is it something to do with Abbie?' she asks her.

Rachel pulls away and looks at her, shocked. 'I don't know what I'd do without Abbie!'

Fran holds up her hands. 'It's just… I don't see you for a few weeks and then you're like this, and the only thing that's changed, apart from dear Beansprout growing, is that Abbie has moved in with you.'

'It's not her!'

'She's supposed to make things easier for you, make you happier.'

'It's me. I'm just all…' Rachel slaps herself on the head.

'Why's Rachel sad?'

Fran looks up. It's Luuk, who is standing hand in hand with Lotte right in front of them, four saucer eyes.

'Is her baby poorly like Noud?' Lotte says.

Rachel sits up and smiles bravely. 'No, no. Baby is happy. Here.' She takes Lotte's tiny three-year-old hand and puts it on her belly. 'Feel her kick?'

Lotte squirms and giggles.

'Can we give Rachel the presents?' Luuk says.

'Sure.' Fran goes over to the big shopper she brought in from the car and pulls out two parcels.

'Can we open them for you?' Lotte asks Rachel.

Rachel laughs. 'Of course!'

They rip off the wrapping paper to reveal the baby video monitor and sweet, expensive hand-knitted jumper and hat set that Fran has bought for Beansprout.

'Little ducks!' Rachel says, running her fingers over the soft wool of the baby clothes. Her eyes fill with tears. 'So tiny!'

'Not very imaginative, but what do you get the woman who has everything?' Fran says, pointing to the baby monitor.

'This is exactly what I need,' Rachel says.

Fran gets up to make the children a snack. She's used to finding her way around Rachel's kitchen, so when she opens the fridge, she is shocked to find that instead of the usual explosion of leafy greens, random leftovers, sourdough starter and home-made nut milks and yoghurts, all she sees is ranged Tupperware boxes with stuck-on labels bearing dates and descriptions, written in a childlike looping hand. It looks like the kind of fridge that keeps medical samples rather than wholesome fresh food.

'That's Abbie's doing,' Rachel says, standing behind her with Lotte on her hip. 'Isn't she a marvel?'

INSTAGRAM POST

6 years ago

rachelhoneyhill
Devon, England
25,804 likes

Image
- Selfie of Rachel, barefaced, no make-up, her green eyes looking directly at the viewer.

Text
Welcome, welcome, lovely people to **@rachelhoneyhill**, my new profile, which I'm growing from @soberachel, because Rachel is now sober: that's a given!

This is my first post on this account, and I'm so excited to be here! Thank you for following. I am so grateful for your love.

If you are looking for support for your own sober journey, please head on over to my old profile, where I list all the beautiful people who have helped me on my path. It's fantastic over here on the sober side and we'd love you to join us!

I'm now all about my life here in Honeyhill Barn, being in nature, with my animals and the trees. It's a simpler way of living, focusing on the really important things.

Visit my RR YouTube channel for a growing collection of Racheletics workouts and fantastic vegan recipe walk-throughs. Link in bio.

I'm also really excited to be showing you some of the products that I love and that will help me – and you! – move towards a more grounded life.

And, if you are feeling lost like I once was, remember: You *can* reinvent yourself. You *can* start all over again.

You are your own person.

We can do this!

#hello #authentic #sober #sobriety #Racheletics #nature #vegan #life

CHAPTER THIRTY-ONE

The look on Charlotte Williams' scarred face when Abbie turns up on the doorstep of the pebble-dashed semi where she lives with her mother and gran is one to be treasured forever. Seeing her in the flesh reminds Abbie why she thought she knew her. Her hair may be pink now, but it was mousy brown three years ago when she briefly featured in Rachel's posts as her friend – for which read employee – @charleywarley.

@charleywarley of course also recognises Abbie from Rachel's posts. Clearly aware that this is not a nice social visit, she tries to slam the flimsy front door. Thanking her stars that she put DMs on this morning, Abbie quickly gets her foot in the way. She leans her full weight on the door, and it falls open.

In a blink, she has Williams pinned up against the coats hanging in the hallway, her silvery gloved left hand up against her throat, her right arm hooked under the basket, as if one side of her body is in *The Sopranos*, the other 'Little Red Riding Hood'.

Williams, who is only about five feet tall and puny to say the very least, squirms under Abbie's gym-honed strength. 'My mum's in.'

Abbie has seen the photographs of Williams' mum on Facebook. She is even smaller and slighter than her daughter. Channelling the scary alter ego that helped her claim high status in the institutional homes of her childhood, Abbie places her mouth too close to Williams' ear. 'Ooh. Frightened,' she says. 'Mum!' she calls out.

No one comes.

'Gran!' Abbie calls again.

No one.

Abbie grabs Charlotte's arm and, her hand over her mouth, takes her on a tour round the house. After having got used to living in style at Rachel's, the sad dinginess of each of the boxy rooms of this post-war semi makes Abbie feel ill. It reminds her all too vividly of the pinched foster homes she was dragged through by the system.

'Where are they?' she says, after they have checked the five rooms and one bathroom. She removes her hand so that Williams can answer.

'Help!' Williams calls out.

Abbie slaps her hand hard back over her mouth. 'Where are they?' she says again, this time only slightly releasing the pressure over her lips.

'On a cruise.'

'Ha.' Abbie drags her back to the kitchen/diner and throws her onto a wooden chair. Pinning her down with one knee, she puts the basket on the ground and pulls out the duct tape and scissors. After first putting a piece right across Williams' mouth to stop her bloody yelling, she winds the tape about thirty times around her arms and torso, fastening her to the back of the chair. She then does a similar thing to her bottom half, taping her shins to the chair legs.

'I'm here to teach you a lesson.' She returns the duct tape to the basket and pulls out the boning knife, the kettlebell, the spirits of salts and the hair straighteners, which she plugs in. 'The lesson being that you can't hide behind your cowardly words.'

Williams tries to say something, but she can't.

Abbie picks up the knife and holds it so the very sharp point is at Williams' throat.

'Where's your phone?'

Williams mumbles something under the duct tape.

Abbie rips off the tape, making her yell as her lips lose some skin. 'If you shout for help, I swear I'll cut you.'

'On the settee,' Williams says. 'By the telly.'

With a threatening point of the knife, Abbie backs out of the kitchen and into the front room to get her phone. She takes it back to Williams and holds it up to her face to unlock it.

'How do you organise it?' she says.

'I don't know what you mean?' Williams' voice comes out as a tiny whiny squeak. Her badly dyed pink hair is the only bit of colour about her. The rest of her is so grey, so beige, that she might as well not exist.

Abbie sighs and holds the knife up once again at Williams' throat. 'You do know what I mean. And you'd be best off if you didn't make me lose my rag with you. You're organising massive pile-ons on Rachel's Instagram. How?'

'WhatsApp,' Williams says in a whisper.

'Thank you.' Abbie slaps another piece of tape across her mouth and scrolls to her WhatsApp. Right at the very top, there's a group called *RR is a bitch*. Just a brief read of it shows her how it works. Williams alerts her group of nasty trolls when she is going to kick everything off, and they just join in. There's all sorts of vile stuff on there, about Rachel, and about Abbie. There are claims of photos that show them having sex. Someone says that Abbie is an ex-con; another says she's heard that she has three children but they've been taken away from her because she was violent towards them. This makes Abbie want to punch a hole in the wall. Another says that she heard she was a drug dealer and was injecting pregnant Rachel with heroin. Someone else says this is true, but they need to have proof, or they will be accused of libel.

Damn right too, Abbie thinks, her hands shaking with rage at all the gossip and lies. She fires off a request to Posh June from Williams' WhatsApp, explaining that it is coming from her and marking it as urgent. June always has an illegal phone on her, so she'll be able to act quickly. All it will take is a message to one of her secret associates.

Checking that the phone's sound is on, and that WhatsApp messages will make it buzz, Abbie puts it down on the breakfast bar, picks up her knife again and once more rips the duct tape from Williams' already bleeding lips.

'Why did you do it?' she asks, the sharp point of the knife back up against the thin grey skin of Williams' throat.

'I'm sorry,' Williams says.

'Sure you are. Why did you do it?'

The skinned lips bunch up, making her mouth look like a skinny cat's arse. 'I hate Rachel,' she says.

Abbie grabs her chin firmly between her thumb and forefinger and lets the knife point just break the skin below where if Williams were a boy her Adam's apple would be. 'Why?'

Williams swallows. There are tears in her eyes. 'She was a bitch to me when I worked for her, then she went psycho.'

'This is Rachel Rodrigues you're talking about?'

'Yes! I thought she was going to kill me.'

'Liar!'

'It's true!' Williams' voice is a tiny squeak. 'I made one mistake and she lost it and dug great chunks out of my cheeks. See my scars? See?'

'You're making it up. You're such a coward, Williams, hiding here like a slug, putting out all those disgusting things about Rachel and about me. Thinking you can get away with it. You just couldn't believe she didn't want you to work for her any more, could you?'

Williams shakes her head wildly.

'Have you looked in the mirror?' Abbie says. 'Rachel probably only employed you because she felt sorry for you. Look at you. You can't even wash properly. You stink.'

Williams snatches a body-shuddering sob.

'You're just a stupid nobody, still lives with her mum, no life of her own, aren't you?'

Abbie takes the knife and slashes open the sleeve of Williams' hoodie, all the way from wrist to shoulder, exposing her musty skin. She puts the knife down on the breakfast bar and picks up the hair straighteners. The red light has turned to green, which means they are now nice and hot. In one deft movement, she presses them firmly around Williams' puny upper arm.

Williams screams. Still holding the straighteners tight, Abbie slaps her free hand over her mouth to shut her up. The smell of burning tickles her nostrils. As she lifts the straighteners, they bring with them a small piece of skin, which for a moment reminds Abbie of the bacon she is no longer supposed to eat.

Williams whimpers.

'Now *that's* real,' Abbie says. 'That's not hiding and tapping out anonymous words on a phone. I'm just doing it to teach you the difference.' Again she clamps the hair straighteners over Williams' arm.

Behind her hand, Williams yelps again.

'Ew.' Abbie wipes the spittle from her palm and releases the straighteners. 'Do you get my drift, *charleywarley?*'

Williams nods.

'Good. Because the other part of the lesson is that words have consequences. Rachel is a real person, and so am I, and there's little Beansprout to take into consideration, too. We are innocent people just trying to go about our lives, and you get right in the way, upsetting Rachel so much that she has to spend most of her days in bed. Did you know that?'

Williams shakes her head.

Abbie puts down the hair straighteners and tapes Williams' mouth again. She picks up the scissors.

Williams squeals.

Driving her hand across the nasty troll's scalp, Abbie hacks away at her hair. The result is an uneven mess of bald patches, mousy bristles and pink tufts.

'It might grow back nicer, you never know,' she says. 'Again. Real-world consequencces. Perhaps when it does, you'll be a better person.'

At this point, just because it feels right, she deals a sharp, hard Doc Marten kick to Williams' shin.

Williams is now snivelling and crying, the simp.

Abbie picks up the spirits of salts and squeezes out a tiny drop onto the back of Williams' immobilised hand, where it sizzles and makes a nasty red patch that quickly turns dark purple, with a little blister erupting in the middle. Again bacon comes to Abbie's mind. Which is appropriate, because Williams squeals like a little tied-up pig.

Before Abbie gets any further with the spirits of salts, the phone buzzes.

'Saved by the bell.' She picks up the phone and walks round behind Williams, staying close enough that her terrified subject can still feel her presence. Posh June has come up with the goods, and an accompanying message:

Don't view. It'll make ur eyes bleed.

Abbie does take a look, of course, just to check. The video June has got one of her associates to forward to Williams' phone is a horrifying example of a despicable form of pornography. Abbie turns down the sound so she doesn't have to hear and holds the phone up in front of Williams, so close that she can't help but see what's on the screen. She presses herself against the back of Williams' plucked-chicken head so that she can't move. With the thumb of her free hand, she pulls up one of her eyelids, so that it is impossible for her to close her eye. Then, her own eyes averted, she presses play.

'Look at it, Charley. Look. This is the logical conclusion of what you are doing. Anonymous hate and violence, abusing others to satisfy yourself. That man is what you are. What he is doing is what you are doing to me and Rachel.'

Williams is really fighting against Abbie's hold, trying to move her head so she doesn't have to watch, but her puny little body can't beat Abbie's new gym-bunny, kettlebell-swinging strength.

By the time the horrible video plays out, Williams has given up struggling, and is slumped in appalled resignation.

'So I'm going to do this now,' Abbie says. She keeps the screen in Williams' eyeline as she forwards the video to the *RR is a bitch* group. For good measure, she finds MUM and GRAN on the contacts and, with Williams squirming under her duct tape, sends it to them as well. She then deletes the conversation between herself, Posh June and PJ's associate.

'That's probably going to make everyone think twice about trusting you in future, *charleywarley*. Sorry about that. Wonder what the police would think about it too, if they were to find out that you had that sort of stuff on your phone, and had distributed it to others? If I hear you've said a single word about this visit to anyone, or if you dare go anywhere near Rachel, me or her channels with your nasty poison, I'm going to have to tell them about this phone. OK?' She rips the tape from Williams' mouth one more time. 'OK?'

Williams nods and mumbles through bleeding lips, 'OK.'

'Good. Well, I think that's probably enough.' Abbie looks over the equipment she laid out on the breakfast bar. She's used everything she brought with her, except for the kettlebell. It would be a pity to have lugged that heavy fellow all the way here and not put him to use.

So she picks him up, and without warning slams him onto the fingers of Abbie's right hand.

'To stop you texting until this lesson has fully soaked in.'

She puts everything into the basket, makes sure she has left nothing on the floor, then leaves the room. Williams is still taped to the kitchen chair, but Abbie's certain the little snake will wriggle herself free at some point.

She stuffs the phone underneath the cushions of the settee in Williams' front room, wedged right down between the base and the back, so it looks like it has been hidden. Just in case she needs to call the police about its contents.

It's been years since Abbie's done anything like this, but it's amazing how the skills stay with you. As she drives away in Rachel's eJeep, she can't hide the exhilaration. She's going to have to do a big workout when she gets back, to clear out her system, and then she'll cook supper for Rachel. Then perhaps, while it's in the oven, they can do a hot tub together.

Already the thought of that, and how she has cleared away one of the obstacles to Rachel's happiness, makes her feel lighter, clearer and cleaner.

INSTAGRAM POST

rachelhoneyhill
Devon, England
6,304 likes

Image
- Luuk, Lotte and Mila, running in a circle on the Honeyhill lawn, chasing bubbles in the sunshine.

Text
This just happened right now. Surprise visitors. Aren't they sweet?
#FriendFran's three beautiful children. They are going to be such fabulous friends for my little Beansprout.
Can't wait!
#friends #children #Beansprout #brother #sisters

CHAPTER THIRTY-TWO

When Rachel intercepts Abbie as she comes in through the front door, she gets a little stir of excitement, like someone in love might feel when their partner returns from work.

'Come in here,' she whispers, dragging her into the room formerly known as Wanda's and shutting the door.

'What is it?' Abbie looks over at the computer with a frown. 'Have I done something wrong?'

'No!' Rachel laughs. 'I just wanted to give you a heads-up that Fran's here with the children.'

'Oh.'

'I don't want you to get the wrong end of the stick, but she's just got a few concerns, so she's come to make sure that everything's OK here with me.'

Abbie looks puzzled. 'What concerns? Why?'

Rachel shrugs. 'She says I'm looking a bit peaky, and she wants to check that you're on it.'

'I hope you told her where to go.'

'What?' Rachel can't work out if Abbie is serious or not.

'Sorry. It's just I'm trying my best here, and we're doing really well. Aren't we?'

'Of course! So we just show her how we are. How everything's going great.'

'How I'm helping you with the work and everything. Taking the pressure off.'

'Exactly. So if we can just be on our best behaviour…'

'I'm always on my best behaviour.'

Rachel smiles. 'I'm sorry if you're offended.'

Abbie holds up her free hand. 'Not at all. I just think it's a bit weird, when just a couple of days ago she asked me to keep an eye on you.'

'She what?'

'She's very controlling, isn't she?'

Again, is Abbie joking? She's smiling, but is there something cold about it? 'It's so complicated. I can't even…' Rachel sighs. 'Look. I just wanted to warn you. She might leave the children with you for, say, half an hour or so.'

'That's not my job.'

Rachel nods quickly. 'But could you just do it? Just this once? Show her how good you are with them?'

'She's using her children to *spy* on me?'

Rachel winces. 'No!' She doesn't want to tell Abbie that they've rigged up the baby video monitor Fran brought with her, but she has little choice.

'More camera spying?' Abbie says. 'Really?'

'It's not my idea.'

'So that makes it better?'

Rachel takes her hand. 'Please, just play along. We just want Fran to go away happy, yeah? Then we can get on with our lives.'

Abbie smiles again, but this time her eyes are deep and mossy. 'All right then.'

An inexplicable little shiver goes down Rachel's back. To fight it, she points to the basket Abbie has in the crook of her free arm. 'What you got there?'

'Just stuff for my journey. Snacks and things, gloves, jumper. In case I got stuck out longer than planned.'

'Where'd you go?'

'Like I said, just a couple of errands.' Abbie smiles. 'All done now.'

Rachel nods. 'Good. It's good to get things done.'

'It's a pity, though, that she doesn't trust you enough to believe that you trust me.'

'What?'

The door to the office opens and Fran pokes her head into the room. 'Hey, Abbie!' she says. 'I'm so glad you're back. Could you bear to give the kids tea while Rachel and I run into town? There's a few expat treats I need to pick up to take back with me.'

Abbie glances at Rachel, who nods.

'Sure,' she says. 'No problem.'

Fran and Rachel drive the hire car up the lane, then pull over in the passing place. The monitor Fran bought is top-of-the-range, so they can still get a signal.

'I don't feel comfortable about watching her like this,' says Rachel. Conspiring like this with Fran feels far worse than just glancing at Abbie on the pre-existing security system.

Of course, Abbie is the perfect Mary Poppins. She prepares the tea Fran has provided according to her detailed instructions. She makes sure that Luuk has the gluten-free bread, and that Mila's food is cut up for her. She sings 'The Wheels on the Bus' with them and asks them to sing her a Dutch nursery rhyme. They teach her 'In de Maneschijn', and find her hammed-up attempts at pronunciation hilarious.

After the meal, she wipes their faces and helps them down, and they all cuddle up on the sofa for a couple of stories. Then she sets them to work with pens and paper, telling them to draw their family while she washes up and wipes down the table.

'Well, that's almost nauseatingly perfect,' Fran says. 'Almost too perfect. Hey!'

The camera is on top of the fridge, half hidden in the leaves of a cascading spider plant. As Abbie passes it, she stops and, after appearing to smile directly up into the lens, she reaches up as if to touch it.

Fran gasps and looks at Rachel. 'Does she know we're watching her, Rach?'

'No!' Rachel says. 'She hates dead bits on house plants, always pulls them off.'

Sure enough, Abbie brings her hand back down with a fistful of brown leaves. She puts them on the kitchen surface and heads off to the dining table to praise the children for their efforts.

'Can we go to the pub?' Fran says. 'I need a gin.'

As Fran puts the car into drive, Rachel spots a tiny wren disappearing into a blackthorn bush, a dead worm dangling from its beak. The hot flush of this new deception she has just played out on her best friend threads across her skin.

When they get back, Abbie has the children bathed and in their pyjamas. They're all on the sofa like a family with a big sister, watching a cartoon about an elephant and a fox.

'What're you watching?' Rachel says as she sits down and puts her arm around little Mila.

'*Crazy Pig*,' Luuk says.

'I don't know that one.' Fran sits at the other end of the sofa to cuddle Lotte.

'It was on CBeebies about four years ago. Every morning at six,' Abbie says.

Fran turns to her and speaks across Lotte and Luuk's heads. 'You were watching children's TV at six a.m. when you were in your early twenties?'

Rachel watches Abbie turn her unreadable face towards her. 'I had to get up early for work. Watched it with my toast and tea.'

'Not with the children you were looking after?' Fran asks.

'I was looking after a lady with a tiny baby at the time,' Abbie replies.

As Abbie turns back to watch the TV with the children, Fran throws Rachel a significant look and mouths, 'She's lying.'

Rachel has no idea what Fran can possibly mean. 'Did you have fun with Abbie, guys?' she asks the children.

'Yes!' all three shout.

Lotte turns her big brown saucer eyes up to Rachel. 'Can we stay here forever?'

'We love Abbie,' Luuk says.

'I don't know what Papa would say if he didn't get you back,' Rachel says.

'You can come back to meet Beansprout as soon as she's born,' Fran says.

The children cheer.

'Is Beansprout going to be my sister?' Lotte asks.

'No, silly,' Abbie says. 'Beansprout is Rachel's baby. She would only be your sister if she was your mum's baby, like Mila is.'

Rachel checks Fran, but as far as she can make out, her face appears to give nothing away.

'But she'll be a very, very special baby for you,' Fran says, her voice a little choked.

'Almost like a sister,' Rachel adds.

Abbie's face, when she looks across Luuk and Mila to Rachel, is so blank that Rachel wonders if she has just worked something out.

She puts it to the back of her thoughts, just in case, on top of all her other skills, Abbie might also be able to read her mind. Nevertheless, something beyond her conscious brain draws an unbidden silent shudder of pleasure as she remembers Wim's hands on her.

INSTAGRAM POST

rachelhoneyhill
Devon, England
1, 315,765 likes

Image
- Fran and Wim, standing on a quay at Rotterdam harbour in their Flow & Glow running gear. Fran is pregnant.

Text
This is my lovely #FriendFran with her wonderful husband Wim, a wildlife cameraman.
Not only is he a silver fox, but he's also a total diamond.
#FriendFran and Wim, who are expecting twins very shortly, have started a charity to fight for a persecuted minority in China.
It's terrible that people elsewhere in the world don't enjoy the same freedoms we take for granted.
Next month I'm going to run a total of 100 **@logmyrun** miles to raise money for their charity.
Do you want to join me?
It feels so good to do something good!
What do you feel strongly about? Let me know below, or post and tag me so I can see for myself!
For background, how to get involved and to sponsor me in my efforts, follow the JustGiving link in my bio.
#charity #politics #hottie #notallmen #LogMyRun

CHAPTER THIRTY-THREE

Abbie clears up the tea things and gets the supper on. When Fran and Rachel come down from putting the children to bed, she tells them she is going to take a plate up to her room and turn in early so they can have a chance to catch up.

'Thank you, Abbie,' Rachel says, kissing her on the cheek.

'We've found a proper gem in you,' Fran says.

But the look she gives Abbie isn't as kind as her words suggest. Abbie strongly suspects that she's just humouring Rachel. She wishes she hadn't said anything about *Crazy Pig*, and she could kick herself for looking straight at the baby monitor like that. But she hates someone thinking they can get the better of her.

It goes against every instinct in her body to leave Rachel with Fran, because she's sure she's poisoning her against her, but she needs to appear to know when to fade into the background. Also, she hopes she's wrong, but that weird moment between Rachel and Fran earlier has set her brain whirring, and she needs to do a bit of digging around about it.

For security's sake, before they came down, she slipped the receiver for the baby video monitor out of Rachel's bag and into her own, which she now takes upstairs with her along with her supper. She leaves the camera on the top of the fridge.

Back up in her rooms, she lets Barney out of his cage. He sits on her head while she watches Fran and Rachel on the monitor and eats the miso-baked aubergine she cooked for supper. Never having cooked with either ingredient before in her entire life, she's pleasantly surprised at how tasty it is.

While she eats, she picks up her emails on her Galaxy. Ms Dafé has been in touch again.

Good news, Abigail.

I have secured permission for you to meet with Zayn at 10 a.m. this Saturday, 20 August, at the contact centre in Bristol, which I think you've been to before. Please can you confirm that you will be able to attend.

At last! Abbie fires off the confirmation and uses the iPad to let Rachel know, via iCal, that she's got a doctor's appointment that day.

Feeling like a superhero, like she has power coming out of her fingertips, she places Barney back into his cage and slips out of her room. She tiptoes down to the first floor and silently makes her way along the corridor towards Rachel's bedroom. Pausing at the top of the stairs, she hears her name being mentioned.

'Abbie's certainly got into her cooking stride,' Rachel says. 'This is really quite good, yes?'

'It's OK.'

Abbie wants to storm down the stairs and tell Fran that it's bloody delicious in fact, and that if she has any beef, she should take it up with Anna Jones, whose recipe she followed to the letter.

She continues on along the corridor towards Rachel's room, where she knows, from Rachel's many posts, she keeps her gratitude journal.

She opens the door and breathes in the scent of Rachel – a mixture of the mandarin, coconut and sandalwood products she uses. It's a few days since she's been in this room, and the first time ever on her own. There's an unwritten rule – made by Abbie, admittedly – that this is Rachel's sanctuary, her private space, to be used only by her. But even so, as she steps in and is greeted by the piles of clothes dumped on the floor, the damp towel on the unmade bed, the three used mugs with chamomile tea bags lurking inside them like discarded innards, her first urge is to dash around and tidy up.

'Leave everything as it is,' she whispers firmly to herself.

She sets the baby video monitor up on Rachel's bed while she searches for the journal, so she can get out of the way quickly if they decide to come upstairs.

It doesn't take long. In fact, she knows Rachel's mind so well, she feels as if she has absorbed part of her spirit, as if she just needs to close her eyes and she'll know exactly what Rachel's thinking, how she's feeling, what she's doing. Their bond goes deep.

She rummages in the drawers to the side of Rachel's bed. The journal isn't there, but she does find a vibrator. Abbie doesn't know why this shocks her so much. Of course she'd have a vibrator. In fact, she even ran a story on them once. But the thought of Rachel masturbating is too much for Abbie to bear, as it would be for any sister.

Laughter from the video monitor reminds her that she has limited time. She stuffs the vibrator back in the drawer and carries on searching.

She soon finds the thick hard-bound notebook, tucked under the mattress. She eases it out and, with trembling hands, flicks backwards through pages sparsely covered in Rachel's slightly italic handwriting. Disappointingly, it isn't the in-depth personal record that Rachel has led her followers to believe it is. In fact, it's mostly lists: food she's eaten, things she's done, plans for her posts and website. The only references Abbie can find to herself are factual: *Abbie out all day. Move Abbie to next training tier.* There's nothing searching or personal, which is a bit of a let-down.

But now is not the time for reading all this current stuff. She needs to go back further. Thankfully, Rachel writes so little in the book that even though it is only two-thirds full, it dates back two years.

And then she finds it. The proof that, because of their special bond, she knew was going to be here. That strange foreign-sounding name: Wim, pronounced Vim. He came here, to this house, for three days in December last year. Noted, in Rachel's no-nonsense style, is the record of what they did while he was here, no doubt in this very bed that Abbie is sitting on.

Sex x 5. Orgasm: me x 7, Wim x 5.

Seven! Running up to that moment, Rachel has left notes to herself to get waxed, buy scented candles, champagne, oysters and Scotch. Abbie works backwards to find similar visits noted four more times, roughly three months apart.

She feels a bit queasy reading this. She has not met Wim, nor now does she want to, however good he clearly is in bed. She's no great fan of Fran, with all her double dealings and spying on both her and Rachel, but how could Rachel do this to her best friend? In some way, perhaps that explains Fran's paranoia.

Abbie knows from experience how the suspicion that a partner is doing the dirty comes way before any concrete proof. Three times it's happened to her. Three loads of grief with three no-good men who were only after one thing until they got bored with it and went after someone else. Perhaps *this* is why Fran was asking her to spy on Rachel.

To be fair, looking at Fran and then at Rachel, there's no comparison. Fran is so uptight. How many times does *she* make Wim come in three days?

Abbie sits with the journal on her lap and looks at herself in the mirror opposite Rachel's bed. What has that piece of glass seen? She tries to picture it: Wim as a young Willem Dafoe, lying on top of Rachel, pumping into her. No, Abbie thinks. That's not how it would be. She rearranges the image so that Rachel is on top, riding him, her perfect body arching into one of those seven orgasms.

She feels a bit sick.

How could Rachel do that? How could she do the dirty on her best friend?

And, of course, sex and orgasms with Wim answer the question on everyone's lips about Beansprout. She does a quick calculation. With it being mid-August now, and Rachel being eight months pregnant, that December visit was when conception took place. And those other times? Always the same time of the month, around the twenty-third, so she wasn't even doing Fran the honour of having a passionate affair with her husband. Instead, she was using him for his sperm. Abbie confirms her suspicions by flicking forward through the book. No more sex with Wim after December, because, of course, Rachel had got what she wanted.

Those poor children of Fran's. They'll be playing with their half-sibling and they won't have any idea. Abbie knows only too well how that feels, with her dad being so prolific around this part of Devon. In fact, one of her half-sisters dated one of her half-brothers before their mums, having first admired their cute matching noses, had a chat and put two and two together.

She breathes out slowly. All these little disappointments about Rachel are beginning to come together. Rachel has had every advantage in her life, every possible chance to help her over that one sad part of her story, the bit about her mother dying – although better surely, thinks Abbie, to have a mother who is dead rather than a shell of herself. And yet she has taken this road of lying, dishonesty and deceit, not only to her followers, who she has enchanted into believing everything she proclaims, but also to her best friend.

How might she turn out to betray her sister?

For a very brief moment, Abbie wants to run round this luxuriously appointed room, smashing all the shells, feathers and driftwood Rachel has placed in artful arrangements, spilling the perfumes and essential oils, tearing up the clothes upon clothes upon clothes.

She turns to the baby monitor screen. Rachel has her hand on Fran's shoulder and is telling her something that both of them find hilarious, but there is too much giggling going on for Abbie to make out what it is.

No. She can address this more positively. She thinks back to the time Rachel turned a bit political and got people to sponsor her for Fran and Wim's charity. Like a good follower, Abbie looked up the links she provided and read up about how the minority group she was raising money for were being sent to re-education camps, where they were taught to think differently about things so that they would toe the government line and not cause problems.

The political activism wasn't well received, and Rachel dropped it pretty quickly – the next day she was back to her more popular subjects with a 'surprising ways with coconut oil' story. At the time, however, Abbie was shocked to realise that this sort of thing was going on in the world. Opening her eyes to the woes of others when her own life was going pretty pear-shaped is one of the things for which she truly has to thank Rachel.

Scandalised as she was at the time by this discovery, though, what she has found out about Rachel more recently makes her think perhaps that the government in question was on to something. Not in aiming the enforced re-education at an entire ethnic group, of course. Abbie knows that is fascism.

But certain people at certain times could certainly benefit from a bit of reprogramming.

Especially if that certain person is the linchpin of your future happiness.

Lessons must be learned.

Before she has a chance to mull this over any further, she sees, with alarm, that Fran and Rachel have stood up and are making 'time for bed' moves. She only just manages to get to the children's room, and is standing there comforting little Mila – who she had to pinch awake – when Fran finds her and praises her for hearing the baby cry and going to her.

'Let's take the children for a walk tomorrow,' Fran says to Abbie. 'Give old Rach a rest, eh?'

Abbie is well up for that.

INSTAGRAM POST

rachelhoneyhill
Devon, England
3,313 likes

Image
- Selfie of Rachel, storm clouds over Honey Hill in the background.

Text
So hot. So humid. Storm's a-coming.
Don't you just love a storm?
Like the world's detoxing.
#storm #stormclouds #detox

CHAPTER THIRTY-FOUR

18 August

'Careful, Luuk!' Fran calls out as her little boy hares down the steep cliff path towards the beach at Red Anchor Bay.

She has Mila in the back carrier, and Lotte is being helped by Abbie. Since last night, Lotte has become Abbie's biggest fan. From waking at six this morning, she has followed her around the house, asking her a constant string of questions, some in Dutch and some in English, in that muddled up way of bilingual children who can't grasp that others don't quite possess the same skills.

'*Waar zijn uw kinderen, Abbie?*'

'I don't know what you mean.'

'Where are your children, Abbie?'

'I haven't got any.'

'*Wat is je favoriete snoepje?*'

'I don't know what you mean.'

'What is your favourite sweetie?'

'Oh, Crunchie bars, definitely.'

'*Wat zijn dat?*'

And so on. All morning, as Abbie trailed around, playing, tidying and making the children little pancakes with the *poffertjes* pan Fran brought as a present from the Netherlands. For all that there's something odd about her, she certainly has the patience of a saint, and a magic touch with the little ones.

If it were just looking after Beansprout when she's born, Fran would have no worries about Abbie. It's what's happening right now between her and Rachel that concerns her. She was alarmed to hear about Wanda and The Team being given their cards. However capable Abbie is – and Rachel seems to be convinced that the sun shines out of every one of her orifices – Rachel needs other people around, or she runs the risk of disconnecting entirely from the outside world. This is one of the reasons Fran wants to bring Abbie to this beach. She needs to explain why Rachel is how she is and why, for the baby's safety, she must keep an eye on her at all times, particularly after the birth. She hopes then to work out, from Abbie's reaction, whether she is the right person to be in their lives.

'Come on, *treuzelaars*,' Luuk yells.

'Eh?' Abbie says to Fran.

'He's calling us slowcoaches,' Fran explains. 'Don't be so rude, Luuk!'

Ahead of them, the sea heaves, bluey-black and foam-crested, pulling a muggy storm up the mouth of the English Channel. The sky, which was shining blue this morning, has, over the last couple of hours, shaded gradually from pale grey to ink. For one instant, Fran thinks she hears ghost schoolgirls singing on the wind:

O hear us when we cry to thee
For those in peril on the sea.

A whole-body shudder rides through her, making little Mila wake on her back and bat at her hair. This is the beach, strewn with boulders from the striated granite cliffs above it, where she and Rachel, aged just sixteen, had their lives changed forever. She needs to be on this spot, with her children around her to give her hope and courage, to tell Abbie what happened that night, when young girls behaving badly went very, very wrong indeed, and why Rachel is a hero who needs special care.

Although she barely admits it to herself – mostly because it would cause a massive practical headache – part of her hopes that when she hears the whole mess that is behind Rachel, Abbie will want to resign.

'Rachel means a lot to me,' Fran says as they step down onto the sand. Luuk and Lotte run ahead towards the sea.

'Me too. Stay back from the water, you two!' Abbie calls to the children. 'Those waves can be lethal,' she adds to Fran.

'I know.'

'Yeah. You and Rachel used to come down here.'

They have caught up with the children and are walking between them and the breakers.

'First one to find five pink shells gets a prize,' Abbie says to them, pointing to the area above the tideline. She turns to Fran. 'You don't mind a little vegan gummy bear reward?'

'Not at all. Not even if they have half a cow of gelatine in them,' Fran says. 'We eat everything.' The children run off, and she and Abbie stroll along the sand. This is her moment.

'Did Rachel tell you what happened down here?' she asks.

'You used to bunk off and drink and smoke.'

Fran nods. 'But did she tell you about The Event?'

Mila, in the backpack, is fussing, tugging at Fran's hair. She wants to join her brother and sister on the shell hunt.

Abbie shakes her head.

'Rachel doesn't talk about it,' Fran says. 'But you need to know, to understand why she is like she is.'

'Mama, Mama, Mama!' Mila yells, pulling Fran's hair. '*Ik wil spelen.*'

'*Ja ja,*' Fran says. 'She wants to get down and play. Could you, Abbie?' They have arrived at a semicircle of boulders, a perfect back rest on top of a clean stretch of sand. Abbie helps Fran off with the baby backpack and produces a picnic blanket from her own rucksack.

'So organised!' Fran says.

'I've got snacks, too,' Abbie says. 'Always good to be prepared for bribery or coercion.'

Fran laughs. 'The number-one parenting tools.'

Freed from her bondage, Mila toddles up the beach to help Luuk and Lotte, who are scouring the sand like little detectives, looking for the pink shells.

'So what happened, then?' Abbie asks. 'What was this "Event"?'

'During the holidays, when we were practically the only pupils in the school, we'd come here and get out of it. Not just cider, but also weed and the occasional pill, whatever we could get hold of.'

Fran wonders if, given the sheltered, comfortable upbringing she described in her interview, Abbie might be a bit shocked even by this part of the story.

Her own teens, and much of her twenties, were threaded through with various illegal substances. It started, as it had with most of the people she hung out with at university and beyond, at boarding school. Pupils returning from the outside edges of the old empire – Kenya, say, or Jamaica – would ship in local weed or hash amongst the lacrosse sticks, rugby shirts and worsted skirts in their trunks.

If Fran had done it herself coming back from Dakar, the colour of her skin might have led to a different outcome, but the white kids – pupils at illustrious schools, the offspring of diplomats and the like – made perfect smugglers.

In any case, Fran's parents were too busy at home to have their daughter in the way, so, stuck at Mothcombe year-round, she had no opportunity to test smuggling opportunities. Bonded over their respective abandonments, she and Rachel became tight partners in crime, grand consumers of the imported wares of their more cosmopolitan peers.

But the pills were more a local matter. 'You know Westbourne Parva, so you're probably aware of the shady side of the village, on the other side, round the appropriately named Dicklands estate?'

Abbie nods.

'Lowlife city. Although we found it terrifically exciting at the time, of course. The thrill of the forbidden. We'd score E's and whiz there. And there were a couple of lads we'd hang around with. Just flirting and that, and rich fantasies afterwards. We liked a bad boy back then.'

'Careful, Mila!' Abbie calls out. Mila thumps down on her padded bottom. 'Hold on.' Abbie jumps up, runs across the sand and stands the toddler to rights.

'Anyway,' Fran goes on once Abbie is back with her. 'One full moon in the summer holidays, Rachel and I came down here with a ghetto blaster, dropped a couple of Doves and drank and danced ourselves stupid.'

She looks over at Abbie, who is watching the children like a locked-on missile. Fran knows she has to forge on, so she braces herself and plunges in.

'It was low tide, so we had the whole beach as our dance floor. And it was one of those rare hot summer nights you get down here. So after a couple of hours we were sweating down to our underclothes, and then they were off and we were dancing starkers, loons in the summer moonlight.'

'It's where the word comes from,' Abbie says.

'Eh?'

'Lunatic. From *la lune* – the moon.'

Fran nods at this strange interjection and random fact. It's as if Abbie doesn't want her to go on. But she must.

'What we didn't know was that we weren't alone. Over the years, the school had had a few problems with local men following girls, exposing themselves, peeping in through dorm windows. It's not nice, but it's what happens around girls' schools, even out in the far-flung countryside. We always assumed they came from the Dicklands. Well, you would, wouldn't you?'

'I guess.'

'Anyway, there we were, dancing naked on the beach, Shamen, Prodigy, LFO banging out the tunes, when we realise there's this man standing between us. Just like he had appeared from nowhere. He seemed to be as out of it as we were, and started dancing with us. Even though he was much older than us, we were so loved-up that we just took him in, and everything was OK for a while. Then he grabbed Rachel.'

Fran looks over at Abbie, who is still watching the children. Nothing has changed in her demeanour, so she goes on. 'Well, I didn't know that's what he had done, because I was off in my own little world, eyes shut, communicating with the universe, stupidly trusting – for the last time in my life – that we lived in a safe little bubble and nothing could touch us. But then I turned, and there they were. He had her down on the wet sand, hand over her mouth, and she was trying to scream and escape. I jumped on top of him and went at him with my fists, trying to get him off her, but he just pushed me off like I was a piece of seaweed. He picked up a stone and smashed Rachel in the head until she lay still on the wet sand. I thought she was dead.'

Abbie flicks a glance towards Fran. 'That must have been bad.'

'Then he started on me. I'm not going to go into details, but, Abbie.' Fran closes her eyes. She hasn't told this story to many people, and finds this part particularly difficult. 'He raped me and nearly killed me. Would have killed me, if Rachel hadn't got to him.'

'Got to him?'

'She saved my life. She came round, and even though she was so badly injured, the minute she saw what was happening, she grabbed the rock he'd used on her and she saved my life.'

'What did she do to him?'

'The point is that we were horribly attacked, and Rachel stopped it. Despite being so badly beaten that she had a bleed on the brain that damaged her permanently, she saved my life.'

'Damaged her?'

Fran nods. 'Haven't you ever wondered why she has no friends other than me?'

Abbie looks blank, like she doesn't understand the question.

'She's special, Abbie. She can't read people. She transmits, but she has had to learn all sorts of techniques to receive. Everything has to be thought out. It's exhausting for her. I owe her everything, so I will look after her forever.'

'Right.'

'And she has this rare sort of epilepsy – usually brief moments when she doesn't know what she's doing, when things can get out of hand. She fell off the medical radar in her messy twenties, so learned ways of self-managing it without prescriptions – she prefers it that way. But even so, things can get quite sketchy, and you need to be on the alert. If it were to happen when she's around the baby…' Fran stops herself, unable even to think about that.

'I know this may sound pretty shitty, Abbie, but at this point I just want to remind you about the NDA you signed when you took this job. You are now just one of a handful of people in the world who know about this. But it's important that you do know. Because looking after Rachel places these special demands on you, and I don't know if—'

But Abbie doesn't appear to be listening. 'When was this?'

'When we were sixteen. What, twenty-two years ago?'

She turns to Fran. 'What happened to the man?'

'Because of the state we were both in, we couldn't hide what had happened to us from the school. We went to our favourite teacher – Miss Chamberlain, our house mother – and told her.'

'The "you can do this" teacher.'

'Yes! Rachel told you? We realise now that the school made hiding the truth a habit – a lot went on there that never got out.'

'The kiddy fiddler.'

'She told you about that, too? Well, yeah, in the same way, the attack was never made public, for the sake of the school's reputation. Not even our parents found out, and we were happy for it to be like that at the time. Rachel collapsed the day afterwards and spent weeks in a coma, and we said she had been hit by a boulder falling from the cliff. No one at the hospital questioned it. Why would they? My rape was sorted with kind words, a morning-after pill and Matron running an STD check on me. It was not, she implied, the first time this sort of thing had happened. That was news to me, and I realise now with deep regret that because of my own silence around what happened, it would also be news to the next girl who saw her in the same situation.'

Fran purses her lips and digs her fingers into the sand. 'Not that our particular attacker was in any position to do anything to anyone after that night.'

She shivers. She hadn't meant to tell Abbie all of that, but she needed to explain the reason Rachel is the way she is, and why their relationship is so co-dependent. She wanted also to show Abbie what a hero Rachel had been during The Event. She doesn't tell her, however, about the years of therapy she went through before she let a man go near her again, the therapy that brings her back to the beach every time she visits Rachel, like an arachnophobe confronting a jar of spiders. Even so, she still has nightmares from time to time, and has no idea how she will cope when her own daughters reach puberty.

'What happened to him?' Abbie asks.

'He got what he deserved.' Fran looks out at the waves, now heaving with all their Atlantic force onto the shore. 'We stayed away. The sea dealt with him.'

'Five pink shells!' Luuk runs towards Abbie, his little hands cupped around his treasure.

'Clever boy.' Abbie hands him a vegan gummy bear. But her voice, her face, her whole demeanour are so strange that he looks to Fran as if to ask her what's wrong.

Perhaps Abbie is too sensitive. Perhaps Fran has told this story – which she sees ultimately as one of survival and hope – in the wrong way and it has frightened her. In any case, Fran wants to leave the beach. Saying the words down here, remembering the graphic details she held back from Abbie, has been too much for her. It's an absurd impulse, but she wants to see Rachel again, to make sure she's all right.

So unsettled is she that she lacks the focus to pursue the issue of whether, given all she has told her, Abbie feels up to looking after Rachel. In any case, as they head back up the path to the top of the cliff and on towards the house, there is no more conversation.

It's like Abbie has shut a door on Fran. She seems barely even to notice the children.

INSTAGRAM POST

rachelhoneyhill
Devon, England
12,873 likes

Image
- Rachel meditating, a little smile on her face. Sam lying beside her.

Text
How can you love your enemy?
Try the Metta Bhavana, the Buddhist Loving-Kindness meditation.
It's really easy!
You start with the love you feel for yourself and you grow that love, moving through other people to your worst enemies and on to the whole world!
If we all did this practice, we would be in a far better place!
You don't have to be a Buddhist to do it, either.
Float over to the RR YouTube channel meditation playlist, where I gently talk you through the Metta Bhavana, with chilled ambient sounds to help you on your way.
Link in bio.
Let me know how you get on!
#love #lovingkindness #MettaBhavana #Buddhism #meditation #peace

CHAPTER THIRTY-FIVE

As Abbie trudges back to Honeyhill with Fran and the children, the hot day hauls the big storm up behind them and she feels like her skull is stuffed with week-old scrambled egg.

If there's one event she can identify as the beginning of the falling-apart of her childhood, it's the death of her uncle Daz. After a lifetime of family mystery, Fran has just revealed what happened to him.

She doesn't want to believe it. In *so many* ways she doesn't want to believe it. She knows, through family stories, that Daz was no angel, but she couldn't imagine he was capable of doing that – an act almost worthy of Da in its horror.

Well, they were mates at the time.

But what Fran says Daz did pales into insignificance beside the big, shocking fact that has just been dealt out to her. That the person who killed him, and thus set Abbie's misery in motion, is the very person Abbie has been relying on to set her free.

When she gets to the house, she can barely look Rachel in the eye.

There's no two ways about it. She is clear what she has to do. Even though she knows it looks weird with Fran and the children leaving in a couple of hours, once they are out of the way packing their things, she tells Rachel that she has to go out on a family matter.

'Oh no. Is it serious?' Rachel asks, her hands twisting, her face all concern. *Her two-face*, Abbie thinks.

'Don't know yet,' Abbie mumbles, unable to meet her eye.

'Well, you must use the car.'

'I'm OK, thanks,' Abbie says.

Rachel frowns at her, clearly wondering what family business Abbie might have so close by that no car is needed. Truth is, Abbie doesn't feel like being in Rachel's car at the moment, nor her house.

Nor anywhere near her, for fear of what she might find herself doing.

So she ignores her, fills her water bottle and straps on her trainers.

'Aren't you going to say goodbye to Fran and the children before you go?' Rachel says, hovering by the front door, almost dancing for her, unable to disguise the pleading tone in her voice. 'They loved you so much.'

Abbie ignores her. 'I'll take Sam,' she says instead, unhooking his lead from the peg by the door and whistling for him to join her. Without a backward look at Rachel, who she knows is standing in the doorway, still twisting her fingers around and around, she sets off, half walking, half running, across the fields towards Westbourne Parva.

The storm finally arrives. It pisses down, soaking her through, but she barely feels it.

It's mid-afternoon when Tracey answers her Dicklands front door with a 'Wot?' She is wearing the faded pink dressing gown she had on that time Abbie and Rachel saw her striding across to her neighbour's place with a bag of dog poo. From the look on her face and the force with which she pulls open the swollen front door, she is expecting trouble.

When she sees it's Abbie, she stops like a woman who has had the existence of ghosts confirmed to her.

'Oh,' she says, her features unreadable in that way Abbie has always found so infuriating. She lifts her hand to her face and pushes back the tangle of greasy hair that covers her eyes.

'Can I come in?' Abbie says.

Tracey pushes her head past her to take a look around for nosy neighbours clocking Abbie's presence on her doorstep. For someone with a more conventional upbringing, the scent of a particular brand of perfume might spell 'mother', but for Abbie, it's Tracey's stench of unwashed tights, cigarettes and stale beer.

'Suppose so. Bring him in, poor thing,' Tracey says, meaning Sam. 'Mind the floor, though. You're both sopping.'

She leads Abbie down a corridor cramped with bulging bin bags and piles of local free-sheet newspapers and through into a back living room where the furniture is almost invisible under heaps of clothing, takeaway containers, empty glasses and bottles and overflowing ashtrays. Sam has a field day, sniffing around at everything. On top of the obvious odours of the visible detritus, the place has a strong undercurrent of cat piss about it, as well as a tang of dog shit explained by the scrappy back garden – just about visible through the blown and mildewed double glazing – which is more poo than patio. Outside, a pit bull snarls and rattles its chain.

Although Tracey loves animals way more than her own children, she is just as incapable of looking after them.

'Take a seat.' She points at the sofa. Abbie moves things aside, trying to touch them as little as possible.

'Cuppa tea?' she says. 'Or something stronger?'

Abbie shakes her head; the idea of tea in a mug from Tracey's kitchen fills her with dread.

'I thought it was you the other day poking around with Miss La-di-dah from up Honeyhill. What you done with your hair? Looks a fucking mess.'

With her own wispy mullet, Tracey could take a look in the mirror, but even so, Abbie tries to smooth the curls Rachel has encouraged her to grow back in.

'Lost some of that blubber, though,' Tracey says. Again, pot, kettle, black, but Abbie tries to be the better woman.

'I've been doing a diet and exercise plan.'

'Ooh, posh. What you doing with that one up there, then?'

'I'm working for her. Mother's helper.'

'A what?'

'I'm helping look after her, and, when it comes, the baby.'

'You?' Tracey says. 'She's paying *you* to look after a *baby*?'

Abbie bristles. This is not going the way she wants, so she comes straight to the point. 'What happened to Uncle Daz?'

Tracey, who is lowering herself into an armchair so well-used that it bears the imprint of her body, looks up at Abbie like she has just shot her. She lets herself fall the last few inches into the seat, and yelps with the pain the sudden movement shoots through her lardy arse. She is forty-two, but outside the Dicklands, she would pass for late sixties.

'Why the fuck you asking about that?' she says.

Abbie looks at her feet. 'I just need to know.'

Tracey lifts one buttock and fishes her fags out of her dressing gown pocket. She flips open the pack with a trembling hand and works a cigarette up so that she can pull it out with her teeth. Then, without looking, she rummages on the table beside her until she finds a lighter.

'Coming here, stirring up all the shit.' She lights her cigarette, inhales deeply, coughs, spits phlegm into a hellish glass reserved for that purpose, then plants a rheumy look on Abbie. 'He was murdered.'

Abbie nods. 'But was it ever proved?'

Tracey reaches down the side of her chair and pulls up a can of Special Brew, pops the ring and takes a slug. 'Course it was never proved. What do the bacon ever care? One less of us to bother about. It broke me, it did, losing him.'

Abbie knows. Tracey's grief consumed her. She quickly became addicted to tramadol, at first prescribed, then procured wherever she could find it – and it was everywhere at the time. Mixed with her high alcohol intake, the drug made it impossible for her to care for her four children, all by different fathers. When Abbie, the eldest, was six, in an act to be repeated later on her own children, one of the 'nosy neighbour bitches' called in social services. To be fair to the neighbour, the house had become party central, and the kids were more or less feral. The result was that they were all taken into care.

From the state of Tracey's track-marked arms as she pushes up her sleeves as if preparing to punch fate for the injustices suffered by her family, the tramadol has now been upgraded to a less medically approved method of dealing with the pain of living.

'When was it, exactly?'

Tracey looks at her with intense hostility, as if it's a personal insult that Abbie doesn't possess the same detailed knowledge of the event that so thoroughly rocked her own world. 'Wait there,' she snarls. She hauls herself out of the armchair and, with a great deal of grunting and moaning, takes herself out of the living room and up the stairs.

Left alone, Abbie tries to remember her early childhood in this house.

It's strange the way the mind blocks out the really bad stuff. She can only bring back laughter, freedom, rough-and-tumble and the strange and intense love she had felt towards her half-siblings and her mother. If anyone, up to a few months ago, had asked her what family meant, she would have answered with something scraped up and put together from her time here.

Now, of course, family has a different definition. Or at least until a few hours ago it did. It meant her, Rachel, Beansprout and everyone, all together under one roof. Sisters and cousins. But that picture of perfection is beginning to be spoiled, dirtied by what she is finding out about Rachel.

Why does real life always have to torpedo everything?

'Where are my grandkids, then?' Tracey asks, as she levers herself back into the living room. She has a very old shoebox with her.

'They're all right,' Abbie says, lips tight. She doesn't want to talk about this.

'When did you last see them?'

'I'm meeting with Zayn soon, in fact.'

'You shouldn't have had them taken off you.'

This is too much for Abbie. 'You can fucking well talk.'

'Mind your fucking language. And don't answer me back.'

Slapped down like a little girl, Abbie sticks her quivering bottom lip out and tries to tuck Zayn, Harry and Taylor away again, beneath her consciousness, where she keeps them safe.

'This is my Daz box,' Tracey says, placing it like it's the Holy Grail on top of the debris on the coffee table.

Abbie wonders if she has an Abbie box. She isn't going to ask.

Leaning forward, panting with the effort, Tracey slowly picks out the contents and lays them out. There's a handful of newspaper cuttings, a small pile of photographs of Daz looking chipper and cheeky – every single one of them with a beer in his hand – a St Christopher – 'They took that off his body,' Tracey says, wiping away a tear – and, last out of the box, a rubber fish.

'What's that?' Abbie asks.

'Sand eel lure. He loved beach fishing.'

'Where did he go?'

'Red Anchor Bay, of course.'

Abbie picks up the newspaper cuttings. They're dated the last week of July, twenty-two years ago. *Search for Missing Local Man* quickly turns into *Body Found at Red Anchor Bay Identified as Missing Westbourne Parva Man*. The dates all work out.

'They said he must have been out of it and got trapped by the tide,' Tracey says.

Abbie's done some bad things in her life, and she's hurt a couple of people, one of them – that Kieran – quite badly, hence her spell at Her Majesty's pleasure. But to kill someone and walk away as if nothing had happened? No matter what he did to you or your friend. The life kicked off by Daz's death and Ma's subsequent breakdown means that Abbie has been sexually assaulted on numerous occasions. While she hates the men who did it to her, and wishes them all colours of ill, killing them wouldn't do anyone any good. To Abbie's mind, if you did away with every man who ever sexually assaulted a girl or woman, you'd be left with precious few in this world.

'He liked to party, did Daz,' Tracey wheezes. 'A proper one for the ladies and all. Proper young buck.'

The same word Da uses about himself as a young man. Abbie looks up from the press cutting. 'Says here they found drugs and alcohol in his blood.'

'Hardly surprising, innit. He liked a drink, did Daz. We all did, back then.' Tracey knocks back the dregs of her Special Brew and opens another. 'He was a lovely big brother, always there for me, always looking out for family. He gave your dad a proper hiding when he buggered off and left me up the spout.'

Abbie winces. She doesn't like all that bad-mouthing of her da.

'Well, they say Daz was arseholed, but then read what they says about the head injury after they done the post-mortem,' Tracey goes on. She throws a load of stuff from the sofa onto the floor, sits next to Abbie and points at the clipping.

This is physically the closest they have been since Abbie was taken into care, and the animal part of her wants to throw herself into her mother's arms and fold into her. The more conscious layer of her brain, however, edges her a little away, towards the sofa arm.

'"Police say that the cause of death was a serious head wound rather than drowning",' she reads. '"A spokesman said that it's likely Darren 'Daz' James may have been struggling but still alive when the waves caught him and threw him against the rocks."'

'You see, that's bollocks for a starter.' Tracey stabs the newspaper with a dirty fingernail. 'Daz was a strong swimmer, and he knew the water there like the back of his hand.'

'Didn't you tell them that?'

'They took no notice. I was shitting rather than speaking as far as they were concerned.'

Abbie picks up one of the photos of Daz, from the bottom of the pile. In it, he has a child on his shoulders, his meaty hand right hand resting at the top of a chubby little thigh.

'Look how handsome he was, my bro.' Tracey grabs the photo. 'Hey. Is that you there, Abigail?'

Abbie squints at the photo. No one but Tracey and that Ms Dafé calls her by her full name. The child in the photo is clearly a boy. 'It's Terry, Mum. He's got blonde hair, look.'

Tracey looks up at her. 'That feels so strange, you know,' she says. 'You calling me that.'

'What?'

'Mum.' The bloodshot eyes mist over.

Despite her clean-freak revulsion at the state of the woman in front of her, Abbie takes her hand. 'Mum. I think I know who killed Daz. And don't worry. I'm not going to let them get away with it.'

'Are you going to tell me who?'

She shakes her head. If Tracey gets involved, everything will go to pot. This is Abbie's job, and she's the one to do it. Lessons need to be learned. Punishment needs to be meted out. But it's all good. In fact, it's even better, because it puts her firmly in the driving seat.

Despite her clear obsession over the death of her brother all those years ago, Tracey seems to be happy with Abbie's assurances that justice will be done. Either that, or she just can't actually be bothered to do anything about anything.

Abbie takes her leave of her mother in a positive mood. But as she and Sam tramp back towards Honeyhill over the newly muddy fields, rain driving in their faces, her head starts to feel hot. All that turning it round, positive thinking, creating opportunities out of threats doesn't change one insurmountable fact. Piled on top of all the disappointments she has encountered since starting at Honeyhill, Abbie's fury at Rachel for messing up her life by killing Daz is as raw and real as a slab of steaming meat cut from a newly killed cow.

Right now, all she wants is to make Rachel pay.

The question is: how?

And niggling away in her chest is the fast-germinating seed of another question: does Rachel, with all her lies and misdemeanours, deserve to be a mother? Or, worded another way, a way that is all too familiar to Abbie, having had it quoted at her by social workers and courts until her head felt like it was exploding: is she fit to be a mother?

Abbie has to conclude that the answer could, in all possibility, be no.

INSTAGRAM POST

1 year ago

rachelhoneyhill
Devon, England
1,378,207 likes

Images
- Photo series from Rachel's drinking years, made to look like old creased Polaroids:
- An idyllic Thai beach
- Rachel downing shots in a Thai beach bar
- Rachel bleary and drunk, stumbling out of the bar.

Text
The past is another country. One we can never visit again.
The future is all we can control.
Move on, into the light.
#livefornow #inspiration #inspirational

CHAPTER THIRTY-SIX

Rachel lies on the sofa, having seen Fran and the children off. Although she can barely admit it to herself, she was, in the end, glad to see them go. Fran had returned from Red Anchor Bay even more rattled than usual. Rachel hopes she didn't freak Abbie out by coming over all PTSD while they were down there. It gets to her, Rachel knows.

However, in some respects, Fran dropping by has had a good outcome. Even though it took a little belt-and-braces intervention, she thinks Abbie has made a good impression, convinced Fran that she's a safe pair of hands.

She cradles Beansprout and rubs a knobbly lump that could possibly be a knee, then lifts her laptop to rest on her bump. It's really time to work.

Outside, the storm howls. The rain is coming so thick and fast it feels like her trolls have got together to fling buckets of water at her windows. She wonders where Abbie is, and hopes that she's OK out there in it. By disappearing so suddenly, she nearly undid all her work at impressing Fran.

'What family business? Where?' Fran asked when Rachel told her.

'All I know from the FitSo is that she's heading towards Westbourne Parva.'

'Westbourne Parva? But her family moved away when she was six.'

'We don't have any right to know all the ins and outs of her life,' Rachel said, the irony that she had just located Abbie by her fitness tracker not entirely escaping her.

Not wanting to think about it further, she turns her attention to her GridSmasher planner. It's Thursday, and the posts for the rest of the week look fine, all set up and ready to go until the end of Saturday. She flicks to her account and checks the responses. Her slimmed-down community of followers seems to have returned to more positive commenting, and her special software that flags up abusive words reports none for the past two days.

She exhales slowly.

Perhaps this'll give her a decent out for not using that terrible video of Abbie. Putting up a defence if you're not under attack is just asking for trouble.

Having taken nearly three days off, she really needs to plan next week's posts, but instead she scrolls back through her online life over the past year. So much care, so much energy, so much work. Just looking at herself exhausts her. She doesn't know if she can live up to that any more. The idea of carrying on, reinventing and building her brand, messing around with scheduling, hashtags, filming, talking to partners, it all seems too much.

'But how else am I going to feed you?' she asks Beansprout. And with Abbie saying that money is tight, it's not like she has much spare cash flow to slacken off or diversify. She can't believe how Wanda has let her down, stealing from her, sitting on potential partners, mismanaging her money. Perhaps she should look into taking legal action of some kind…

But no. That would be too much stress, with the potential for it to go public. Anyway, it's water under the bridge. To carry on worrying about Wanda is too much effort.

She closes her eyes. Breathe, Rachel. Breathe. A lot of this disquiet must be hormonal. Nothing is important but you, your baby and living your best life.

'And recording it and showing it to your followers,' she says to Beansprout. 'And monetising it.' She laughs, but it sounds a bit desperate, even to her.

Turning her attention back to next week, she pulls up her recent photo stream. Luckily Fran's visit resulted in plenty of images that can get her on to talking about children. She could feature some kids' meals and meditation for little ones. Perhaps use that snap of them looking at Beansprout's nursery, to give the cot maker their pound of flesh. Fran has signed release forms so she can now feature Luuk, Mila and Lotte without blurring their faces, which will add value, as they are very pretty with their brown skin and amazing hair from Fran, and their Dutch blue eyes from Wim. She wonders what colour her own baby's eyes will be.

No matter that the schedule is telling her she promised some more posts for Gossip Yum, and to do that she has to engage her younger, yoga-clothes-buying followers, seventy-two per cent of whom, her data shows her, are not parents themselves.

Why should she let herself be so led by what she's supposed to do? She should follow Abbie's advice to be truer to herself.

She scrolls over to her now dormant SobeRachel account, where she used to do just that. In the old days, she posted whatever took her fancy. There was no strategy or theme to what she did. She didn't even curate her grid, or base her hashtags on marketing potential, or have them dictated to her by partners.

She looks back on that time like the early days of a love affair, when you can't keep your hands off each other, when all you want to do is be with that person, before compromise and familiarity get in the way.

Not that she has anything to judge this by, never having been able to let anyone get close enough to find anything approaching love.

Outside in the hallway, the front door slams shut, bringing with it a gust of stormy wind. Abbie is home! Rachel feels like a

1950s housewife whose husband is back from the office – a major component returning to the family unit.

'Hi!' she calls out. But there is no response. She tries again. 'Abbie?'

Perhaps Abbie has her earbuds in, that incongruous Lady Gaga music blasting. Sam's claws scuffle on the tiles, then cupboards open and shut as outer clothing is taken off and hung to dry. But instead of a hungry or thirsty Abbie charging into the kitchen for refuelling, Rachel hears her climbing the stairs.

'No. You stay there,' Abbie orders Sam in a voice Rachel has never heard before. It's a new one on Sam, too, because Abbie has to repeat herself. 'Stay!' she says again, making Rachel squirm, like it's her that's being told off.

She holds her breath as Abbie's footsteps continue up to the second floor, to her rooms.

This is remarkably unusual behaviour.

Feeling the need for connection with some living creature, she calls out for Sam, who comes running to her. Abbie has towelled him off, but he's still pretty damp. He jumps up onto the couch and curls in beside her. His breathing settles and becomes slow and even, a little whiffle catching on the in-breath, and soon he is fast asleep, pressed up against Beansprout. Rachel is not long to follow.

'What makes a person fit to be a mother?'

Rachel peels her eyes open. Abbie is standing over her, ruddy from a shower, dressed in a brand-new F&G tracksuit, which fits her perfectly. But it's not so much what she's wearing that Rachel notices. It's the look in her eyes, which are greener than ever.

Perhaps it's because of Fran having been in such a state earlier, but for one brief and horrible second, that look brings someone else back to Rachel. He's bearing down on her from a similar angle, twenty-two or so years ago, in Red Anchor Bay.

All that expensive therapy, all those drugs, all that oblivion had, she thought, finally put that away, but here it is, so present that it makes her heart race and Beansprout turn an outraged somersault inside her.

Gasping, Rachel tries to fight the image away, back to where it belongs. As she pushes herself up to sitting, she accidentally shoves Sam off his perch next to her.

'Mind the fucking dog,' Abbie says.

'Sorry.' Rachel is woozy and confused. Daytime napping does that to her. 'What did you say?'

'I said: what makes a person fit to be a mother?'

Rachel pinches the bridge of her nose between her thumb and forefinger. 'Why?'

'To check. See if you know.'

'Of course I know.'

'What is it, then?'

'I've just woken up!'

Abbie leans in again. 'What is it?' she says, her fists curling.

Rachel holds her hands up to shield herself from those eyes. What is this? 'Can you give me a bit of space, please?'

Abbie takes a small step backwards.

Rachel blinks. 'OK, then. Good mother: warm, loving, kind, always there for her kids, puts her kids first, looks after them, cuddles them, reads to them, makes them strong and confident, teaches them love, security, that they are important, that they deserve the place they take up in the world…'

She stops, because she realises she is sobbing.

All of this – this image of what a good mother is and does – is what she has come to understand, rather than what she has ever experienced.

In better times, she imagined that as a tiny child she did know mother love, even though she can't consciously remember it. But reading and memorising the toxic press around her mother's life – the parties, the papped photographs of her tumbling out of nightclubs at three in the morning – makes her question that. Many of those stories date from after her birth, so where was she when her mother was having this high old life? Who was looking after baby Rachel? Whose arms, if any, were around her?

Through her tears, she looks up at Abbie, whose attitude hasn't changed one bit.

'Isn't that the answer you wanted?' she asks her.

Abbie narrows her eyes so that they are just emerald slits.

'Should a mother tell lies?'

Rachel frowns, gives her head a tiny shake. 'No!'

'Should a mother be a fake?'

'Abbie, if this is about my work, I've told you it's not real life. It never pretended to be that.'

'Tell that to your followers.'

'It's just a game, an entertainment, like an actor playing a role.' And she's back to her mum again, who she always pictures like Isadora Duncan, standing in a sleek convertible, scarf flying, hands thrown in the air, a picture of freedom and joy before she was snuffed out. 'Everyone knows that.'

'Should a mother be self-deluding?'

Rachel frowns at Abbie. 'What is this?'

'Should a mother have a history of violence?'

'I—'

'Should a mother have killed a man?'

Rachel swallows. 'What?'

'Fran told me what you did. Down on the beach. When you were at school.'

This hits Rachel like a punch in the head. 'What?'

'She wanted me to "understand" you.'

'I had to do something, or he would have killed her. He thought he'd killed me, I—'

'"He" was my uncle. Remember? You probably knew it after I told you about him, but of course you didn't say anything. You killed my uncle, which sent my mum mad, which meant I ended up in care and basically my whole life went to shit.'

'But you had a lovely childhood, a happy family.'

Abbie pushes her face up against Rachel's. 'That's what I told you. Do you think you'd have employed me if you'd known the truth about how I was dragged up?'

Rachel's heart roars in her head. 'I would have understood. My own childhood was very similar in so many ways—'

'Don't give me that. Going to one of the best schools in the country? Having all this? All this money, all this privilege, all this entitlement? And yet you still can't be honest about your life or the way you live it.'

'I… I…'

'I expected so much of you, Rachel. I loved you. I thought we were going to be perfect. And now I don't know if you're fit to have that baby. Lying to Fran, and to Wim, as well as the whole world.'

'Lying to Fran and Wim? I never—'

Abbie nods her head. 'You did. I know. You used him for sex to get yourself pregnant. You betrayed your best friend. You lied, and lied, and lied.'

'I didn't, we—'

'JUST SHUT UP, RACHEL!'

Abbie looks so dangerous that Rachel picks up a cushion to shield herself. 'What are you going to do?' Her voice is small.

'I need some time and space to think things through,' Abbie says. 'You may have seen that I have an important appointment coming up day after tomorrow, and that I need to take a day off.'

'That doctor's appointment,' Rachel says.

'Oh, so you do have it in you to think about someone else. Yes. Doctor's appointment, in Bristol. So tomorrow I'm taking the car, and the credit card, and I'm going to stay in a nice hotel and have a think and make a plan.'

'You're not going to tell anyone, are you?'

'I'm going to give you a chance. We're going to do this, Rachel. And I'm going to stand by you. But if you want to give Beansprout the best beginning – a beginning like you and I never had – things are going to have to change.'

'I'm sorry.'

'I expect you to stay here and not contact anyone,' Abbie says. 'Because I don't trust you, I'm taking the router, the laptops and all the iPads and phones.'

'But—'

'I'll also lock and alarm all the windows and doors, which means you can't go outside the house.'

Rachel is on the edge of panic. 'What about Beansprout, what if—'

'I'll keep the security system on, with all the cameras online. If you get into trouble, I'll be back in time to help. If you contact anyone while I'm away – and that includes Fran – I will go to the police with the story of what you did, and how you hid it from the authorities, and that will be very miserable for you, and for Beansprout. Same thing applies if you try to disconnect the cameras or the security system. Understood?'

Rachel nods, her eyes shut.

'When I get back, I'll have worked out what is going to happen, and we'll take it from there. Understood?'

Rachel nods again. Her shame is complete. She knows she deserves this.

'Good.'

'I'm truly sorry about your uncle,' she says.

'So am I.'

Rachel wants so much to add the 'but', to say he deserved everything he got. But her own lies, cover-ups, inability to truly ever face what happened are also inexcusable.

Abbie climbs on a chair and reaches up to the router, which is on a shelf high up in the kitchen. She pulls it down, rips out all the wires and places it on the kitchen worktop.

'Hand me your laptop,' she says.

INSTAGRAM POST

rachelhoneyhill
Devon, England
8,265 likes

Image
- Luuk, Lotte and Mila, sitting cross-legged in a line in the Honeyhill studio, wearing flower garlands, their eyes closed.

Text
You're never too young to learn to meditate!
#meditate #meditation #kids #children #spiritual #friends

CHAPTER THIRTY-SEVEN

19 August

Abbie checks in to the Marriott on College Green in the centre of Bristol. It's only a mile or so away from her old flat, but as she pulls her suitcase full of Rachel's tech through the glittering marble reception area, she feels like she is on a different planet. As coolly as if she has done this before, she hands over the credit card to put it on record for charging room service, takes her key card and allows the bellhop – she remembers seeing them being called that in movies – to take her bag upstairs to her four-poster suite with stunning city views. She tips him a fiver then throws herself backwards onto the big bed and gazes out of the window at the fat, damp Bristol sky.

The drive up – cathartically fast, with her now not giving a toss about whether Rachel gets a couple more points on her licence – has worked out some of the rawness of her fury. The plan she had for their life together had been so perfect, and now it's spoiled. She was hoping for a leader, someone to guide her, someone to look up to. Now it seems that, as usual, it's going to be down to her to make things work.

Nothing's ever easy for her. Like meeting Zayn tomorrow. She had to fight so hard to make it happen. Why can't a mother see her son when she wants to? It's inhumane.

To stop herself getting any more worked up, she sits up on the bed, crosses her legs in Sukhasana and finds a Rachel-guided meditation video on the RR YouTube channel. But only a couple of minutes in, Rachel's soothing tones start to grate. They're so different from how she normally speaks, so artificially softened. For Abbie, the effect is the opposite of calming. It becomes yet another disappointment.

Instead, she puts on the towelling dressing gown and slippers she finds in the wardrobe and goes downstairs to the spa area. She buys a swimming costume from the little boutique down there, frets by the pool, sweats it out in the steam room and finishes off by taking advantage of an available drop-in spot to have her toe and fingernails done dark scarlet. As everything else has been thrown up in the air, she readily accepts the offer of a glass of Prosecco while the manicurist kneels at her feet. The pampering brings back the BabyMoon – happier days, before Rachel messed everything up.

In an act of rebellion, she decides against buying some workout gear and doing her Abbie's Journey weights session.

Upstairs, she uses Rachel's laptop to fire off an email to Sue at the Baby2You private midwife service, saying that she has decided to go with the NHS and asking that she immediately sends her all her medical records. This will mean the end of the partnership, and they will probably try to make Rachel pay for the care she has had so far, but the service has featured in five posts already, so Abbie is up for a fight on that one. She's met Sue on two of her visits and didn't like the way she breezed in and took over. If Abbie's got to drive everything, she's going to drive *everything*.

Time for room service, she thinks.

Sitting on the bed watching telly and tucking in to a meat-feast pizza with a large glass of wine and a slab of chocolate gateau for pudding, she decides that in her future life, she's going to stay in hotels more. Bring the kids along. And Barney and Sam. She misses Barney and Sam.

'The body of a woman has been found in a house in Exeter in what appears to be a bizarre torture murder.'

The newsreader's announcement makes Abbie pause, a slice of pizza halfway to her mouth. A reporter is on screen, speaking outside a familiar pebble-dashed semi.

'Last night, Elaine Williams and her elderly mother returned home from a fortnight's cruise to find the body of her daughter Charlotte, twenty-three, bound to a kitchen chair in what appears to have been a bizarre execution, with injuries that suggest torture. A mobile phone was found at the scene that points to further criminal activity. Police are appealing for anyone who may have seen anything here in the St Loyes area of Exeter in the past two weeks, however insignificant they may think it, to call 101 immediately.'

Abbie bunches up her lips. This is the last thing she needs. The stupid girl can't have managed to work herself free. What if the police identify her as Rachel's ex-employee and troll? Would that bring them to Honeyhill?

Then she remembers another of Posh June's mottos: 'The pigs ain't half as clever as they scare you into believing they are.' Of course they won't make the link. And even if they do: Sweet Rachel Rodrigues? Murderer?

She laughs and laughs at that one. Because of course that's exactly what she is.

She knocks back her wine and orders another large one to be brought up to her room. By the time she's drained that, unused to alcohol as she now is, she passes out on top of the bed. It's only in the middle of the night that she actually manages to slip between the thousand-thread-count sheets.

The light through the curtains she never closed wakes her at dawn.

Hung-over, she staggers through to the bathroom and stares at herself in the mirror. It's not too much of a disaster. A quick shower, a bit of make-up and a change into one of the silk dresses Rachel bought her and she'll pass as an entirely respectable mother. Any social worker would be happy to hand three children back to her in that lot.

The decidedly non-vegan hotel buffet full English still repeating on her, she climbs Park Street towards the Clifton Child Contact Centre. As she walks – noting how easy she finds the hill compared to how she used to wheeze up it before Abbie's Journey – she tries to internalise her smart, capable good-mother appearance.

'This is who I am,' she says, much to the consternation of a passing man.

But all the tough talk in the world can't stop the butterflies in her stomach. Halfway up the hill, she stops and stares into a jewellery shop window, just to calm herself down. Inside, she sees a series of small silver pendants shaped like abstract women with tiny breasts. The pendants have words on them like *Strong*, *Peace*, *Calm*, *Clarity*. Just reading them makes her feel warm inside. She pulls her courage together, rings the shop entry doorbell and, to her amazement, rather than being turned away like she half expects, she is let in with a warm welcome. The pendants are forty-five pounds each. She has never spent so much on a piece of jewellery before, but she chooses one with the word *Safe* etched on it in gold.

'Would you like a silver chain with that?' asks the young female assistant – so coolly dressed and pierced and tattooed that Abbie feels tongue-tied in front of her. 'We have a range, starting at forty pounds for sixteen inches.'

Abbie shakes her head. It seems like a needless extravagance, when all she wants is that word, in solid silver, to hold onto.

'How about one of these?' The girl pulls out a long leather shoestring. 'They look lovely on.'

'How much?'

'A fiver.'

'OK then.' But as Abbie gets out Rachel's credit card, a thought strikes her. 'Get me another three, will you?' she says, recklessness rushing through her.

'All the same?' The girl smiles, like she knows what's on Abbie's mind. Which she can't, of course, Abbie tells herself firmly as she nods. 'Well, I think we can throw in the thongs for free, then. Do you want me to gift-wrap them?'

Abbie glances up at the clock behind the counter. She has fifteen minutes and would rather die than be late, but gift-wrapping seems essential, so she nods and watches as the girl works with scented black tissue paper and smart gold-embossed boxes.

She runs the rest of the way, swinging her cool little jewellery shop carrier bag, feeling like she is in a movie.

Stepping into the Contact Centre takes the wind out of her sails. The attempts to make the place welcoming and homely – cushions, a sofa, books, toys – can't hide the atmosphere, which reeks of desperation and conflict. Abbie is not new to this place. She has been here before on several occasions to see her children, but it has never ended well. She just can't curb her emotions. Plus the need to bolster herself beforehand has meant that more than once she has been turned away for being drunk. In the end, her presence in her own children's lives was deemed detrimental to their well-being, and all contact was suspended, and has remained so through five case reviews.

Until now.

A receptionist behind a reinforced glass screen asks her to take a seat. She does so and waits, her FitSo tracking the time passing and her heart rate rising. Where is Zayn? Where is Ms Dafé? Why doesn't anyone tell her anything?

Her nerve-shredded English-breakfasted bowels grumble. Reluctant to leave the waiting room, but unable to hold on, she goes to the toilet. Completely voided, she returns to find a woman with a yellow batwing top, clipped hair and red lipstick looking around the empty room as if there's a nasty smell, as if she might find a bit of rotten food lurking somewhere, or perhaps a decaying corpse.

'Abigail Speakman?' she says. They exchange a nod. 'Ayo Dafé. Follow me, please.'

Despite her familiarity with the machinations of this system, the formality almost winds Abbie. Ms Dafé knows all about her past: all her misdemeanours, all the history of these meetings going tits-up. She is led into a small room, empty except for a table with what looks like a walkie-talkie sitting on it.

It's only when Ms Dafé asks her to blow into it that Abbie sees the white tube on the side and realises she is being breathalysed. She is being checked for sobriety before seeing her own child.

Luckily, the wine from the night before doesn't affect the reading. Ms Dafé leads her on to a medium-sized room with a 'homey' sofa just like the one in reception and a dirty window looking out over Hotwells and the river. It's a nice view, but Abbie's eye is drawn to the boy, small for ten, sitting at a table staring out at it. He has his back to her and doesn't turn when she enters. Someone has shaved lines into his cropped hair. Abbie hates them. They scream 'thug'. This will have to change when he returns to live with her and Rachel and Beansprout. She'll let it grow out and she'll cornrow it, like she did when he was little.

'Zayn, your mum's here.' Ms Dafé sits in an armchair near the door. 'Don't you want to say hello?'

The boy doesn't move.

'Hello, Zayn love,' Abbie says. She moves round him and sits at the end of the table, where, even if he doesn't turn his head, he can see her in his peripheral vision. Where she might once have shouted at him – even slapped him – for not acknowledging her, she feels able to sit and wait him out. She grudgingly admits to herself that this new aptitude for patience and calm is one good thing she has learned from Rachel.

Eventually Zayn turns to look at her.

'How are you doing, babe?' she asks him.

'All right,' he mumbles into his collar. His voice sounds deeper than she remembers. It hasn't already broken, has it? She can't believe that.

'How's the home?' she asks him.

Ms Dafé pipes up. 'He's with a foster family right now.'

This is news to Abbie. She tries to swallow down her anger at not being told. 'Are they nice, your foster parents?' She hopes they aren't like any of the people who took her on, who were either abusive or unable to control her rage, or, more usually, both.

Zayn shrugs and looks at the floor. It's like she is a stranger to him. And she is, in a way. Two years it's been since they last let him see her. Almost a quarter of his lifetime. She can't bear it.

Something inside her breaks. She stands so suddenly that she sends her chair flying, grabs his arm and pulls him towards her. She clasps him and puts her face in his close-cropped hair, smelling coconut shampoo and boy sweat. She is aware that Ms Dafé has sprung to her feet and is tugging at her, trying to get her away from her son. But she's not moving.

'I love you, Zayn, and I love Harry and Taylor, and I'm working hard to make sure we'll all be back together, living under one roof in a big house in the country, with a dog and a horse and your auntie who you've never met and your little baby cousin who isn't born yet.'

'You have to let go of him.' Ms Dafé pulls at her. 'Help! Help! Interview Room Two!'

Zayn squirms in Abbie's arms, trying to push her away, but she keeps going. 'I want you to know that the reason I was how I was was because life was shit to me and broke me, but I've changed. I'm a different person now, a good person. I've made it all better and I'm getting all the proof of that together. I'm going to take you back and I'm going to make sure that you get all the good bits that I missed out on, and we'll be free of all this – the courts and reviews and social workers and places like this that just chip away at us until there's nothing left—'

'Step away from him.' A male voice now. A giant pair of hands are on her, forcibly prising her away from her son. Even the new, fit Abbie can't match this strength. She finds herself panting, her arms pinned behind her by this suddenly materialised security guard. Snot and tears gloss her face, making her look every bit the broken person she has just sworn no longer exists.

Zayn, now cowering under Ms Dafé's batwing, looks at her with round, frightened eyes.

'Have you heard me, Zayn? Have you heard what I said?' Her little boy flinches, and she realises that she is screeching. She breathes and lowers her tone to something more level. 'They can't stop me.'

'You promise?' he says, his voice tiny.

'With all my heart,' she says.

'We're going to have to stop this here,' Ms Dafé tells her, disapproval oozing out of every pore.

'I've got him a present,' Abbie says, as if this is a point in an argument.

Ms Dafé looks at the security guard – who is still restraining Abbie – like he is some authority sent by God.

'You probably don't get many presents, do you?' Abbie asks Zayn. Although she remembers birthdays and Christmases, she's not always been in a position to send him actual gifts. And she knows herself what a big deal it is if you're a child in care and someone bothers to give you something.

'Is that all right with you, Zayn?' Ms Dafé asks.

Zayn nods, looking back down at the floor.

'Can I?' Abbie asks her guard, who reluctantly lets go of her arm. She can sense his alertness, though, so she moves slowly and deliberately towards the jeweller's luxury carrier bag. She pulls out one of the beautiful boxes and hands it to Zayn.

All three adults watch as he opens it, his face betraying nothing.

'Sick,' he says as he pulls out the little pendant.

'Here, let me.' Abbie tries to go to him to show him how to tie the leather thong around his neck, but the guard steps in between them. 'See,' she says, around the side of his bulk, 'it says *Safe* on it. That's what you'll be soon, Zayn. I've got one and I'm going to make sure your sister and your brother get one too, and soon we'll be able to take a photo, all of us together, all wearing our little *Safe* people.'

Realising she is ranting again, she stops talking and watches, tears in her eyes, as her boy touches the pendant. She wishes she was that little bit of silver. How much simpler her life would be.

'Time to go now,' Ms Dafé says. She is clearly still on high alert for Abbie kicking off again. She turns to Zayn. 'That's a nice necklace, isn't it?'

'Yes,' he says. He's not making eye contact with anyone now.

'Would you mind going out to reception with Barry here, please?' Ms Dafé says to him, before turning to the security guard. 'I'll be out in a second. I just need a word with Mum.'

'I'll see you soon, love,' Abbie cries out as Zayn is hustled through the door. 'I'm going to win this for us, you'll see.'

'I'll have to write a report on this, Abigail,' Ms Dafé says, once they are alone. 'I'm not unsympathetic, but I have to look at what just happened from Zayn's point of view. You've not done yourself any favours.'

Abbie can't speak. Despite wanting with every molecule to not lose any more dignity in front of Ms Dafé, her lips are wobbling, the corners turning down like they are weighted.

'I've got presents for Harry and Taylor, too,' she says. 'Can you get them to them for me?'

'I'll see what I can do.' Ms Dafé doesn't sound too certain.

'If you're not sure, I'll find another way.'

'No, leave it with me.'

'You promise?' She takes out one of the boxes and hands over the carrier bag containing the remaining two.

'I promise.' Beneath her professional veneer, pity weighs in Ms Dafé's eyes.

Abbie wants to smash her face in.

She howls all the way back down the hill to the hotel. Glad that she's booked in for two nights, she once again makes use of room service. This time, though, it's a steak and a bottle of champagne, because they are the most expensive things on the menu, and right now, she couldn't care less.

INSTAGRAM POST

rachelhoneyhill
Devon, England
paid partnership with **baby2you_**
2,348 likes

Image
- Selfie of Rachel, taken from below her naked belly. Her linea nigra, popped navel and stretch marks are on full show.

Text
Just had my 36-week check with Sue, my lovely midwife from **@baby2you_**, who is going to see me and Beansprout right the way through… until Beansprout's 18, I hope!
Beansprout is blooming, as you can see.
This is what 36-weeks pregnant looks like.
#pregnant #belly #stretchmarks #nofilter

CHAPTER THIRTY-EIGHT

21 August

Rachel makes herself a spirulina matcha smoothie and forces it down her throat. It's her second breakfast alone in the house, and her ears are ringing with the silence and the emptiness.

If she had known Abbie and that monster on the beach were related, she wouldn't have allowed her anywhere near her house or her baby.

But then of course, had Abbie known about her role in her uncle's death, she wouldn't have applied in the first place.

And now the secret is out on both sides.

'What are we going to do?' she says to Beansprout. She has shaken all the doors and tried all the windows, but Abbie has taken her fingerprint off the locking system. Unbreakable glass and deadbolts running through the frames into steel tubes in the wall mean that she can't even smash her way to freedom.

Poor Sam has tried to hold on, but he's had to resort to the printer paper she has put down on the utility room floor. Even though she's double-bagged the results, the ground floor has acquired a distinctly animal fug.

Without the internet, she is unable even to watch TV, and looking for old phones is not an option because there is no reception at all here, not for phone or for data. If the house were to burn down, she would go with it. If she were to go into labour…

Despite Abbie's assurances, it doesn't bear thinking about.

As it has several times over the past two days, thinking about her situation brings the panic up. Her fingers tingle. If she were to suffer an episode here, alone, God knows what would happen. She hurries to her meditation room, lights some incense and tries to work through a calming yoga series. But offline, and with no physical means of playing music, she only has her uneven breathing for company, and she can't find her flow. She sits and tries to count backwards from a thousand. It's her last-resort meditation technique, but she keeps losing count as her mind drifts to how everything has been upended. How could she have been so trusting? What is Abbie's game?

It's time to find out.

Rachel's bedroom wing has a panic-room function, which means it can be sealed off if ever an intruder were able to penetrate the house's ring-of-steel security. However, the other rooms in the house are secured only by physical locks with old-school keys. Abbie has locked her own rooms and taken the spare set from the key cupboard. But what she doesn't realise is that there is a master set of internal keys in the secret safe that Rachel had installed, because as recent events are proving, you can't fully trust anyone, however well you think you know them.

With shaking hands, Rachel opens Abbie's door and lets herself in. It's the first time she has been in here since Abbie's arrival. It is so well looked after, looks so much like the home of a sane, well-balanced mind, that if it weren't for the proof of her current situation, she would leave, lock the door and put aside any of her worries about the occupant.

A breeze hits her face. Over in the far corner of the room, a window is open. Sensing an opportunity to escape, she rushes towards it, but it is firmly locked on a limiter, with just a fifteen-centimetre gap. She presses her face up against it, drawing the fresh air into her nostrils. While the house is air conditioned, it's a relief to reconnect with the smell of outdoors.

'You look lovely!'

Rachel wheels around. There, right behind her, locked in its cage with plenty of seed and water, is Abbie's bloody budgie, cocking its head sideways and setting one beady eye on her. Wary of her allergy, she backs away.

Searching the rest of the living area, she finds a knitting bag containing a half-made baby coat almost identical to the horrible one she tried to lose. On the coffee table is a pile of recipe books with Post-its stuck in them – *Sauté = to fry; Add salt 2 onions 2 draw out liquid; How 2 make a roo* – and a couple of manuals on make-up and photography. More disturbing is what looks for a terrible, fleeting second like a head severed from its body. Closer inspection reveals that it is in fact just a life-sized make-up practice head, covered in inexpertly executed contouring and ghoulish eyelash extensions.

Rachel rolls her head, clicks out her neck, then moves into Abbie's en suite. The inside of the bathroom cabinet looks almost identical to her own. The same brands are here – from toothpaste to make-up remover to perfume. This does not surprise her. What does give her a shock, however, is that there on the top shelf, above all these familiar bottles and tubes, is that pink jar edition of her special bespoke DNA moisturiser. The one she thought she had lost. The one she – sucker of the century – has on order as a present for the very person who stole it! As she lifts the cream out of the cupboard with the reverence it deserves, something metallic shifts behind it. She reaches up and hooks it out with her forefinger. So familiar is the shape and feel of her discovery that she knows from first touch what it is. There in her hand is her beautiful amber spider ring. Admittedly, she hadn't even noticed it was missing, but even so.

'You little bitch,' she says. The term she would never normally even think about using against another woman seems just about right in this instance.

She slips the ring onto her finger. Then she opens the lid of her moisturiser and inhales its Frankincense essential oil smell like it's a long-lost pal. She reclaims it by patting a small scoop onto her cheek.

Bracing herself, she takes a look in the bathroom bin. It appears to be full of bloodstained toilet roll tampon bundles. But looking closer, she sees that something else is lurking underneath all that.

Covering her hand with toilet roll, she rummages around and is rewarded with an empty packet of Kataquel, a drug she has never heard of. The prescription wrapper bears Abbie's name, and the information leaflet is still inside. Rachel reads, and her eyes grow wide. The drug is an antipsychotic used to treat several illnesses, including bipolar disorder, mania and schizophrenia.

Before today, Rachel would have felt compassion for Abbie. But the fact that she has hidden this from her, the fact that she has lied her way into occupying such a central position in her life, stealing her trust, looking after her precious baby…

It's too much.

As though it's a poisonous snake, she flings the empty packet on the ground and stamps on it. She has to stand still afterwards, hands on Beansprout, breathing and counting to bring herself back under control.

She looks out of the window, at the woodland beyond, no human intervention in sight, hence no need for obscure glass. Never has outdoors looked more attractive. Perhaps she'll die here, shut in, and not be found until someone wonders why she hasn't posted for a while…

Fingers tingle, vision swims.

No.

She mustn't panic. Whatever Abbie's plan is, it involves Rachel and Beansprout being well and healthy. She will be coming back.

Won't she?

And if – *when* – she does, Rachel must remain calm, keep her cool, until she sees her opportunity to raise the alarm or escape.

She moves through to the bedroom, which again, in its tidy and ordered state, looks decidedly unpromising. The bedside table offers no surprises other than that Abbie has a taste for young adult novels written – or ghosted – by influencers.

Having grown up in dorms where privacy was at a premium, Rachel knows where a girl might hide her secrets. As if she's saving the best for last, she gets down on her knees and lifts the bed throw. And of course: underneath the bed is a box. She pulls it out. But before she opens it, she also visits that other place beloved of girls with personal lives they don't wish others to know about. Reaching under the mattress, she is immediately rewarded with the gift of a fat exercise book, its pages crinkled with writing and use.

Book or box? Box or book? She sits for a couple of moments deciding. Then, her back twingeing, she carries them both through to the living room and sits on the sofa.

'May I come out, please?'

Once again the bloody budgie makes her jump out of her skin. But as she looks at it, she realises that she and it are both in very similar situations.

'Poor thing, all locked up,' she says.

'You're gorgeous.'

She's not getting any allergic reaction, and they've been in the same space now for a good fifteen minutes. Perhaps she's got over it. It is, after all, years since she last had an attack. And it's not like he's a big bird.

'Let's set you free, then.' She goes over to his cage and unclips the door. The bird makes no move to escape.

'Stockholm syndrome?' she asks it.

'Nice tits,' the bird says.

'Thank you.' She goes back to the sofa, trying to picture Abbie teaching the bird to say such things.

She opens the lid of the box and is confronted by a picture of a young woman with two grubby children – one barely a toddler – and what looks like a newborn baby hanging off her. The woman looks tired. She has a black eye and stringy hair, and her pale, fleshy body seems to be seeping out of her stained clothes. She scowls at the camera as if it has just caught her out. Rachel holds the photo up to her face and realises those green eyes could only belong to one person.

The whole set-up of the photograph – Abbie's clothing, the state of the children, the state of the room behind them – tells Rachel that this is not a picture of her at work with someone's else's children.

Her heart thumping, her hands shaking, she lifts the photo to find many more pictures of the children at different ages, each telling the same sad story. And below them, more nasty baby knits, three tiny snipped-off hospital bracelets – Zayn, Harry and Taylor James. The tattoos. Poor children. Named for pop stars. And where are they now?

Where are they now?

Rachel grabs the book and starts turning the pages. This is Abbie's gratitude journal – probably started at her own suggestion.

The early pages of the book, dating back a couple of years, are full of pasted-in pictures and paeans to Rachel, who seems to have been the sole source of gratitude for Abbie at this time. About ten pages in, the whole spread is taken up with the proclamation *I AM RACHEL'S BIGGEST AND BEST FAN EVER*. The hairs on Rachel's forearms prickle.

She turns the page and comes to a pasted-in A3 sheet. Unfolding it, she sees that it contains a family tree drawn in coloured felt-tip. Some of the individuals have photographs stuck above their names, including Abbie's father, who has no name other than Da, and who sits right at the top. His face looks vaguely familiar, rings a dull sort of alarm for Rachel, like he is someone to watch out for and not in a good way. But since he is not named, she has nothing else to go on. It appears that 'Da' has sired at least twenty offspring, which is remarkable in itself. But what really draws Rachel's eye is the photograph of herself at the bottom of the page. It's not just that it's outlined in glitter pen. It's also because this family tree places her as one of those twenty children. The trail of glitter leads from her to Abbie, the word *SISTERS*, in bold capitals and with five exclamation marks, threading along the line.

Rachel gasps. This cannot be true. But however impossible, Abbie has dreamed it into a fact for herself. Flicking quickly forward through the journal, she comes to the part where Abbie has read about the mother's helper post, where she formulates the plan for the fraud she will commit in order to get the job, including contacting someone called Posh June.

Then there's a drawing, which looks like it's been done by a child, of three children and two women sitting on a sofa. Both women look like they are supposed to be Rachel, but while one has a shirt with an R on the front, the other is wearing an A. The one with the A is holding a baby.

Rachel would have read on, but she feels a pair of claws dig into her hair.

'Hey, angel,' the voice above her sings, followed by the sound of a beak preening deep into feathers.

Like someone has pulled the plug on her lungs, Rachel's chest seizes up. Her throat feels like she has a fist jammed down it. Her face grows like it's the moon, and despite a thin, distant voice in her head telling her that she mustn't collapse leaving the book and the box's contents strewn all over the sofa, she falls to the floor, unable to breathe.

Perhaps knowing he has given his best shot for Abbie, once his perch has collapsed beneath him, Barney heads towards the open window.

He only just fits through it.

CHAPTER THIRTY-NINE

One touch of Abbie's fingerprint and the Honeyhill fortress opens with a series of whirs and clicks. As she steps into the house, there's a loud thump upstairs, like a statue has fallen over.

But Rachel doesn't have any statues.

She is later back than she intended. In need of a pee and some fresh air to work off the agitation built up crawling down the grockle-jammed Devon so-called Expressway, she had sailed past the Honeyhill turn-off, carried on for another mile and took the exit for the winding lane down to Red Anchor Bay. By the time she pulled up in a lay-by opposite the isolated school building, she had to fall out of the car to relieve herself on the grass verge. Taking advantage of the lack of passers-by, she changed into her running gear, then headed off, jogging round the top of the semi-tropical valley towards the coast path.

Just being there up on the cliffs, looking down at the scene of the act that ruined her life, made Abbie's face itch. The disappointment trickling into her almost since the day she started working for Rachel had finally filled her up, matured into resentment and was now, she swore, overflowing through her ears, eyes, nostrils, fists.

Above her, one seagull fought another for a dead fish skewered on its beak.

When life gives you shit, fling it back.

She climbed down the crumbling path to the strand, where the sea today was as calm and clear as she remembers the Mediterranean from that one trip to Spain. She took off her trainers and socks and waded in, so that the tiny wavelets kissed her shins. Filtered by the crystal water, her beautifully painted toenails looked so perfect she wanted to cry. This clarity, this calm, contrasted too violently with what was going on inside her.

She took a deep breath, stretched her arms above her head, her fists clenched, and yelled up at the clear blue sky, 'Fuck you, Rachel.'

And then it came to her, simply and clearly. She needed to teach her big sister the great lesson her own life has taught her:

Don't believe you're so bloody special.

The humility bred by such an awakening would make Rachel a better person, and she would finally be able to live the truly authentic life she'd always banged on about.

And then, perhaps, she would actually be worthy of being a mother.

Abbie promised herself that she would be patient, that she would help Rachel with this process. Rachel's Journey, in fact.

'No outside interference, just me and her,' she said out loud to the sea. 'Keeping it in the family.'

She would have swum, if she could, as a sort of rebirth. But she's not one for going in the water. Not even swimming pools, unless she has to.

The sheltered valley was too humid and steep to run, so she picked her way up towards the car. By the time she arrived, she was soaked with sweat and thirsty as a dog in a desert. She took her water bottle from the holder by the driver's seat, but it was empty.

The old school gates loomed up behind the car, the *Keep Out* signs ramming home how she had been excluded from the privilege Rachel had enjoyed. How could anyone be miserable growing up in such an amazing big mansion, in such a beautiful setting?

Remembering how Rachel had drunk from a tap in the school – back in the happy days, she thought mournfully – she walked round the perimeter until she found the hole in the fence. But at the front door, she remembered that Rachel had the key.

Of course Rachel had the bloody key.

This tiny but massively symbolic fact made Abbie's rage bubble over.

It was all Rachel's fault. Every reason her life had gone to shit was down to Rachel.

As she stepped back to see if she could spot a way in, she stumbled on a stone fallen from a rockery edging the overgrown gravel driveway. The shock, and the pain in her palms, which took her weight as they broke her fall, made her suddenly burst into tears.

This, in turn, brought back the many times as a child she had fallen and cried and received no comfort whatsoever from any of the adults paid to look after her.

This, too, was all Rachel's fault.

She looked up at the building, all grand pillars and ivy and tall arched windows, like some Greek temple landed in the Devon countryside. Fury flashing through her, she picked up the stone that had tripped her and, taking a running jump at one of the beautiful windows, flung it like a Russian girl with a shot-put.

The window smashed, raining glass onto the stone terrace beneath it.

'Wicked,' she said, smiling.

Her thirst forgotten, she headed back to the car.

The statue thump is followed by a noise like someone is vacuuming up there with a wheezy old hoover, banging the furniture.

Rachel says it is against her religion to do housework. And anyway, Abbie thinks, she should be sitting in her meditation room reflecting on all the things she is doing wrong in her life, not procrastinating or deflecting by floor-cleaning.

Abbie's mood is not good right now. The privilege that annoyed her down at the school is also seeping through the walls of this building, irritating her like a rank stink.

'Down, boy,' she snaps at Sam, who has run down the stairs towards her and is agitatedly trying to tug at her sleeve. He obeys her order, but still stands at the bottom of the stairs, whimpering.

'What do you want?' she asks him.

He starts back up the stairs.

'Rachel? What are you doing?' she calls out as she follows.

The noise isn't coming from Rachel's floor, though. When Sam leads her up to her own rooms, she sees with a stab of fury that the door to her private space is wide open. There on the floor, her head banging against the coffee table leg, is Rachel, her lips all swollen, her hands at her throat like she's trying to rip it open.

'Help!' Rachel says, her voice a tiny rasp. She looks like she is drowning under the weight of her big round baby belly. 'EpiPen!' she cries, then arches her back and goes horribly still.

Abbie turns and runs down the stairs to Rachel's bedroom. Thanks to her housekeeper's knowledge of the contents of the house, she knows exactly where to look. Unwrapping the EpiPen as she goes, she returns to her living room, kneels beside Rachel, pulls down her running tights and whacks the big needle into her thigh.

'Please, please, please,' she says, slapping Rachel's cheeks, seeing everything she has worked for falling apart if she doesn't come round. 'Come on, Beansprout, come on, Rachel…'

Suddenly the adrenaline hits Rachel's heart, and taking a massive in-breath, she sits up with such force that Abbie is knocked flying.

Her joy at having saved Rachel and Beansprout is slashed by what her receding tunnel vision now allows her to see, spread all over her coffee table and sofa.

'You bloody snoop,' she snarls at Rachel.

'You bloody thief,' Rachel wheezes, struggling to her feet, her fists swinging like a prize fighter readying for a knockout blow. 'And you bloody liar.'

'I saved your bloody life.' Abbie jumps up, ready to weigh in herself, and in doing so, she sees Barney's cage propped open, and the window she left ajar just enough to allow him some nice fresh air.

'Where is he?' she says.

Rachel looks round at the cage. 'He landed on my *head*.'

'You've let him fly away!' Abbie is at the window, staring out, trying to spot the little speck of green that has been her anchor, her saviour, over the long, lonely days since her children were taken away from her.

She turns, her vision swimming in red, but Rachel is heading for the door. Sensing Abbie's distress, Sam has taken her side, and is now all ears back, snarling at his former mistress.

'Don't you dare,' Abbie says to her.

But Rachel picks up speed, holding on to Beansprout as if she is going to fall out of her.

She's not fast enough for Abbie, though, who is on her before she can even reach the door. Sam has circled round and is barking at Rachel from the front.

'You're not going anywhere,' Abbie says. 'I don't trust you as far as I can throw you.'

She pulls Rachel backwards to the kitchen area, where with her free hand she opens a wall cupboard, pulls out the saucepan in which she hid the items she used on Charlotte Williams and tips them out onto the work surface.

'Didn't find this lot nosing through, did you, eh?' she says to Rachel as she sorts through them.

'What are they for?' Rachel asks.

'My secret.' Abbie spits the words at her. 'Just so you know, though, everything I did with them, I did for you.' She elbows Rachel's head down onto the worktop, and with one hand holding her arms behind her back, she uses the other to wind duct tape around her wrists.

'What are you going to do with me?' Rachel says.

But Abbie covers her mouth with tape so that she can't ask any more difficult questions. Her fingers itch as she looks at the knife, the spirits of salts, the hair straighteners. She really wants to hurt Rachel, but she knows she can't, not with Beansprout there.

Barney's empty cage stands over on the other side of the room, a warning sign of what could happen if she ever trusts Rachel again.

It's a massive responsibility.

How is Abbie going to teach her sister about humility, privilege and comfort?

A plan starts to form in her head.

Take it back to where it all started.

CHAPTER FORTY

'Please. I'm sorry.'

Rachel is exhausted. After her anaphylactic attack, she's worried about Beansprout, and she's worried about herself.

But Abbie continues to silently wrap duct tape around her ankles, to add to the strip she wound around her wrists up at Honeyhill before she drove her down here to the school. As she works, she tells her the story of her three children and how they were taken off her.

If it wasn't for the situation she's in, hearing all that, Rachel would feel truly sorry for her.

'All done.' Abbie stands up and leaves the house mother's room, shutting the door and leaving Rachel alone, curled up on the floor.

As she lies there in the dusty, mildew-scented room, she can hear Abbie dragging something large across the floor of the dorm outside. The giant suitcase she brought with her in the car and lugged through the hole in the fence sits against the wall, directly in Rachel's eyeline. The thought of why Abbie has brought her here, and what she plans to do with the suitcase, fills her with terror.

'Are you going to kill me?' she asks outright, as Abbie opens the door and drags in one of the beds from the dorm.

Abbie stops what she is doing and looks at her. 'What kind of monster do you think I am?' she says, her lip just slightly curling.

Turning back to the bed, she drags it against the wall next to Rachel. She moves over to the suitcase, hoists it up onto the ancient mattress and starts to unzip it. 'It's actually got stuff in it to make you more comfortable.'

She pulls out a clean white duvet, pillows and sheets and makes the bed with them. 'There. I checked and there aren't any peas under the mattress, so, Your Highness, you should be able to sleep quite soundly.'

She drags her up and levers her over so that she is lying on the bed, uncomfortable on her back, Beansprout pressing on her sciatic nerve.

'You're going to leave me here?'

Abbie sits on the duvet and folds her arms. 'You can't be trusted up at Honeyhill.'

'I'm sorry it was your uncle on the beach. And I promise I'll not snoop in your things again. I'll buy you a new bird. I'll do whatever you want. I'll stop posting—'

'I don't want you to stop posting. I just want you to post *better*.'

'I'll post better, then.'

'You just don't get it, do you? You actually killed my uncle and never owned up to it.'

'He thought he'd killed me. He would have killed Fran.'

'Why should I believe you? You lie about everything else.' Abbie breathes in so quickly, her nostrils flare. 'And about the snooping: basic decency should mean you wouldn't even think about looking in my stuff. And that wasn't any bird you can buy a replacement for. It was Barney. No. You're going to have to change, Rachel, and prove to me that you've changed, before I can let you be mum to Beansprout.'

'What?'

'You heard what I said. I'm keeping you here so that you can really think about what you've done and how you can do things better, so that you're not lying and misleading people all the time.'

'I don't!'

'Oh, you do.' Going back to the suitcase, she lifts out the sharp boning knife sent to Rachel by that idiot PR. Rachel flinches and closes her eyes as Abbie steps towards her, the sharp blade held in front of her.

'Don't be mental, Rachel. I'm not going to hurt you,' she says. 'I'm cutting you free so you can have a cuppa.'

So, instead of slicing Rachel's throat, Abbie uses the knife to cut through the duct tape around her wrists. Rachel looks at her newly freed hands, flexes her fingers, makes sure everything is working. But then Abbie takes her by her shoulders and pulls her top half forwards. Along with stomach acid from her poor squeezed innards, she feels a ball of panic working up into her throat. 'Please…' she says.

'Just making you comfy,' Abbie says as she plumps the pillows she has put on the bed and places them behind Rachel's back. 'Nice?'

Rachel almost laughs. The situation she's in couldn't be further away from 'nice' and 'comfy'.

'Not speaking now? Suit yourself.' Abbie returns to the suitcase and pulls out a kettle, a loaf of bread, apples, oranges, peanut butter, a plate, bowl and mug and a handful of cutlery.

'This is just enough to keep you going,' she says, laying them out on the mantelpiece of a once-grand fireplace Rachel remembers Miss Chamberlain lighting a fire in in the winter. 'I'll be down at least twice a day with food for you.'

She returns to the suitcase, grabs a roll of toilet paper, a towel, soap and shampoo, and puts them in the little shower room off the main room. 'None of your fancy high-maintenance products here. You're going to learn how to live with just a few simple things. Enough to fit in a suitcase, or a bin bag, like when you get moved between foster parents, or from children's home to children's home. Then perhaps you'll start to learn a thing or two.'

She fills the kettle and plugs it in. 'I'll make us both a nice cup of tea, though. I'm not a complete brute.' She smiles at Rachel as if she has just cracked a joke.

'Why is how I behave so important to you, Abbie? If I offend you so much, why don't you just leave?'

'As you know, from all your poking around in my private business, you are in fact my sister. I owe it to you to help you change.'

'Tell me how you think that's true.'

'Although with me being your little sister, it's *you* should be setting an example to me.'

'Why do you think we're sisters?'

'We've got the same colour eyes.'

'But—'

'We've got the SAME COLOUR EYES.'

Abbie pushes her face up against Rachel's and Rachel is too scared to say anything more. The kettle boils and Abbie turns to it. She pours boiling water over two tea bags that she has placed in two RR branded mugs. 'My da is your da. He's got lots of children round here. Our half-brothers and sisters, although you won't want to meet any of them, they're all tossers and losers. He had your mum and she got pregnant with you.'

'Who is your da, Abbie?'

'You saw him when you were snooping in my stuff. Didn't you recognise him from the photos?'

'I thought I'd seen his face somewhere.'

'Does the name Wayne Speakman mean anything to you?'

Rachel takes a deep breath. Her face prickles. Any woman her age would remember Speakman, the man who made the streets of Bristol off limits after dark. Even visiting the city by day, you would have your guard up. Speakman's reign of terror lasted five years, leaving at least three women dead. He didn't cooperate with police, so they reckon he could be responsible for the fates of up to ten others – on top of the countless others left traumatised by his attacks. 'That's your father?' she says. One rapist uncle is bad enough, but to come from this monster? This is the blood Abbie has brought into Rachel's house?

As she processes this, she realises with a stab of horror that the somewhere she thought she had seen Abbie's da before wasn't news reports from over twenty years ago. It was her own living room, the time Charley forgot to lock the gates and a muddy freckled stranger wandered in.

Was that really Wayne Speakman standing in her house that evening? 'He's still in prison, isn't he?' she asks, praying that she's wrong and he's still safely locked away, and not some twisted part of this grand plan of Abbie's.

'He's in a special hospital,' Abbie says. 'But he's clever. He got away a few years ago, came back this way.'

'They caught him again, though?'

'After three whole days.'

Rachel's mouth is so dry it tastes like dust. 'They need to lock him up and throw away the key.'

'Hey. That's our da you're talking about. He's just got something wrong in his head. Like you.'

'That's because of an injury. Your uncle hit me, over and over…'

But Abbie isn't listening. 'Blood is thicker than water, Rachel.'

Rachel shakes her head. 'He can't be my father.'

'You may not like it, but it's true. He knew your mum really well. She went to the Shepherd and His Pack, and they had a great romantic fling, and the dates work out. He's got to be your da. And he's not such a bad man as they make out; it's more complicated than that. He's clever and he's funny, and he knows all the right things to say.'

'But I was adopted.'

Abbie stops talking, her hand half extended with the mug of tea. 'What?'

'My mum wasn't able to have children. She adopted me as a baby. It's one of the reasons Beansprout is so important to me.'

Abbie turns away and puts the tea on the floor. She walks over to the far wall and leans against it, her back to Rachel. 'What.'

'It's why my grandparents didn't want anything to do with me. In their eyes, I wasn't theirs. Not really.'

Abbie hits the wall with her clenched fist, again and again, until her blood smears the pummelled plaster. With each blow, Rachel curls further into herself, a foetus around her foetus.

Abbie turns to face her. 'You're lying. I know we're sisters. I knew from the first moment I saw you that we're linked, that we are part of the same thing.'

Rachel knows she has to keep Abbie talking, or that force she used on the wall, on her bleeding knuckles, will be turned against her, and she is in no position to defend herself. So she sits still as she talks, her fingers secretly working away at the duct tape around her ankles. 'Tell me about that first moment, Abbie. When was it? What happened?'

Abbie tells her about a workshop she once ran, ten years ago, in Calstock, for looked-after children. 'You remember me, yeah?' she says. 'Well, you might not think it was me, because I looked very different then, skinny, with really short, bleached hair. But you must remember the connection we had. The way we looked at each other, the charge that passed between us. You recognised it in me so much that you called me into the tent.'

'What tent?' Rachel says.

'The tent you were running the workshop in!' Abbie says it furiously. 'Don't pretend you don't remember. Don't!'

Rachel really doesn't remember.

'Thing is, Abbie, I did a lot of those sorts of things back then. I'd just qualified as a yoga teacher and personal trainer and was just starting out and I needed to earn money.'

'You remember me. Look!' Abbie scrapes her hair back, sucks in her cheeks, pushes her face towards Rachel and stares into her eyes. 'Look!'

Rachel looks at her, and all she can think is how la-la scary crazy Abbie actually is. She has no memory whatsoever of this event, and like the authentic being Abbie is trying to force her to be, she can't hide the fact. She starts to try to explain.

'Ten years ago was a hard time for me—'

'It was a hard time for me, too.'

'I was still struggling with my addictions.'

'You qualified as a yoga teacher.'

'As you so rightly point out, I'm good at being two-faced. I spent six weeks in Goa to get my qualification, stoned or drunk most of the time, and no one suspected a thing. You'd be surprised, anyway, how many of my classmates were doing this or that drug. We were all in some way needy.'

'Poor little rich girls going all the way to some beach in Thailand.'

'India. And it's not like that. It's the cheapest way—'

'Spare me yet another sob story, Rachel.'

'So when I did this workshop in Plymouth—'

'Calstock. It was in CALSTOCK.'

'My perception was still shot, as was my memory.'

'So what are you saying?'

'I'd probably had a few drinks. It helped with my nerves. Early on, I got a sort of stage fright. You would have been a blur to me.'

'But our eyes. They met. Our matching green eyes.'

Rachel reaches up and pinches her right eyeball. A tiny flap of green-tinted plastic comes away, squashed between her thumb and forefinger.

She looks back at Abbie with one pale grey iris, then proceeds to do the same thing to her left eye. She hit upon inserting the invisible barrier of monthly green contact lenses when, after The Event, she couldn't look herself in the eye.

'This is me,' she tells Abbie. 'This is the authentic me you want me to be.'

'You *liar*. You *fake*.' Abbie is backing away, shaking her head.

'I know.'

'You don't deserve me.'

'I'll do whatever you want me to do,' Rachel says. 'I will change my profile. I'll not lie any more. I'll hand over all my savings. I'll welcome Zayn, Harry and Taylor into my home—'

'Don't even put their names in your filthy mouth!'

'—if you'll just let me go. Let me go back to Honeyhill, and we'll live happily ever after. It doesn't matter that we're not related, it—'

Abbie's cheeks are grey. Her whole body trembles with rage. 'You're my fucking sister!' she yells. 'And you're going to stay here until you admit it.'

'Please—'

'If I don't go now, I don't know what—'

She storms towards the door, takes the key and leaves, locking Rachel in.

'Please!' Rachel cries out. 'Please don't leave me! My baby! I…'

But she hears the door to the dorm slam shut, and Abbie's footsteps retreating out of the building. A few minutes later, the artificially composed sound of the electric Jeep breaks the silence, and Abbie is gone.

Rachel is on her own, locked in her old school building. The darkness she is so scared of is falling, and as it does, the ghosts move in. She looks up at the ceiling, her heart pounding in her ears. Even if there was electricity, the overhead fluorescent is smashed.

She lies on the bed, trying to make a plan. But her lines of thought are disrupted by a hot, squeezing pain in her belly.

There is no one to hear her scream.

In the delirium of the agony, she imagines she feels a hand on her forehead.

A whisper in her ear.

'You can do this.'

INSTAGRAM POST

OmCrystal_3487
Bromsgrove, England
23,560 likes

Image
- OmCrystal in her local Bromsgrove park, her hand at her brow, peering into the distance.

Text
Looking for **@rachelhoneyhill**.
Where's today's post?
Anybody seen RR?
#wheresRachel #wheresRR #wheresrachelhoneyhill

CHAPTER FORTY-ONE

Abbie storms into Honeyhill. What is she going to do now? What is going to happen between her and Rachel? She spends an hour in the gym, looking at herself in the mirror as she runs on the treadmill, at the sweat sticking her little *Safe* pendant to her chest.

She wants to rip the leather thong from her neck, but manages to stop herself.

'Defeat is not an option. You can do this,' she says to herself, as instructed by Rachel back in the days when Abbie thought she could teach her things. 'You are strong.'

She dead-lifts eighty kilos, swings the heaviest kettlebell, then sluices her body underneath a shower so hot that it nearly raises blisters on her arms.

Yet still her worked-out abs clench in anger, channelling all her energy towards her centre, where it builds and festers like hot pus in a boil.

Still steaming from the shower, with Sam sitting faithfully at her feet, she perches on her sofa, clearing up after Rachel yet again by putting her special things back in their special order into her special box.

Barney's empty cage looms over her.

Everything she has been working towards is broken.

She unfolds her pasted-in family tree. All those brothers and sisters, all of Da's children. Like a brainwashed cult member whose leader has been shown to be a fraud, she still can't shake off the belief that has been the centre of her being for so long. There *has* to be a connection between her and Rachel, despite what Rachel says. Perhaps her birth mother was from round here, slept with Da and—

'Don't be stupid, Abigail.' In one sharp movement she rips the family tree from her journal and tears it to shreds. Then she looks at her five-point plan, which seemed so clear to her when she wrote it after hearing about Rachel's pregnancy:

1. Buy a nice interview suit and get your hair done.

2. Get the job with Rachel.

Both of these items have ticks against them. Tears stinging her eyes, she reads on.

After Beansprout is born:

3. Tell her the truth about being sisters.

4. Get her to vouch for you so Zayn, Harry and Taylor can come and live with you.

5. All live happily ever after.

'All live happily ever after.' Abbie turns back to her box and looks at the photograph on the top, of herself sitting with her children.

'What a mess, Sam,' she says, pointing at the picture. And her scraps of children, the damage already there in their eyes. Even she can see that. She looks at them, and all she feels is tired. The fights she's had over them, the crying she's done. Her son in the Contact Centre in Bristol. Is there ever any hope he will love her, respect her? Will she ever be able to turn the clock back?

'The past is another country.' She quotes the Rachelism at Sam. 'One we can never visit again.'

She rips up the photograph, rips up the five-point plan, rips all the pages from her journal and shreds them into tiny pieces.

Sam likes the destruction of her past. He thinks it's a great game.

She gathers together all the bits of paper and stuffs them into her waste-paper basket. With Sam running beside her, she carries the basket down the stairs and out of the large bifold door onto the back garden, where she empties it onto the fire bowl. She goes back into the house, finds matches and firelighters, plugs the router back in and tells Google to play Lady Gaga at maximum volume.

She sings once more that she's on the edge of glory, and dances around her past as it goes up in flames.

Perhaps she really is.

She falls panting to the ground and watches the last charred pages curl and turn to smoke, enjoying the way the bonfire smell obliterates the farm stink from next door. Out of the blue, something light and scratchy lands on her head. Any other person would flinch. Some might even scream. But Abbie knows who this is.

'Hello, stunner,' Barney says, as he rootles his beak through her hair.

Her spirit soars up into the sky from which he has just descended like a little feathered Jesus.

It's a sign.

Anything is possible, she thinks. Anything at all.

The real sign happens next, though, when Sam, guarding his new mistress, the most important person in his world, acting with all his doggy instinct, leaps into the air and with one quick, brutal snap decapitates the little green bird.

That makes Abbie scream. She screams and rages, and tries to catch poor bewildered Sam, but he reads the signs and makes himself scarce. With her bare foot she kicks over the white-hot fire bowl, burning her toes and sending embers flying all over the dry lawn.

She hobbles into the house, shutting the glass wall behind her so that the murdering dog can't get in. Then she flings herself face down onto the sofa.

Why does everything have to turn bad?

Why does everyone turn against her?

She pummels the cushions until there is no more punch left in her.

Safe, indeed.

Eventually, Sam scratching at the window makes it impossible for her to ignore him. When he has her attention, he sits there patiently, waiting for her to let him in. Someone who knows nothing about dogs would imagine that the sheepish way he is looking at her implies remorse. But he is only feeling bad because she punished him. He was only following his dog nature, doing his best for her, when he attacked poor Barney.

While she can't forgive Rachel for letting Barney fly out of the window, she can just about find it in her heart to forgive Sam. In fact, she thinks, the fury stirring at her insides yet again, it is all Rachel's fault that poor Barney is dead.

Abbie looks at Sam. Sam looks at Abbie. He melts her heart.

In the end, she lets him in, and his gratitude, displayed through low-status crawling towards her, holding out his paw and nuzzling into her leg, entirely resets her feelings towards him.

'You're hungry, boy,' she says, now down on the floor, holding him tight in her arms. Him and her both. She hasn't eaten since her feast the night before.

She opens a tin of the meaty beef chunk dog food she bought for him when she went to visit Da. He tucks in like it's all his Christmases come at once.

'She used you to earn money to flog that shitty VeggieDog, didn't she, Sam? And did she get your consent? No she didn't.'

As she makes herself a massive plate of spaghetti with a whole jar of pesto stirred into it and half a block of Rachel's emergency non-vegan Parmesan, she mulls over this idea of consent. She had to give hers, signed, on a form, in order for Rachel to use her. And boy, how Rachel used her.

She sits down with a fork and spoon and mechanically works her way through the mounded bowl of gluten-rich, animal-fat-enhanced carbohydrate. 'And how will Rachel use Beansprout?' she asks Sam, who is waiting at her side for any scraps she may throw his way. It's a bad habit, one that demonstrates how unqualified Rachel is to own any animal.

Or, indeed, any child.

'She'll use her right from the moment she's born,' Abbie says. 'And she won't even give a second's thought about whether the poor baby would consent or not.'

She chews and thinks about this. It's another big negative for Rachel. Another point to prove that she shouldn't be allowed to keep her baby.

'Imagine,' she says to Sam, 'if the Abbie of two years ago had tried to plaster her children all over social media to try to make money out of them. Social services would have been all over her in an instant.'

Despite it setting a bad precedent, she dangles a strand of spaghetti in front of Sam's nose and watches how gently he takes it between his teeth. So different to the treatment he meted out to poor Barney.

So much loss Abbie has had to deal with.

Why shouldn't she gain, just once?

She closes her eyes and, like she did when Juno took her picture, transports herself back to the place she was happiest, with the foster parents who took her to Spain and showed her the respect she had craved all her life – until she tested them one too many times by attempting to set their house on fire a few months later, but she glosses over that.

She puts her 'now' self into the vision, adjusting the eyelines to her own adult level. White sand, calm sea, and sky so blue you wouldn't believe it. The sound of happy children laughing in a little shaded play park. She's walking along the palm-fringed promenade, stepping in sand-gritted sandals on the lozenge-shaped pavers. In her mouth, the taste lingers of that special Spanish chocolate milk. Everything feels good, in a way it never has again since that holiday. She's pushing a state-of-the-art buggy. In it, cosy in a leopard-print fake-fur snuggler – too warm for the weather, but hey, it's a fantasy – is Beansprout.

'Hey, Daz,' she coos at the imaginary baby in the imaginary buggy in her imaginary Spain. That's what she'll call her. In honour of her late uncle, so wronged. Short for Darlene, perhaps, if Rachel is right about her being a girl. Darren, of course, if it's a boy.

Fuelled by this vision, she gets up from the table, does the washing-up, dries it and puts it away like a civilised person.

How can she make this dream come true?

What would Da do?

It all suddenly becomes clear to her. She hangs up her tea towel to dry and heads for the office. 'Time for a little admin,' she tells Sam. 'And don't worry,' she adds, 'I'm not going to leave you behind, even though you are a dirty bird murderer. We all do unpleasant things from time to time.'

Thanks to Wanda's inefficiencies, it takes a while, but after scouring the office computer and going through the filing cabinets, Abbie manages to locate and log on to all of Rachel's savings accounts. She has Rachel's phone beside her to get through the double security process, and within two hours, she has tipped two hundred thousand pounds into the current account. It seems that Rachel wasn't as broke as Abbie initially thought. Never having had any spare cash, the possibility of savings hadn't really occurred to her until Rachel mentioned it a couple of hours ago. This – rather than Wanda's bank account – is where all the money was disappearing to, but Abbie refuses to feel bad about that.

Two hundred grand is an unimaginable amount, more than enough to set her, Daz and Sam up for their new life in Spain.

She writes a new five-point plan: a list of details to be taken care of.

1. Sam: pet passport? Jabs?

2. Daz: passport.

3. Me: passport.

4. Flights to Spain.

5. Rachel?

Next, she fires off a text on her Galaxy to get Posh June on to the issue of paperwork – including a passport for herself under a fake name: 'Take your pick,' she tells PJ. She's decided that in order to keep the trail minimal, she'll just get a train to the airport after she picks up the papers, and buy plane tickets when she gets there – she supposes that's what you do. That's everything worked out except that last item. Rachel. She draws another, massive, question mark beside it.

What would Da do?

She sleeps on it, and in the night she has a few ideas.

In the morning, she whizzes up a protein smoothie, packs up the leftover pasta and the rest of the Parmesan and two large bottles of water. With everything in a large rucksack, she takes Sam off for a walk across the early-morning fields, towards the old school.

INSTAGRAM POST

NelWarrior_06
Aberdeen, Scotland
230 likes

Image
- Graphic RR, followed by a question mark.

Text
Where is **@rachelhoneyhill**?
#wheresRachel #wheresRR #wheresrachelhoneyhill

CHAPTER FORTY-TWO

22 August

Rachel barely sleeps all night. She rides three episodes of hot, squeezing pain radiating down the backs of her legs – which at least she has released from their duct-tape bonds – and out into her fingertips. She spends the time in between praying they are just practice-run Braxton Hicks.

But she is shocked and floored by the pain. She remembers telling Abbie her theory that with the right breathing, labour is like an extended orgasm with a bit of period pain.

'We'll see,' Abbie said, counselling her not to rule out pain relief entirely. Of course, Rachel realises now, Abbie *knew* what it was like. What a fool she must have seemed to her.

If this is a taste of what's in store, then rather than the natural water birth she's been preparing with Sue at Baby2You – and, she thinks, in a moment of hope, won't they raise the alarm if she's not around for her next appointment? – she now wants all the drugs and gas that modern medicine can throw at her.

But while she is going through the pain, at least it takes her mind off the cold fear of being alone in this ghost of a building, with no light and no one to hear her scream.

Each time something of her better self tries to breathe through the fear, and then through the pain, a rising panic takes over, and she finds herself dizzy and short of air. Speckled shapes form and haze away in the darkness, strange rustlings and scratches move around her. Outside, the wind brings the distant roar of the sea, reminding her there is a world out there that she can't reach.

Then she explodes in a cascade of prickling nerves and loses herself and time.

She comes round to find her bedding torn, the kettle, the plates, the mugs smashed on the floor, her feet bleeding from the crockery shards all over the floor.

Why did it have to come then, to be exerted on inanimate objects, rather than later, and on Abbie?

But oh, thank God she hadn't given birth, and…

No.

She doesn't want to think of it. It conjures hideous images of herself, like that awful Goya painting she remembers seeing at school that gave her nightmares for years after: *Saturn Devouring His Son*.

'I'm not fit to be a mother,' she says, riding the next wave of contractions, crawling towards the bed through the cracked china. 'Not fit to be a mother…'

Coming round again, she finds her mind on her profile. What's happening out there? Her work must be falling down all around her…

But then the cold white realisation comes to her: for the first time in many years, all that is an irrelevance. What she needs to worry about now is that she is captive here in this abandoned building, with her baby on the verge of being born.

Perhaps, she thinks with a laugh that would be read as manic were there anyone to hear it, *this* is Abbie's lesson.

How much more in-real-life-authentic can you get?

She howls like a wolf as she is taken on another ride of white-hot pain.

She thinks she hears a voice in her ear: 'You can do this. You can do this.'

'WHAT?' she screams into the dark, empty building.

It is only when the thin grey dawn arrives that she can finally close her eyes and spin a few moments of static oblivion.

She's on the toilet, clutching herself, holding her belly in place as the squeezes of another contraction subside, when the dorm door thirty paces away clangs. In a second, she is blearily on her feet, the bottle of cheap shampoo Abbie left with her somehow in her hands, the intention to use it as a weapon fully formed in her brain.

Her knees still shaking from the onslaught of the last contraction, she stumbles to the locked door of her room, and stands to one side with the shampoo bottle open and ready.

The key rattles in the door and Abbie steps carelessly into the room. Instantly Rachel squeezes the bottle so the thin shampoo squirts straight into her eyes. She follows that up by swiping the bottle across Abbie's face, the hard plastic spout gouging into her cheek. Abbie screams and swears and rubs at her eyes. Rachel dances past her and pelts across the main dorm, moving surprisingly quickly for a woman in her position, belly, bloody feet and all. Sam is on her heels, barking at her, trying to stop her.

'No, Sam, down!' she says, but as with everything else, it seems like she has also lost control of him. He sinks his teeth into her calf, so she reaches down and punches him away.

'Don't hurt the *dog*!'

Abbie's roar behind her tells her she needs to move fast. Using the momentum of her weight, she lurches forward and through the dorm door, out into the long corridor. Her bare feet pick up speed along the murky parquet, and it feels like she is flying towards freedom. She has run this stretch of the building many times as a girl, late for breakfast in term time, bored and racing with Fran in the holidays when the school was almost as empty as it is now.

'Stop *now*, Rachel, you come back here right *now!*' Abbie's yelled commands, close behind her, just spur her on.

She slams through the door at the end of the corridor and out onto the grand landing. Leaning on the banister, she half runs, half falls down the sweeping staff-only staircase. Thanks to adrenaline, her relatively greater fitness and, possibly, the instinct of an animal in urgent need of a safe place to give birth, she is managing to put distance between herself and Abbie. There before her is the front door, slightly open, fresh air and morning light filtering through. She pushes on it and stumbles out onto the gravel driveway, pelting across the brambled lawn, not even feeling her feet, which, in addition to her crockery injuries, are now studded with thorns.

Abbie is barely through the door, and Rachel is nearly at the hole in the fence, nearly at a point where she can either run down into the jungly valley and find a hiding place, a nest to do her birthing, or try running uphill to the lane and then to the road to hopefully flag down a passing car. These are her two plans, and she doesn't know which one she will take. But before she has to make the decision, a giant wave of a contraction sucks her in from her feet to her head, pulls her inwards and outwards and stops her in her tracks. She falls to her hands and knees and roars.

There is no release. A kick from behind floors her. As she rolls over onto her back to protect her belly, a large stone, held between two hands comes down again and again on her lower right leg, which is already bloody from dog bites.

'You do *not* hit Sam,' Abbie is saying, over and over. 'You do *not* escape.'

'Help me!' Rachel screams.

A massive contraction rocks her, takes her far away, and she thinks she is by a roaring fire in a ski lodge somewhere in the Alps, her legs burning from a day out on the slopes…

'You're having the baby?' Abbie finally realises.

'YES I'M BLOODY HAVING THE BLOODY BABY.'

'Save your energy for the important things.'

Abbie's voice cuts through the howl Rachel realises is coming from her own throat.

Somehow, her surroundings have changed. She is back in the house mother's room, her body a total expression of pain – inside, outside, her edges blurring into the air.

Propped up on pillows and naked from the waist down, she tries to move. But her legs are taped to two chair backs tied up against either side of the bed, a sort of makeshift stirrups. A numbness, though, tells her that beyond her right knee, something is very wrong indeed. Her elevated right foot looms in her eyeline, floppy like a dead fish, and she realises she can't move it, not even to flex it against the roller coaster of this next contraction, which is building through her until she doesn't think she can bear it…

'BREATHE.' Abbie is yelling at her. 'YOU HAVE TO BREATHE.'

Rachel clamps her lips shut and nods. She knows this. She's seen all the YouTube videos about how to give birth. Abbie coaches her through the breaths until she's out the other side.

'I need to mobilise,' she says. 'I need to be up, to walk around, to allow gravity to play its part.'

'This is all stuff you've just heard about, Rachel. It's not true. I did it three times on my back, in a bed, just like this.'

'It hurts.'

'It's meant to.'

'I can't do it.'

'Woman up, Rachel!'

'My leg hurts.'

'It will do. But you won't be running away again. We need you close, for the best start for baby.'

Another contraction rises inside Rachel and takes over from the thudding dull pain in her cracked shin bone and ankle. She is dimly aware of Abbie lifting her phone and taking a photograph of her.

How much time has passed? She has no idea. All she knows is that Abbie is now looking at her from between her legs, telling her to pant lightly, and she feels like she is splitting open.

'Here.' Abbie reaches up and grabs her hand and puts it between her legs. Her fingers meet a hard, hot, rough-textured lump that seems to be part of her, yet she can't feel her own touch.

'Baby's head. Weird, isn't it?' Abbie grins up at her. 'When you feel the need to push, give it all you've got. You can do it, Rachel.'

And then it comes on her again, like there's some brute pressing down on the top of her diaphragm, squeezing her inside out.

'Good girl. Push, push, push,' Abbie says, her voice rising and not helping Rachel at all, who wants to shout at her to shut the fuck up. But even in her current state, she knows this is not a wise move. She knows it is in her best interests to be that good girl.

And then when she thinks she can't push any more, one thing gives and another thing slithers out of her, and Abbie is suddenly very busy doing something, scooping and patting and rubbing and then slapping…

'What – what is it?'

But Abbie is too busy to answer. And then at last there is a strangled cry and the baby breaks air and yells. Two little fists punch up, and Rachel tries to lever herself upright to get a better look, but her exemplary abs are broken, and there's this big pancake thing in the way, which she realises is what is left of her emptied sack of a stomach.

'It's a boy,' Abbie is saying, stroking the baby. 'A lovely little boy. A lovely little Daz.'

'Give him to me.' Rachel doesn't recognise the voice that has just come out of her own mouth. She reaches out and grabs for her baby, but Abbie has him as far away as she can, given that the twisty, bluey-white umbilical cord is still attached to his placenta, which is still inside Rachel.

'He needs to be wrapped first.' Abbie reaches down for Rachel's hastily removed running tights and binds him up in sweaty old Lycra, which is about as different as it's possible to get to the hand-knitted cashmere blanket Rachel has stashed away for exactly this purpose. But then nothing about this experience is what she planned.

She didn't even get to listen to her Spotify playlist.

'There we go, Mum.' Abbie finally places Rachel's baby on her front. 'Latch him on now. He needs that first milk.'

'Hello, baby,' Rachel says through her tears. For one moment, everything bad about this situation recedes. She even forgets that she was certain Beansprout was a girl. 'Hello, my sweet little baby. My Ethan.' The baby squirms, then, like the wisest Buddha, knowing exactly what to do, he wiggles his way to her nipple. She unwraps the leggings.

'His name is Daz, and he needs to be kept warm,' Abbie says, looming over her.

'Put a blanket over us then,' Rachel says, a touch of fierce in her voice that makes Abbie immediately do as she says. 'Skin on skin is the most important thing.'

Abbie picks up Rachel's trainers and pulls out the laces. When they are free, she ties them around the baby's cord.

'Wait till it stops pulsing,' Rachel says.

'Sooner he's free of you the better.' Abbie once more takes that boning knife from her rucksack and, to Rachel's horror, cuts the cord and gives a tug on the non-baby end. A shuddering contraction goes through her once more and the placenta slithers out.

Abbie scoops it up in her hands and puts it on the floor. She laughs. 'You probably wanted to turn that into a pâté or something, didn't you?' Then she whistles to Sam, who, still smarting from the punch Rachel dealt him, darts in, snatches it and takes it to a corner of the room.

'Least you can do for him, in the circumstances,' Abbie says.

Rachel would feel sick, but the post-birth endorphins flying round her body make her forget everything else except her baby, who is here, at last, in her arms.

She has no idea what Abbie is planning for her, or for him. But one thing she is sure about.

She will do anything to keep him.

'Smile, Rachel. Look happy. Show Daz to us!'

'He's Ethan.' Wrapped in the bliss of her baby boy, Rachel looks up and smiles, and Abbie, who has her phone in her hand, snaps her.

INSTAGRAM POST

RosyPosy1234
Hove, England
58 likes

Image
- Graphic RR followed by a question mark.

Text
Where is **@rachelhoneyhill**?
#wheresRachel #wheresRR #wheresrachelhoneyhill

INSTAGRAM POST

Carlalalala_1999_
London, England
830 likes

Image
- Graphic RR followed by a question mark.

Text
Where is **@rachelhoneyhill**?
#wheresRachel #wheresRR #wheresrachelhoneyhill

CHAPTER FORTY-THREE

Abbie puts her hands under the rucksack to take some of the weight of the birth-soiled sheets off her back. As she and Sam tramp over the gorse and fern back to Honeyhill, her fingers itch to cuddle that baby.

But right now, for his healthy start, he needs his mother. After that, Daz is going to have a perfect life. Unlike her own poor children, who were exposed to so many awful things so early on – the drugs and alcohol in her system when she bore them, the violence they witnessed when their little personalities were being formed, the neglect she put them through because of her own sorry situation.

Looking back, the children *were* safer out of her reach. The damage has been done to them, and she's right not to give herself – or them – any more heartache by pursuing them. Time to move on. Fresh start.

She's helped Rachel wash, made sure she's eaten something, and tucked her up in a freshly made bed. This is how things are going to be for a short while. A few days of breastfeeding, that should sort it out. Then little Daz will be set up and she can take him away to Spain and start all over again.

It has become clear to Abbie that Rachel needs to be fully out of the picture. Her attempt to escape is an example of what could happen if she leaves her behind. Even if she's too scared to go to the police for fear of her evil past coming out – and Abbie would make sure in that instance that it absolutely would – she would come after her and Daz, and they'd never have any peace.

And peace is what's needed.

It's not like this will be Abbie's first time, not after Charlotte Williams. However accidental her death was, Abbie knows it was her responsibility. Also, she supposes, by asking PJ to set her associates on her, she was, in a roundabout way, behind the killing of that journalist Jane Roberts

She turns and takes in the view, which is magnificent. The sea is like shifting mercury, stained orange by the setting sun. Today has been a great day. This sunset marks the end of an exceptionally trying period of her life. A new beginning is on its way.

Really, it's the kindest thing to do.

She'll do it gently, with sleeping pills and alcohol. Rachel will just go to sleep and never wake up, and it will look like she has done it to herself. By the time they start asking about the baby, Abbie, Daz, Sam and the cash will be well out of the way.

The breeze whips her hair as she stands in the grassy meadow with Sam sitting at her side, and she feels like the very embodiment of Gaga. Above them, swallows put on their evening show, hoovering up the midges and gnats. Abbie watches the sun until it is a vanishing red line on the horizon.

'That's all, folks,' she says.

But it's not. It's just the very exciting beginning.

Nicely bathed, all Rachel's gore washed from her, she sits at her desk in no-longer-Wanda's office. Speak of the devil, there's an email from the former occupant to Rachel's private account.

I just want to make sure everything is OK with you, Rachel. I would love to talk to you, tell you my side of the story, but it seems Abbie is blocking all my attempts to contact you. I still think she's bad news. I have never, ever stolen anything from you, Rachel, I swear. I'm getting really bad vibes about what she's up to.

I think she is trying to take you over.

Please call me.

Love W x

'Bad vibes!' Abbie puts the message in the trash, which she empties immediately. 'Hippy dippy.'

Then she starts to prepare the biggest Instagram post of Rachel's online existence – her last.

Let her call Daz Ethan if she likes. Abbie knows what his real name is. And no one will be looking for a Daz, will they?

Once she has completed the draft, Abbie selects four photographs from the sixty or so that she took over the course of the birth. She crops each one carefully, so there is no hint of where it has been taken, or of her own presence. The cropping also abstracts the more graphic images – of what Abbie heard Zayn's father, in his brief presence in his son's life, call 'the business end' – so they have a greater chance of not being censored.

These are not glamorous pictures, and Rachel would probably die early if she saw the parts of her body that are being held up to the world. But, if there were any point now in her learning anything, it would be a good lesson in how it feels to have your image exploited without your consent.

While Abbie is working, GridSmasher flashes up a warning that there were no posts yesterday, and there are none lined up for today. For the first time in @rachelhoneyhill's online life, a day has passed with no posts.

'You had one job, Rachel…'

She needs to find something to put up, to avoid people – Fran, mostly – getting suspicious. Looking into the drafts section, she sees that Rachel has worked on a couple of posts but not yet assigned them to days to go live. One is a photograph of her with little Mila in her arms. The other is notes for a series of pictures of Fran and the children looking round the nursery, with links to the partners who have given her the baby furniture and equipment.

'Using Daz even before he was born,' Abbie tells Sam. But she lines the pictures up to go live anyway over the next couple of days, with the Mila one ready for tomorrow. She just copies the words for the nursery post from something Rachel ran a month ago, but no one will notice. Seeing her brats up there on Instagram will no doubt keep Fran sweet.

To her annoyance, Abbie can't find her film defending Rachel against trolls anywhere on the GridSmasher, even in the rough notes section. While it may all be academic now, she wouldn't mind enjoying a little limelight one more time before she disappears into Spanish obscurity.

After a good hour searching, she finds the video in the trash bin on Rachel's photos. She hauls it into the library and, after some deliberation, runs it through the PerfectMe filter. While she would prefer the video to be #nofilter, the lighting is harsh, and shows up that big spot she had on her chin last week. Had she known she was going to be filming, she would have used concealer on it, so by using the app she's just doing the same thing, but digitally.

She drags the enhanced film into GridSmasher and sets it up to go live immediately, a move the program finds so challenging that she has to tick three boxes to verify that she is certain about it. Oh, she is *definitely* certain. She wants her moment of fame before she has to slip into obscurity.

There it goes, with one final click on OK.

Instantly, the comments and likes come flooding in, and she feels a surge of power and possibility that makes her fingertips tingle, a small glimpse of what it must be like – have been like, she corrects herself – for Rachel.

She lines Rachel's farewell post up for three days' time. Daz will have had the benefit of the colostrum, so Abbie will be able to start him on the bottle and make her move.

She's quite excited about the stir Rachel's going to make with that final post. Pity she won't be around to see it.

She sleeps well that night. The sleep of the dead.

INSTAGRAM POST

rachelhoneyhill
Devon, England
2,578 likes

Image
- 60-second video of Abbie, saying how happy she is to be taught by Rachel about healthy eating and exercise, hair and make-up.

Text
Listen up, party people!
Abbie is happy here with me.
Let her tell you in her very own words.
#nofilter #AbbiesJourney #fitness #MothersHelper

CHAPTER FORTY-FOUR

Enclosed in her baby bubble, Rachel barely notices the darkness as it falls. She is an animal in her nest, and her only concern is the survival of herself and her baby.

The post-partum endorphins are wearing off, and the throb of her broken leg is doing battle with her opened-out insides and torn perineum for most painful body-part prize.

Abbie gave her a bed bath and replaced her bedding with dusty sheets and blankets rescued from the other dorm beds, so she is clean, but she will probably need stitches if she can get herself seen to soon enough. She has had an exploratory feel around and her hand comes up bloody, but it doesn't feel excessive.

She doesn't *think* she is going to haemorrhage and die.

But she doesn't know.

She doesn't know what is going to happen.

For now, all she can do is marvel at the little starfish fingers, the tiny fingernail perfection of this beautiful creature she and Wim have created. He looks very like his daddy – it's common with babies, she has read, a safeguard in case there is any doubt about paternity.

No doubt here, just a fact that's hidden to the outside world. She's glad that Wim will have no paternal rights or responsibilities, that it's only her and Ethan, here to face the world, the two of them together.

In the last light of this day of his birth, she gazes into his inky eyes and plays a story in her head of the two of them in an open-top car, him about five, her happier than she has ever been. They are driving up the Pacific Coast Highway, from LA to San Francisco, a journey she has always dreamed of taking, and the wind is in their hair. They have no worries except where they are going to stop to eat. She is not recording this journey for any purpose whatsoever. She is just being in the moment with her boy and they are living their best lives for themselves.

In this moment, there in the future, she is free.

But it's brief. The smell of the dust on the sheets that cover her and her baby, the drip of the tap in the bathroom, the spectral silence, underscored by the distant sigh of the sea hitting the shore in *that* bay just a kilometre away: it all brings her back to her appalling present.

Is there a future? What is going to happen? Abbie's plans, like her face, are unreadable.

But Rachel fears the worst.

No, she realises. Not the very worst. For the first time, her own death is not the most awful thing that could happen.

'You will survive,' she whispers to her baby. 'Whatever happens to me, you will survive.'

He looks back at her with those eyes, and she realises that she owes it to him, more than to anyone in the world, to make sure that she also gets through this.

She will not let her son be a motherless child.

The tiger in her rises, and she knows that whatever it takes, she will get out of this. She is, after all, a proven survivor.

She has form.

With this sure knowledge, she allows herself the practical measure of sleep. Whatever the next days or weeks may hold, broken bits notwithstanding, she has to be in the best possible shape for whatever circumstances are thrown at her.

*

When Abbie arrives in the morning with her food for the day, Rachel makes sure she eats everything on offer.

Just a couple of days, and she'll work something out.

There has to be a way out of this.

There is a way out of everything.

INSTAGRAM POST

rachelhoneyhill
Devon, England
paid partnership with **cotsandco**
18,356 likes

Images
- Fran, Luuk, Lotte and Mila looking at the cot in the nursery
- Selfie of Rachel with the others, their faces peeking through the cot mobile.

Text
Everyone is looking forward to little Beansprout arriving!
I can't wait to lie little Beansprout down in this fabulous cot! It's handmade in Cirencester by **@cotsandco**, who also make these adorable matching mobiles and this totally organic bedding.
Admittedly, it's not cheap, but you want to give your baby the very best start in life, don't you?
#baby #cot #nursery #green #organic #cotsandco #friends

INSTAGRAM POST

rachelhoneyhill
Devon, England
28,278 likes

Image
- Rachel, barefoot in the Honeyhill garden sunshine in a filmy Indian dress, with baby Mila in her arms.

Text
Isn't little Mila gorgeous?
Can't believe that in one year's time, Beansprout will be this size.
Photo captured by my #FriendFran.
#baby #authentic #nature #nofilter

INSTAGRAM POST

rachelhoneyhill
Devon, England
2,870,925 likes

Images
- Rachel, eyes closed, sweating and panting through a contraction
- Rachel, face strained in pain
- Close-up of the umbilical cord emerging
- Rachel with the baby in her arms, sitting on dirtied sheets, smiling.

Text
This is me, Rachel Rodrigues, giving birth to my beautiful baby boy, Ethan, yesterday, at a secret location. I have taken myself away from Honeyhill to make sure we get the peace and calm we deserve.

My baby is perfect. My life is perfect. I have everything I need. And now that I have set out on this new chapter, the time has come to move on.

I had hoped to carry on, take some of you with me and build a new set of followers who were interested in motherhood and babies. But I have realised that I don't want that for my son. It is his right to remain anonymous, his right to not have his life displayed for your entertainment, or to sell products I don't really believe in to people I know nothing about.

So, in the #nofilter vein of these photographs, which, when you swipe, you will see show the reality of giving birth – the blood, the pain, the difficulties as well as the joy – I am turning my back on my digital profile and I am going to live my real life only. You will not see me here again, nor anywhere else on social media.

This is me, Rachel Rodrigues, signing off.

#nofilter #authentic

CHAPTER FORTY-FIVE

25 August

Fran rushes downstairs from her office to the living area, where Wim is just serving up breakfast for the children. They're early starters in this apartment.

She tries to speak, but the words just aren't coming. All she can do is point at her phone.

'Mama!' Lotte says, holding up her arms.

'Just a minute, Lots,' Fran says, thrusting the phone at Wim.

'What is it?' Wim slides the pancakes onto the serving plate and sets the frying pan back on the stove. He takes the phone and swipes through the photographs that have just appeared on Rachel's Insta.

Fran watches her husband's face as he looks at the no-holds-barred images of Rachel giving birth.

'Good,' he says, handing the phone back to her.

'But the baby's two weeks early!'

'He looks healthy. And handsome.'

'Is that all you can say?'

'What do you want me to say? I hope we get to meet him soon.'

'And she's not at home, but she's not saying where she is. And why hasn't she let me know? I was supposed to be there!'

'Perhaps she has other things on her mind?'

Sometimes his cloggy pragmatism, his inability to get worked up or react to *anything* is a nice antidote to her tendency to go to the worst-case scenario. But today there is no calming to be done. This to her screams emergency, and her brain is going into overdrive trying to make sense of it, trying to make a plan.

'For one thing, she would never allow these sorts of images to go live. And for another thing, read it! She'd never say all that.'

'She's just had a baby, Fran. Remember how it was for you.'

'It says she's closing her account!'

Wim turns to the fridge and pulls out chocolate syrup, butter and buttermilk, which he ferries to the table. 'That's a good thing, *ja*? You're always saying how she needs to "row back", get a grip, live her life for the joy of living it. That's what you say, isn't it?'

His reasonable tone means she has to work hard to stop her rising panic diverting into an attack on him.

'But she'd never do any of this without letting me know.'

'Perhaps that girl you got, the mother's helper, whatever, is enough for her right now?'

Fran closes her eyes and sways.

'Isn't that what you wanted?' Wim asks her. 'Not to be so duty-bound?'

'What if I've made a terrible mistake?'

'What if Rachel actually wanted to go away, wanted to close her account?'

'She would have spoken to me. You know that.'

'Have you tried to call her?'

'She's not answering.'

'Have you tried the girl?'

'Not answering either.'

'Just perhaps they're busy with the baby?'

Fran wants to scream. This is not right. The spark of concern she felt when she left Rachel with Abbie just six days ago catches like a bushfire. It almost takes her breath away. And she's worried to death now about the baby. She knows too well how precious and fragile a new life can be. What if Rachel had an attack during labour? She closes her eyes.

'What is it, Mama?' Luuk reaches up and takes her hand, but she is too taken up to even register his touch.

'Fran!' Wim touches her arm and draws her attention to her little boy, who is on the verge of tears because he is being so ignored.

'Sorry, Luuky, I'm miles away.' She reaches down and picks him up, swinging him round onto her hip.

'Is it Rachel?' Luuk asks, and Fran and Wim share a glance that holds not a tiny drop of pride at their preternaturally perceptive son.

'Her baby's come early,' Fran says.

'Oh no!' Luuk says.

'Oh no!' Lotte echoes, her face smeared with chocolatey pancake, picking up on the mood, if not the meaning, of what has happened.

Luuk curls a strand of his mother's hair around his finger. 'You must go and see her.'

'I don't know where she is, though, Luuky,' Fran says.

'You must find her. You're a good finder.'

Fran looks at Wim again. He is nodding, slowly.

'Go, Fran. You have good instincts.'

She smiles at him. He has utterly redeemed himself. He earns bonus points by handing her a plate with a pancake on it.

'Now,' he says to the children. 'Who wants *hagelslag* on their pancakes?'

They all do. But Fran, pancake plate in hand, is taking the steps up to her office two at a time.

No chocolate sprinkles for her.

*

It takes her an hour to reschedule her appointments for the forth-coming week. Luckily she has nothing she can't either postpone or offload on a colleague. And happily, Wim is in between contracts, so he can look after the children.

Within two hours she is clearing passport control at Schiphol. Two hours after that, she is driving down the M5 from Bristol airport. While she was waiting for the plane, she kept trying to contact Rachel and Abbie, but with no luck. It's as if they have slipped off the edge of the planet.

Fran feels like she has ants crawling over her arms and face. After making sure that her children survive and thrive, picking Rachel up and making sure that she does the best she can is the most important thing in her life. Rachel saved her life, and while Fran knows that she didn't escape The Event unscathed herself, she is thankful beyond belief that she wasn't damaged in the way Rachel was.

Everything she does is motivated by that thankfulness.

She has stepped in and saved Rachel so many times – from getting her out of scrapes with unmentionable men who took advantage, to her addictions to drugs and alcohol, to her various run-ins with people due to her brain injury.

'What can I do with my life?' Rachel had wailed after she got clean in her late twenties. 'I don't want to be a waitress forever.'

Fran lent her the money to do the yoga teacher training in Goa. Shortly after this, the death of Rachel's grandparents and the farm falling into her hands sealed the deal of her recovery. Fran encouraged her to build her online brand so that she could stand on her own two feet. And Rachel thrived, she really did.

But over the years, the whole RR thing started to eat itself, and Fran could see she was unhappy. The baby plan was part of giving her something else in her life, another point of focus.

And now look what monsters that plan has unleashed.

Fran puts her foot down and the hire car hits a hundred miles an hour, overtaking even a boy racer in a stupid noisy Porsche.

After nearly barrelling nose-on into a tractor as she whizzes along the high-banked lane from the main road to Honeyhill, she finally draws up at the locked gates, her mouth dry, her face hot.

She opens the car door and the smell from the pig farm next door does battle with the artificial air freshener in the hire car. She gets out and stretches, then girds herself and places her finger on the keypad by the gatepost.

Nothing happens.

She tries again. Again, nothing. Rachel – or *someone* – has taken her fingerprint off the security system.

She thinks about pressing the videophone buzzer but decides against it.

Instead, she pushes her face up against the wooden slats of the high fence. But only a tiny chink of light is visible between them.

So that's the polite part over.

Still in the clothes she was wearing at the beginning of what she thought was going to be a day full of meetings with politicians, Fran removes her I-mean-business heels and pulls her trainers out of her suitcase. She glances around, then changes out of her tailored dress and into her running gear, which, out of habit, she always slings into any suitcase she packs. Now more suitably dressed for house-breaking, she drives the hire car to the end of the lane, just before the pig farm, and parks it in a disused driveway, where it is sheltered by trees and invisible from Honeyhill.

She slips the car key onto her key ring and zips it into the pocket at the back of her running tights, then jogs back to the house and reaches up to the first branch of the ancient sycamore that grows just to the side of the gate. She knows it has a good view of the house, because at one point she tried to have it cut down for security purposes. Rachel begged her not to go ahead. She was always sentimental about plants.

Fran shakes her head. She's thinking about Rachel in the past tense. She has to stop that right now.

Swinging herself up onto the branch, she climbs farther up into the tree to get a better view through the picture windows and down into the galleried hallway. Nothing looks out of place, except the fact that, it being Rachel's house, nothing *is* out of place.

She glances along the perimeter of the fence. If she were to jump down on the other side, she would set off alarms and lose any advantage of surprise.

She thinks about calling the police. But what would they say? A grown woman has posted on social media that she is well and has had a baby. If anything, they would be suspicious of Fran wanting to find her, perhaps thinking she is some sort of crazed fan or something. There would be too much explaining, which would lead to too many police-type questions, and neither she nor Rachel can afford that.

But she *knows* there is something wrong. She knows it in every inch of her. She holds her breath and strains her ears for any sound. Apart from a crow somewhere behind the barn, and the distant rumble of farm machinery in a field over towards the village, there is nothing but silence. The eJeep isn't on the drive, but it could be in the garage.

She's just wondering what her next step will be when the front door opens, nearly shocking her off her branch. Sam comes out first and trots towards her tree. He can smell her, but thankfully, because her scent is so familiar, he only wants to greet her.

'Go away, Sam,' she mouths as she shrinks back into the leaves. 'Just ignore me.'

'Sam! Come here!' Abbie's shout rings out against the stone of the old barn building. She whistles and Sam is instantly at her heels, following her towards the gate. 'You and your squirrels,' Abbie says. She's in her running gear and has a large full rucksack on her back, the kind you would use for a fortnight's backpacking.

She blips the gate open, then, when she and Sam are on the outside, she uses her fingertip to close the front door and the gate and reactivate the alarm system. As she does so, a magpie lands in the tree, right next to Fran. The black and white flurry, followed by a series of chattering ticks, draws Abbie's eye upwards, and for one frozen second, Fran's blood stops in her veins; she is certain she is looking straight at her.

She closes her eyes and readies herself. She's not scared. After the attack on her and Rachel, she learned tae kwon do, and has used it on three occasions to teach men that, contrary to what they clearly think, a woman walking through a city at night is not theirs for the taking.

So Abbie poses no physical threat. But if she's forced to jump down and take her on now, and Rachel isn't in the house – which she's pretty certain is the case – Fran may never find out where she is.

'Hello, Mr Magpie. Toast and marmalade,' Abbie says.

Fran opens her eyes.

Abbie is walking away, with Sam at her side.

She can try to ward off the bad luck from this lone magpie all she likes, but she's going to feel a whole parliament of sorrow if she's harmed Rachel or her baby.

'Hello, Mr Magpie,' Fran whispers. 'Pancakes.'

The second Abbie is out of view, she silently slips out of the tree and darts along behind her.

But Sam catches her scent. He stops still, looks back and whines.

'No squirrels, Sammo,' Abbie says, pulling him on.

They are heading towards the sea. Fran slips from bush to bush, following them along the hedgerow-lined footpath.

When Abbie and Sam reach the coastal path, they take a left towards Red Anchor Bay. They're out in the open now, so Fran stays hidden in a little clump of trees, watching as they turn inland, taking the path round the top of the valley.

Her heart leaps. She knows exactly where they are heading.

'Poor Rachel,' she whispers. She knows how scared her best friend is of the dark; how spooky, dirty, decrepit and crumbling – dangerous, even – the building is. To spend the night in there alone would be Rachel's idea of hell. To give birth there – with all her plans of warm pools and curated playlists and special cashmere blankets – how awful must that have been?

Once Abbie and Sam dip into the hollow that leads from the cliff path to the school, Fran sprints round the track towards them. As she runs, she does a quick inventory of the situation. If Rachel and her baby are captive in the school, she has to get them away from Abbie. Abbie is strong and, Fran now realises, clearly deranged. But Fran has surprise on her side, plus the fact that she can kick and punch like a machine.

What if Abbie's armed, though? How else would she have been able to overpower Rachel, who is taller and, even in the late stages of pregnancy, strong from all her body work?

Fran needs to get it right. Again she thinks about calling the police – here is the proof that Rachel is being held captive – but she knows without even looking at her phone that there is no reception whatsoever here.

Desperate to stay out of sight, she slips blindly towards the school, hoping that she has made the right assumption and that Abbie and Sam haven't gone beyond it. As she lets herself through the hole in the fence, she is rewarded by the sight of Abbie's arm pulling the back door shut, and the sound of a key being turned in the lock.

But this isn't a problem for Fran. She still has one of the keys she and Rachel stole back when they were boarders, and she keeps it on her key ring as a sort of memento mori.

She counts to thirty to allow Abbie to be clear of the hall, then she unzips the pocket at the back of her running tights.

CHAPTER FORTY-SIX

Over the days since Ethan's birth, Rachel has tried to gather her strength. She has forced herself to eat everything that Abbie has given her, even though her appetite is stunted by the dread that fills the place Beansprout used to take up in her belly.

She has no idea what Abbie is planning. Only that, since Ethan was born, she has said very little, coming in silently each morning, not even looking at her or her baby while she deposits the food, nappies and baby clothes she ferries down from Honeyhill. She even brought the cashmere blanket, for which Rachel was stupidly grateful.

What worries her, though, is that there have been no items for her own care. Even though she asked, there have been no sanitary towels, no changes of clothing beyond the nightdress Abbie brought down on her first visit after the birth, and nothing in the way of postnatal care.

Why is Abbie looking after Ethan and not her?

She has a theory, and she doesn't like it.

Her nipples are sore as raw blisters, she is suffering from agonising haemorrhoids, and in the night, she started to run a fever, which could be due to a blocked milk duct – she vaguely remembers reading something about 'milk fever' – or, and she doesn't really want to think about this, she might be infected where she tore giving birth.

Or it could be her leg, of course. If it weren't for the pain in other parts of her body, her snapped and dog-bitten shin bone and crushed ankle would be the sole focus of her being.

She has asked for painkillers, but they will be bad for 'Daz', apparently, a response that only adds fuel to her terrifying theory about what Abbie might have in store for her. The one concession to her comfort has been that when two days ago she mentioned that she was having difficulty getting to the bathroom – hopping in her condition is all but impossible – Abbie found an old tea trolley in the kitchens, which she now uses to shuffle across the floor, dragging her dead-fish foot behind her.

For many hours, Rachel has lain in this dusty bed, holding her baby and turning over the possible conclusions to her situation. Despite the horror it holds for her, she has decided that she would do anything – anything – rather than let her baby be brought up by Abbie.

Whatever the risk, she knows she has to try to get out of here, for her own sake and for Ethan.

So last night she splinted her leg with a couple of wooden bed slats and the leggings that were Ethan's first swaddling. She could never previously have even imagined the pain she experienced as she shifted the mattress to get at the slats, but she knew she had to do something if she was going to have any chance of getting out of this mess.

While this makeshift splint doesn't mean that she can put weight on her smashed leg, it will keep it out of the way when she makes her move.

She also removed two more slats, to use first as weapons and second as crutches.

Abbie is singing that damn Lady Gaga song as she and Sam come down the corridor at lunchtime. This, thinks Rachel, is a very bad sign indeed. She congratulates herself on deciding that today is the day for action.

Because of that decision, she awaits Abbie's entrance standing behind the door with the gorgeous cashmere blanket wrapping Ethan tightly to her front. She has unboxed and moulded an entire pack of nappies under the duvet, so it looks like she and Ethan are still asleep in bed. Her plan is to knock Abbie sideways with the door, follow it up with the trolley, then whack her senseless with the bed-slat crutches.

It sounds horribly violent, but she has reckoned that as she doesn't have speed on her side, her only chance of escape is to have Abbie pretty much unconscious.

'Anyway you've done worse before,' she said to herself as she was working it all out during her fever-tossed night. 'Haven't you?'

CHAPTER FORTY-SEVEN

It's a great day.

Singing, Abbie runs over her plans as she and Sam head down the corridor towards the dorm and the house mother's room.

Posh June has pulled out all the stops and has, amazingly, arranged for a drop-off of the documents Abbie, Sam and Daz need to get to Spain tomorrow morning. They will be on the plane and away before anyone notices anything wrong.

She's going to be ever so gentle with Rachel. In her rucksack she has a thermos of hot herbal tea into which she has crumbled a month's worth of her own prescription drugs. She's set aside another month for herself, until she and Daz and Sam get settled in Spain. The last thing she needs is another withdrawal episode while she's in charge of a baby.

She also has a bottle of vodka and a funnel, which she intends to use once Rachel is asleep, as a sort of belt and braces. And the boning knife is tucked into the back of her running tights for quick access. Just in case she meets any resistance.

Then she'll scoop up Daz and walk him away to their perfect future. Back at the house, she's got the car in the garage, packed up and ready to go, and a nice bottle of formula ready to be warmed to see him through till they get to the hotel in Swindon for the passport pick-up. She could have driven to the school today, but she didn't want to draw any attention.

Also, she is looking forward to walking back across the fields with Daz. She has Rachel's brand-new beautiful baby sling – something she never dreamed of being able to afford for her own babies. Depending on how long it takes Rachel to die, they might even catch the sunset.

It will be like a great romantic movie scene: a scene of victory, she thinks as she walks through the dorm to the house mother's room.

'Come on, Sam,' she says. He's hesitating at the far end of the room, like he knows what she's planning to do. 'It won't hurt her, I promise,' she whispers, so Rachel can't hear. 'Anyway, *you* can talk, bird murderer.'

She opens the door. Rachel and Daz are still fast asleep in the bed in front of her.

She steps towards them, but before she is over the threshold, she is swung off her feet by the door slamming back into her.

The trolley she left TO BLOODY HELP RACHEL crashes across her.

Something whacks down on her head, again and again and again.

Abbie roars. She springs to her feet, her vision blurred but her instincts clear. She reaches out and her hand just misses Rachel as she jounces past her, a bobbing, lumbering ghost, into the dorm room beyond.

But Abbie's on her, and so is Sam, who is tugging at one of the pieces of wood Rachel is using as crutches.

'Mind the baby!' Abbie and Rachel cry out at the same time.

But it's too late. Rachel screams and flies forward, her right leg crumpling beneath her.

'No!' someone yells from the other end of the dorm, and Abbie and Sam freeze. Even Rachel, mid-fall, appears to pause as she looks up, startled.

CHAPTER FORTY-EIGHT

It's like an invisible hand at her back.

She doesn't know how it happens, but somehow Fran reaches Rachel in the split second necessary to stop her falling and crushing her baby.

As she scoops her up to standing, they catch each other's glance, just for a second. For the first time for over twenty years, Fran sees Rachel's grey eyes.

'Help me,' Rachel croaks.

Fran nods and moves past her, hoping her friend will be able to regain her balance and get herself and that baby as far away as possible.

'Down,' she says to the snapping, barking Sam, using her most assertive voice. 'Go,' she says, pointing to the corner of the room.

He does exactly what she tells him, and sits.

'Stay,' she says, and at the same time spins around and kicks Abbie full on the jaw.

Taken by the force of her foot, Abbie spirals away and staggers towards the dusty parquet floor. But it's clear to Fran that this is not the first time she has taken a beating, because she uses the force of her fall to roll onwards and get herself up again.

The two women face each other. Fran readies herself. She has her keys clenched in her fist, protruding from her fingers, but apart from that, she is unarmed. Abbie, she notices with alarm, seems to have got hold of a knife.

'What the fuck are you doing, Abbie?' she says.

'I'm making the world fair.' Abbie lunges with the knife.

Fran tries to fend her off with a blocking arm, but Abbie gets her in the shoulder, plunging the knife so deep that Fran can feel the bone of her upper arm stop its progress.

In the second it takes for her to absorb this, Abbie has tugged the knife back and is off, haring after Rachel, who has nearly made it to the dorm door.

Fran goes to catch her and fails, but by some good chance, Abbie trips and goes flying, up into the air and down onto the floor, the knife falling out of her hand.

Rachel disappears through the door, and Fran launches herself onto Abbie, grabbing the knife, rolling her onto her back and straddling her. With one hand she pins Abbie's arms above her head; with the other, she holds the knife up to her throat.

'Life lesson, Abbie,' she says. 'The world isn't fair.'

'Sam!' Abbie calls. 'Help!'

'No!' Fran says to the dog.

'Now!' Abbie says.

When it comes down to it, Sam obeys Abbie's voice. He launches himself across the room and sinks his teeth into Fran's back. The shock makes her relax her grip enough for Abbie to work herself free, knock Fran's knife arm aside and deliver a head butt.

Fran roars and puts her hand to her nose, which feels like it is broken. Abbie continues on her upward trajectory to push Fran backwards so that the situation is reversed, with Fran on her back, lying on screaming flesh mangled by Sam's bite. Abbie is on top of her, and with both hands she digs her nails into Fran's pinioned hands until she finally lets go of the knife.

'I don't know why you're defending Rachel anyway,' she says to Fran, once she has the knife at her throat. 'You know she was fucking your husband all last year?'

Fran looks up. Abbie has her back to the dorm door. She can make out the word *Safe* on a silver pendant dangling in her face from a leather thong around her neck.

Despite her situation, she forces herself to laugh. 'Yes. Yes, I knew that!'

Abbie frowns. 'You knew?'

'Wim and I have an open relationship. Rachel wanted a baby. She didn't want a partner. The chances of conceiving are much higher with actual sex than with a turkey baster.'

While Fran is desperately holding Abbie's stare, she is aware in her peripheral vision of Rachel creeping closer and closer.

'He made her come, though,' Abbie yells. 'She counted the times!'

'Even better for conception. It's practical, Abbie.'

'You're mad. All of you.' Abbie lifts the knife and brings it down into Fran's chest.

A sound like a cartoon rush, a big bird flying into the room, makes her look round.

'*We're* mad?'

Through the helpless eyes of a woman who knows she may well be mortally wounded, Fran watches as Rachel, her baby somehow disappeared, swings one of her bed-slat crutches with the superhuman force her fugue states seem to summon. It lands on the back of Abbie's head, knocking her sideways.

One of the last things Fran remembers of that moment, as she lies with the knife sticking out of her chest, is the scandalised look on Abbie's face as all three women hear the sickening crack of her neck snapping. It's a look of realisation that despite all her best-laid plans, she has been thwarted. Fran reaches out and tries to catch her in case, somehow, she rallies. Her hand grabs the leather thong, but it breaks, and Abbie is on the ground.

Sam snarls and snaps at Rachel, who is bringing the slat crutch down again and again on Abbie's head.

'Sam, sit,' Fran croaks, blood accompanying the words in her mouth. 'Rachel, stop now.'

The dog, realising that the object of his loyalty is no longer relevant, obeys.

From the corridor outside, the baby cries, making Rachel snap out of it.

She hobbles quickly from the room.

As she clutches Abbie's *Safe* pendant to her stab wound, that is all Fran knows.

CHAPTER FORTY-NINE

25 October

'I swear it was Miss Chamberlain who made the phone reception appear at the top of the teachers' staircase.' Rachel winces as she adjusts her foot on the stool in front of her. She's been in this cast for two months already, and it's driving her crazy, although Rotterdam is a lot easier to get around in a wheelchair than rural Devon.

'It was the new 5G mast, Rach. I looked it up – they finally turned it on.'

Just out of hospital and under doctor's orders to take it easy herself, Fran sits next to Rachel on the sofa by the massive windows overlooking the Nieuwe Maas harbour. Over the other side of the vast living space, the children squirm on the rug with their new baby brother. It's rather sweet to see them all obsess over him.

Wim, who is clearing up after supper, laughs. 'Convenient!'

'Whatever it was,' Rachel says, 'it saved your life. And mine and Ethan's too, probably. We'd still be there, rotting away, if I hadn't been able to call the police.'

Wim winces. 'Did the money arrive yet?' he asks.

Rachel smiles at Fran. It's ironic that Wim, usually the straight-talking Dutchman, always tries to divert their conversation away from what they are beginning to frame as The Day.

'Yup. Honeyhill Farm and Honeyhill Barn are now officially reunited under a new owner,' Rachel says. 'They're going to Airbnb it. There's a lot of interest from my old followers.'

Fran makes a face. 'Macabre.'

'Well, y'know.' Rachel holds up her hands. 'Nothing to do with me any more. And at least it's the end of the pig farm.'

Fran shudders 'I'm so glad we're finally completely away from that place.'

Sam, who is on the floor by the sofa, worn out from playing with the children, gives a little whine in his sleep.

'You don't want to think what his dreams are about,' Fran says.

'Got a pretty good idea, from my own,' Rachel says. 'Poor Sam. All he knows is loyalty. The way he sat by Abbie until the police arrived.'

Her own dreams are getting better, though. She finally came clean with the doctors about her episodes. They have put her on a new drug that is keeping everything in place. She has been told that so long as she keeps taking it, and continues to refrain from recreational drugs and alcohol, she will never again lose herself.

That's quite a promise.

Wim looks up from wiping the table. 'Any more thoughts about what happens next, Rachel?'

'I'll get me coat right away,' she says, laughing.

'Idiot. You know you're welcome here as long as it takes you to decide what to do,' Fran says. 'Once more, I owe you everything.'

'Babe,' Rachel says, 'if it wasn't for you, I'd be rotting in the house mother's room, and Abbie would have got away with Ethan.'

'Instead of lying dead on the dorm floor.'

Wim sighs and shakes his head, clearly resigned to the fact that all roads will inevitably lead back to The Day.

'Perhaps I'll go to LA, live in Venice Beach,' Rachel says, to appease him.

'Cool,' he says. 'What'll you do there?'

She shrugs. 'Dunno. Work in a restaurant? Or a shop? Bring up Ethan and live a real life, though, that's for sure. Stay off social media.'

Fran puts a hand on her good leg. 'No filter.'

Rachel laughs. 'Hashtag nofilter!'

'We'll come and visit often,' Fran says.

'You'd better.' Rachel looks out of the window at the water reflecting the sharp red sunset back into the room, grateful that she has the freedom to do whatever she wants. 'We were so lucky the police believed us about what Abbie did,' she says.

'Why wouldn't they?' Fran says. 'It was our word against hers. And what was her word worth?'

Rachel looks down at her hands, at her nails, which are bitten to where they meet her flesh. 'What chance did she ever have?'

'A father like that Speakman beast,' Wim says. 'Right from the start, poor child, she was doomed.'

Fran puts her hand on her husband's knee. 'Ethan's so lucky.'

But Rachel is miles away. She's thinking about the pile of post that greeted her when Wanda, in a fit of I-told-you-so helpfulness, wheeled her and Ethan back into Honeyhill Barn after her hospital stay. Most of it went straight into the bin unopened. But there was one interesting-looking parcel. Opening it, Rachel found the big pink pot of expensive face cream she had ordered for Abbie. Hardly surprisingly, what with everything that had happened, she had completely forgotten about it.

She unscrewed the lid of the beautiful jar. The cream inside smelled exactly the same as her own, which Wanda had retrieved for her to use in hospital. After feeding Ethan, she lined up the two pots, each with its unique intricate mandala of the DNA result from which each special blend of oils was concocted.

The images on her own and Abbie's jars were identical.

Of course, it could be that the whole face cream thing was a con. That there isn't a unique formulation according to the DNA from your paternal line, but just the one, same cream, the one, same mandala.

Or it could be that her mother had lied about her being adopted, or perhaps her birth mother had been one of Wayne Speakman's many conquests.

In which case, not only does she have Speakman's blood in her veins, but she has also killed her half-sister.

Looking at her beautiful son playing with his half-siblings, Rachel has chosen to believe the first theory.

In any case, she's in no hurry to mention anything about it to anyone else, ever.

She threw both jars away.

Outside the vast window of the warehouse apartment, it's a glorious autumn evening. The beautiful young people of Rotterdam sit among the forests of parked bicycles outside the Fenix Food Factory, sharing global street food and knocking back craft cider.

Rachel closes her eyes and runs her fingers over the word etched on the little pendant that Fran gave her as a present for saving her life.

Safe.

Ethan's five, and they're driving in an open-top car up to San Francisco, the ocean on their left, the mountains on their right, and this will be in real life.

A LETTER FROM JULIA

Dear reader,

I want to say a huge thank you for choosing to read *The New Mother*. If you enjoyed it, and want to keep up to date with all my latest releases, just sign up at the following link. Your email address will never be shared and you can unsubscribe at any time.

www.bookouture.com/julia-crouch

At the centre of this story is one of the big questions for our times: what do we really need in order to make us happy in this world?

When I had the first of my three children, as well as falling in love with my baby, I was shocked by two very tangible changes in my life. The first was the way small freedoms I had always taken for granted – for example, uninterrupted baths, running out to the corner shop if I needed milk – were now not available to me. The second, and most shocking, was how I had become part of a demographic to be sold to. This pre-dated social media, and I can only imagine how much more acute this is for first-time parents today.

Social media can be such a positive, democratic way of communicating with the world and keeping in touch with far-flung friends. It can also have massively negative consequences

– reducing dialogue to one-liners devoid of nuance, spreading misinformation, hate and hysteria. Sitting in the middle of all this are the influencers, helping, selling and seducing, at best being our intimate friends/big sisters, at worst feeding the pain of our perceived shortcomings. It's a brand-new job description, with no precedent, and like all jobs, it can make you or break you.

In *The New Mother*, I peel back the skin of the digitally projected perfection of Rachel's online persona, and examine the gulf between her life and those of her fans. Where is the integrity, the authenticity? Where the acknowledgement of her multiple privileges?

With the arrival of Beansprout and Abbie into her life, reality bites. The awakening is brutal, for Rachel and for Abbie.

I hope you enjoyed the ride, and I'd love to know who you found yourself rooting for, and why! I've really enjoyed connecting with readers through my other books, *Cuckoo*, *Every Vow You Break*, *Tarnished*, *The Long Fall* and *Her Husband's Lover*, so please, if you have any comments or questions, do get in touch on my Facebook page, through Twitter, Instagram or my website.

Finally, I hope you loved *The New Mother*; if you did, I would be very grateful if you could write a review. I'd love to hear what you think, and it makes such a difference helping new readers to discover one of my books for the first time.

Thanks,
Julia Crouch

JuliaCrouchAuthor

@thatjuliacrouch

@juliageek

www.juliacrouch.co.uk

ACKNOWLEDGEMENTS

First off, I have to categorically state that @rachelhoneyhill is a fictional character, and absolutely not based on anyone at all on Instagram (although seek and you may find her, along with @soberachel).

However, I would like to thank all the YouTube/Insta stars I have enjoyed following for my research. In particular, @adrienelouise, whose YouTube yoga (with Benji, who is clearly way more loved than poor Sam) has kept me going through the lockdown years; @zoesugg, aka @zoella, a YouTube pioneer who has shown that it is possible to grow your profile through time; @me_and_orla (Sara Tasker) for her beautiful book on how to succeed at Instagram, *Hashtag Authentic*, and her honesty on her blog, meandorla.co.uk; @deliciouslyella, whose recipes Abbie could take a look at; and the marvellous @celestebarber, whose parody account makes me snort daily, before leading me beyond @gwynethpaltrow and @goop to the even more enjoyably narcissistic parts of the 'Gram, who I won't mention here but who have given me such joy.

Special thanks to @oliviamaycxo, a younger, up-and-coming YouTube (Olivia May C)/TikTok (oliviamayc1)/Insta star, who was so generous with her time and tolerated my nosiness about her life and career.

My lovely friend @samtoftartist, who talked me through how she has built her following on Instagram, and the long dog-walking chats about engagement with followers.

My niece @elsietao for the Bristol details.

My friend @petrusursem for Dutch language advice (any errors my own).

My children @nelcrouch @owencrouch and @joeycrouch_ for giving me all the material I need on what it's like to be pregnant.

The general crime-writing scene, full of wonderful writers who have seen me through a lot of ups and downs over the years, and the many incredibly engaged readers and bloggers. Special mention here for Colin Scott: next drink's on me!

My wonderful editor @ruth_tross and the team @bookouture. Getting to work with Ruth has been one of my writing goals for longer than I care to remember.

My über agent @taffyagent @curtisbrownbooks for keeping the faith, moral support and amazing editorial input.

My long-suffering and supportive husband and first reader (poor man), @thistimcrouch.

My cats, #Keith and #Sandy, for their herding of the new puppy #Uncle, so that I can write.

My students @uea Crime Writing MA, who help me sharpen my own practice, and Prof @henry.sutton.980 for supporting my long-stay visiting fellowship (I'm a bit like a cousin in a Victorian novel in that respect).

The Royal Literary Fund (too venerable for an Instagram account), for whom I worked for two years as an RLF fellow at Brighton University. Top employers, and a great help to writers in need, as well as the students they support.

My dear friend and mentor @diana_porter_jewellery, 19/11/43–28/2/21, who gave me my first proper job and whose beautiful, inspirational Sybils, which I helped to sell around thirty years ago, are among the very few real products in the whole novel.

Printed in Great Britain
by Amazon